The Murder of Medicine Bear

SUSAN HALEY

The Murder of Medicine Bear

Gaspereau Press · Printers & Publishers · MMIII

Many thanks to Dila Houle & Vern Yellowhorn
for their hospitality and help.

I

1983 · Marina

❦ IT WAS A MONDAY MORNING WHEN MARINA AND HER THREE kids took the bus to Bitter Root. Marina had wakened the girls early, getting them off the single bed they shared in the rented room, sleeping head to toe, packing their backpacks for them and helping sleepy Jasmine, who was only six, into her clothes. Rose held the baby while she was doing that, feeding him a can of evaporated milk from his bottle.

The little girls slept on the bus and her baby was not much of a problem, wide awake, but not lively. He was a good baby. Marina had not thought of a name for him yet, even though he was ten months old. They called him Baby. She was not going to name him after the father.

In Bitter Root they took a country taxi from the bus stop out to the Reserve. Marina was conscious of how much money this was taking; it was taking all the money and once they were there, there would be no going back. She would go straight to the Band office and find the social worker. There was no way they could refuse to help her. She was a Native; she was from this Reserve.

The social worker was not there, so Marina talked to the Band manager, a young woman. She explained everything about the kids, the welfare, about her boyfriend, how he wouldn't leave them alone, how they had to move every couple of weeks when he found them again.

"Well, you can go to the drop-in centre," said the Band manager dubiously. "But I don't know whether they can put you up there overnight."

Marina went to the drop-in, which was in the basement of the

Catholic mission, carrying the baby, holding Jasmine's hand. The housing situation on the Reserve was tight, the Band manager had said. She was going to look into the question of eligibility. She had been surprised, taken aback even, when Marina had asked to see the forms, to fill them in for herself.

However strange it was here, people with strange presumptions about your literacy, strange hill-country scenery, strange roads with deteriorating pavement or no pavement at all, it was a safe place. It felt safe to her. Things had slowed down; now that she was here, she could breathe again.

Marina did not think of the Reserve as home. She had been away for more than thirty-five years. She had been taken away from it as a child and never returned. On the other hand, it had been a kind of place inside her all along, a place of security, which gave her security, because she knew she could get back there if she ever needed to. It was a real place, after all, the home of her people, where she had been born.

The girls were okay with the drop-in, but Marina was not. It was full of teenage boys, for one thing, and she didn't like the way they talked, every other word a swear word. There was nowhere to change the baby. They sat on a bench by the wall in a little cluster.

"I'd like to send my kids to school," she said to the elderly man who seemed to be the caretaker of the place. "If we're going to live here, they should be in school."

He looked at her blearily.

After they made some sort of meal—they still had change to buy chips and pop out of the vending machines at the drop-in—Marina took the girls by the hand, and leaving the baby sleeping on a coat under the eye of one of the teenagers in exchange for a pop, they went to school.

The girls were excited. They had been yearning to get back to school, particularly Rose, who was eight, and had a very strong sense of how things should be done. She should have been in grade three, but she had been unable to start school at all this year because of their continual moving, and it was now October.

The grade three teacher was a pretty young Native woman, which was a surprise. Rose actually stared at her. Then she turned around and looked at Marina. Marina smiled and so did Rose. So did the teacher.

"I think she's going to like it in your class," said Marina.

"I think so too," said the teacher, taking Rose's backpack to hang on a hook, then leading her to a seat with a couple of other little girls in braids and overalls, like Rose.

Jasmine had a failure of nerve when Marina tried to leave her with the grade one teacher (although since she had not really finished kindergarten it was not surprising.) She clung to Marina, crying and whining—and as the teacher in this case was a young man, the fact that he also was Native did not much help. Jasmine did not trust men.

Then Rose's teacher looked out the door and said Jasmine could come in with Rose till she got used to school, and Marina was able to leave them together, Jasmine happily scribbling with an orange crayon over a picture of a Halloween pumpkin, and Rose already showing the teacher that she could read and write. It seemed like a good omen, how easy that had been.

Marina went back to the drop-in to collect the baby, then walked over to the Band office again to see whether the social worker was there yet. She was, but there was something dreadfully wrong.

"You aren't eligible for housing."

"I'm a member of this Band!"

"You say you were married to this George Cartwright?"

"Yes, and the kids are his kids. That's why—" It was not entirely true because the baby was not his, but George was not here to contradict her.

"Well, then, you're non-status."

"What the hell does that mean?"

"It means you lost your status when you got married. You aren't a Band member."

"But—but—I'm—I got un-married."

"Does he have status on some other Reserve?"

"No."

"Then it's clear-cut. You don't have status. The kids are white."

"The kids aren't white!"

In the middle of this exchange—it was becoming an

argument—a tall, slim, handsome young man wearing braids and a headband came through the outer office they were in and went through an inner door marked "Chief."

"Was that the Chief?" asked Marina. He seemed too young, somehow, in his early thirties.

"Yes. Now the best thing you can do is go back to the Social Services office you were—"

"I want to see the head guy. I'm not going to talk to you any more."

Marina went over and knocked on the Chief's door. Then she opened it. The Chief was inside, his feet up on the desk, talking on the phone—probably to his girlfriend, she thought.

"Hey!" said the Band manager.

A moment later, both the social worker and the Band manager were screaming at her.

The Chief hung up on his girlfriend. "What's going on?"

"Nothing." Marina had sat down in a chair in front of his desk. All the screaming had got the baby going too. He was probably hungry, but she was out of everything now except fruit juice. She began groping through her backpack for a bottle.

"Nothing?" He raised his eyebrows.

"Yeah. That's what I've got. Nothing. No milk for this baby. No money. I just thought I'd talk to you about that, Mr. Chief, rather than these hysterical women."

She was nearly hysterical herself. The baby was going strong; one of the women was actually trying to lever her up out of the chair by her arm, and it looked as if there was no juice in her backpack.

The guy in braids had his feet on the floor by now. He said to the other two: "Maybe you'd better leave this to me."

The social worker let go of her arm. Marina found a bottle of juice.

The two women went out of the office, leaving the door ajar.

The baby was taking the juice. He was a wise child already. He knew there was no point in holding out for something she hadn't got.

"So what's the story?"

"Shut the door, okay? I'm not talking to them any more."

His eyebrows shot up again, but after a moment he got to his feet and went around his desk, then around her chair, to shut the door.

"Well?" He had got back behind the desk again. It was a safe place, behind a desk.

"I'm a Native. I'm a member of this Band. I was born here," she said.

"Okay. I'm with you so far."

"I made the mistake of marrying George Cartwright about ten years ago."

"A non-Native?"

"Is that what you call them? I thought he'd kicked his habit, but he hadn't. So that left me with two kids, girls."

"Where are they now?"

"In school. I took them over there this morning."

"When did you get here, incidentally?"

"This morning."

"Wow. That was quick."

"Maybe they'll like your school. That grade three teacher was pretty nice to Jasmine."

He nodded. "Native teachers."

"Yeah. So now I came over here to see the social worker and she tried to kick me out."

"So I saw. Why?"

"She says I'm non-status. I'm not eligible."

"The Indian Act—"

"I don't really care," interrupted Marina. "So save the explanation. Tell it to your girlfriend."

He grinned.

"Is that the whole works?" he asked, when she didn't go on.

As a matter of fact, she had stopped because she thought she was going to burst out crying. Apparently it was true; even this guy, who was otherwise so friendly, so nice—even good-looking, although too young for her—he thought so too.

But how could she be ineligible? The Reserve had been on her mind for so long as the place of last resort. What if there really was no last resort?

He was shoving a box of tissues at her across the desk. Marina took one, fumbled, then angrily threw the whole box on the floor.

"Let's start again," he suggested. "What's your name?"

"Marina Smythe."

"Smythe?—Okay, you were born here. Then what happened?"

"I was in a couple of foster homes."

"One of them was the home of the Smythes? Should I write this down?" He took up a pen and looked at her with ironic expectancy.

Marina laughed, then blew her nose angrily. "I got out of that and spent ten years on the street."

He put the pen down and began lighting a cigarette instead.

"Then I went into detox, got the booze out of my life, did some upgrading, and married one of the counsellors in that place."

"You had two kids, but in the meantime he went back to his habit?"

"Did I say all that?" She was surprised. He really was listening.

"You did. But why are you here, though? Sounds like you can take care of yourself. Upgrading. You're on social assistance, I guess."

"Yeah. But I can't stay anywhere."

"Why not?"

"I've got this crazy murderer following me around."

"The husband?"

"No."

"The baby's father? He's a murderer?" He spoke thoughtfully.

"Well, he hasn't murdered anyone yet. It's me he's going to kill. But I've got lots of evidence that he means what he says."

"You told your social worker, I guess. What about the cops?"

"I tried to get a court order. But the cops are worse than useless. You think they're going to save my life? I moved six times in the last three months. Rose didn't get to start grade three. Jasmine never even finished primary."

"What makes you think this place is safe?" he asked.

[16]

"He won't know I'm here. He doesn't know about this. Where I'm from. He'll look all over Calgary, that's all."

The Chief was silent for a short while, frowning. Then he said:

"Would twenty bucks help?"

"Yeah. I told you. I'm broke."

"I could probably see you to the bus ticket too."

She stared at him in outrage. "No!"

"Well—" he shrugged. "What else can I do?"

"You're the Chief in this place. Get me somewhere to stay. It doesn't have to be great. We can stay just about anywhere. We were staying just about anywhere in Calgary already."

"And then what?"

"I'm on welfare. Maybe I could get them to send my cheque on. Does it matter that I'm out here?"

"Yeah. We handle our own social assistance payments."

"You're saying I can't be on welfare here?"

He shrugged again. "Look, I didn't write any of these rules. This is Canada you're dealing with, not me."

"I'm dealing with you." She folded her arms. The baby was sitting forward on her knee, apparently quite happy just to watch this guy, although he had not had enough to eat this morning; he had not had any formula for several days.

"Look, the way things are, if you go off the Reserve, marry a non-status man—"

"Are you married?"

"No." He looked startled.

"Never went off the Reserve, huh?"

"As a matter of fact I grew up out there, like you. But—"

"Of course, you're a man, I forgot. If a man gets married to a non-status woman, I bet he doesn't lose a thing."

"That's true." He had the grace to look slightly ashamed as he said it. "There's a big argument going on about this. Maybe they're going to change it soon."

"And maybe I'll be dead soon. But I've got kids. I can't afford to die."

To her annoyance he was taking out his wallet; he began

looking through the compartments. Apparently there wasn't any money in it, because he put it down on the desk. He drummed his fingers on the blotter for a moment. Then he got up.

He was not going to listen to her any more.

"I can probably borrow some. Look, stay here. I'll be back," he said, going out.

The office was full of expensive equipment, so it surprised her that he had just left her there like that. What if she became irrational and began trashing the place? There were filing cabinets, expensive panelling, a phone deck, fancy computer equipment on the fancy desk.

She put the baby down on the floor. He couldn't sit up without some support, and it seemed as though he was always on her somehow these days—on her lap, in her arms, on her hip. The floor was clean. She laid him down on it on his back and he kicked placidly. He would be all right like that for a few minutes. Then she went over behind the desk to look out the window.

Outside was the Reserve, dry and brown: brown roads, brown grass, no trees, just brown dirt, brown houses, a brown school. The kids were getting out; she saw them straggling down the road. She supposed Rose would take Jasmine back to the drop-in. Then eventually, they would bring them over here. They would have to bring them over eventually.

What if they didn't bring them?

She should have thought of that. It was necessary to stay together. She should never have taken them to school. She wasn't able to get them because she would never get back into this office if she left now. But if they didn't bring them; if they called in social services and the girls were taken away from her—

Almost panicking, Marina leaned on the broad sill behind the desk, her mind searching frantically for a solution, some trick—

The social worker and the Band manager had come into the office. The social worker grasped her by the arm again. The other woman had picked up the baby. "You can't stay here."

"He said he'd be right back."

"He isn't coming back."

"Where did he go then?"

The women looked at each other in exaggerated ignorance, pop-eyed, shrugging.

"I don't know! Home?"

"Okay." Marina shook off the hand on her arm. "Where's he live?"

"Where does he live?" they repeated.

"I'll go there."

Again they exchanged a look. The Band manager gave Marina the baby. He was beginning to fuss.

"Show me. Out the window. Does he live in a house?"

"He lives right over there," said the Band manager. She pointed, giggling suddenly.

It was a brown house like the others, among the others, but nicer than some of the older ones. Split level. High cement front steps.

Marina now saw Rose and Jasmine coming hand in hand down the road, walking a little uncertainly towards the drop-in.

"I'm going now. I'm going to get my—my other kids." Her panic was still there, but she was determined, also. She had said some things and she thought he had understood her. He had gone out to get money, not that this was what she wanted. But she felt that he was sincere, at least. He had been intending to come back.

She went out of the Band office and met Rose and Jasmine just as they were about to descend the cement steps into the church basement.

"We didn't have a snack," said Jasmine, taking her hand and looking up. But she was not whining. Her face was placid.

"The teacher shared," said Rose. "Her name is Miss Running Horse."

"Where are we going?" Jasmine asked.

"To a house."

As she had imagined, the Chief was not a man who locked the back door. He had said he was going to borrow the money, so she had not expected him to be there. The kitchen was empty.

Empty and very dirty. Dishes in the sink. Not too many, but covered with food moulds. The floor was blackened with the marks of rubber boot heels. The automatic coffee maker on the counter stood half full of inky coffee, a week old at least.

The other room on the main floor was not so dirty. It was almost empty of furniture. A sofa with a throw over it. One picture on the wall, kind of a dark-looking oil painting of a girl, unfinished.

They were accustomed to moving as a phalanx. They wheeled, Jasmine on one side, Rose on the other, and went out of the cold, empty room and back to the kitchen. "We going to live here, Ma?"

"The baby's hungry."

He was eating his blanket, stuffing it into his mouth, whimpering softly.

"Look in the fridge."

Jasmine looked in the refrigerator, since Rose was holding the baby. It was almost empty, but there was a carton of milk in there.

"How old is it?"

"It's okay." Rose read the date out loud. "We could have some, right?"

Marina was already washing dishes. Almost all of them were cups. The guy never cooked, this was obvious. She laid out three clean mugs on the table and poured milk.

"He wants it in the bottle."

"Better change him too, Rose. I didn't change him since this morning."

"Okay, Mom." Rose was happy. "Mom" was a happy name.

There were some stale cookies in the cupboard. They ate them all. Marina finished the dishes. There was ground coffee in the cupboard so she made coffee in the clean pot.

Rose and Jasmine explored the rest of the house, taking the baby with them. "There's three bedrooms. Does someone live here? One of them has clothes and stuff in it."

"It's a guy who's letting us stay here. He's the Chief, as a matter of fact."

"What's a Chief?"

"A leader. Kind of like a king."

"Oh. An Indian Chief?" asked Rose.

"Yeah. He's an Indian Chief." Marina began to smile. It was funny. She must not laugh, however, she reminded herself. Hysteria was still very close to the surface.

The clock on the stove said 5:00. They opened a can of tomato soup and cooked it with the last of the milk, then Rose set the table with bowls and spoons and they all had some. The baby loved it. He had liked everything they ate: cookies, 2% milk, tomato soup ... However, she was going to be out of diapers by tomorrow.

Marina turned on the radio and they listened to the news.

"He's got a TV in his bedroom."

"Can I have a TV in my bedroom?" asked Jasmine.

"Can we watch TV in his room, Mom?" asked Rose, the realist.

"Okay. Don't touch anything else."

"There isn't anything," said Rose. "He hasn't got anything else."

It was blissful to be alone, even for a short while. A little later she went down to see. They were all asleep, the three of them, lined up on the pillows, the baby in the middle for security.

It was true that there was nothing else in the room besides the mattress on the floor, the TV on top of a bureau, some shoes and shirts in the partly open closet, other stuff on the shelf. The place reminded her of a hotel room. The drawers of the bureau were probably empty; it stood there only to support the TV.

The other two bedrooms were completely empty. They had carpeting on the floors; that was the only furniture.

Marina went upstairs again and lay down on the sofa. She pulled the throw over herself after a while. It was not entirely comfortable, but it was much better than anything she had had lately: a jacket on the floor with the baby.

It was getting late. She didn't dare go to sleep, however. She was going to have to fight for this. She needed to steel herself, so that she wouldn't give in.

She fell asleep. She couldn't help it. It had been a long and eventful day.

She woke up at about 6:00 the following morning. At first she was not sure where she was. Then she remembered yesterday. The guy must not have come home last night.

She was not cold, only a little stiff from lying on one side all night, but glad to be sleeping alone, without the baby. She rolled over the other way and slept peacefully for another hour or so.

School. She was awake again and she remembered school. When did it start? 8:30, probably. She sat up and stretched, tidied the sofa. It was not that late yet.

She went into the kitchen. There was another can of soup that they would have to make with water this time. They could eat that. Diapers were going to be a problem, she remembered. Perhaps it was time to wake the kids. She turned on the coffee maker to heat up what was left in the pot.

She went downstairs. The man was asleep in all his clothes, lying diagonally across the bare mattress.

She nearly panicked, but then she saw the bedclothes lying on the floor, covering up her kids, who were now laid out in a row on the carpeted floor, each one with a pillow and blanket. He had used a large towel to cover the baby.

She stood in the doorway and the tears came into her eyes and rolled down her cheeks like marbles. At the same time she wanted to laugh, but again she forced that laugh back and down.

She was looking at him now, almost covetously. He was good—not just young and good-looking. He must have lifted the kids off the bed without waking them and the care he would have taken in doing that—this alone showed that he was good.

Rose sat up suddenly. "Momma!"

"Sh!" Marina put her finger to her lips, but the Chief had already rolled over with a groan.

"Oh yeah," said Rose, craning her neck to look at him too.

He sat up on the edge of the mattress and yawned into his hand. Then he fumbled in his shirt pocket and took out a pack of cigarettes.

"You can't smoke," Rose pointed out.

He paused, lighter in hand and looked at her interrogatively.

"The baby," she said. "And because of us too."

"Well, okay. I forgot."

These two seemed to have met already.

"There's some coffee," Marina remarked, as he got to his feet.

"I know. I had some last night."

Jasmine was waking up with her usual unhappy whimpers.

The baby had begun to cry. The Chief escaped past her, through the doorway.

He reappeared in the kitchen as they were finishing the soup. She had known he would have to come back, as he had departed in sock feet. Unfortunately the can of soup could not be stretched to five people. They had eaten it all. He disappeared downstairs to the bathroom.

Rose and Jasmine left for school. It was time, and Rose had been agitating to go. She took Jasmine's hand carefully as they got off the bottom step of the porch, then turned around to wave. Marina waved back.

Marina did the dishes and went to change the baby into the last diaper. When she returned to the kitchen, the Chief was having a cup of coffee.

"Have some yourself," he suggested.

"I can't drink much of that stuff these days. Maybe I have an ulcer."

She sat down opposite him, carefully setting the baby in front of her feet so that he was supported by her legs. Then she rested her elbow on the table and put her cheek in her hand.

"I really did go out to borrow some money the other day," he said. "I borrowed a hundred." He took out his wallet, withdrew the bill and put it on the table in front of her. She didn't touch it.

"I figured twenty wasn't going to get you very far."

"No," she agreed.

"I can give you a drive to the city too. Wherever you want to go."

They both stared at the hundred dollar bill.

"Please take it."

"I can't," said Marina. She wanted desperately to take it. She could still stay here. He would not be able to make her move. Not unless he called the cops, and she was fairly sure that he would never do that. But it seemed that she could not take the money and stay as well.

"I'm out of diapers." Her voice came out in a strange, hoarse whisper. "There's no more food, not even cookies. The baby— he's hungry."

Marina was not a fat woman, nor a large one. But she had become a bit chunkier after she quit drinking and had kids. Her bottom had widened, her shoulders had become broader, she had a bosom of sorts for the first time. Now she felt herself becoming heavier and heavier. She felt that she could not actually move from the chair; and she would be too heavy to lift.

"Oh for God's sake!" He got up and walked around the room. "Okay," he said, turning around. "What do you want me to do?"

Again, she felt the pressure of her dilemma. She could not leave because she would never get back. But without leaving, she could not get the things that they needed, the food, the diapers, the milk.

They stared at one another. Marina's chin was only a few inches off the table. She rested it on her fist. He leaned back against a kitchen counter. Then he came over to the table again and took up a stance like hers, opposite her. They stared at one another like buffaloes.

"Okay! Okay!" He snatched up the bill. "Tell me what you need! You need food? You need diapers? Milk, right? What about him? Does he eat something special?"

"Yeah. He needs formula. I've just been giving him milk because—"

"Maybe you'd better come, you know? Let's make this simple."

"You'll bring me back here? The girls, they're in school ..."

"I'll bring you back. What do you think? Think I'd dump you on a street corner with a truckload of groceries and diapers?"

They drove to a supermarket off the Reserve that was some distance away. It made Marina uneasy. However, he had stuffed the hundred dollar bill into her jacket pocket, so at least she had that. They drove without speaking, but he came into the store, he even pushed the cart. On the way out he bought a pack of cigarettes with the change.

"Hurry up," she said. "I think they come home from school for lunch."

The baby was cheerful; he had slept on the way. But he ate all the time they were in the store and all the way home: cookies, a can of formula, pieces of fruit. The man kept glancing at him.

"What's his name?" he asked.

[24]

"He doesn't have a name."

"Really? But don't you have to register them—I mean, at birth? Isn't there some form you have to fill out?"

"Yeah. When you don't have a name you just write Baby Boy. I didn't feel like naming him after his dad."

"Oh yeah. The future murderer." He glanced at them again. "Okay, it's not a joke. But I like to laugh at a lot of things that aren't funny. You'll get used to it."

She would get used to it? He seemed unaware of the presumption behind his own words.

He left the truck running while he helped her lift the grocery bags out of the back and up the porch steps, Marina coming and going with the baby on her hip. Then he got back in front and drove the hundred yards over to the Band office. He waved briefly, looking her way, then disappeared inside.

The little girls came home before she was unpacked. Rose was in her glory, surrounded by cans—of meat, of stew, of tuna, of beans. She piled them up in pyramids on the floor, on the counters.

They had some beans for lunch, although none of them liked beans very much. It seemed like a conservative approach. They all agreed that stew was something to save for supper. Then the girls went back. Jasmine was going to go into primary again; the teacher was a woman, not a man.

Marina lay down on the sofa and slept away the afternoon, the baby sleeping too, blissfully full, face down upon her chest. When she woke up it was to the sound of the tv downstairs. The girls had come home and gone down there without disturbing her.

The Chief did not come home that night.

AGAIN, THE FEELING GREW IN HER THAT SHE WAS TRAPPED. HE was trapping her. The food would not run out for a long time, but it was now her sense of isolation. She knew no one here but him; there was no one she could trust. She was trapped on the inside, this time.

But on the afternoon of the next day, he showed up again, driving over in his truck, which had been parked in front of the Band office all this time. She had been keeping watch.

"Where were you?" She was glad to see him; she couldn't keep it out of her voice.

"Working. I have a job."

"Oh yeah. You sleep there?"

"Sometimes I sleep with women," he replied. He looked at her coolly, his eyes half-closed.

It made her mad to hear him say it. This had been on her mind. How had he guessed? She had even felt twinges of jealousy. Jealousy of this stranger, with younger, more attractive women.

He had said "women." Several of them. Many women. This made her feel better suddenly.

"The kids are watching TV."

"That's okay. Could I sleep on the mattress, though?"

She laughed. "You haven't been in anyone's bed, have you? Slept in a chair, probably."

"I kept thinking of all those cans of Spam and Irish stew. It began to make me hungry. Finally I had to come back here."

"I'll cook for you," she said. "There's no need to move out."

The kids usually ate supper in front of the TV, but she made them come up this time. They sat around the kitchen table. Rose fed the baby on her lap.

Marina had begun cautiously to expand her cooking a little now, and they had mashed potatoes with the stew. She washed the bowls and then they divided up a can of peaches.

"He wants his bed," she told the girls, with a certain irony.

"We could bring the TV upstairs."

"Maybe you guys could sleep in the other bedrooms," he suggested.

"Oh, sure. We slept on the mattress. But that was just while you were away."

"While we're at it," he said, "let's name the baby." He had been watching the kids, an amused smile on his lips.

"Let's," said Rose. She looked at Marina. "Miss Running Horse thinks he should have a name."

"Miss Running Horse?" He laughed. "Angie?"

Marina thought of Rose's pretty young teacher. Maybe she was one of the many women.

[26]

"Athanasius. You don't like that one? Balthazar."

"What's your name?" they demanded.

"Tim," he said, surprised.

"That's a good name."

"Oh no! You're not going to name him after me?" He looked from one to the other in surprise and mock horror.

Marina felt her lips settle into an ironic smile. It served him right, for bringing it up.

"Tim," said Rose to the baby, giving it a try.

Marina was slightly cross now. Tim was a good name, but the baby had gone without one for so long that nothing seemed appropriate. And a name could hang around reminding one of things and people one might not like to think of later.

"Bring up the TV," she ordered Rose.

"I'll get it," said Tim. "They're kind of small, you know, Marina."

He went out of the room and she was in the grips of another kind of name-anxiety. He had called her by her name. She had actually forgotten that he knew what it was. He had never called her anything before.

The voice of the TV came now from the living room. Marina turned to the dishpan. The kitchen was considerably cleaner than it had been. The floor was washed, several of the cupboards washed and stacked with cans, the stove and refrigerator were spotless. Rose had been a big help.

She made coffee and as she was finishing up wiping the counters, Tim came out and poured himself some. He prowled around the kitchen, cup in hand.

"What's the matter?" The sound of her voice was sharp and brittle.

"Nothing. I want a cigarette."

This little thing—that she could tell him not to smoke in the house—made her feel good.

"I tried." He spoke abruptly. "I called just about everyone I could think of. But it's here that I couldn't get any kind of agreement. It's a political issue, status. And the housing situation on the Reserve—I had no idea how tight that is."

"You have a house," she pointed out.

"Look, I'm the Chief. I get a house."

"With three bedrooms?"

"That's the way they build 'em." He was distracted, however. "God, if only I didn't have a house," he said with a wry smile.

"Yeah. Like you said, there's plenty of places you can sleep."

"Let's get off me, okay?" He paused. "I called Social Services."

"You did?"

"Yeah. I pointed out that nobody was doing much for you. Jesus, if somebody wants to live on a Reserve just to be safe, what are they coming to, anyway?"

"They're a bunch of deadheads. Where'd they send you next? The Calgary police?"

"No. I talked to your social worker."

"What?" Marina was outraged. "What'd she tell you about me?"

"You're pretty uncooperative. They set you up in an apartment. But you took off. You don't do what you're told."

"Where does she get off? Where do you get off talking to that scum about me!"

"Okay, but I'm with you, remember? I said you were scared, your ex-boyfriend was after you, you'd been moving around. Apparently she knew all that."

"Cow! So what about my cheque?"

"You can't get it here."

"Why not? Whose fault is that?"

"I don't know. Mine, I guess." He shrugged. "I already told you. We administer our own welfare. I explained all that to you. She explained it to me a few times too." He sighed. "But finally, I got it. The cheque."

"You got it!" She jumped up in agitation.

"No. But she agreed to give it to you. I could take you there."

"Oh yeah. Then you drop me off on some street corner, eh?"

"The kids'll be in school here, remember?"

"That's what scares me. Maybe we'll get separated and I'll never see them again. Maybe they'll never see me again. That was what happened to me. One day I'm saying goodbye to my father. The next day I'm in foster care and they tell me he's dead."

He was looking at her sombrely.

She remembered that he had grown up off the Reserve. "Well, maybe something like that happened to you too."

"Maybe it did."

They were both silent for a moment and Marina was curious. But nothing really bad had ever happened to this guy, she could tell.

"Look, let's just get the cheque."

"So, after that, I can't stay here?"

"I didn't say that."

"I can stay here? You're saying that? Why?" she demanded suspiciously.

"I don't know. You're safe here. You'll have some money." He made a gesture of tearing his hair. "Why do I do anything?"

"They're probably going to cut me off now."

"She said that. But there's a cheque. Let's get it. Then I'll get on the phone again."

Marina was not sure what to say. She was not used to expressing gratitude. And for some reason he was looking sad. He wasn't like other men, who would have been boasting about beating the system this way, celebrating. His whole outlook was odd.

◖ TIM TOOK THE GIRLS TO SCHOOL IN THE MORNING, TAKING Marina and the baby as well, all of them pressed together in a jumble on the front seat of the truck. After he dropped Rose and Jasmine off, he continued on out the main road of the Reserve, the way they had taken to go to the store in town.

It was a very nice day for late October. There was still no snow on the ground and the sun was shining into their faces, making the cab of the truck hot.

Marina leaned back against the seat cushion. The truck was not new and it seemed to have an exhaust problem. There was quite a lot of noise. He wasn't saying anything; it was too hard to compete with the muffler noise.

The baby was taking an interest, not sleeping. He could sit up without any help now, and he bounced on her lap in the hot sunshine.

Marina suddenly realized that they were on the highway travelling east, away from the mountains, not towards the little town.

"Where are we going?"

"To Calgary. To pick up your welfare cheque."

"I can't go there!"

"Hey, wait a minute. We talked about this. You need the money, don't you?"

"Yeah, but I can't go to—to that office."

"Why not?"

She could not tell him. Her stomach was churning already, just at the fact they were heading in the direction of the city. Lionel was there, he was waiting for her; he knew she would have to see that social worker sometime. He knew the place and one day he was going to be there. That was what he had said the last time she had picked up the phone.

"She said you'd have to get it yourself."

"Bitch!"

"Well, it makes sense," he said patiently. "I'd have picked it up already, but she can't give your cheque to just anyone. Who the heck am I? She doesn't know me."

"I can't go in there."

"Tell me why not, okay?"

"Maybe he'll be there. And maybe he'll kill me."

"Oh, I see. But he wouldn't have any way of knowing you'd come today. In the morning." He had actually found the inner city street where the building, a storefront, was located and was looking for a place to park. He found a spot and pulled into the curb.

Marina sat still, the baby no longer bouncing. He knew something was wrong too.

"You can leave the kid. Or maybe you can't. He'll cry, won't he?"

It was comical how little he knew about children. She smiled faintly.

"So what's the problem? It's a bright, sunny day. No one on the street but a few bums. You don't think he's actually in her office, do you?"

She did not reply. She was paralysed, her stomach in turmoil.

"All right, I'm coming with you."

He got out, then came around and opened her door. She got out. He was the only person who had tried to help in a long time.

They went in and sat in the outer office. Tim was impatient, but clients were processed slowly. It was part of the strategy, in Marina's opinion, wearing people down so that they didn't want welfare; they wanted to die of an overdose instead.

"What is the crazy murderer's name, incidentally?" Tim asked, not bothering to lower his voice. Several people, including the receptionist, looked up at them.

"Shut up."

"Okay. Sorry." He sat back restlessly.

After about an hour, she saw her social worker, who talked to her quite severely about "Choices." She was making a "Choice," apparently, which would cause her to lose her welfare status. Her address was wrong. This was welfare-worker-code for sleeping with a man, Marina knew. Sleeping with someone was always tantamount to losing eligibility for welfare, even if the man himself was on welfare. She didn't bother to argue. Her new address was the only good thing that had ever happened, the way she saw it now.

They went out of the building and down the street to the truck. Marina got in quickly and slammed the door. "Hurry," she said.

"Why?"

She felt like crouching on the floor. She had her head bent low over the baby.

"Okay. I'm hurrying." They pulled out of the parking place.

"So what was that all about?" Tim asked as they began to get out of Calgary, going west again at last, the sun at their backs. "What was the big hurry to get out of there?"

"Lionel was there somewhere."

"He was? I didn't see anyone."

"I could feel it. He's lying in wait for me."

"Look, don't you think that this is paranoia? There wasn't anyone there except some women in the office, a drunk or two outside in front of the beer parlour. He wasn't there. And I don't see how he could know you were coming."

"That fat cow talks about me. She talked to you!"

"Oh yeah. Well, you have a point. She has a big mouth."

She was very surprised by his agreement. Somehow she had expected to have to go on fighting with somebody.

Instead he was looking out the front window, driving calmly. The baby bounced again. He was beginning to sit very strongly by himself.

"What if he got the license number?" she asked.

"The license number? Of the truck, you mean? How's that going to help him?"

"I don't know. Couldn't he find out where I am?"

"If he was there—maybe he just wanted to see the kid."

"Are you serious? He tried to kill me the night I told him I was pregnant. I had to go to Outpatient for stitches."

"Was that when you took off?"

"No."

Tim was silent for a while. The mountains were pretty in the sunshine, a few white puffy clouds above them in the high blue. As a child, so long ago, it seemed to her now, Marina had dreamed of flying up there, landing on them like a bird.

"It was brave of you to go in there," Tim said.

"Yeah, but you just think I'm crazy. You don't think there's a guy who's trying to kill me. You're another one—like that social worker, the police. You don't believe me."

"I believe you," he said, and again she was surprised.

The muffler was making even more noise than before and they stopped talking. But she sensed that he was thinking hard about something. It made her uncomfortable.

She knew that she was not brave. And the social worker was right. She had simply latched onto another man. This one was good, strong, faithful, even loving—but he didn't love her. He wasn't anything to her. How was she going to hold onto him?

It was strange to find everything so normal when they got back. Tim went to work. The girls came home from school. Rose had brought a drawing of a spotted dog. The TV was on. The baby was happy, chuckling, playing with the girls.

Tim did not show up at suppertime. They had fried Spam and mashed potatoes. The good food was making everything better.

Even Jasmine was more cheerful. She had brought home a book from school and Rose was trying to teach her to read some of the words.

"Were you allowed to take the book?"

"The teacher gave it to her, Ma."

"They didn't give us anything when I was in school." Marina examined the inscription inside the front cover. It said—sure enough—For Jasmine, Love, Miss MacPherson. Miss MacPherson was the primary teacher's name.

"Where did you live when you were little?" asked Rose.

"On this Reserve."

"Right here?" demanded Jasmine.

They were both gazing at her, wanting to know more about her life. Marina was not used to letting that out; only in desperation to a social worker, if she had to.

"Yes," she said.

"With your mother—and your father?" asked Rose. She was aware that fathers might not hang around.

"With my mother and some guy," said Marina. "But I had a father—a wonderful father."

"Why didn't you live with him?"

"My mother—I could only see him sometimes."

"But he gave you things. He wanted you to stay with him. He loved you best of all," contributed Rose.

Marina nodded. It had been that way. He had given her things—once a stuffed rabbit at Easter. But she could hardly remember anything now. Only the last time she had seen him. She was already in foster care, but he had got down on his haunches; he had told her he was coming to get her soon. He had promised—and then sometime later—was it months, or maybe even years?—she was told that he had died. He drowned. Why had it happened?

"What did he look like?"

"Oh—tall. And handsome."

"Like Tim?"

She was startled. Tim was far from her thoughts.

"Does he live here too? Maybe Tim knows him."

"No," she said sharply. "I told you. He's dead."

It had not occurred to her before that she probably had some living relatives here, aunts and uncles, maybe even a living grandparent. The thought frightened her. There was really no refuge anywhere. It would be better, perhaps, to drown. To be away from all the people who were following her and persecuting her, who would know or guess things.

But she was going under the name Cartwright. And before that, Smythe. No one could possibly know who she was. The kids were so used to having nobody but her for family that it had not occurred to them that there might be anyone else. And what she had told them was so limited, so sterile, that they would not remember, or it would not matter if they did.

She sat still, her hands stretched out upon the kitchen table as the kids went into the other room. They had seen from her face, from the grim set of her lips, that she was not going to tell them anything more, that she would snap at them if they asked; and she was hardly conscious of their leaving, filing through the door, first Rose, with the baby on her hip, then Jasmine, trailing behind as usual.

It was now apparent to her that their being able to stay here depended upon one thing.

Tim had not come home and he did not come home all evening. After the kids had gone to bed Marina sat in the kitchen waiting. His truck was not in the parking lot at the Band office and she was vaguely aware that it had not been there all day. He must have gone somewhere—maybe to sleep with one of his women.

Finally she went into the living room and lay down on the sofa. She was not asleep though, when she heard the distinctive roar of his truck outside; but she pretended to be asleep. That way, when he came through the room she did not have to talk to him. He paused, apparently looking at her, but she kept her eyes closed.

He went downstairs then and she heard him taking a shower. She heard the water running and was glad, because it put off what she was going to do and any reprieve was something to be grateful for. After this, she would know, after all, whether they really could stay or not. There would be no more doubt about that. And right now, doubt seemed a good thing, a hopeful thing.

She heard the bathroom door click open and then there was a moment when he must be looking in the open door at her kids lined up on the floor of the other room with his pillows and blankets. He crossed the hall and went into his room then, for she heard his footsteps on the linoleum floor in front of the bathroom.

She lay on the sofa, frozen. She couldn't do this, it was too deliberate, too much of a trick; he would see through it immediately. But on the other hand, it was also not a trick, for when she thought of him going to another woman she felt jealousy. And at the sight of him, his long nose, his introspective eyes, the length and breadth of him too, she felt a quickening of her breath, an intake of air that tensed her diaphragm. Sometimes she could not even look at him for fear that he would notice her attraction.

She was wearing jeans and a flannel shirt; she really had no other clothes but a jacket, some underwear, another pair of socks. These clothes, like herself, her stocky middle-aged body, would have to do. Something inside him might do the rest; it had worked that way so far.

She went downstairs silently; the carpeted treads made her soundless. She too stopped to peer in at the kids. They were fine, baby in the middle. It was a great relief now to sleep without the baby. Even though he woke early.

Then she pushed on the half-open door of Tim's room and entered quietly. He was lying face down, flung across the bed, with clothes on—there were no blankets, of course. He was asleep.

She sat down on the edge of the bed. And then she knew he was awake. It almost seemed, in the tension of his apparently casual pose, as though he must have been waiting for her.

He half rolled over now and she lay down, her neck on his outflung arm, their knees abutting, their faces only a few inches apart. His eyes were open; he was wide awake. He must have been awake, waiting.

"Marina," he said.

She had that heart-stopping intake of breath, like a stab in the chest. It was because he had said her name. But at the same time, she was afraid that if he said anything more, it would be to stop her.

She pressed herself more fully into his arms. Against his upper body, although his knees prevented her from coming much closer. She put her lips against his lips. And felt his lips give way, but only in a smile.

He said: "I've got to tell you something, Marina."

Their lips were still only two, maybe three inches apart. It was only his smile that prevented her from trying again.

She said bitterly, "I could love a man like you." For she knew now that all was lost.

Surprisingly enough he did not move away. He even put his other arm lightly across her shoulders.

"Listen to me, okay?"

He paused and she nodded mutely. He was going to tell her something to get her out of his life, but at least he was kind, he was doing this decently. She could listen. While he went on holding her this way, there was plenty of time to listen.

"This is hard to say, you know?" He laughed. "Marina, I think you're my sister."

Marina suddenly rocketed upright. She was sitting on the edge of the mattress with her back to him.

"It's strange how hard it is," he went on. "I've thought of you all my life. I've even dreamed of you. But only as someone like Rose, not—you know—a woman."

"I can't be," she said, speaking through stiff lips.

"Well, I do have a sister."

"I don't have a brother!"

"You did, though. You were six, younger than Rose. And I was a baby. Like little Tim. That was me, Marina."

"But I don't have a brother!" She was in tears. She put her hands over her face. It could not be true.

"Listen, Marina." He was sitting beside her now, and again, unbelievably, he put his arm around her. "I know you're my sister. I know your name. You were on the Band list back then."

It was a nightmare. It was the thing she had just begun to dread that afternoon. And yet it could not be true that Tim, of all people, was her closest relative. It simply could not be true.

"I was already wondering—" he said. "You know, after you moved in. Even before that, when you were in my office, when I went to find you that money, I kept thinking: this could be my sister."

"But it isn't possible. You should have said! You should have asked me then!"

"But you'd have said no, wouldn't you? Just like you're saying no now." He was laughing at her, teasing. "What's the matter? Is there something wrong with me?"

"There's nothing wrong! I just—just tried—!"

"Oh yeah. But that's okay. I know why you had to do that."

"It isn't true! You aren't my brother!"

She got up and blundered for the door, banging into the back of it. He followed, and caught her, cowering now, behind the door. He looked down at her quite seriously for a moment, turning her face around with the palm of his hand hard against her cheek. Then he kissed her on the lips, also hard, the kiss then becoming gentler and more insistent; it was what she had been trying to elicit from him.

It was a wonderful kiss, that would have spread fire through her belly a few minutes ago; but now she found it repellent, horrifying, disgusting. It broke the oldest of all the rules.

Completely revolted, Marina tore her lips away, disengaged herself from his grasp, and flung herself somehow around the door and up the stairs.

In the kitchen, he said coolly, "Mind if I smoke?"

They were a mile apart.

"Smoke. I don't care what you do."

He lit a cigarette, looking at her curiously. He was going to ask her questions now—about their mother, about everything. But then, perhaps it was still a possibility that he knew nothing about all that. He had been taken by Social Services too; and he might have read his file, but she had seen her own and it contained nothing about the trial, only the stark facts of her passage through the family courts.

"Your name. It's Tim—Tim Steen. That's the wrong name," she said.

"I'll tell you the right one then. It's Medicine Bear. And I am— I am Medicine Bear," he said.

She turned her head away, unable to endure hearing him say it.

He said, "I didn't have what happened to you. I was adopted, not fostered. It was a good place. I had a father, a whiteman. Named Tim Steen. Nothing bad happened to me."

"I'm glad. Real happy for you then," she said in bitterness.

He seemed to be trying to reassure her about his own history, as though it might have bothered her. Whereas she had never thought about it, never wondered what had become of him. Her own nightmare had been enough. She had never thought of him as growing up, becoming a man, until this moment.

"The man who took me was the defense attorney at the trial of my father," Tim went on steadily. "So I know, Marina. I know the whole works."

"You can't know!" she shouted. She stared at him, then turned away abruptly, covering her eyes. These memories were the most recurrent nightmares of all: whitemen, telling her she was lying, trying to trap her, to trick her, to trip her up.

"You don't know anything! You were a baby! You weren't there! You didn't see what happened! I was the only one who saw it!"

"You'll wake your kids," he said softly. "Just talk to me."

"Oh God! I wish I had never come here!"

"I'm glad you did, though."

"So you can torture me!"

"No. So we can have this—" he came around to the other side, facing her, and put his hands lightly on her shoulders. Marina stood, weeping and shaking, unable to look up. "Look, Marina. You're my whole family."

She was shaking her head still, even though she realized that she had given it away now.

"Of course, I have my adopted father. And then there's this place. I just came back here about five years ago. Everyone here is some kind of third cousin of everyone else. I can be part of that. But I never had—you know—this."

[38]

He had actually taken her in his arms again and for a moment she had some of the feelings of protection and safety that being with him had given her before. But she flung herself away.

"Your father murdered my mother."

"I know," he said.

"I saw what happened. I still see it." She shook her head. It was true; she saw it sometimes, as a still photograph. As a child she had been able to run it like a film. "I was there."

"I know about that."

"I hated him. Your dad. He killed her. You had a murderer for a father."

His eyes dropped but he nodded slightly.

"I sent him to prison. They hanged him because of what I told them. I'm not sorry."

"Well—I am. I'd like to have known him." He had looked up again and they were standing facing each other with the whole kitchen floor between them, he by the outer door, she by the inner.

"So this is between us? You can't forgive me—for what he did?"

Actually, it was he who could not forgive her, that was what she knew. And now she had nowhere to go at all. This last place had been taken away too, and now she was truly lost.

"Look, Marina, I admire you. You're a brave woman. You've got guts. The way you came at me. My house." He gave a wave round the place, the clean kitchen with the cupboards full of cans, the kids sleeping downstairs. "You've got the whole works now. You probably could even have got me to go to bed with you. Except for this other thing—which is even better, as far as I'm concerned. I like you. I even love you. You're my sister." He was listing these things on his fingers. "Doesn't it add up to something? For you too?"

It did add up. But she could hardly believe he was saying it.

Of course, he had had an easy time of it. He had never been verbally and physically abused as a child, or sexually abused, even tortured, by boyfriends on the street who turned out to be pimps disguised as boyfriends. He never been placed in a mental hospital against his will, and given electroshock treatments, or wrapped in hot and cold sheets. He had not had a drug habit and been in detox; he had probably never spent a night in a drunk tank. He had never married a drug addict, nor had he escaped an abusive relationship only to find himself in another one. He had not been stalked; no one was trying to kill him. And he had never been on welfare with three kids. Nothing like all of that had ever happened to him. She could almost hate him he had had such an easy time of it.

She was still twisting and turning, trying to find, in the shifting ground of her mind, some rational basis for her anger and humiliation, which was actually at the rebuff which he still had not given her, but that must be coming, she felt, any minute.

He had lit another cigarette right after the one he had just put out. He leaned now against the sink drain, smoking it and looking sad. She had no idea what he was thinking.

She sat down at the table, slowly, shakily, and put her head down on her folded arms.

"I don't want any of this coffee," he remarked. "Hey, Marina, do you like herb tea? I had some kind of rosehip stuff here in this drawer. Some girl gave it to me."

He put water in a pot on the stove while she raised her head, staring at him.

Together they watched the pot as it slowly, interminably, came to the boil. Then he poured an envelope of pink powder into the pot and again they watched while the tea was brewing. Finally he found a couple of mugs and poured out the cloudy pinkish liquid, full of floating debris.

It occurred to Marina that perhaps he was trying to poison her. She stared at the dirty-looking substance in the mug.

"Well, I don't know. I thought she made it that way. It tasted better, though. Maybe she strained out all this junk." He took Marina's untouched cup away, and poured it, with his own, down the sink. "Well, sorry, now there's nothing to drink because I poured it out."

Once again he was laughing, he was amused, he was teasing her. Making tea and taking it away before she had even tasted it. Lighting one cigarette after another. He had just lit another one.

"I make some kind of a salary," he remarked. "Do you think you and the kids can live on that?"

She nodded, not believing it, still watching him closely.

"Well, that's good, because you don't have much of a welfare file any more."

"What?"

"Maybe you're not going to like this. But I guess I'd better tell you about it. I went back to argue with your social worker this afternoon. I made an appointment. She says that they don't handle your boyfriend or whatever he was as a client. He wouldn't know where you pick up your cheque. In her opinion, you're having delusions about being pursued."

"That bitch!" shouted Marina. "How does she get off saying those things about me!"

"Well, she's not a good person, is she?" he remarked. "That's what I'm telling you. According to her you're paranoid and you have a history of delusions. And—oh yeah—she left me alone with your file. I guess she wanted me to read all that stuff about mental hospitals. She left it in the room with me."

"You saw my file!" It was a nightmare. "You read it? You had no right—! It was none of your business!" She had jumped to her feet again.

"I didn't exactly read it. Anyway, no one else is going to."

"What did you do to it?"

"I ate it." He touched his flat belly. "It was really hard to eat. It was lucky she had a water bottle on her desk. I could make it into little pills and chew it up. When she came back in I was eating it."

She laughed suddenly. He shrugged.

"I figured it would be hard for her to explain. 'I left this guy in my office with a file kind of accidentally-on-purpose and when I came back he'd almost eaten the whole thing.'"

"My God, what did she say?" They were both laughing now.

"I don't really remember. She was pretty annoyed."

It made her strangely lighthearted to think that the file, or at least part of it, had disappeared. Of course they had computerized records. But there were some things in there—letters, handwritten reports—that were gone. They were inside him; right now they were probably still being churned up in his stomach. Then they would be gone for good.

"Ugh!" he said, holding his belly. And they both began to laugh again.

After a moment he said rather plaintively: "Could I go to bed now? It's after 2:00. And I haven't really been to my office in three days."

"Okay."

He came over and stood in front of her. After a moment he took her hands and drew her to her feet.

"I've been looking for you—for a long time." He was holding her hands, looking down into her face.

"I came to live here, then I got elected to this job. I thought—maybe I can find my sister. But you weren't here. There wasn't a trace. The old people are dead. No one knew. I'd given up really. And then—there you were. Ordering me around. Messing up my life."

She smiled faintly. He laughed.

"Is the sofa where you want to be? I guess I'll have to get a couple of mattresses. There are plenty of rooms."

She nodded. He let go of her hands and went out of the room; she heard him running lightly down the stairs.

Marina lay on the sofa and did not sleep, staring into a picture that she had in her mind from long ago.

2

1983–4 · The Future Murderer

MARINA FELL ASLEEP AS IT WAS GETTING LIGHT. IT WAS LATE when she woke up. The kids were going to be late for school. She had no watch or clock, but she was used to telling time by the quality of the light; it was after eight. They were all in the kitchen already.

"I gave the baby his bottle, Mom."

"Did you have something to eat?" Cold dread was gripping her stomach. Something had happened last night; something she didn't understand. "Better go to school. You're going to be late!"

"It's Saturday, Mom."

She began making coffee, recalling the rosehip tea of the night before. It seemed like a dream, both of them sitting there so solemnly, watching the pot slowly come to the boil. And then how funny he had been, not even letting her taste it; teasing her like that.

But she still could not think of their conversation; her mind approached it, then shied away.

She said to Rose, who was cooking Spam, dreamily poking at it in the pan with a fork, "After breakfast we'll get packed up."

"Are we going someplace, Ma?"

Jasmine looked up anxiously. Only the baby remained in bliss, banging a spoon on the floor. He was sitting up very well these days.

"Where are we going?" Rose was frightened, she saw.

She did not know where they were going, that was the trouble. And she had no more money. The hundred was invested entirely in canned goods.

"He'll take us someplace."

"Oh. We're going with Tim."

Rose was completely placated, and Jasmine, who had been looking up in apprehension, hearing the note of panic in her mother's voice, in Rose's, returned again to reading her new book.

Grimly, Marina began to put some cans in her backpack. Rose, meanwhile, was serving out the slices of Spam. She sat down with a spoon to eat her portion.

"Have some too, Mom." There was an extra slice on a plate.

Marina sat down, but could not eat. She pushed away the plate.

Tim arrived suddenly in the kitchen. Marina could not look at him. All she felt was fear. Fear and disgust at what she had tried to do last night.

"Do I get this?" He was looking down at the plate of Spam.

"It's Ma's. But I guess she can't eat it."

"I want some coffee. That's all I usually have." He looked at Marina. She was no longer packing. It was a kind of stealing, to take those cans. But they would need food, wherever they went.

"Who drew the picture?"

"Oh!" said Rose. "I did." It was the picture of the spotted dog. Rose had carefully attached it to a cupboard door. There was no tape or thumbtack to hold it up; she had slid it into a crack.

"Is it a horse?" he asked.

"It's a dog!"

"Oh, I see. It's kind of like a dog. It has dog ears." He had taken down the paper and was holding it in his hands.

"Have you got a pencil?" he asked Rose.

"In my backpack." She got up instantly to get it for him and Marina felt a flash of jealousy and dislike of her daughter.

"I'm going to draw."

"Draw a horse!"

"Draw a dog and a horse and some kids in a field with the sun shining."

He took up the pencil and Marina turned away, biting her lip. She could never explain this to the kids; they would just have to get along with it somehow. He was not as important to them as other men who had gone out of their lives and there was no reason why they should remember in a few years that this had ever happened.

"What is it?"

"It's just lines."

"No. It's Ma. Look. It's her hair."

"Mom! Come look at this! He drew you!"

Marina looked. She couldn't help it. They had brought it over and were standing clustered around her insistently, holding out the paper.

He had not drawn her face but her body, twisted away, and the fall of her magnificent hair. It came down nearly to her waist, and right now it was loose. She had let it out of the clip but had not had time to comb it.

The picture was only a few lines, yet she saw in a flash that it was herself; it represented how conflicted she was, her fear. Her turned-away face, just shoulder and hip and hair, one arm and hand lifted as though to ward away physical attack.

She seized it out of Rose's hand and tore it across, then threw the pieces on the floor. Then suddenly, her stomach constricting, she burst into tears and fled for the bathroom.

❦ FOR A LONG TIME THERE HAD BEEN NO SOUND FROM THE KIT-chen. Marina had combed her hair and washed her face. She had crept upstairs and sat for awhile on the sofa, looking at the painting of the girl over the false mantel. Perhaps he had painted that. But it was unfinished. The girl had long hair as well, and downcast eyes, and she was gazing at something in her hand, a bright blur. Marina could not make out what it was.

The fear was growing in her again. This time she was afraid that he had done something to her kids. She should not have left them with him; she should not have gone even as far as the bathroom.

She crept to the kitchen door. No one was in the kitchen but Tim.

"I was going to my office and then Rose told me it was Saturday."

"Where are they? Where is Rose?" She was gripping the door frame and she heard the high shrill note in her own voice.

He shrugged. "She took the kids outside."

Marina plunged forward and went to the back door. He didn't stop her. She looked out and there were all three kids and another one whom she had never seen before, with a spotted dog. There was a horse grazing uphill. It was strangely like Rose's picture, the one she had asked Tim to draw.

Marina turned around, the door safely at her back. Now he was inside; she had an escape route.

"Look, it's okay," he remarked, holding his hands palm out. "See? No paper. No pencil."

"We're leaving. I—we can't stay."

"Oh God—what is this? You fill my house up with stew and beans. You take away all the bedcovers and hang underwear and baby clothes in the bathroom. You totally mess up my life, my job—even my mind. And now you can't stay?"

It was one of his comedy routines. She had forgotten about the underwear.

"Your dad killed my mother." His eyes went blank. He turned his head aside for a moment and Marina felt triumph. He had not denied it.

"She was my mother too," he said.

He spoke again after a moment. "Tim. I mean the little one. His dad is the future murderer, isn't he?"

"The guy who's stalking me, yeah."

"Do you blame your baby?"

"Of course not!"

"Then maybe you can see—" he spread his arms wide. "Why blame me?"

There was logic in it. And now that she was looking at him again she found that she was not afraid of him. Everything about him was mild; he was crazy, but he was harmless.

"So, okay. Do we understand one another—finally?"

"I just don't get why you are doing this!"

"Why not? You got it when you thought I was a total stranger. Now that it turns out I'm your brother you have to leave quick?" He was laughing. She smiled. She really had to.

"They've got some stake in this too, don't forget," he went on, indicating with a wave at the door behind her that he meant the kids. "I'm their uncle—God! Am I an uncle? Besides a hundred dollars worth of canned goods, they get me."

She nodded slowly. It did make sense. The kids liked him.

"You named the baby after me." He was smiling at her.

She smiled back. The wave of nausea that had come over her in his presence was behind her. Everything—or so it seemed at least while he was talking—could be put in perspective. She was here now, and strangely enough, she was safe.

"You'll stay? Then maybe I can go to work now."

"I thought it was Saturday."

"You don't know Indian Chief, sister. They work Saturday, Sunday, all night, all day. It's like being at a meeting that never comes to an end."

He was going out the door as he spoke. She watched from the porch as he climbed into the cab of his truck. He backed down the short gravel driveway, then turned and drove the hundred yards to the Band office, disappearing inside with a wave.

Left alone, Marina went back into the house. The kitchen was a mess, with dishes, the remnants of cooking on the stove, Tim's coffee cup on the counter. She sat down slowly in a chair, and after a moment, picked up the two halves of the torn picture and fitted them together into a spotted dog. Then she turned it over and inspected with amazement the drawing he had made of her, the terrified twist of her body and the fall of her beautiful hair.

Over the next few days Marina began to houseclean more seriously. The kids were in and out all the time with other kids. They tracked in dust and mud.

She had plenty of time to herself. Tim had an erratic lifestyle. He never ate at home. He ate in restaurants, at the café on the Reserve, ordering pizza to his office at midnight, at six in the morning. He was usually gone all day, till late at night. But then she thought he was used to sleeping in as well. When school resumed on Monday, he got up with the kids, but only because they woke him up.

At the end of the month he got a paycheque, apparently, for they went shopping for groceries again and for furniture. He bought

Marina a bed and a bureau. He got a couple of mattresses for the kids. Bedclothes. Even some toys: crayons, a bicycle.

Now she had a bedroom, the kids had one. There were more dishes. They ate canned fruit every day. Marina had money.

She surmised that Tim took his paycheque and turned it into money every month, then spent the whole thing. He must often run out before the month was up; he had been broke when she arrived. And he was probably broke again, or nearly so. Of the two of them, she had started out with the most cash, since he had given her hundreds of dollars the day they went shopping.

Slowly, timidly, she started to venture out onto the Reserve. To school in the morning with the kids, once to the small store for a video, with Rose; and to Tim's office, where she was stared at by the Band manager and the social worker. They did not actually stare—they peeked at her instead of staring—and she realized that he must have told them that she was his sister. So they knew who she was, then.

She was annoyed, fearful, overly aggressive—but she wanted him to buy her some diapers. She had to give him the money for them; he did not seem to have any.

Back home she was a little bored. The kids were at school. Life had been such a struggle for her recently that she was not able to relax. Even in the luxurious new bed she didn't sleep well.

Tim's room. She contemplated the open door, coming out of the bathroom. Her own room, so recently occupied, was already cluttered with clothing, both hers and the children's, bags of diapers, baby wipes, zinc ointment, her rudimentary makeup, a book, books belonging to the kids, drawings by Rose, a magazine.

His room was empty and as impersonal as it had been when she first saw it. She went in and sat on the edge of the mattress, thinking with a certain horror of the night when she had tried to seduce him.

What she had felt for him then had been very straightforward. Strong attraction, even love—love that derived from the feeling of safety that she got from him. Now her emotions were more complicated. She had never had a relationship like this with anyone.

It seemed like a kind of paradox, to love a man and not want to sleep with him.

She remembered how she had looked into this room the first day and thought it looked like a room in a motel. Furniture which was just there to support other furniture. Nothing actually in use but the bed.

She went over to the bureau and pulled out all the drawers to test this theory. There were two magazines in the drawer; she almost did not look to see what they were, it was so obvious that they would be there. But then she was surprised to see that they were women's fashion magazines, one of them a copy of *Vogue*, as thick as a telephone directory, and stinking of perfume samples.

Marina stared at this in bewilderment. This was not something for a man to have in a bedroom drawer. She remembered how he said that he slept with women. But there was no evidence that a woman had ever come to this house. She remembered the filth in the kitchen, the blackened floor, spattered stove, mouldy dishes.

The magazine in her room, also a woman's magazine, had actually been bought by Tim, she remembered. He had looked through it briefly, then thrown it in the shopping cart. She had thought it was a gift for her. But perhaps it had been for him?

She went back to her own room, taking the *Vogue* with her and sat on the edge of the bed, looking through it. There were pictures in it that she regarded as obscene, ads, movie stars with no clothes on. But the magazine he had bought for her in the supermarket was just an ordinary women's magazine, with recipes, crafts, pictures of people's gardens, many ads.

He came in later that night with the diapers.

"Kids in bed?" he asked. He liked the kids, especially Rose.

He threw the diapers in a corner, went for a cup of coffee, propped the back door open a crack, lit a cigarette, had two puffs, threw the end out into the snow—which had finally arrived—then came to sit opposite her at the table with a smile.

"You've got to take up—bingo or something, Marina. This place is pretty boring unless you're interested in politics. You aren't interested in politics, are you?"

"No."

"That's something else I like about you then."

He caught sight of the two magazines now and the quality of his smile changed. A slightly guilty look came over his face.

"You read these?" she demanded.

"Well, there's nothing much to read in them. I look at the pictures."

"Why?"

She just didn't get it. He said he slept with women. Miss Running Horse: she remembered how he had laughed, said, "Angie," in that teasing voice, yet he liked to look at fashion magazines? It seemed like some sort of obscure perversion to her.

"Look at this, Marina." He took up the *Vogue* and leafed through it to a full page ad, just of a woman's face. "Tell me what you see."

It was a very exotic-looking face, a young face, high cheekbones, dark hair; the eyes dark, enigmatic, innocent, but also wild.

"Some fashion model."

"A beautiful girl, right?"

"Yeah."

"If you went next door, would you see a woman like this?"

"Of course not."

He was leafing again, this time through the other magazine from the drawer.

"What about this?"

"Same girl?"

It was full length this time. Long, high-heeled boots, some kind of wild animal fur on the collar of the coat. She was running, looking over her shoulder, an expression of alarm on her face.

"Do you know her, or something?" It had dawned upon her that it was this girl he wanted to look at.

"Yeah. I know her. I know her," he repeated, looking down at the picture. He looked up again, not smiling. "She's Vicky Boucher," he said. "One of the Bouchers from this Reserve."

"Are you kidding?"

"No. It's because of her—because of her that I'm here now. I ended up here after she took off."

"She took off on you?"

"Do you think I kicked her out?" He was unsmiling still.

She wished to hear that he had. She was seized with a wild jealousy of this woman, much crueller and more violent than anything she felt for Rose's teacher. She wanted to tear the page out of the book and mutilate it, stamp on it.

"Well, she's far away and famous now. I just keep her around to look at sometimes," he remarked, closing the magazine and sending it skimming into a corner of the kitchen.

"You weren't married?"

"No." He was smiling his teasing smile again. "I never told you I used to be an artist, did I? I smoked dope and made art. That's how I got together with Vick. We did a bunch of stuff together."

"Here?" She was still having a violent reaction, concealing it as well as she could.

"Oh yeah. Here. Political art. That's how I got into politics. Vicky drove me into it. Then she got out. Good for her. Bad for me." He laughed.

Marina was thinking of the picture he had drawn of her. Rose had come home with tape and carefully reattached the two halves. It was up on the wall now, dog side out.

But there was another picture of a woman hanging in this house, she realized.

"Did you think I had a couple of wives in the background, trying to kill me?—The way you've got husbands?"

He really didn't take her seriously about that. But she didn't want to argue. Lionel only seemed like a probable kind of threat now when she was alone in the afternoon—or late at night. She could accept his skepticism right now—even share it to some extent, just because he was present.

"I just didn't get it. About the magazines."

"Well, now you know." He paused. "Look, Marina, there's another person you need to know. My dad."

"That whiteman? The lawyer?"

"I told him about you. How you showed up."

"Has he seen me? Has he been spying on me?"

"He hasn't seen you. He lives in Calgary. I talk to him on the phone every once in awhile."

She had jumped to her feet and was actually cowering on the other side of the kitchen.

"Why are you scared of him?" he asked gently. "He's good. He won't hurt you."

"He asked me questions. Tell me I'm lying. I dream about it."

"He wouldn't—Did I ask you anything? For God's sake, Marina."

"Call me a liar. Try to trip me up. Over what I say in court." When she was frightened like this, her voice rose and she spoke in sharp staccato sentences. Like herself as a child. The memory of herself as a witness was choking her.

"Look, he's getting old. I see him sometimes. He comes out here and hangs around. He likes this place. Don't ask me why." He widened his eyes and shrugged.

"He'll come here?"

"Sure. Why not. You'll give him a cup of coffee."

"When?" she demanded.

"I don't know. It'll happen. This is for me, okay? I don't like to keep my life in compartments."

FOR A MONTH SHE KEPT THE COFFEE POT GOING AND HE didn't show up. Then suddenly, it was Christmastime.

Marina was not prepared for the Christmas concert. The kids had told her about it, but at first she thought it was just something at school. This sort of thing had happened at various schools Rose had attended and Marina had always ignored it. Here on the Reserve it was harder to ignore. Everyone was going. The kids took it for granted that she was going. They were excited about costumes; she heard them singing their songs.

Then it emerged that Tim was going. He mentioned it casually. Apparently he always went. "I'll pick you up at 6:30," he said. The school was a hundred metres from his house. But Tim never walked anywhere.

"I'm not going to that."

"Why not?" Tim was just going out the back door to go to his office. It was the last day of school.

"There might be somebody."

"Sure there'll be somebody. And they'll all be staring at you too." He paused in the doorway, the cigarette already between his fingers.

"Maybe they'll know who I am."

"Sure they know who you are."

"How?" her alarm was choking her.

"Let's see." He began listing the points on his fingers. "Everyone knows who I am. I'm the Chief in this place, I have to remind you. You're my sister. Therefore, everyone knows who you are too."

"I can't go!"

He sighed patiently. "It's a school concert. And in this place, if you don't go to the school concert, that means you're sick. Or drunk. Or else—oh yeah—crazy."

She stared at him, her eyes dilated.

"You want people to talk about you? Don't go. Take my advice."

"But would they say—? Why would they say—?"

"People say whatever comes into their heads. It's a herd animal, didn't you know that? You get to be leader if you just happen to be up front one day." He lit the cigarette and began to run down the steps. "So I'll pick you up at 6:30."

The kids left right after supper, very excited. Jasmine was going to be an angel. She even had a white dress.

Tim picked her up at 6:30; he just waited for her outside, with the truck running. She came down the back steps, carrying the baby. He was a handful these days, beginning to creep around all over the place, pulling himself up on chairs and staggering from handhold to handhold.

"This is Dad," said Tim, pressing her into the cab. A shadowy figure stood to one side, holding the door open. "He always comes to this."

"To hear your speech," remarked the whiteman. In the flickering light as they passed under a street lamp, Marina caught a sidelong glimpse of his face: big nose, ten gallon hat. It was an ironic comment, apparently: his lips had a humourous set.

In the gym she had to sit beside him again. Tim deposited them in the front row and disappeared. Marina was busy with the baby, who twisted in her arms, arching his back until she had to put him on the floor. He rose to his feet by way of her knee and then began to creep along the line of chairs, still empty since they were right up front. Marina caught him and tried to hold him on her lap again. He gave an energetic twist and she put him down. This time he took to the other side, holding onto the whiteman's trouser leg.

"What's his name?" asked the man.

"Tim."

He picked up the baby, who seemed, suddenly, quite sanguine about being held.

"Tim, eh?"

Recorded Christmas carols were pouring at them through the speakers on either side of the stage. The large echoing room was full of noise: the cries of babies and young children, the rustle of conversation and scraping of metal chair legs against the floor. She didn't have to talk, and right up front where they were, she didn't see everyone looking at her. Aside from keeping one rigid shoulder and the fall of her hair towards her companion, Marina began to relax her defences.

Tim made a speech; it was the first item on the program. At first it seemed like a fairly simple speech of welcome, but he got onto something he called an issue and wrestled with it for some time. Marina was not listening, but from the restiveness of the audience, she felt that no one else was either. They all just wanted to see their kids in the pageant, the choirs.

"Well, that went down pretty badly, didn't it?" whispered Tim across her. He had come to sit on her other side.

The pageant had begun. Marina was stunned to see that Rose, her Rose, was playing the Virgin Mary. A big boy was Joseph; it upset and frightened Marina to see her daughter with a boy.

But the real surprise was Jasmine. With her hair flowing, her floating white costume, her bare feet, a halo made out of twisted brass wire, she looked like an angel. Her dark eyes were wide and shining, her lips solemn.

Tim whispered: "Hey! Look at Jasmine!"

"Which one is she?" asked the whiteman.

"The cutest angel."

The show was long; every class in the school had a play or a song. Marina's attention flagged after the pageant. Tim was sitting slumped in his chair. Only the whiteman on her other side sat bolt upright, apparently watching the whole thing, while the baby ranged along the empty line of chairs and then back to his knee.

She had a bad moment when they got up to leave. They turned around then and went into the crowd. People spoke to Tim and she was surprised to see that they also talked to the whiteman on her other side; some of them shook his hand. But they ignored her. Glances were veiled; Marina was afraid.

And then she saw a woman whom she knew from Calgary. Someone who had been in upgrading with her, who knew George and worse—Lionel. The woman stared at her across the crowd and it seemed to Marina that her stare was malicious; she had certainly been recognized.

"Hey, Marina, it's okay," whispered Tim. "Just think of it as a herd of elk or something."

Outside, he said to his dad, "Want to come home for a cup of coffee?"

"I want a drink, that's what I want."

Tim shrugged.

"Okay. Coffee it is."

Jasmine and Rose came running out the door. Jasmine's face was flushed, her long hair flashed loose under the light shining out from the gymnasium door.

"Stars of the show," said Tim. He was heading for his truck, even though the parking lot was clogged with vehicles backing out.

"We won't all fit in the cab," said his father. "Don't you ever walk anywhere?"

"Did you like it, Momma? Rose was good, wasn't she? Did you like the songs? Miss MacPherson said I could keep my costume. I wish I could wear it to school."

"Look, you guys, this is my dad," said Tim. They were walking home now, strung out along the road. "Rose, Jasmine, I don't know. What are they going to call you?"

"It's kind of a problem," agreed the whiteman.

"He's Tim too," said Tim.

"He is?"

"There's too many Tims," said practical Rose. "I think we should call him Grandpa."

"You okay with that, Marina?"

Marina was still rigid with fear. When Tim took her arm, she actually jumped away from him. "Hey, what's the matter?"

He stopped on the road while the others went on ahead.

"I saw somebody. A woman I know," she said. Her voice was hoarse. "She knows I'm here."

"Sure. Like I told you, everyone knows you're here."

Marina was silent. It was an emergency. But she saw again that he, like everyone else, really didn't believe in the danger she was in.

"Come on. Let's catch up with them." He took her arm again.

Up ahead, under a street light walked the whiteman with a prancing little girl on either side.

She didn't know this whiteman, she had not recognized him, and now the fear of Lionel overlaid this other fear. Lionel loomed in her mind's eye, larger than anybody else. She saw him, in his undershirt in a Calgary rooming house, cleaning his gun.

The girls had some juice and then went to bed, unresisting, taking the baby with them. They were still very excited, but the presence of Tim's dad made them shy and obedient.

"Sit with us, Marina," said Tim. She had been about to go down with the kids. She came back to stand just inside the inner door of the kitchen.

They had already started to talk about something, even while the kids were still there. Tim did not really live in the same world as the kids. He liked them, he talked to them sometimes, especially Rose, but he had nothing to do with dirty diapers, spilled juice, tantrums, putting to bed, getting dressed, night terrors, preferred or unpreferred foods. All of that simply did not exist as far as he was concerned; he was never in the same room with it. The father seemed to be more aware of the juice-baby-bottle-new-diaper-glass-of-water-kiss-goodnight scene than Tim was. He had been watching all that with a smile.

And with her too: Tim cared about her, but he did not know exactly what to do with her. If she had been a woman he had slept with she would very probably have been out of his life again by now. This stuff—the indigestible stuff of his speech, of this conversation he was now having with his adoptive dad: this was what he lived for.

"There has to be some kind of definition," Tim was saying. "If you let everyone into the club it ceases to exist. That's assimilation, really. It's a way of forcing us to assimilate."

"All I'm saying is that the Charter of Rights should apply across the board. It's a great thing. Let's let it work."

"Oh sure, that's the white liberal point of view. But maybe there's another level. Your country made a deal with my country; then it becomes illegal under some law you enact later. Did my country make that law?"

Tim's speech had been about this. But she had been too distracted, too nervous to listen to it.

"Okay, you're right. Justice is not just the law. But this is unjust. Why should a woman lose her identity just because she gets married."

"I don't know—She kind of consents to assimilate, doesn't she?"

"Does she cease to be the same person, with the history and background that she has?"

"No. And if it were only a question of that one individual, I'd say she shouldn't lose status either. But what about the husband? And the kids? Especially the kids? How do they fit into this?"

"But why does it only happen to the woman?" asked the white-man.

Marina had grasped finally what they were talking about. They were talking about her.

And at the same time, she suddenly recognized the lawyer. She had been standing there, looking from face to face in bewilderment. They were arguing hard, their untouched cups in front of them, and Tim had the abstracted, dreamy look he got when he was thinking. The whiteman spoke quietly, incisively, and finally it was that, something about his articulation, the way the words fell off his lips, that made her remember.

She must have made a sound, maybe a loud cry, for they were both looking at her. Then Tim got up and moved her into a chair,

[57]

putting her down into it quite firmly. A moment later he was standing beside her with a glass of water.

"She's pretty nervous," he was saying over his shoulder. "Too many people, maybe."

Marina even felt now that she had seen the old man attacking Tim. It had been like that. That quiet contradiction was a form of attack—a devastating form of attack.

"Marina," he said now, and hearing her name uttered by that voice, she knew again that she was right; this was the one.

"Maybe you'd better not try to talk to her, Dad. There's a whole bunch of stuff going on with her tonight." Tim was holding her hands, looking down at her with concern, while she struggled with her terror.

"Okay. I should go home anyway." The man got up and the kitchen seemed to be full of him. Only Tim stood between them, and he was both shorter and slighter than the big man, now putting on his huge hat.

"I'll just say this—I'm glad you found her. I'm glad you've got each other."

"I know. Thanks. Want a drive? Your car is over there."

"No. And besides, you can't drive me. Yours is over there too," he remarked in good humour, going out.

◖ SHE BEGAN AGAIN, VERY TIMIDLY, OVER THE NEXT FEW DAYS, to go out with the baby. At first she walked to school to collect the girls at lunchtime. Then she went with them in the morning as well.

She needed to go to the store again. They were finally beginning to exhaust their supply of cans. It was not just diapers she needed but coffee, spaghetti sauce, toothpaste, apple juice, milk, potatoes, eggs. And clothes. No one had clothes that fitted any longer except her.

Tim tried to give her the keys to his pickup so that she could go to the store. But she had never learned to drive a car. He was surprised and horrified that she had no driver's license. "How did that happen?" he demanded.

"Never had the money to own one."

"But what happened when you were a teenager? Those people you stayed with must have had cars. Didn't you get driver education in school?"

"I told you. I never finished school. Not till I did upgrading ten years ago."

"Well, okay. I should teach you to drive."

"When are you going to do that?"

"Starting right now. It'll take less time in the long run than driving you everywhere."

They began driving all over the Reserve in the mornings. The baby had started going to daycare a couple of mornings a week and this helped to make their driving lessons possible. He said she was a fast learner.

There were only about seven miles of pavement in the place, but the country roads went out into the hills, rutted, barely drivable. They went on these and Tim seemed to know them all. It explained the condition of his truck.

"There's a lot more to this place than that little cluster of broken-down houses, you know?" he remarked. He threw his cigarette butt out the passenger side window. Marina was driving slowly and carefully down a winding rutted trail on the river cliff.

It had been a winter of little snow. The hills were barely skimmed with it. A biting January wind blew it into the valley below, where the river lay, locked in ice.

They had come to the end of driveable road. She began backing and filling to turn around.

"Sometimes I look at the River and wonder if that is really what it's all about," he continued.

"What it's all about?" They were fully turned around now and the landscape they looked across was harsh and bitter. The buck-skin browns of late summer and fall had become grey with snow, drifted in around the houses, which looked, even from a distance, brown and broken as he described them. They were facing east, over the rough land, a less optimistic prospect than the vision of mountains with cold blue sky above.

"Let's go down there," he suggested, and Marina began to drive carefully back down onto another trail. The River was hard to get to; it did not flow through the little town of the Reserve, which was out on the prairie where the government had put it.

They came to an outlook and she stopped, keeping the motor running for the sake of the heater, which was barely competing with the wind.

"What does it all mean? Why do I want to stay alive?" he asked. "Because of this thing called I, this brain or mind? Why am I attached to that?"

She shrugged.

"That's what modern life is trying to persuade us of anyway. That all we've got is this little me-thing, which only exists for this short span of time. The thing is to get as much as possible right now—because that's all there is, that's all you're going to have."

"You don't have kids."

"Kids—." He pondered. "Do they make you feel immortal, or something? A bit of you that goes on after you die?"

"No. You know you have to live. To protect them," she said. "Sometimes it keeps me awake at night—what would happen if they lost me. What it would be like for them."

He turned to look at her, interested, lively, no longer pensive, vague, the way he had been.

"But did you want to have kids, Marina? Did you know you wanted them?"

"No. But now I've got them—I'd die for them if I had to." She spoke fiercely.

"So having kids gets you beyond that me-thing?"

She nodded. She was having an easier time understanding him than she usually did.

"Well, I guess I missed it then, Marina."

She wanted to say something which would serve to deny this, or at least to hide it from him. For she felt it was true.

Of course he was still young enough to marry. But she had seen the way he studied the girl in the magazine. And a woman like that was never going to settle down with him in one of those little houses and have kids. Marina felt this with fierce joy. He would never have kids; he would never have them with that girl.

"I guess that's kind of what I get out of the River," he went on, now turning to look down upon it, frozen, snow-covered, with the crazy wind blowing wisps and puffs off the drifts into the air. "It's had meaning for us since—well since pre-history. The River came first, then we lived here. You and I, Marina—we lived here all this time."

She had an inkling of what he meant, at least the 'you and I' part of all that. It was impossible to make sense of the 'you and I' that they formed unless it was of some importance that they were brother and sister, that they belonged to this small group of people who lived on this River, to whom this place had had significance since tribal memory failed. In all the years she had lived in the city, Marina had never cared for one place over any other—some apartments were, of course, markedly worse—some rooms utterly wretched. But all that time this Reserve was in her heart. Perhaps the life or death of the individual was of no importance, but the River reminded them that they belonged to something.

"See, I think you don't know—" he was saying. "But they've been trying to take this River. Actually they've been trying to do that since the settlers arrived. First they drove us out here. But then they wanted the water for irrigation. Now the government intends to dam the River upstream of the Reserve and take the whole thing. But they aren't going to get it." he added. "Not while I'm alive."

◀ TIM HAD BEEN SURPRISED TO DISCOVER THAT THERE WAS A daycare.

"Well, I guess it's been going on for a while," he said. "I don't know where they get the money, though. We don't fund it. Some drug program, probably."

Marina thought that this was typical. He was discovering some things he needed to know, in her opinion. For she saw him as sheltered, naive in certain ways. It was partly because of his background, his whiteman's education, the fact that he had never married, had no kids—but most of all, she considered, it was that he was a man.

What she was going to do with the baby while she was learning to drive—or taking a federally-funded, computer course on the

Reserve, which she had begun doing—he had never asked himself a question like this before.

She finished the computer course in very short order and got a part-time job with the housing authority, helping to computerize their records, which were in a mess, as she discovered.

Tim found her having this job a great irony, as he was now conducting a long struggle with the housing board about his house. It had been allocated to him when he became Chief; but Marina's living there—especially with her kids—suddenly put the question of why he had been given so much space under the microscope. He pointed out that if he had married, or even just been living with a whitewoman, there would have been no dispute over his entitlement. The fact that Marina was Native, was his sister, his closest blood relative, seemed to count against her occupying the house, rather than for it.

And there was a similar dispute going on with the school, which received no federal funding for the attendance of non-status children. Tim had taken now to driving the kids over there every morning. The teachers loved it when he came in with Rose and Jasmine.

Marina got no feeling from him that he was under any pressure on account of her. He fought these battles easily, with humour, without anger—winning on every front, at least locally. But it was a paradox, because when she remembered his speech at Christmas and his conversation with his whiteman father, he was with the First Nations leadership on this question of status; he was with the other men.

Tim's father did not come to the house, but the children sometimes told her that they saw him, that he came to the Reserve. He had worked for the Reserve as a lawyer, and even now that he was semi-retired, he went to the Band office, he saw Tim—and gave Tim advice in the struggle over the dam on the River that Tim sometimes took and more often did not take.

Rose was talking about an Easter dinner, an actual turkey dinner, not something from cans. She began planning it weeks in advance.

Marina really hated cooking and had never done a turkey, but on Easter Sunday she found herself being woken up early by Rose

[62]

to put it in the oven. Real mashed potatoes—not from a box. Jello salad, not just canned fruit. Rose was relentlessly conventional.

Rose, of course, was the only one who could remember their more or less normal life before Lionel came into it. She remembered George—and Marina was convinced that she secretly grieved for him. However, there was nothing that could be done about that; if George was not dead, he was untraceable—without an address or a job, probably without anything but a needle in a back alley.

They put the huge meal on the table—which was scarcely large enough for all the food—and then suddenly Tim turned up with his dad, who was wearing a cream-coloured three-piece suit and cowboy boots with his huge white hat.

Marina realized that someone had planned all this. Rose had arranged it through Tim, probably. She would certainly have had to invite Tim specially, who otherwise would never have come to a meal in the middle of the day like this. He had no schedule for eating at all.

"You know, I have to go to a Band feast tonight.—I guess you didn't," Tim remarked good-humouredly.

The girls sang the grace that they sang at school. Then everyone had a piece of turkey. There were not enough chairs. Marina stood over by the sink, not eating. Tim perched on a kitchen counter, nibbling on a wing. His dad and the kids occupied the table.

The dad seemed to be on perfectly easy terms with the kids, and here again, she felt that there must have been something going on behind her back. He produced chocolate eggs for all of them from his coat pocket after they had finished with the turkey. Tim looked at his egg, lying on the counter, with a pensive smile.

Marina took hers from Tim, who passed it over. She was still afraid of his father, but less so. There was a kind of tacit agreement—she saw that he was a party to this—not to mention the past. And by now, with Tim and the kids, there was so much of the present to talk about, that this did not feel like any kind of omission.

"Why don't you have a phone here?" the whiteman was asking Tim.

Tim shrugged. "Too much trouble. I have one at the office. Bad enough."

"Yes, but Marina and the kids are living here. I should think it would be useful for them. For instance, we could have called up to ask what time to come to dinner."

"Rose told me."

"Well, maybe Marina would like to use it sometimes. You don't leave a woman with kids alone in a house without a phone."

Tim's eyebrows shot up in ironic surprise. "I didn't think of that."

"Okay. Now you did."

When Tim came back from the feast it was nearly midnight. His dad had gone with him, and so had the kids, but Marina was still shy of public events. Even though Tim was right; everyone on the Reserve knew she was here, knew who she was. She was still afraid of being seen by that woman, the woman who might tell Lionel she was here, who might have already told him she was here.

"Wait a second," said Tim. "I've got something for you. I left it in the truck."

He went out the door to get it as Marina began shooing Rose and sleepy Jasmine, her thumb in her mouth, downstairs to bed.

She had been waiting up for them, feeling anxious, as she always did when they were away. Now she merely felt irritable. He should have brought the kids home earlier. But he had no sense of time.

Tim came back in, carrying an oversized Easter bunny, pink and white, fluffy and vulgar. It was not like him to buy such a thing; she immediately felt his difference from it. But she was thinking that the baby might like it—or Jasmine. Rose was too old—too smart.

"Where did this come from?"

"Dad," he said. "It's for you."

Marina gazed at the Easter bunny, now perched upon a chair, its floppy ears, its crazed expression, the polka-dot bow tie it wore. And suddenly a cold wave swept over her—a wave of recognition, of nauseated recollection. It was so like, so very like, the stuffed bunny her father had given her long ago. Was the whiteman giving her this to taunt her somehow, to torment her?

"What's the matter?" said Tim.

Marina really could not speak. She wanted to bury her face in the bunny's fluffy fur and weep. But another part of her wanted to tear it apart, to pull out its polyester insides and jump and stamp on it.

He had not come back. He had not rescued her. Her father had taken the easy way out, got drunk or stoned, and drowned, leaving her to the courts, the juvenile detention system, the streets and the hospitals.

This was the only present, the talisman, that had meant so much to her, that had sustained her through so many years of bitterness and terror. How could the whiteman have known?

"Look, what is this? I think he just felt kind of stupid about actually giving it to you."

"No!" said Marina. She was clutching the bunny now, digging her fingers into it.

"Honest, Marina. I was with him when he bought it. There was some stuff like this in the gas station. He said he gave you one a long time ago. He wasn't sure you'd remember."

Marina made a loud inarticulate sound, her face buried in the toy.

"Well, I guess maybe you do remember," said Tim helplessly.

She felt that she was going to cry all night. She cried in the kitchen while Tim tried to remove the bunny from her grasp. Then she cried on the sofa while they sat together, his arm around her.

"Well, maybe all this can be true at the same time," Tim suggested. He had been able slowly to piece together what she was crying about.

"Maybe my dad bought it, but your dad gave it to you."

But Marina shook her head, turning her face into his shoulder in misery. She knew now that she had put the whole thing together herself; someone had given her this bunny and she had thought, she had hoped, that it was her father. That picture she had, of him on his haunches, giving her the enormous rabbit—it was gone. She had made up that picture and held it in her heart for years. It seemed impossible that a picture could be untrue, but that one was.

"Well, perhaps there was more than one of the stupid things then. The world is full of them," he was saying.

Again she shook her head. But she was just about empty of tears.

"Okay. Here's what he said. Maybe I shouldn't tell you; I don't want to start you off again. He said he felt pretty sorry for you. That's why he bought you the rabbit back then. He said he always wondered whether you got it. You were being kept away from everybody by that team of prosecution lawyers. And he knew—I mean, of course, he must have known—how you felt about him. He took me, in the end. But he couldn't take you."

She was too far gone for denial. She merely stayed where she was, pressed against Tim's side. After a long while she fell asleep like that, woke briefly to find him covering her up with a blanket, then slept again till morning.

◖ THE PHONE WAS INSTALLED THE FOLLOWING WEEK. MARINA had stopped working for the housing board, not because of conflict of interest—for everyone understood very well that housing disputes could go on for years and everybody who worked for the board was in any case, more or less in conflict. She had taken a less interesting job in the daycare to keep the baby in. The daycare was agitating for funding, with Tim, as usual, on the wrong side of the question even though he drove Marina and the baby over there on Tuesday and Thursday mornings.

Marina was incredibly, disbelievingly happy. Jasmine had finally learned to read, the baby was walking, they had new things in the house every month—furniture, new clothes, toys; nice things, pretty enough clothes to satisfy even Rose. But the best thing of all was the devotion of Tim. He showed no signs of irritation or boredom with the kids, although he still functioned in an essentially abstract universe, in which food scarcely figured, let alone bathroom stops, drinks of water, favourite blankets. Whatever he did all day when he was working, she had his complete attention when he came home, when they sat together late at night in the kitchen and he talked to her, while she struggled to understand, about the Reserve, about aboriginal rights, about history and ecology, about native spirituality, about capitalism and Native socialism. About the River—and the dam.

It had been started in the 1970s, then stopped, while government-sponsored inquiries followed upon one another. In the meantime, the River continued to flow down through the Ochre Reserve, undiverted. The dam site that had been identified and prepared fell more and more into the purview of the Natives, who although excluded from its initial construction, had gradually become its guardians, its watchmen and janitors.

There was hardly any other type of employment for men on the Reserve. Surrounded by ranch country, the Reserve had no farms. A café that was open intermittently, the gas station and the little store beside it on the highway; these were the only businesses. There was no oil, no other revenue from natural resources. These people had only one thing that anybody wanted: the water of the River.

"You'll hardly believe this," Tim said. "But there's a whole faction here now that wants me to plead with the government to build the dam on the Reserve. We already get a bit of revenue from leasing out our land, but if we could irrigate, it would be more valuable. Farming. It's money." He shrugged. "Well, they'll have to get me out first. But maybe they will."

◀ THE PHONE RANG. IT WAS TIM. IT WAS TIM'S FATHER LOOKING for Tim. Once it was Rose calling from school to say that Jasmine had vomited.

This time it was nobody.

Marina put the receiver down and stared into space for a few moments.

It was probably a wrong number. There were telephones in many houses on the Reserve and they still functioned on a tiny obsolete circuit, using four digit numbers. To call in from outside required eleven digits, always a long distance call, even from Joshua's garage on the highway. They weren't in any phone directory—it was like calling a foreign country from Alberta.

It had to have been a wrong number.

Marina forgot about it almost immediately, for everyone came home at once, Tim from work, Rose and Jasmine from school.

Tim was going to Edmonton to make a speech. He left, wearing his usual clothes, and carrying the bearskin robe that he wore on ceremonial occasions.

She was alone all night, sitting up, waiting for him, then realizing that he was not coming, but watching, waiting beside the phone. Which did not ring.

Tim was back early in the morning. "I went to some shindig with the premier. He liked my dress," he said. He took a shower and then went to work.

All was normal. Marina went to work, taking the baby.

In the afternoon she took little Tim and they went to a play-group one of the daycare mothers had organized. Many of these women were actually relatives of hers and most of them were aware of it. About her history, her background, they had nothing to say at all. The little community absorbed her as it absorbed most things that happened, knowing, but not saying what it knew.

The playgroup was in an ordinary house, a smaller, shabbier one than Tim's. The mothers clustered around a coffee table in the living room, chatting, drinking pop and tea, while the older kids played outside on tricycles, the little ones with large plastic blocks at their mothers' feet. Marina was older than most of these women and she did not have much to contribute.

Later, some of the women would begin to play cards and she would take little Tim home. Cards often went together with liquor and Marina was careful about that. She stayed away from trouble.

She noticed, bored, the guns above the sofa. It was an open rack: someone's handiwork, for the guns rested on fretwork notches. Those guns lying there made her think of Lionel's guns, his hunting rifles; but he had a handgun as well.

It was hard to believe that he had been very attractive to her once. He had seemed like a way out of all the dubiety and hardship of her former life, although he worked as a janitor. He had tried for the Mounties but had not got in, because, as she now suspected, the suppressed violence in his character had put them off. He had once been a security guard—but when he lost the job, he had kept the gun.

They had no guns at home because Tim did not hunt. He was

one of those new-style chiefs who had an education, who dealt with the whiteman on his own terms. She supposed that his prestige derived from his cleverness, for he had no old-time skills.

Later, she took the baby and went home. The girls were already there, eating peanut butter on toast.

The phone rang. Rose picked it up and said hello. After a moment she put it down again.

"Who was it?"

"Nobody." She returned, unconcerned, to her piece of toast.

That never happened again. From then on the caller concentrated on the morning and early afternoon, times the caller knew that only Marina would be home. He seemed to know—he had guessed—that there was a man.

Tim was spending time in Edmonton these days. Another environmental hearing about the dam was going on, and Tim was attending.—Was that really why he was away? Marina wondered whether there was a woman.

She told Tim about the calls. He was preoccupied. "Some whacko," he remarked.

"I think it's Lionel."

"Well, so what? You're with me. He'd have to know that in order to call you."

"That's bad."

"You're on the Reserve. You're safe."

"He could come here. Then he could—could just ask."

"Yeah, but look, Marina." He led her to the window. "House over there. House on the other side too. Strange whitemen don't come here. Out here, they're scared of us, not the other way around."

She shook her head. She knew she wasn't safe.

"Do you want me to get rid of the phone?"

She didn't want him to do that. The phone was Lionel's way of harassing her; but she might need it. She might need it if he actually came.

It did not occur to either of them to get the police involved. The police were not the friends of anyone on the Reserve.

The fourth call came very late at night. Marina had been sleeping on the sofa, waiting for Tim, or for Tim to call. When she got the silence on the other end, she tried to talk into it, to negotiate with it. "All right. We're here. But you should be glad, Lionel."

The silence was intense, a listening silence.

"It's my brother Tim I'm staying with. I found my brother."

It was important to try to explain the relationship. Jealousy was one of the things that fuelled his hatred. Whoever had told him she was here—if it was that woman—had probably heard of the relationship. He could verify that what she said was true, that she wasn't living with a lover.

"I'm not doing you any harm. Why are you following me?" she cried.

But he still did not speak. And finally she put the receiver down. Then went around the house locking doors and latching windows. Undoubtedly he had been calling from Calgary. Just calling to see if she was here; although someday his call would be a prelude to his coming.

He had beaten her up a few times. Once she had stabbed him with a paring knife. The knife had gone into the muscle of his upper chest, above the heart, about an inch away from the arm. There had been a lot of blood, but luckily, she missed the artery. He had been very sore there for weeks, but oddly enough, it had put him in a good humour. They even joked about it. Her taking him seriously enough to snatch up a weapon in self-defence; this had flattered him somehow.

Their relationship had only lasted about a year, long enough for the baby to be conceived and born, long enough for Marina to have to protect her huge belly—and her other kids—while being pushed and kicked and slapped. She had not had anything like this with George Cartwright, who simply slipped away from her into his habits, plunging deeper, leaving her to cope with increasing financial desperation. When Lionel had come along he seemed like someone who cared, whom she could depend on, whom she desperately needed at that time. It seemed ghastly now, to look back on it and to realize how abject she had been, how she had been willing to crawl to him on her knees, to plead and cry.

He would allow no friends, no contact with her husband, even though the kids missed him; and she had obeyed. Now she realized that the fact that Tim was her brother would not allay his consuming jealousy. He wanted her to have no one.

He would be coming out here soon. Tim was in danger too. It was not just herself and the kids.

The next afternoon, at the playgroup, she asked the woman, now almost a friend, Mary Tall Grass, if she would teach her to hunt.

Mary was a woman in her thirties with two kids, a little boy about Rose's age and a toddler. She lived alone, although her boyfriend, who was the baby's father, slept there intermittently. The guns were hers, and she was actually rather famous on the Reserve for her independence, her ability to shoot and trap, which she had got from being the oldest in a family of girls brought up by a widowed father. Tim had mentioned this when Marina told him about the playgroup; and Marina gathered from his smile, from the way he said her whole name, "Mary Tall Grass," that he liked her, that he had probably slept with her.

She thought that he must have slept with every pretty young single woman on the whole Reserve. But she overcame her jealousy; she liked Mary Tall Grass too.

They went out on the hills, now emerging from snow cover and beginning to exhibit a verdant green in patches, and the brief spring flowering of the dry land. They took advantage of daycare mornings; Marina had quit her job there now. Daycare bothered less about status than Housing did. They walked the tracks on which Marina had learned to drive Tim's truck, looking for targets to shoot at with the .22: crows, rabbits, pop cans set up on distant rocks.

Mary was having a good time. "I never get out like this any more," she said.

She was only about thirty, and she had lived her whole life on the Reserve. She had gone to a residential school on the Reserve, then later she had gone to Abercrombie for a year or so, before quitting high school. It was a sheltered life, from Marina's perspective, an easy life.

About her boyfriend, she confided, "I kind of love him, but I want to stay single. I'm freer that way."

To Marina she seemed very free, very innocent.

It was the place that sheltered her, as it was now sheltering Marina. A kind of benign neglect existed here; she was able to see how it functioned now. To the men, the place had a political existence. It made a claim, a statement to the outside world. It also existed in the world of nature, as Tim had pointed out to her; a tract of land surrounding a river, threatened from the outside but still preserving the people who had sprung out of the place, with a nexus of beliefs, the fragments of a language, a tradition of resistance to the whiteman's society all around them.

To the women, however, it provided welfare in the truest sense, a place to raise a family with the help of an extended family of grandmothers, sisters, cousins and aunts, and with the occasional preoccupied male also functioning as a babysitter.

Mary had been to Calgary; she went occasionally into Abercrombie or Steamboat, but she was surprised to hear that Marina went outside for groceries.

"Too many whitemen," she said. "Since Joshua started selling milk and stuff I usually go there for everything but meat."

The meat, Marina gathered, had been got by hunting in the days when Mary had gone hunting with her father and had run a snare line.

"We used to go after elk sometimes. Back in those days we used to hunt for food all the time. My sister's husband took the 30-30. I got the .22 and the shotgun."

"What is a thirty-thirty for?"

"Oh—deer. Antelope. Those buck elk can get pretty big. You really need something heavier. Don't you know anything about guns?"

"I grew up in the city," said Marina.

"Why do you want to learn to shoot, anyway? Hardly anybody does much hunting these days. The big herds are gone."

"To defend myself," she replied. "To defend my kids." And she thought of Tim, too, who had no concept of the malice of a man like Lionel.

"No kidding," Mary was saying. "But you're safe here. No one comes here." The younger woman looked at her in perplexity. "No whitemen, I mean."

"I'm afraid of my ex-boyfriend, the baby's father. He's phoning me."

"What does he say?"

"Nothing. He does it to scare me. When I was living in Calgary I had to keep moving."

"Why don't you just hang up?"

"I do. But he's found out."

"Found out?" The other woman was concerned.

"Found out things," Marina said vaguely. But she felt no doubt about it. He found out when she was there and when she wasn't, who else lived in the house, whether the kids were in school, what happened late at night.

"Tim's there, isn't he?" asked Mary.

"He's there." But she could take no comfort in this. Tim was more unaware of the real threat that existed than this girl. And he was not always there nowadays.

They started walking again. Marina had the .22 now. Mary had been shooting rabbits. She had three in the bag. When they went back home they were going to skin them for stew.

Suddenly one started almost from under their feet. It was a good hill for rabbits; Mary had said that. Marina took aim, quick, but clumsy, even with the light little gun. The rabbit was in her sights. She could kill it. She squeezed the trigger.

The rabbit sprang up in the air, twirling, as if in a dance, then fell down on the harsh grass. When they came up to it it was still breathing. Its eyes glazed over as Marina stared down at it and it was dead.

That was all there was to death then. Death by gunshot. It was easy.

Mary hoisted it up by the back legs and dropped it in the bag. "Good for you."

She took the gun now and aimed it at an old stump. Marina caught a glimpse of her absorbed face as she took aim, then slowly lowered the barrel of the gun again with a wistful expression. "It's kind of like the good old days," she said.

They had a small, two-family feast that night with their four-rabbit stew. Tim came home unexpectedly.

"I'm still hanging in there," he remarked. "Between the people in Edmonton who want to kill me and the people out here who want to kill me."

Marina was more worried about the food. Mary's boyfriend brought his friend, William Hogan. With five adults and five children, the four rabbits were hardly enough. They supplemented the meat with buns, pickles and canned peaches.

Marina saw that Tim was glad that she was getting to know people on the Reserve, that she had a friend. He had been surprised and pleased by her various jobs too. Seeing him together with Mary she was sure that there had been something between them. Whatever it was, it lingered a little with Mary, who looked at him shyly, her face slightly flushed.

Mary's boyfriend, Don, and his friend William, were quite different from Tim. A few years younger, used to the same sheltered culture as Mary; they rarely took off-Reserve jobs. William Hogan was working off-Reserve as a bear monitor for the Ochre River Dam project.

The two younger men were talking about hunting bears and Marina began to listen intently.

"Some of them suckers are as big as a house."

"What calibre rifle would you need for a grizzly?" asked Marina.

They were sitting on the floor around a sheet that had been spread out in the living room. Tim was lying on his elbow, coffee cup in hand, listening with a smile.

"Hunting stories," he remarked to Rose, raising his eyebrows.

"Aim for the head," said Don. "If you hit a bear in the chest it just makes him wild."

"Slows him down when he gets hit, though."

"Yeah, but it's like having a gravel truck coming towards you, down grade, fully loaded. Think you can really stop that?"

"He doesn't change his mind once he gets after a man, that's for sure."

"But it's a funny thing. They don't usually eat the corpse. Just maul it a bit, roll it over and over, tear off a few things." Don grinned.

"You have to speak to the bear," contributed Tim.

Don laughed. He looked at William. "That'd give him all the time in the world to claw you up," he said.

"There's an affinity between bears and men," said Tim. "They aren't cannibals."

"Affinity—what does that mean? They sure don't stop to talk."

"They don't talk. But they can understand human speech."

"Oh, come on!"

"I'll tell you what you have to say to the bear." He jumped up and Marina suddenly remembered the tattered bearskin he always lugged off with him to meet the whiteman. In its downtime it lay around on the floor of his bedroom closet.

He began to chant, and the two younger men, heavier and chunkier, looked up at him in naive surprise.

There was a kind of magic in the moment, the falling shades of evening in the room, yellow electric light streaming in from the kitchen doorway, Tim standing above them, solemn and gracile, singing his bear chant. It went on for some time; even after he stopped they were somewhat spellbound.

"Where'd you learn that?" demanded Don.

"I'm Medicine Bear, remember," said Tim lightly. He sat down cross-legged.

"You going to teach me that?" asked William. "I might need it."

"Sure."

"Yeah, but what does it say? What does it make the bear do?"

Tim shrugged. "The bear does whatever he's going to do, my friend. The song doesn't have much to say about that."

"So he claws you up anyway." William was disappointed.

Yet they had been in the presence of some kind of magic, they all knew it.

Tim was looking at his watch. Then he was going out the back door. Going to Edmonton with his ratty bearskin under his arm. The dam was drawing him there—the endless argument that was going on about that; Marina believed this now. It was not women that he cared for, but something in his own thoughts, in the power of his persuasion.

But would he be able to practise his brand of magic on white-men in suits at long tables with microphones? And she wondered, as with the bear, whether he would get clawed up anyway.

THAT NIGHT SHE WAS ALONE AGAIN. LYING, WAKEFUL AND terrified on the sofa, she knew that she was going to have to get hold of a gun somehow.

The following day she and Mary borrowed William Hogan's car and took it to the big supermarket in Abercrombie. Tim had taken his truck with him to Edmonton. It was almost always gone nowadays; but William's car was easy enough for Marina to drive, an automatic. She had become quite confident about her driving these days. It was a big old Chevrolet with a shattered offside front window and no reverse gear. Marina pulled it through a line of parked cars some distance away from the store, so that they could drive straight out. Little Tim had stayed behind on the Reserve with Mary's baby, safe with Mary's grandmother.

The store was full; it was Saturday morning. Mary was rather shy and uneasy. She stuck close to Marina, sharing the cart with her. They both had only a few purchases, mostly meat bargains, since Marina had taken to buying milk and sliced bread at the gas station store.

Mary went to the pharmacy to get a bottle of hand lotion and Marina lingered by the tiny post office in the front of the store. There was a glass-panelled room in front of her where the store sold videos—the place was really four or five stores in one—and through the glass she caught a glimpse of Lionel's head. A man with Lionel's head was renting a video. A moment later, he turned around and she was certain: his short, clipped hair, his blue eyes, the determined, fierce set of his lips.

He saw her; she was sure he had seen her. His eyes were on her, but they did not seem to register recognition. He paused, glancing down with a frown at something on the counter beside him. It was almost as though he were giving her a chance to get away.

Marina had frozen there, her grocery bags hooked over her

fingers. When he came out, carrying the video, he brushed past her, pausing just to whisper, so that only she heard him: "Bitch! Now I have to kill you!"

"I had a hard time finding the good stuff," said Mary breathlessly. "The store had so many brands. What's the matter, Marina?"

"I saw Lionel."

Mary looked all around. "Where is he?"

"He's gone."

"Oh!—I just thought—if I saw him too—"

It was always like this, Marina knew. With social workers, police, friends, with Tim, with everyone she had ever told about Lionel. Whether they had met him or not, after only a short while her fear began to seem excessive and paranoid to them. Then they disbelieved her, or at least didn't take it seriously. Yes, he might have said he was going to kill her, but people said such things. He had abused her; it was natural to be resentful and nervous after such experiences, but to fear for her life—this was really all in her mind.

"Let's go," said Marina.

She did not doubt he was watching her to see the car and it occurred to her that seeing this car would lead him only to William. It would not help him to trace her. But then, he knew where she was anyway. It was only a matter of time.

William Hogan was still employed as a bear monitor and since he was making good money and was friends with Mary and Don, he began taking them all out in his car from time to time, including Marina. They went to a drive-in movie, as the warm weather had begun to arrive, and Marina found herself in the front seat with William holding hands. He was very shy. Holding hands, that was it.

The following week he quit his job as a bear monitor. It seemed to Marina that he might have done this because of her—to have more time to get to know her. Then she thought this must really be her imagination. Sitting in Mary's kitchen over coffee, he scarcely looked at her.

It was Mary who suggested that he take her out hunting and show her how to shoot his heavy rifle. They all went in the end,

Don, Mary, Marina and William, and had a long walk over the rolling hills, taking turns with the .22 and the rifle on all the stumps and rocks and crows in the uplands.

William Hogan said she was a good shot. She had very good eyesight; it was still good, even though she was in her forties.

Marina told him she wanted to borrow the gun.

"What do you want it for?"

"To sleep with," she said.

"To sleep with!" He found it fascinating, even sexy, she saw, the idea of her sleeping with his rifle. The sexiness would have attracted Lionel too, and this thought nauseated her. For a moment she thought she might even throw up.

"Marina's got a crazy boyfriend and she's worried that he's after her," interposed Mary. "You could let her have the gun, William. You don't need it for work any more."

He did let her have it and she took it home and hid it under the pillows on her bed. She knew that Tim would not like to have it in the house; she didn't want the kids to see it either. But sleeping with it under her head, with her hand under the pillow just touching the stock, gave her the deepest security she had felt in months.

It seemed to her that William Hogan could not have any real interest in her. The trip to the drive-in had not been a date exactly; nothing had happened, and in any case, like Mary, he was still only in his early thirties. But when she went to bingo the following Saturday, he showed up at her table; he was soon sitting beside her. He bought her cards, a bottle of pop.

Later, walking home, Mary asked, "Hey, William, are you still staying at your mother's place?"

"Yup," said William, beside, although slightly behind Marina.

"William looks after the whole family," Mary remarked. "And he's not even really one of them. He was adopted off another Reserve. He doesn't come from around here."

"Grew up in the place though," said William gruffly.

An outsider. She had been thinking for a moment that he was an outsider like herself, when she realized that she was not an outsider at all.

Mary broke away and continued walking towards her home

with a brief wave, leaving Marina standing in front of her own doorstep, with William, stock-still, shy and nervous, at her side.

He couldn't come in. The kids were not there; they were with Mary's grandmother, who was often the babysitter these days. But he couldn't come in anyway, because she didn't want him to. She was not attracted to him, slow-spoken, unsophisticated, not old enough or smart enough. He was her very opposite, in many ways, and she thought this was probably the source of his interest in her.

Irritated, she allowed him to kiss her, a shy, inexperienced kiss. But she went up the steps and inside without a word after that, leaving him standing on the gravel pad of the house in the darkness, staring after her.

She was aware, in the presence of this difficult courtship, how much she was still in love with Tim. She could not have Tim, she knew; but she had not forgotten, could never forget, how he had said that she might have had him—how he had kissed her. But despite the fact that love between them had to be familial, she was in his magic circle and she did not want to leave it. If she had a relationship with another man, however fleetingly, she felt that all of that would go away. Tim would withdraw his attention and she would be on her own again.

So she simply could not even consider William, who was unsuitable in so many other ways. He had kissed, but she had not kissed back; and she thought of him without regret, now plodding back to the church hall to collect his car.

Once she was in the kitchen she was almost instantly aware of danger. There was nothing different, nothing was wrong, she tried to convince herself. But she went through the house, searching for a sign, even a slight disturbance of the air, a scent—the scent of a man.

Nothing had been moved. The light was on in the front room, in the kitchen. She moved through the rest of the house turning on lights, then locking the doors. There was no one here. It was her imagination.

Marina sat down suddenly in a kitchen chair. All at once she was having a hot flash, which she got occasionally these days. A wave of heat spread outward from the interior of her body; it was like a rash of fire on the surface of her skin. Even her eyeballs felt hot and swollen. She was sweating so heavily that she wanted to tear and claw at herself, to get out of her constricting clothes, out of her skin, if possible.

Like the hot flash, was her fear the product of some internal state, physical or psychological? Was it all just her imagination really? Had she actually seen Lionel in the supermarket and heard his muttered threat, or had it been some weirdo making a strange pass, or perhaps even a delusion—for she had had delusions. She had been in hospitals for that; she knew she had been crazy.

The heat wave was receding, going back the way it had come, a dragon returning to its cave deep inside her. Marina got up and began to make tea. She boiled the water in a pot, the same pot Tim had used to make the rosehip tea. Putting in the tea bag, she even began to laugh foolishly, remembering. Her madness had been diagnosed, but the paper evidence of that was eaten—and had been long ago digested—by Tim.

It seemed that she could have it one of two ways: she was paranoid, she made things up. Or else it was really true that Lionel was coming for her. Which one would she prefer?

She tasted the tea, then poured it all down the sink. It was a crazy kind of ritual, but it was going to help her to sleep.

But she woke up in the night and she was again in the grip of that unreasoning fear. Why had she come back to this house all alone? Why had she not gone home with Mary—or with William Hogan? Even if that had meant that she was going to sleep with him. Gone somewhere, where there were other people who could reassure her by telling her she was a fool.

Now she was inside. And Lionel was outside somewhere. But even the sense of their separation by the locked doors, the walls of the house, gave her no reassurance. She remembered the feeling she had had when she came in that he had been here. He had been inside the house, although he was not here now. She put her hand under the pillow and the cool dull metal of the gun barrel met her fingertips, smooth and soothing like hand lotion, like balm.

She slept again.

And then woke up in a nightmare. It had seemed as though she were hearing the sounds of sirens, as though the flashing lights of a police car were being reflected off the bedroom ceiling. She lay still, trying to distinguish the sounds heard in her dream from real sounds, the flashing lights from the phosphorescence of nightmares. Soon all was silent; it was still dark.

She lay for an hour—or perhaps it was only a few minutes—unsure whether she was really awake or still asleep.

The phone rang suddenly. Marina got out of bed and, taking the gun, crept very quietly up the steps and into the front room. She stood in the doorway between the rooms, thick darkness of the night still complete, the cocked and loaded gun in her hands, as the phone rang and rang. He was calling, to check, to make sure she was there, she was alone—and she didn't want him to be sure.

She wanted him to be dead.

Finally she crept to the back door, almost paralysed with fright, and unlocked it. The only way she could do it was this way. She was the bait, the living bait, in the trap. Crouching in the doorway between the rooms, she waited. It seemed a long wait.

There was a slight scuffle outside on the gravel pad, a footstep. Then silence—a long silence, followed by a stealthy sound by the back door. Someone must be trying the handle, someone who expected it to be locked.

Marina dropped to her knees, and lifted the gun sight to her eye. There was still nothing to see. The door, metal and cheap, with no window, filled the doorway blankly and the darkness in the room was still almost absolute.

It was too late to go back on this idea of the baited trap. She realized that she now had no choice but to follow through with it. There might be time to reconsider later, to rearrange hatred into some kind of decent regret—also, if necessary, she realized, to rearrange the body somehow. But she had set this thing up so that she had to go through with it now. Whatever the outcome for herself, the kids were safe; none of them was here to see this. It was something that would only have to be done once; then they would always be safe.

The back door cracked open.

She had already decided that she was going to shoot without

speaking. To speak would only give him time to get the gun away from her, by force or some kind of trickery.

The person coming in was now framed in the open doorway, with the faint light of the coming dawn behind him.

She took aim, but could not aim for the head. At the last moment before she pulled the trigger she dropped the barrel a little, realizing even as she did it that she might not kill him, that she could go to jail if he was not dead, if he became a witness.

"Marina, are you all right?" Tim spoke rather loudly. He turned back to shut the door behind him.

As she fired.

3

1975 · Coming Home

HIS FATHER SAW HIM AT ONCE AS HE GOT OUT OF THE TRUCK.
Dominique was pleased, yet apprehensive. He had been away from
the farm in Steamboat for nearly four years.

There seemed to be a party going on; Robbie had a beer in
his hand.

"Dominique! You've come home?" Robbie was beaming, and
Dominique found himself grinning crazily as well.

"I guess so." They were almost the same height, Dominique
noticed. Robbie was a little heavier than he had been, now that he
was in his forties.

"It's Sonya's birthday!" Robbie put his arm around Dominique's
shoulders lightly, leading him forward. "Somebody's going to be
glad to see you, Dominique. I don't know if she could be gladder
than I am, though."

His father's wife, Sonya, came out the back door, wiping her
hands on her apron, and he saw that she too was older. But she
was still pretty, with the soft, plump prettiness of middle-aged
whitewomen.

"Dominique!" She ran towards him and hugged him.

"You're home!" There were tears in her eyes. She wound her
arms around Robbie's arm, her cheek close beside his shoulder.
"Have you seen your mother yet?" A little frown suddenly wrinkled
the creamy skin between her eyes.

"No."

"But you're going to stay here, aren't you?"

"Sure."

"Oh, Dominique! So much has happened! Look! Here's Harry. He's four!"

Dominique looked down at a light head beside Sonya's knee. The pale, thin-skinned face, lightly sprinkled with summer freckles, was turned up to stare at him in curiosity.

Sonya knelt beside the little boy. "See, Harry. That tall handsome Native guy is your big brother." She lifted him up to put him in Dominique's arms.

"And Marian. Marian, here's Dominique, do you remember?"

"Marian does, but Laura doesn't," said Sonya.

"I do so!" said Laura, who was five, and Dominique kissed them all. It was a family that did a lot of kissing.

A little later, he took a walk around. The place was much the same. He had always thought Robbie was rich. Now he saw that it was just a good farm—although it needed irrigation.

He was ignoring the party. Some curious stares had come his way, but Sonya's relatives meant nothing to him.

Harry ran after him the way the little kids always used to. They were standing beside the corral. There was a bunch of boys out there, showing off to each other. A very pretty girl was riding a big horse with a white blaze on its face. She rode like a maniac, wild, and a little cruel to the horse. Dominique picked up Harry, who immediately pointed, saying: "Thunder." It was the horse's name.

The wild young girl was racing towards them and she reined in just in time on the other side of the fence, her dark hair falling down over her bare shoulders in the sunlight. She sidled the horse down the fence towards them. She was looking at Dominique, who was glad he had Harry to hold up like a shield against her brightness.

"Dominique? I'm Emma, don't you remember?"

He already knew who she was. He gazed at the clear face, the straight little nose, the widely set, slightly slanting blue eyes, the round determined chin, the pink mouth, triangular, like a cat's.

"Want to come ride with me, Dominique?"

She was his cousin Emma, and she seemed to have grown up. She had once been one of the kids tagging along after him. There were four years between them; she must be eighteen now.

Dominique helped Harry over the fence, then climbed over himself. He lifted Harry up on the neck of the tall horse.

"I meant just you," she said.

They set off at a decorous trot. Emma put her arms around his waist. "I guess you haven't been riding for a while, Dominique."

It was Robbie's old stallion and Dominique wondered whether the horse remembered him. He thought probably Emma did not have permission to ride this one—but no one was paying much attention to the kids on Sonya's birthday.

"I want to gallop. Put Harry down. Harry doesn't like to go fast, do you, Harry?"

Harry turned up his face and grinned at Dominique. He didn't think much of Emma, it was plain, and he thought Dominique would agree.

They went right around the field and he could feel Emma fidget, the round knobs of her hard little breasts coming in contact with his back through the thin fabric of his shirt, her hot hands twisting and flattening against his stomach.

Harry got off on the fence. "Bye-bye," he said cheerfully.

"Let's go out of the corral." She wanted to disassociate herself from the younger ones playing in the field.

Dominique felt a moment of crazy joy coming over him and they galloped all the way to the windbreak. Emma was kicking as the horse began to slow down

"Hey! Quit that!" Dominique brought the stallion, quivering and blowing, to a full stop. He jumped down, holding the bridle.

Emma slid down in front of him, only an inch or two away. The horse was between them and the field, the field and the corral separated them from the people at the party, in the house and yard.

She kissed the same way she rode a horse, wild and mean. Dominique let go of the bridle and the horse walked forward a step or two, bending his neck to graze.

Her eyes were dilated to blackness. She was violently excited.

"You ride like a bad dream," said Dominique.

"All right, Uncle Robbie!" She put out her tongue.

She wasn't innocent, and she never had been, but from another point of view, she was. Very innocent. Ignorant of fear. The other

[85]

people around her had protected her all her life. She leaned against one of the poplars, her hands tucked in under the curve of her behind, looking at him provocatively. "Aren't you going to kiss me again?"

"Maybe."

"You can if you want."

He pulled one of her hands out from behind her back and she let him raise it unwillingly. She was a little uncertain; he could see her long dark lashes against her cheek as she looked down at their hands. He bent over and kissed the pink palm.

"Hey! What are you doing?—Is that all?" She seemed to be trying to dare him, provoking him—the way she had when she was younger. They both knew this was bad; that he shouldn't fool with her like this.

He was still holding her little hand. And then Emma seemed to understand something. A soft, shiny look came into her eyes, and when he took her in his arms, her body was soft and pliant. Their lips met and then her mouth relaxed its aggressiveness, and became soft and yielding. It was a good kiss, and this time it was she who stopped first.

"Oh, Dominique, Dominique! You came back! And I love you, Dominique!" She began to cry, passionate Emma, who had cried so many times before when he wouldn't kiss her, now crying because he did. "Oh Dominique! I never thought you were going to come home!"

"Well, I did come home. So stop bawling."

"Yeah, but I'm not—I'm not—Oh, Dominique, if only I could have known, if I'd known you were coming home, I wouldn't have—!"

"Jesus, Emmy. Did you have to tell me that?" He let go of her in irritation.

He sat down on the edge of the ditch, and after a moment, she sat down beside him, childishly wiping her eyes on the heels of her hands.

"I wanted it to be you," she said, looking away.

"Look, it doesn't matter." He wished he had not said this; it made it sound as if it did matter. Did it? He had never really wanted Emma this way before.

"But I did it with more than one—I mean—" Her voice quavered.

"Did you bite them, too, like you were doing to me?"

"No!" She was mad again. "I never bit you!"

"Well, when a girl's had all that many guys, I guess she figures she knows it all."

"It wasn't all that many!" She stopped wriggling. "Didn't you have a girlfriend?"

"Not really," said Dominique.

"Not really?" Her eyes turned towards him, blue and amazed. "That means—?"

"It means she wasn't really my girlfriend."

"Oh." Her mouth opened a little and they gazed into each other's eyes.

"Do you like me, Dominique?"

He could see down inside her blouse to the shallow curve of her breast. She was like a little piece of acid candy, sweet and sour. He undid the top button and she gasped and put her hand up against his cheek.

"Oh, Dominique! I love you, Dominique!"

He slipped his hand inside the vee of her blouse and the little breast curved softly against his palm. Her tears fell into his mouth and trickled down his chin as he kissed her again.

"Jesus, Emmy, what are you doing?" All at once they were almost wrestling. She wouldn't even let him caress her; it had to be right here, right now.

Dominique let go of her and closed his eyes. It was not going to be like this. She seemed to get the idea, for after a moment, she left off her frantic efforts to undress him.

He opened his eyes. Beautiful Emma was kneeling beside his head and he marvelled for a moment at the sun glistening on the curves of her body, the bloom of her skin. She wore a halo: the shine from the crown of her black hair. Her face was vulnerable, her eyes wide open, her lips parted and quivering.

"Those other guys? That's the way it was with them?"

[87]

She nodded, looking at him doubtfully.

"Don't tell me anything, okay? Because you don't know anything, Emmy." He put his arms around her and made her lie down beside him, pinning her to the ground with his leg across her thighs.

She put her arms around his neck.

"Do you love me, Dominique?" she whispered.

He had always refused to say. When they had played together as children, she had teased him to kiss her, to say he liked her, even that he loved her, but he had always refused. In the past, he had found it annoying—boring, really—the way she showed off, the way she threw herself at him.

She still wanted to stir him with her badness. But instead he felt a deep desire to protect her, so young and wild, so reckless. And there were things he knew already, that he could show her, to make up for the way those other guys had used her.

"Yeah. I love you, Emma."

"Really? Did you always? The way I did? I always loved you." Her hair was tickling his cheek, her little breasts rose and fell quickly, pressed against his chest.

"I just started to." He laughed. "But I guess I'm not going to stop."

❧ EMMA CAME TO THE BARN THAT NIGHT. THE PARTY WAS GOING on, long and drunken, and Sonya had given Dominique Robbie's arctic sleeping bag to take to the haymow.

He was almost asleep, but he had been awake, wondering if she would come.

"I went down over the porch roof," she whispered. "Sonya made me sleep with the girls." Kneeling beside him, she began to pull her thin summer nightgown off over her head.

"Hey!" He pulled the nightgown back down. "What did you tell them?"

"You won't make me go back?" She tried to sound piteous, but he could hear the devil in her voice.

"No. I want to know what you told 'em. And I'm going to take that thing off, not you."

"Oh." Emma snuggled down beside him in the hay. "I just told 'em—told 'em I was going to sleep with you." She giggled.

"Marian said you're nice and Laura thought there wouldn't be room in the sleeping bag. I told her it'd be better than being kicked by her all night."

"Great," said Dominique. "So now they know."

"I made 'em swear not to tell," she said.

Dominique lay still for a moment, wondering what would happen. Robbie would act to defend Emma if he thought she was coming to harm. This was a fine thing on his first day home.

"Nobody'll find out," said Emma. "I guess you're worrying about Sonya."

"I was worrying about me."

"Mother says you were in love with Sonya." She kicked up her legs discontentedly and he saw them glimmer, long and fine. "That's why you left home, isn't it?"

He rose on his elbow and grasped her around the waist. The nightgown had fallen back, exposing her naked thighs, pearly in the dim light of the haymow.

"Isn't it?" she insisted. She liked to torment people in the way that hurts the tormentor most in the end. He remembered her with her brother Howie, slapping and kicking, then running away in hysterical tears after she hurt him and he cried. Howie tried to ignore her and stay away from her. He had to, out of self-preservation.

"Listen Emma. I told you something this afternoon I never told anybody before. Or if I did, I didn't mean it. So now you know."

"Really?" She clung to him. "Oh Dominique, Dominique, I can hardly believe it's true!"

❡ DOMINIQUE WENT WITH ROBBIE AND SONYA TO EMMA'S highschool graduation. Emma wore a white dress, a white robe, a white, four-cornered hat, and white shoes. All the other participants were white as well. White and in white.

The perfume in the high school gymnasium was making Dominique feel slightly sick to his stomach. Robbie was dressed, like all the other men, in a suit, a string tie and a ten gallon hat. Sonya wore a pastel-coloured cotton dress and Emma's mother's corsage. Emma's mother, Mollie, wore a pantsuit with an indecent skimpy tank top; no brassiere. This too revolted Dominique.

[89]

"Oh, for God's sake! Mollie!" said Robbie to Sonya, in disgust.

Dominique momentarily tried to visualize himself and Emma going to the future graduation of a child of their own, dressed as Robbie and Sonya were dressed. It was an impossible thought.

"Isn't Emmy pretty?" said Marian, looking up innocently. "Don't you think she's pretty, Dominique?"

Laura, too little to be taken in by the miraculous transformation of a white dress, merely put her hand in Dominique's and rested her head on his sleeve with a sigh of ennui.

"I'm not going to that stupid dance," said Emma mutinously to Dominique.

"Yes, you are." He was implacable. He had already refused to take her. She had to finish this all by herself.

"I wish I could go." Marian was envious. "I wish I were you, Emma."

"Well, you're not!" snapped Emma. She looked pleadingly at Dominique.

"You'll have a good time, Emma," said Sonya.

"Yeah, and stop bugging Dominique," directed Robbie more sharply. He had already noticed some things. But he blamed Emma for them. Emma was turning out like her mother, in his mind.

"Damn you," said Emma softly to Dominique. "And damn him, and damn all of them, even your precious darling Sonya."

DOMINIQUE HAD A RESTLESS EVENING. ROBBIE WAS MENDING horse tack, wearing his glasses. Sonya read aloud to the little girls. He gave Harry a bath.

"Emmy don't have one of these," Harry confided cheerfully, exhibiting what he meant.

"Yeah, but they've got something else. It's good too." Dominique proffered the towel.

Sonya put the children to bed.

"What're you going to do with yourself this summer, son?" asked Robbie. "Want to keep on working for me?"

"Yeah. As long as I'm living here. But—"

"Well, you just stay and do what you want."

"I've been thinking about getting a job as a spray pilot."

[90]

Robbie looked at him in surprise. "You've got to have a license."

"I've got one. Maybe I can't get a job," said Dominique. "But I might as well try."

Sonya came down the stairs and Robbie stood up. "Go kiss the girls and make them cry," she said, and he kissed her lightly in passing.

She sat down and Dominique started sewing the harness where Robbie had left off.

"You've seen Eliza—" she began hesitantly.

He had been out to the Reserve to see his mother, who was drinking. Not right in front of him, but she had a hangover, the house was in a mess.

That flat and broken land, rising in the west to foothills. The little broken house. He had not forgotten what it was like out there.

His sister Vicky came home from school and had hung around looking at him, her eyes soft and haunted. He hadn't been imagining her as a teenager, somehow, although she had been nearly thirteen when he left.

"You're staying with Robbie and Sonya?" asked Eliza.

Vicky had looked quickly at the floor. She was jealous of Sonya and Robbie, angry that Dominique had deserted her, years before, left her with Eliza, when he went to live with Robbie and Sonya. It wasn't fair, but he had been trying to save himself, and she was at least safe at home on the Reserve, safer there as a child than he was as a teenager.

"I'm going to try to get a place of my own," he said quickly. "You'll come stay with me when I get that, won't you Vick?"

She raised her eyes again, and a look of pure joy—of love—irradiated her face.

He couldn't help noticing what a beautiful girl Vicky had grown up to be. It made him nervous. She was no longer safe at home, in his opinion. The Reserve was a wild place, and a girl who looked like Vicky, with the faint blush of happiness on her face ... She wasn't safe anywhere that he knew of.

Sonya was still gazing at him, a worried look on her face, while he thought of this.

[91]

"Things are going from bad to worse out there. With Ma."

"Poor Eliza." Sonya knitted her brows. "I love her, but—"

"Well, I don't," said Dominique. "Not the way she is now."

"She can't help herself."

"She's drinking again. And what about Vicky? No food. Ma out all night."

Sonya was silent. Their eyes met for a moment. She thought she'd saved him from life with Eliza, he knew. But there was so much that she didn't know, that he couldn't tell her.

"You don't have to worry about me, Sonya. I can take care of myself now."

"Yes." She looked at her hands, twisting her big diamond ring. "But you're not all alone, Dominique. We're here."

He smiled. "You're just the same, Sonya." The worried look left her face and she smiled back at him.

Robbie came back into the room again, and Dominique thought of the years when, sullen and miserable, he had not been able to look at Sonya. Robbie had walked just as calmly into rooms thick with Dominque's anger and lust.

"Bedtime for me," said Sonya. "Do you want to stay up with Dominique and have a beer?"

"I don't drink beer," said Dominique. He stretched. "I don't drink at all."

"That's good, if you're going to be a flyer."

"I guess I'll go out." Dominique got to his feet. "Maybe I'll drive around."

"Do what you want, son," Robbie put his arms around Sonya. "I'm going to bed with my wife."

"Who is, once again, pregnant," Sonya made a face.

◖ "WHY, HELLO," SAID MOLLIE. "THIS IS A SURPRISE." THERE was a cynical gleam in her eyes. Dominique thought again with revulsion of her drooping breasts in the tank top. Tonight she was wearing jeans, an ordinary T-shirt, with a brassiere underneath.

The kitchen was clean, although dark and small. The house was painted white, minimal—a settler's house—on a tiny 160 acre farm tucked down in the river valley. Mollie had always lived alone on this place with her kids, Emma and Howie. Something had happened to her husband years before. No one had ever told Dominique what.

"What can I do for you? Want a drink?" She paused, raising her eyebrows, then gestured him into a kitchen chair. When Dominique shook his head she poured herself one anyway. "Waiting for Emma, are you?"

He nodded. "What's Howie doing these days?"

"He's off digging dams." She sighed impatiently, blowing through her nose like Robbie.

"Tell me. Have you screwed Emma yet or did you think you were going to after this big drunk-I-mean-dance—" she waved her hand, "is over?"

"I'd say that was my business." He was startled. This woman was hard to deal with.

"Well, maybe it is, but I pay for the pills. Or did you get around to asking her whether she's taking them?"

"She said it was all right," Dominique replied evenly.

"Ah. She did, did she?" Mollie's voice was harsh. "Well, just keep asking, will you? That way we can keep the half-breeds in this family down to one."

"Me, you mean."

"Yeah. You." She smiled, looking him over curiously. "You seem to have grown up, Dominique. I guess you're about the most fascinating thing that ever crossed Emma's little small-town field of vision. I've got eyes myself."

She was trying to embarrass him. He said nothing. Women had done this to him before, trying to get a rise out of him, as though just any response at all were a sexual one.

She lowered her eyes and took a sip of her drink. "I guess you know that there's nothing I can do about you and her. I wouldn't do anything even if I could. But Robbie'll have something to say, believe you me. He's not going to like this much."

"I know."

"Yeah, and Sonya'll be pushing him around as usual. But I guess you know about Sonya already!"

"Maybe I'll wait outside."

Mollie glared at him for a moment. Then she said, "Well, I'm going to bed. I don't have to wait up for Emmy now, do I?" She laughed, a sharp laugh. "You may not realize it yet, kid, but I'm the only one who's going to be on your side in this deal. Just so we know where we all stand."

She left the room, carrying another drink.

Emma did not get home till 2:00. There were car noises and rowdy sounds from the bottom of the driveway. Then he could hear her screaming furiously, "Screw you! Screw all of you! And don't you come looking for me any more, 'cause I don't know you, see!"

She was still crying fiercely when she came in the back door. She looked at Dominique in disbelief, then went to the cupboard where her mother kept the whiskey. She sat down at the table with a tumbler full of raw liquor and wiped her blubbered face, trying to compose her expression.

Her dress was torn at the hem, and one shoulder strap had been pulled awry. There was no other damage besides the black marks of her tears, runnels of the mascara she put on her dark lashes.

"Want some?" she asked, holding out the glass with a smothered sob.

"I don't drink that stuff."

"Well, screw you too, Mister Oh-You'll-Have-A-Good-Time." She took a big choking swallow. "You want to know what that was? An *orgy*."

"I guess that's why you came home."

"Oh yeah. I started saying I wanted to go home about 11:00. I had to say that for *three hours*. And I guess you were worrying about me, weren't you, smarty?"

"Yeah."

"Were you worrying?" She looked happier. "Well, I didn't do anything—except get drunk!"

"C'mere."

She went around the corner of the table and sat down on his lap.

He didn't like drunk women. He put his arms around her loosely, and she leaned in against his chest, breathing heavily and a little fast. She smelled of cigarette smoke and booze.

[94]

"What'd you expect me to do? You must have got drunk lots of times yourself. Want me to drink pop, while they—?" She squirmed around to look up at him.

"I don't drink," he said, resting his cheek against her hair, feeling the thick clean strands slip across his skin. "I hate that."

The tense, nervous energy of her body was draining away. She yawned.

"Want to go to bed now, Emmy?"

"We could go out in the barn," she said. "Mother'll hear us if we—"

"Look, I'm going to put you to bed. Then I'm going to go home."

"Put me to bed?"

"Yeah," he replied, laughing. "Are you coming or do I have to carry you?"

"You have to carry me." She put her arms around his neck and he picked her up easily. She was almost as light as Harry or Laura—and she stank of whiskey.

He carried her up the stairs and put her down on the bed in her room—beside Howie's empty bed. She tried to hold him down, but her arms slipped off his neck and she was yawning again.

He found the nightgown and made her sit up to pull off the demure white dress. Underneath it she wore a padded bra and white panties that made her look even younger and more innocent than the dress. He pulled the nightgown down over her head.

"Want to go to the bathroom? Your face is a mess."

She got up and went out of the room, not even bothering to reply. Dominique sat on the edge of the bed and looked around at the decorations on the walls. Posters of rock stars, one of them a hermaphrodite with a python. A snapshot of a boy, probably a boyfriend, was stuck in the mirror frame. This was torn across, then taped. Someone had drawn on a moustache and a pair of glasses after the taping.

Mollie had gone to bed in a room downstairs. But she was probably aware of what was going on now. And after what she had said, she was undoubtedly expecting him to stay.

Emma came back into the room, her cheeks shiny and pink from the towel.

[95]

"Get in," said Dominique, lifting the triangle of bedclothes.

"Now kiss me good night, Daddy. Or are you going to tell me a story first?"

He kissed her mouth, fresh with toothpaste.

"When my Daddy did this, he was always the one who was drunk." Emma spoke loudly—for Mollie's benefit.

Dominique went to the door and turned off the light.

She sat up in bed. "Can I come over tomorrow?"

"Sure. You won't feel like it in the morning though. Good night, Emmy."

"Good night, Dominique. Oh!—Good night."

He tidied up the kitchen on the way out, putting the whiskey bottle away again and throwing the contents of the tumbler down the drain. Then he went out into the fresh, clean-smelling night air. There was more than a hint of midsummer dawn in the eastern sky and he watched it change from apple blossom pink to eggshell as he drove across the Reserve towards Robbie's farm.

IN THE MORNING DOMINIQUE WENT TO THE AIRPORT. IT WAS a little country airfield in Roseland, about twenty miles from Steamboat. The glider club was there; there was an agro-spray company and a couple of maintenance shops.

Dominique went into the tiny building that was the office of the spray outfit.

"What can I do you for, son?" There were a couple of thick-bodied farmers sitting around; the desk and countertops were littered with coffee cups.

"Looking for a job," said Dominique.

The man stared at him. He was an old man with a beard like Santa Claus, a Polish or Ukrainian accent. "You've got to have a license for this line of work."

"I've got one." Dominique reached for his wallet.

"Boucher, eh?" said the man. "From the Reserve?"

"I've got two-hundred hours. No accidents."

"Where'd you get the hours?" The man was still friendly.

"I paid for most of it," said Dominique. "Then I had a job on a

Supercub, for a while, flying some guy around. He laid me off to hire his nephew."

The man whistled through his teeth for a moment, staring at him.

"Wondering whether I drink? Well, I don't."

"You bet." The man grinned back. "I guess I know who you are. You're Robbie Hallouran's boy. Poppalushka is the name."

"What kind of machines are you using?"

"Oh, just about any old rusty piece of junk we can soup up," said Poppalushka. He stuck his thumbs in his belt. "Want some free experience? See whether you can fly that." He pointed to an old Stinson in the yard.

Dominique went out of the little office building and had a look at the Stinson. He had never flown one of these things before. He discovered immediately that he would have to hand crank it; there was no kick in the ignition. He began looking for some big rocks to chock the wheels.

He had been hoping for a test of this kind. "Get the hell out of here, boy!"—that was the response he had prepared himself for.

He took a good stand, then swung the prop, and it promptly came off in his hands, knocking him backwards into the tall grass, where he lay for a moment, still cradling it in his arms.

He got to his feet and went to look inside the cowling. There was no engine in there. Someone had hung the prop up as a joke. The swallows who lived inside were diving and swooping angrily around his head.

He went back into the little office. They were all smiling; some of them were still wiping their eyes.

Dominique sat down and grinned.

"What's the matter? Can't get her started?" said Poppalushka, prompting another explosion of muffled laughter.

"She needs a few things."

"You know anything about mechanical, son?"

Dominique helped himself to a mug of dense black coffee from the urn.

"I can do that. Got no papers for it, though."

"I've got someone with the papers. Me." The old man pointed at his chest. "You want to help me fix her up, maybe you can fly her."

"You going to pay me for that or what?" Dominique took a sip of his coffee. No one was grinning any longer. The offer seemed to be on the level.

"Pay you when you fly. That okay? You want to show me how you do that, come back this afternoon. I've got a guy coming over from Pinkerton in a Supercub."

◖ DOMINIQUE TOOK EMMA WITH HIM TO THE FIELD THAT afternoon. She would give all those old farmers something else to look at while he took a trial run.

"Where're we going?" she demanded. She was cross; she had a hangover. She had been having a quarrel with Mollie when he arrived to pick her up.

"You'll see." He turned off on the section road to Roseland. "You still look kind of green."

"It's just because of the smelly old truck," she replied sullenly.
Then she smiled.

"That's more like it," he said. "What are you thinking about?"
"I was thinking about you kissing me good night."
They both laughed.
"Hey! Is this an airport?"
"Yeah. I'm going to fly a plane this afternoon."
"You are?" Her eyes were round with wonder, with admiration.
"Who's the young lady?" asked Poppalushka, his thumbs in his belt.
"My cousin, Emma."
"Yeah, I'm his cousin," said Emma. "But this is my boyfriend, Dominique, Mister."

He laughed. "Well, you can stay here with me while he goes up in that." He jerked his thumb at the Supercub beside the Stinson. "She'll be in good hands, son. Just go off and show your stuff."

Dominique looked under the cowling first this time. It was in good shape, oil, gas, everything. He took it far out, to get his feel for flying back, then came in for a couple of touch and goes. Then he pulled in neatly beside the Stinson.

Poppalushka was standing by Emma at the office door. She was looking amazingly pretty all of a sudden.

"Think it's going to rain?" Poppalushka squinted at the sky.

"Guess I'll get to work on that Stinson now."

"Not if it's going to rain. You probably got better things to do this afternoon anyway." Poppalushka winked at Emma. "Come in tomorrow."

"Did he get the job?" demanded Emma, standing in front of the big man, hands on her hips.

"Yeah, he did, sweetheart."

"Wow!" Emma grabbed Dominique's arm.

"Not but what there isn't a thing or two he could maybe learn."

"Yeah. I don't know anything about spraying," agreed Dominique.

"You don't know nothing about nothing yet," said Poppalushka. "But you've got the prettiest cousin I ever saw."

Dominique could feel Emma quivering with excitement. She had her nails dug into his arm. It was a good moment, standing there under the shadow of the approaching thunderstorm.

"Don't get wet." Poppalushka went inside his tiny office.

They walked down the airstrip, looking at the old wrecks parked on either side. Then the storm broke overhead and they raced hand in hand through the lank grass of the field to the pickup.

"Could I come with you tomorrow too?"

"He might not think much of that."

"I think—" said Emma, dimples suddenly appearing in her cheeks. "I think he'd like it if I did."

◖ FOR THE NEXT THREE WEEKS DOMINIQUE WORKED ON THE Stinson, taking Emma with him to Roseland every day. He worked, she lounged around getting a tan, reading the ratty magazines in the office, and going up in an airplane whenever anyone offered to take her, which was often.

Poppalushka seemed to enjoy having her there. He thought—and frequently remarked—that Emma was a smart girl.

"I never saw no Indian like you before," he said, his head inside the cowling, as Dominique stood beside him, handing him a three eighths wrench. "'Course you're Robbie's boy."

"Yeah, but I'm an Indian. I'm on the Band list."

"Well, Jeez. You keep on like this and maybe I'm going to change my mind about you people."

In the grass: "What do you think Poppalushka thinks we're doing?"

"I don't care what he thinks!" said Dominique, gasping.

Merely to see her sprawled among the daisies set his heart on fire. She was the spirit of the place; she was home, she was all his family, she was the reason for everything.

It was a crazy idyllic month of summer, the days so much alike that they seemed to stretch to infinity, like a poplar windbreak going off over the horizon. But he was aware that there was a day of reckoning approaching. Emma knew it too; it gave her a thrill of willful disobedience.

❡ ROBBIE AND SONYA CAME TO SEE THE MAIDEN FLIGHT OF the Stinson. Robbie had been involved all along from afar. His harness needles mended the fabric; it was his welding that fixed the exhaust.

"Hello, Emma. Did you come to see Dominique fly too?" asked Sonya.

An engineer had come over from Pinkerton to watch the test flight. Emma strolled in front of him wearing shorts and a halter top and a slightly more alert look crossed the sarcophagus of his face. Robbie frowned.

"I don't mind telling you, that's a good boy you've got, Robbie," said Poppalushka as Dominique climbed into the plane. He glanced at Sonya, remembering something suddenly, but she merely smiled and waved to Dominique.

Dominique circled the field, did a decorous touch and go, then climbed up, up and away, circling into the sun.

"Yahoo!" cried the Pinkerton engineer, throwing up his hat.

Some minutes passed as they waited for Dominique to come back. Poppalushka looked at his watch. Sonya looked at Robbie.

Emma's face was white. She crossed her arms over her bare midriff, shivering.

Sonya said: "Surely he could land somewhere if—"

"Nothing's happened, Sonya."

Emma whimpered and Poppalushka took her arm. They looked out across the empty prairie. Not even a crow was to be seen in the sky.

There was an advancing roar. The Stinson came in low—very low—hopped a hedge, and zoomed down the dirt strip. Low and fast, Dominique climbed away, did a flashy turn and sideslipped down into a real approach.

"Got yourself a cowboy there, Poppa!"

"Hey, that's not a cowboy! He's an—!" Poppalushka suddenly turned with an oops!-I-did-it-again expression towards Sonya and Robbie, who were standing arm in arm, watching as Dominique got out of the plane.

Laughing and weeping, Emma rushed into his arms. As though they were alone in the world they stood pressed against one another, their lips locked in a long blissful kiss.

Robbie stopped smiling. Sonya's hand, raised to shade her eyes, dropped to her side.

Looking around nervously, Poppalushka took the situation in hand.

"I guess your cousin was real worried about you, young feller," he said, stepping forward. "And while we're on the subject—"

Dominique raised his head, his eyes still other-worldly from the rush of his daring.

"While we're on the subject, you ever fly a plane of mine like that again—I'll—!"

"Oh, it was great! It was so great!" Emma was still hugging him, her eyes shining. Dominique kept his arm around her, looking over her head at Robbie.

Emma now saw that Robbie and Dominique were staring at one another. She twisted around.

"Well, so what, Robbie?" she shouted, breaking free to stand fiercely in front of Dominique. "What're you going to do about it?"

"Emma," said Sonya. Her mouth turned downward deprecatingly.

"You aren't my dad!" she screamed at Robbie.

"No, but he's mine." Dominique breathed these words into her ear.

Poppalushka now erupted into furious activity.

"Well, I guess I can sign out that book now," he said, hustling the Pinkerton engineer, open-mouthed, into his office. "And it was real nice to see you folks," he added in parting. "You're welcome to come along any time. Emmy likes to drop by—uh—every once in a while too."

Dominique let go of Emma, and then he and Robbie walked in silence down the airstrip, side by side.

"So it's like that," Robbie said.

Dominique plucked a piece of timothy. "I know she's pretty young—"

"She's like her mother," said Robbie.

"She's not like her at all!"

Dominique looked at their feet, advancing side by side through the grass. They both wore Western boots. Boots with pointed toes that changed your feet to blind helpless deformed stumps, that made them sweat and stink. These boots were virtue and manhood; they represented something you had to struggle with all your life.

"The point is, you can't have her."

Dominique stopped walking. The charade of their man-to-man talk was over.

"I've got her already."

"You can't say that, Dominique."

"Sure I can. I'm the guy who knows. Not you."

"I was real proud to see you fly today, Dominique. But this is something else."

Dominique folded his arms. "Maybe the world today is different than you think, Robbie. Emma doesn't know anything about—what you think."

"Emma doesn't know nothing about nothing," growled Robbie.

"Yeah, but I do, and I can take it. I've been taking it all my life—"

He looked up and their eyes met. "I'm not scared of what's going to happen."

Robbie shook his head.

"You just think you're responsible for Emma—"

"I am," said Robbie. "And that's another thing. Emma is like your sister, Dominique. You can't screw your own sister; nowhere in the world that I know of."

Emma was not his sister, Dominique thought. He had a sister. His relationship to Emma had never been anything like that.

"This isn't something for us to argue about, Dominique."

"You're just telling me, is that it?"

"Yeah. I guess I am."

Dominique felt tears pricking the back of his eyes. Something that he cared about, that he relied upon, was coming to an end.

"We can send her off for the rest of the summer. Sonya was talking about doing that anyway, getting her a job in Banff, or somewhere a good long way away from Mollie. Next fall she'll be going to college."

"Let's get this straight, Robbie. Emma isn't pregnant. She can do what she wants."

"She's still living at home."

"So am I, is that what you mean, Robbie? Well, I guess I'm moving out."

"Jesus, can't you take my word for it? I did this, Dominique. I screwed up your mother's life. That's how I know."

"Well, I guess I've got to show you that it's different, that's all." Dominique began to walk in the other direction, back towards the vehicles.

Robbie paused, then followed him more slowly.

They could see the two women, standing apart. Sonya was shading her eyes, watching them come.

"Dominique," said Robbie, catching up. "I'm not kicking you out. For one thing, Sonya would kill me."

"I know. But I won't stop seeing Emma, Robbie."

"Seeing her's not the problem."

"Then I guess you didn't look lately," said Dominique.

Emma was gloriously beautiful in her rage. Her eyes snapped

and sparkled, dilated to blackness. Her lips had tightened from their usual slight pout and there was a wild flush in her cheeks. She began screaming at Robbie as soon as he was within earshot.

"Damn you, Robbie! How dare you take Dominique away and talk at him like that! I'm not a doll! You can't push me around! I'm not going anywhere this summer! I don't care what you and Sonya cooked up!"

Robbie stopped in front of her and looked down. She was quite a tall girl, but he loomed over her, broad and strong. "Coming with us now?" he said.

"No!" she shouted, hands on her hips.

"Robbie …"

"Okay, Sonya."

He swept Sonya before him to their truck. Dominique watched him drive off. Robbie was angry, but still he drove slowly. His wife was pregnant.

"What'd he tell you?" Emma had the piercing eyes, the high colour of the Hallourans. In her fury, she looked a lot like Robbie.

Dominique took her by the arm and led her to the pickup; then made her get in.

"It's all because of Sonya, isn't it?" she demanded. "She's jealous of me! She doesn't want you and me to—! She thinks I'm just a kid and she can get Robbie to push me around!"

"Sonya isn't jealous!" He was surprised and annoyed by this interpretation.

"Oh no? You and her—I remember! And Mother says—!"

"I don't give a damn about what your mother says! Leave Sonya out of this!" Dominique restrained himself. "You're the one who's jealous, Emma."

"I'm not! I'm not! How can you say I am when I'm not!"

"Look, just be quiet for a moment, Emmy. You're making everything worse."

Although it was true, Dominique reflected, that the wild forces in this family were harnessed to Sonya. And whatever Sonya thought, she would be telling Robbie now.

They would not let go of Emma the way they had let go of him. She was too young, a girl, liable to get hurt, get pregnant. And this would be a scandal in the countryside; he was aware that it already was one after the scene of the afternoon. It was not only because Emma was still a baby; it was because of his mixed blood, because he was Robbie Hallouran's illegitimate son.

Sonya. He had been born before Sonya even met Robbie, but she had virtually adopted him at the age of fourteen in the face of the disapproval and fear of the whole neighbourhood. She ignored things like that; she had always done so. He knew Sonya would not try to get Emma away from him because she was afraid of gossip and scandal. Whatever happened, though, she would back up Robbie.

He had not intended to come back here and pretend that he was a Hallouran. He had been headed for the Reserve. It had been a fluke that he stopped to visit Robbie before going home to Eliza. But it made no difference anyway, he realized. He would have seen Emma sooner or later. And that myth—that he was a member of this family—had to be wrecked now. Emma was not his sister.

Looking out the front window of the truck they saw Poppalushka seeing the engineer off in the Supercub, back to Pinkerton. He stood irresolutely for a moment, not looking in their direction. Dominique thought he was going to lose this job, before he had even started it.

Emma whimpered, watching him walk towards them.

"I was wondering," said Poppalushka, looking in the window of the truck. "Would you and—and your young lady like to come in for a drink?"

They followed him silently into the office.

Rubbing his hands nervously, Poppalushka got out a rye bottle and a couple of smeary glasses. He poured, taking the dirtiest glass for himself.

"You did a real good job fixing up that plane, son."

"He's going to fly it now, isn't he, Poppa?" said Emma.

Poppalushka looked into his glass.

"He came back with the plane! He was gone a long time but he brought it back!"

Dominique laughed. "I just went over the river valley and did a spin or two," he said.

"You'll get over doing that fancy stuff for fun," said Poppalushka. "You get tired of it."

"I just wanted to know if the plane could take it."

"Drink up, son."

Dominique had another sip. He didn't like the taste of whiskey. Emma had already finished her drink. Poppalushka poured her another.

"Me and Mark Edgerton got a contract to spray a couple of thousand acres out by Orson next week." He looked up. "You keep that craziness of yours under control and you can do it for us, son."

This time Emma had the sense not to say anything. Her cheeks turned bright pink with pleasure.

"And another thing. Once we get going, I can't be here all the time. I have to get out, mixing chemicals, hauling gas. So I was wondering, does Emmy want to look after the phone? I could pay for that too."

"Do I want? Oh Poppa!" Emma threw herself at him, and blocked by his knees jutting halfway across the tiny room, embraced his head.

"Well, since you're here all the time anyway," Poppalushka pointed out in a muffled voice.

❡ DOMINIQUE GOT HOME THAT NIGHT LONG AFTER SUPPER. HE had made love to drunk and joyous Emma in a field, then they ate perogies from a roadside stand, and he dropped her off at her house, sober again, and childishly tired from all the excitement.

Sonya was sitting in the kitchen, her hands lying loosely on the slight bulge of her lap. There was no sign of Robbie. She had been waiting up for Dominique.

Dominique sat down too, not knowing what kind of a showdown this was going to be. The one he had already had with Robbie was straightforward by comparison.

"It was nice to see you fly, Dominique," she said, smiling. "Even that crazy landing. Sometimes you remind me so much of Robbie."

It was very like her to start their conversation by making the greatest concession of all.

She got up. "I'm going to have a cup of tea. Do you want one?"

He shook his head.

"Robbie is very upset about Emma," she said. "She drives him wild sometimes. She's so much like Mollie."

Dominique could not help grimacing. Why did everyone have to tell him this?

"You don't really know Mollie," said Sonya quickly. "She's the most honest person I know. And she's so smart. But she wrecked her life."

"However she did that, it's ancient history. I'm not wrecking anyone's life."

"I don't think you are." Sonya looked at her hands, spreading the fingers. "Emma can do her own wrecking. She was in a mess even before you—All those boyfriends!"

"Well, I didn't hurt her and I'm not going to hurt her."

"Do you love her?"

"Yeah. I do."

"Who am I to say you don't?" She smiled and he realized how defensively he had spoken.

"Robbie thinks it's too—well, too all in the family."

"He said it was like screwing my sister."

"That's not true," said Sonya quickly.

"I think he meant it."

"Maybe he did." She was reflective. "But I think you're really the person he's afraid for, Dominique."

"That's not what he said."

"Well, but it's true. You're on your way up. Anyone can see that. And we're so proud of you, Dominique. Robbie is desperate that you don't throw it all away."

"Yeah. But he doesn't really think I can get anywhere. I'm an Indian."

"No!" Sonya looked shocked. "That isn't what he believes."

"I think it is."

"Look, here's what it's about, Dominique. It's not about you! It's about her! She doesn't know who she is yet. She has to get away from here and—and find out! Find out who she is! I know it sounds so—!"

"I don't know what you're talking about," he said. "Emma is old enough to pick a man. She doesn't have to go away to do that."

"But what is she going to do with her life, Dominique? Maybe she wants a career."

What was she saying? Emma wasn't going to have a career. He barely had one of those himself.

"What is it about really?" he said. "I'm going to marry her someday, Sonya. That's all."

"Well, but Dominique—that isn't all!"

"Anyway, I don't want to make Robbie mad, sticking around. I can go stay with Ma. And I got a job this afternoon. Flying."

"You did! With Poppalushka? Oh Dominique! That's wonderful!" She was surprised—astounded, he saw.

"It is," he said dryly.

"Oh! This family! I hate these fights!" She turned away, twisting her hands together. "I never thought we'd be having one with you! And you just came home!"

"I'm not fighting with you, Sonya." He stood up and she turned back, standing directly in front of him.

It was the first time they had looked at one another as adults, on equal terms. Dominique remembered the guilty feelings he had had for her, that had forced him into sullen adolescent withdrawal. It had become such a burden to live here and continuously ignore Sonya that it became the main reason why he had to leave. He felt none of that now. And he thought Sonya might feel a little wrench in no longer having any power over him.

Robbie came into the kitchen, shirtless, wearing only a pair of old jeans.

"Robbie!" Sonya turned around. "Dominique got that job! From Poppalushka."

"Well, good for him," said Robbie. He glared at Dominique for a moment, but his expression softened as he looked at Sonya in her maternity dress, standing by his son.

"I couldn't sleep," he said, pouring himself some tea in Sonya's cup.

"Well, we're all going to bed in a minute," said Sonya.

Dominique shook his head.

"Oh Dominique! Not tonight! Think about it."

"Thinking isn't going to make any difference, Sonya."

"Well—Jesus!" said Robbie, his fingers tight around the handle of the cup.

Sonya went over and put her hand on Robbie's bare chest. "Maybe this is the best way," she said softly.

"Nothing about this is good, as far as I'm concerned." He covered the hand with his own.

"You can't decide for them, Robbie."

"Them!" he exclaimed. "Who's this them! I never heard of them till this afternoon."

"I'm going now, Robbie," said Dominique.

"Well, go." Robbie continued to look down at Sonya's hand. "Don't come back, either."

And then Dominique was outside, walking towards his truck, feeling sorry, feeling anguish, really; but also feeling liberation. They knew. That was over. He was free. And his life was just starting.

4

1976 · Ochre River Dam

A TV CREW SHOWED UP TO DO A DOCUMENTARY ON agricultural spraying. They lingered for days, taking different shots of Dominique flying, and of his gorgeous white girlfriend. He was the only Native pilot in southern Alberta.

Emma loved the attention.

"Think they'd like to film this?" She giggled, hanging over Dominique in the goldenrod.

"I doubt if that Dick guy could hold the camera steady."

"He told me he had three wives."

"Oh yeah? All at once?" Dominique tried to keep his mind on this, her clover smell in his nostrils, her skin like a ripe peach.

"One of 'em was that woman—she's on TV. She's in shows and everything."

"I don't care! Oh—Emmy!" The hot sun bore down upon his back. The grasses were pressed flat beside her head. Her eyes flew open, then closed languorously.

Later, her lips sweetly parted, she lay on her side, smiling at him speechlessly. A curious bee stepped tangle-footed among the strands of her black hair, searching for the pollen it had shaken down from the dense yellow flower heads above.

Now that it was a job, he was through with flying for thrills. Every day was a challenge in the low-flying, hedge-hopping little plane. The wind blew all the time in that part of the prairies. And every wind was different, every condition of sun and cloud was an updraft or a downdraft, and any fence or electric wire could be death. It did not frighten him, but it was intense. His reflexes were sharp, his ears were tuned to the minute variations of noise in the delicate relationship between the wind and the engine, he could see out of the back of his head.

They were invited to see the rushes of the documentary. Poppalushka put up the money for a dinner in Edmonton and a hotel room.

Emma was in every frame. Kissing Dominique goodbye, reading the barometer, shading her eyes, hair blown back, to look into the sky. There were cuts of her talking to Poppalushka, flirting with the delighted engineer (both of them in grease to the elbows), putting her tongue out at the camera, eating a garlic sausage, and hanging on Dominique's arm when he came back.

They ate steak and lobster in the restaurant on top of the Chateau LaCombe. The lights of Edmonton shone up into her pretty, excited face, where she sat between Dick and the sound man.

There were some women present too; Dominique didn't get their names straight, even though they paid a lot of attention to him. At first he was amused, but he was physically repelled, and he ended up getting slightly annoyed. There was too much to drink; he did not have any of it. Emma was getting drunk.

"They're going to do another show this fall," Emma told him as they took the elevator to their room. "Maybe I'll get a job."

He took her home on Sunday morning and she staggered off to her room to sleep after a brief exchange of insults with her mother.

"You better come in," said Mollie sharply. "I can't eat all these pancakes."

"I guess I could help you out." Dominique came to the table and sat down. He had not gotten much sleep either and he had to fly in the afternoon.

"Now she's going to be a TV star?" Mollie put a plate of breakfast in front of him.

"They said something about giving her a job," said Dominique.

The pancakes were delicious. Dominique drank down a glass of cool thick farm milk from Mollie's cow.

"And what are you going to do in the fall? I guess you won't be working on the harvest for Robbie!"

"I'll see what I can do about getting another flying job. There's jobs up north."

"You haven't seen them since July, have you?" Mollie looked at him curiously. "Robbie and Sonya, I mean."

"Nope."

"Well, Robbie's still hopping mad. He's mad at me too. Sonya's playing her usual little peacemaker game."

"It isn't a game."

"I'm interested to hear that from you," said Mollie. "I thought you got kind of a raw deal from her once upon a time."

"What are you talking about?"

"You got a little hard to handle so they shipped you out," she said.

"Nobody shipped me out," he said. "I left." But that time Robbie had pleaded with him to stay.

She was looking at him curiously. "Well, now you're out on your ear again."

Dominique shrugged. "I guess it had to be this way."

"You're a pretty smart boy," said Mollie energetically. "What I can't figure out is why you picked Emma. You could have had just about any other girl and Robbie would have gone to the wall for you, whether she was white, brown or green."

"He said it was like—" He could never forget this. "Like she was my sister."

"He did, eh?" She gave a cynical laugh. "Look, maybe I'd better tell you a few things. About your family. The Bouchers and—oh yeah, the Hallourans. I bet Robbie never told you much?"

"Not too much."

"Probably he forgot. After he got himself a rich English wife."

"I don't think it was because of that."

"Well, for a start, we lived through the Depression in this house."

Mollie must have been born in the middle of the Dust Bowl. The house still looked old; it looked poor. Even though everyone in this part of the world was rich—from oil, from grain, from cattle. Except the Reserve.

"Dad was an old man of—oh—sixty, doing one more harvest when his heart got him. My mother died of TB back in the fifties—before I got married. Coughed her lungs out in the sanatorium in Calgary. Robbie and I have been orphans for a long time."

They didn't act like orphans. For one thing they were both nearly middle-aged, vigorous, successful—even Mollie, in her own way. And they didn't cry—not the way Dominique's mother sometimes cried, inexplicably, the tears beginning to pour down her cheeks, even when she was sober.

"Dad wasn't one of those dirt poor, Irish labourers. No, he was what they called a remittance man—that means an aristocrat. You'd better believe it! Not that there was ever any money coming in. There was this farm, that was all. That was what made us rich. In the war he was lucky and got a job on the railway. Along with the other dirt poor Irish labourers and the Chinese.

"He was still doing that in 1948. There was influenza around that year. Plus TB, which was always around. Flu hit here, hit the Reserve. We got sick, we got better. We were living on what Dad sent home besides whatever we could scrape together from hens and cattle. Then—I'll never forget that day! During a chinook, bad wind, slush up to your armpits, Indians came to the house. Two of 'em. A man and a boy. The man was carrying a dirty bundle of—something.

"They unwrapped it in the middle of the kitchen floor. My mother was trying to give them food. Anyone could see they were starving. I guess they were on the run from the flu. Taking it with them, but they wouldn't have known that." She paused. "You know what was in the bundle, don't you?"

They were both looking at the linoleum. It had been this floor, apparently.

He shook his head.

"All right. I guess you don't know anything. I just can't believe Robbie didn't tell you this, at least!—Well, it was a little girl. She was so weak from starvation she couldn't walk. Wrapped up in a dirty blanket. No shoes, no moccasins, no leggings. No pants, for God's sake! The old guy just showed her to my mother and got up to go.

"There was no way my mother was going to make him wrap up that blue child again and take her away with him. He left, and the boy went too, with a loaf of bread and a dozen eggs and a bag of tea, just about everything we had that they could pack. They were going south. To see if there was anything better on the Reserves in the U.S. They were walking. Horses died probably—or maybe they ate 'em. Anyway, the girl stayed. And got warm. And started eating right alongside us kids, as soon as the hens laid a few more eggs."

There had been nothing in those winters on the Reserve. The government took the grazing land for their own cattle in the war effort. And at the same time, the beef and flour rations the Indian agent had been giving out since the time the treaty was made were reduced and finally ceased. Dominique had often enough heard all of this.

"They came back for the girl in the summer. They left her because they couldn't carry her, but they weren't deserting her. It was my mother who wouldn't give her back. She stayed on with us and went to school in Bitter Root with Robbie and me. You've guessed who she was by now, haven't you?"

"Ma?"

"Yeah. It was Eliza. The man's name was Dominique Boucher. The boy's name was Henry, but his real name was Two Crows. Your grandfather. Your uncle."

He nodded. He knew he was named for his grandfather; that his mother had had a brother.

"Well, but you don't really know anything," she went on impatiently. "You look at this district now. Farming. Ranches. Oil. The wealth. The cars, the roads. Back then it was a desert. I remember the years when the air was so full of dust you coughed all summer. And all the time the Indians sat out on the Reserve and collected rations. They had the River and the government gave them cattle, but they were too proud to learn to farm. People said they starved because they wanted to starve rather than work. I might have believed it if I hadn't seen Eliza when her dad unpacked her on the kitchen floor.

"Besides—" She laughed. "It was the kind of thing they said about the Irish too."

Perhaps they were too proud—on both sides of his family—to have ever told him the story before.

"Well, I guess you know what happened."

"Yeah."

"Eliza went back to the Reserve and had you," continued Mollie. "And all I know is that it broke my mother's heart. They said it was TB that Mother died of. But nobody remembers what TB was like any more. That long sick decline." She passed a hand over her eyes. "Maybe that's what it means, dying of a broken heart. It means TB."

She looked up. "So now—what Robbie said about you screwing Emma—that she was like your sister? Well, you know, it was what he did. Eliza had been living with us six years."

Horrified and taken aback, Dominique was thinking that he should have known. He should have guessed it was the reason why Robbie had said that.

"Well, Robbie went off and made something of himself in the end. I was busy buggering up my own life with Otto, so I didn't notice he was doing that. Then he came back with Sonya. Smart, rich, well-educated. But the first thing I noticed when I met her was that he was marrying a woman like our mother. Sonya's prettier, she has all her teeth—but you know—there's something special she's got. My mother had it too. She kept us together through those awful years, even though Dad drank and we were poor as dirt. The first thing Sonya did was to go out to the Reserve and find you. It was like my mother come to life again.

"Of course if Sonya was here right now, she'd be papering all this over. What Robbie did—And Dad never drank, he was a wild and charming Irish gentleman. Mother was his true love—well, she was!" Mollie smiled suddenly. "Even I'm not all that bad if you hear the story from Sonya!"

EMMA WENT TO EDMONTON WITH THE PRODUCER, DICK, FOR a job interview in the first week of September. Spraying was over, and Dominique was filling in time as a mechanic's helper over in Pinkerton.

She returned, looking smug as a cat. "I got a job! I know I did!"

"What'd you have to do?" Dominique put an engine part in the Varsol bath. Emma had dropped in on the hangar. She was driving her mother's car.

Emma looked thoughtful.

"Did they want you to take off your clothes or something?" Privately he had thought this might be what it was all about.

"Are you jealous?" She was fascinated, instantly.

"Nope." He straightened up, smiling.

"Actually, they just asked me some questions. Maybe I can be a production assistant," she said. "It was kind of boring really."

Dominique stripped off his coveralls and began washing his arms.

"Where are we going to go tonight, Dominique? It's getting cold out."

Dominique smiled. "It's a surprise," he said.

The surprise was a big old house in Steamboat that he was renting from Poppalushka. It was the family mansion, now almost a derelict; for Poppa went to Florida for the winter, and lived out of his office and his pickup during the months of spraying in the summer.

Dominique had had the idea of fixing it up over the winter. He wanted to move Vicky in too, as soon as school started. Living with Eliza and Vicky during the last weeks of August he had seen for himself that he had to get Vicky off the Reserve. The boys were beginning to notice her and he had found himself acting as her guardian—more like a watchdog, actually—keeping her in at night, keeping the other kids out of the house, hiding Eliza's whiskey and cigarettes.

She was only seventeen, but hardly any other seventeen-year-old girls on the Reserve were still in school. It involved a bus trip to the district high school in Abercrombie. He remembered that himself—first the kids on the bus, then the kids and the teachers at school.

Emma loved the house. She ran up and down stairs, all over it, making plans. "I don't want to go home."

Dominique yawned. He was tired. They had made a fire and were lying on the floor in front of the fireplace. Her head was heavy on his arm.

"I was kind of hoping you'd say that."

She was up on her elbows instantly, her long dark hair falling over his chest.

"No more field!" she exclaimed. "No more cab of the truck!"

He laughed.

"No more Mother yelling at me. 'Clean up your room!' 'Feed the chickens!' 'Eat your meat!'"

"I'm going to bring my sister over tomorrow."

"Oh." She considered this. "Can't she stay home?"

"Nope. This way she can go to school in town. You'll like Vicky, anyway."

"Yeah. That'll be okay, I guess," said Emma generously. "As long as she goes to bed at nine, and helps with the dishes, and stays out of my room." She laughed. "Boy, I sound like Mother."

"Your room?" He smiled. "Do I have to stay out of your room too?"

"Nope. You have to stay in my room." She pressed her little nose down on his nose, her forehead on his forehead.

❡ THERE WAS NO MORE WORD ABOUT EMMA'S JOB, BUT SHE WAS so wild about fixing up the house that she scarcely mentioned it. And Dominique did not expect ever to see Dick, the producer, again.

They gave a housewarming party in the garden of the house on a warm day at the beginning of October. It was a garden gone crazy; Poppalushka's mother or whoever had been the settler here, had ploughed fifty or sixty years of prairie seed catalogues into it, and the tomato vines, gone wild, trailed over rose bushes and giant carrot plants.

They had invited Poppalushka and the boys from the hangar. Steamboat was more cosmopolitan than Roseland or Pinkerton and Dominique was amused to see that everyone wore his best: clean shirts, pressed trousers, slicked-back hair. Mollie turned up, bringing someone else with her.

"Tim!" Emma flung herself into the arms of a young Native man, a little older than Dominique. He was dressed oddly in a light-coloured three piece suit and a plastic dime store headband with coloured turkey feathers in it.

"Who's the Chief?" asked Poppalushka, eating a piece of the

garlic sausage he had brought with him. Mollie had supplied most of the food, which was why Emma had invited her.

"He was my mother's boyfriend," said Emma, passing by with a plate of sandwiches. "But he moved out years ago."

"Does he wear that getup everywhere he goes?"

Dominique went over to say hello to Mollie, who introduced them immediately.

"This is Dominique Boucher, my brother's son. And this is Tim Steen. He turned up again. But, believe me—I won't make the same mistake twice."

Tim shook hands with Dominique.

"How are you, Dominique?" she went on.

"He's great," said Tim, catching Emma in the curve of his arm as she came back the other way with the plate. "Anyone can see that."

The Pinkerton-Roseland contingent was watchful. They had never been to a party before with a guy in a turkey feather headband.

Emma offered Tim a bottle of beer and he took it. "Whoops!" The bottle disappeared and turned into a joint, which he quickly swallowed. Then he withdrew a line of knotted scarves from his mouth, and tucked them carefully into the low neck of Emma's top, withdrawing the beer bottle again from between her breasts.

"Wow!" said Emma. "Can you turn me into something?"

"I could turn you into a frog, but then who's going to kiss you, dear?"

"What kind of drug are you up on, anyway?"

"You saw me eat it with your own eyes."

"Okay, but Tim—! Maybe I got a job—! I'll be on TV!"

"I already saw you on TV. The set wasn't on. But I was watching it anyway."

"Stop showing off and come over here," said Emma. "I'm going to tell you all about it."

Mollie had a thin smile on her lips. "Good with kids, isn't he?" she remarked.

Dominique had seen Vicky watching Tim while he was doing his tricks, her eyes wide, her mouth a little open. Now she was drifting over to the corner where Emma had taken him. It was wonderful to her that there was another Native man at this party, Dominique realized, especially one as dazzling as Tim. He felt an urge to go stop her from listening to whatever he was saying to Emma. Emma was one thing, but a guy like that could be a really bad influence on his little sister.

Mollie was following his eyes. She said: "I'm sorry I had to bring him, but he wanted to see Emma. She was still just a little girl when he was hanging around."

She was wearing an unattractively brief halter top and a pair of short shorts. Dominique found that he could ignore this.

"As for me, I just came out of curiosity. To see what you've got here."

"Come anytime you want," said Dominique hospitably, enjoying his party.

Poppalushka was now staring at Mollie, his eye bulging. He came over, carrying his plate and a small glass of vodka.

Poppalushka rather fancied himself as the father of Dominique and Emma's love affair, having been in on it even before the family quarrel. Dominique had the idea Poppa had come across the room to defend him from Mollie.

"Are you Emmy's mother?" he asked hoarsely.

"Want to make something of it?" she responded immediately.

"I thought you were married to that German feller over in Bitter Root."

"I am married to a German fellow over in Bitter Root. Or do you stop being married to someone who's dead?"

"Oh." Poppalushka was realizing now that Mollie was a different proposition entirely from Robbie and Sonya. "Well—want a drink?" He withdrew a quart bottle of vodka from the lapel of his jacket.

"I brought some myself." Mollie took a forty ounce bottle of whiskey out of her enormous purse.

When Dominique came back with a glass he found Poppalushka and Mollie taking turns with the one they had.

The Ukrainians from Roseland had began to sing in their own language; a powerful male chorus. Drinking songs, then patriotic songs, sad and sentimental.

Looking across the grass from where he sat in a lawn chair, Dominique saw that Tim and Vicky were standing opposite one another beside the back steps. They didn't seem to be talking; they were both looking down at something. He would have got up and gone over to stop it, whatever it was that was going on between them, except that Emma was sitting on his lap and he was too happy to be worried. They were right there in plain sight.

Dominique had never seen Tim before in his life. But since Tim was not from the Reserve, he believed he wasn't likely to show up again.

What they were looking at was Tim's hand. He had introduced it to Vicky's hand a moment ago.

Emma had drifted away and now he seemed willing to give up on the kind of wild patter he had been entertaining her with. They were both just looking down at his hand which he slowly turned over under her gaze.

Vicky knew he was stoned. She had seen him swallow the joint, and even Vicky, who was a child of the Reserve, and therefore almost a prisoner of alcohol, knew about the strange behaviour of people who were stoned.

What she felt for him most of all was a kind of sympathy, a tenderness, because he was lost somehow. Who was he, that he, one of her own people perhaps, had had to resort to children's tricks and turkey feathers?

She looked seriously down at his hand, and he was serious too. Her own hand was not involved. She had removed it almost immediately, not just because she knew that Dominique would be looking. The magician might take her hand and do something that would damage it. He wouldn't want to harm her, but he was not in control of what might happen at all.

He was staring now at his palm.

"I see—I see greatness here," he said, stumbling a bit, even over these simple words.

"Maybe you'll become a great Chief," she said. "Like Crowfoot. Or Poundmaker."

"Or Medicine Bear," he said. "Ever heard of him?"

"Where do you come from?" she said. "Who are you?"

He looked up, and she saw that his eyes were glazed and what he said now was not to be trusted at all. "I am Medicine Bear," he said.

◀ FROM DOMINIQUE'S POINT OF VIEW THAT WAS THE LAST GOOD time they had that fall. Emma went to Edmonton to get a job with the TV station as a receptionist. Dominique kept the house with Vicky until Christmas, seeing Emma on the weekends, and then Poppalushka got him a job as a mechanic up north. He left, Emma went on with her career, and Vicky went back to living on the Reserve, taking the bus to Abercrombie to attend the district high school, and writing not at all, although Dominique wrote a letter every week to her and Eliza as he always had done.

Emma wrote long screeds at first, all about her job, her apartment mates, about how horrrible Dick was and how he wasn't coming through with anything. Her letters were spaced further and further apart.

In April he got a letter from Robbie. He did not recognize the handwriting on the envelope. He had never received a letter from Robbie before.

> Dear Son,
> This is to say I guess I was wrong. The hell with it, Dominique, you are living your own life now. Saw Emma last weekend but maybe she wrote you. The main news is we had a baby girl at the end of February and everybody is just crazy about her. Poppalushka says you're coming back pretty soon so you'll see her. Your father,
>
> Robbie
> P.S. Named her Eliza.

Lonely Dominique in the bunkhouse read this letter several times. Greasy pin-ups from men's magazines lined the walls. In the background the radio was wailing the sad, sad songs of country and western.

He saw Emma sitting dreamily before the mirror into the frame of which the same torn-up boyfriend was forever jammed. He saw Robbie driving Sonya to the hospital and he saw him in a green gown and gloves, holding the baby. He saw Sonya, rosy and pleased, lying in bed at home, saying they would name the baby for Dominique's mother. He saw himself taking off in the Stinson again next summer while they all waved to him from the ground. He rolled over and buried his face in the dirty pillow.

Emma moved away from her mirror and advanced towards him, her vivid face turned up.

He took the bus to Slave Lake. There he picked up a wreck of an old Cessna 182, poured oil into all its orifices, and flew it south to Roseland. Emma could not leave Edmonton till the weekend, which was too bad; he would have liked to fly her home in style. She was busy right now, working in a telethon.

Poppalushka drove him to the ranch. His own pickup was parked at the airstrip where he had left it in the fall, with four flat tires and a dead battery.

Robbie was out in the field, driving a tractor in front of the harrow.

"Want to get out here, son?" Poppa's large brown eyes were humid with sentiment. "I'll just go along and drop off your stuff, I guess."

Robbie came back down the row, looking over his shoulder at the machine behind. Dominique was almost beside the tractor before he turned around. He stopped at once and the tractor stood idling as Dominique swung himself up. They looked at each other, pleased and surprised. Robbie was smiling.

"Going to help me with seeding? I guess Poppalushka won't have anything to do for another month or so."

Dominique nodded. "I got your letter," he said. He stood up behind Robbie as he had when he was a boy, one hand on his shoulder, and they trundled down the field.

"About time for tea," Robbie shouted.

Poppalushka was eating doughnuts in the kitchen with Harry on his knee. Harry jumped to the floor, his arms spread like an airplane, and ran to Dominique, who tossed him up in the air.

"Dominique's never seen Lizzie!"

"Oh Robbie! Don't wake her up!" Sonya gave Dominique a

[123]

distracted hug. He followed Robbie upstairs and they looked down at the sleeping baby in the crib. Harry trailed after them.

Dominique picked up the little boy again and Harry whispered in his ear, "After this, you want to see my rooster?"

◖ DICK DROVE EMMA DOWN FROM EDMONTON AFTER THE telethon was over. They came straight to the farm, arriving in time for lunch. Dominique was washing at the sink, wearing his farm work clothes, a green drill shirt and pants. He turned around, wiping his face and hands on the towel. Emma stood glowing in front of him, in a brilliant flowery summer dress with a short, short hemline, her hair longer now, halfway down her back.

"You look nice, Emma," said Sonya, doing three things at once between the stove and the kitchen table. "That's a very short dress."

"Too nice to wear out to the barn," remarked Dick, with a flick of his eyes at Dominique.

Dominique saw Emma's eyes grow dull momentarily. Her lower lip thickened into a sullen grimace and she turned around slowly to glare at him.

Dick had long hair. It fell over his collar and descended to his shoulder blades. Everyone around the table thought he was a hippie, even though he was quite well known as a TV produc-er—with an even better-known wife.

For a moment, Dominique felt jealous of Dick. But then he pulled himself together; he knew with his rational mind that he did not have to feel jealous. He wouldn't even consider this.

An hour later, Dominique and Emma were in the haymow. The older adults had tactfully left them alone. Dominique had allowed Emma to get rid of Harry; but Harry had been in on this Emma-thing since the beginning and he was not offended.

"Well!" said Emma. She raised her arms and let them drop to her sides, standing knee-deep in the hay. Turning her face a little to one side, she smiled.

Dominique saw that she was making some comparisons. Maybe she wanted to tell him something he didn't want to hear. But Dick was not a real rival. And she was home again.

"Yeah, it's a barn, but—" he was speaking close to her small half-exposed, roseate ear. "Think it'll do?"

"What if I said no?" she teased.

"You'd be missing something!"

He kissed the ear, feeling her quiver. "Dominique, I—"

"Just come here, okay?" breathed Dominique, taking possession of her mouth and she gave a delighted giggle as he pressed her back into the mound of hay.

They lay together under the haystack, watching the swirling motes settle in the sunlight with child-like contentment. She stirred.

"I guess Robbie doesn't know we're—"

"Oh yeah. He knows." Dominique moved his head from the smooth shoulder to the hay beside her neck, relieving her of the weight.

"Dick brought me down in April and Robbie was just as mean as he could be. Sonya had an egg hunt," she added.

Robbie's letter now had an even more complete explanation. Whatever Robbie thought of Emma with Dominique, undoubtedly he hated Dick.

"Robbie told me I ought to stay home. I said I had a career. After all, what does he want? He and Sonya were giving me a bunch of stuff last year about going away and being independent. So now I actually do that and—"

Dominique thought of Robbie's flared nostril and curled lip over the lunch table, passing Dick the peas, the hot buns, and laughed quietly to himself.

"What are you laughing about? I do have a career! I helped make a commercial! That telethon! I've been working all winter."

She rose on her elbow to stare down at him, offended.

"So what are you going to do this summer?" he asked. "Going to go on being liberated and independent?"

"Yeah!" She lifted her chin.

"Want to do that in Steamboat, or do you have to go to Edmonton?"

She looked doubtful. "Are you going to fly?"

"In about a month. I'm living with Ma and Vicky right now, but maybe I could get Poppalushka's house again."

"So—it'd be the same?"

Her hair lay over his arm in a slithery fall. "Yes!" she sang into his ear, against his mouth, making the voiced accompaniment to the pounding of his blood.

◖ MOLLIE CAME TO ROBBIE AND SONYA'S FOR SUPPER, BRINGING A casserole dish full of scalloped potatoes. "So you're back," she said to Dominique, looking him up and down with a smile.

Howie was also there. He was a brown-haired, freckle-faced boy of twenty-one, more like his dead German father than the dark and Celtic Hallourans. The Hallourans made him nervous. He was shy of Dominique too, afraid of the family scandal. Dominique felt a kinship with Howie. He didn't like scandals either.

The baby was circulating. The whole family was mad about her, especially Robbie. Harry sat confidently beside Dominique on the sofa, Emma on the other side.

Howie said, "Are you helping Robbie with the seeding, Dominique?"

"He's going to start working for Poppalushka," said Emma. "As a pilot."

"I'd like to go up in one of them little crates," said Howie. "I only ever flew once and that was on the air bus to Edmonton."

"I could take you up."

"Howie'll be scared. He was scared that time on the air bus. I love flying." Emma spread her arms.

Howie flushed. He was embarrassed.

"You've been working on the Ochre River dam?" asked Dominique.

"Yeah. They started getting ready for that," said Howie sullenly.

"It's tons of cement. Tons and tons and tons. Howie said," contributed Harry, dreamily coasting a toy truck across Dominique's leg.

"Indians don't like it much." Howie was still sulky. "I guess they think it's their water or something. But water doesn't belong to them."

Dominique was silent. Emma, inattentive, lighted a cigarette. She had taken up smoking, more or less as a pose, and Dominique noticed how silly she looked, blowing smoke upwards in front of her nose.

"Want to hold the baby, Emmy? She's so cute. Look, she's yawning!" Laura held the baby up for Emma to see. Emma smiled slightly, but did not hold out her arms.

"Want a beer, Dominique?" Howie was looking at him shyly. He was sorry he had said anything about the Indians.

"Sure," said Dominique, getting up. "I guess we should go have it in the kitchen. Coming, Harry?"

Harry jumped up with alacrity, glad to get away from babyland.

Robbie wanted a beer too. He was sitting on a chair at the table. Dominique took another, with Harry on his lap. Radiating bashful pride, Howie brought in three bottles from the case outside in his truck.

"Been working hard?" asked Robbie.

"Yeah. I'm driving a crane."

"Well, that's good. That dam sure is taking a long time to get started. And we need the water."

Howie's eyes flickered at Dominique.

"They've got a bunch of guys from the Reserve working on the job. The government's makin' them hire the Indians. My boss was mad." Howie was now talking only to Robbie. "They can't keep 'em working because they don't show up. Or they show up drunk. We had an accident the other day because of that."

"Fired 'em, I guess," said Robbie, wiping froth off his lips.

Emma sauntered into the room and looked around at them.

"I want a beer," she said to Howie.

"Nope. Make some money and buy your own. You're so liberated."

"What are you talking about? I am liberated! I have a job."

"Oh yeah. Waitress or something. Think you're going to be on TV."

"I'm doing production!" screamed Emma. "That telethon—! I worked on a commercial!"

Harry sat solidly on Dominique's lap, not moving an inch. He had stopped playing with the truck, however.

"Hey now!" said Robbie. "What's this all about?"

Dominique said suddenly: "Have my beer, Emma. I don't drink anyway."

Howie turned scarlet.

"I guess you're scared I'm going to get drunk on one beer." Emma took a defiant mouthful out of Dominique's bottle. "But you're the one who's going to turn out like Dad, not me!"

"That's enough, Emma," said Robbie.

But Emma was once again indifferent. A fight with Howie was just a fight with Howie to her.

"That dam's sure going to make a difference to the farmers down here," Robbie said, trying to pick up the pieces.

"Yeah, but like I said, Robbie, there's going to be trouble." The colour fading from his thin pale skin, Howie looked down at the bottle in his hand.

"There's been trouble over that since I was a kid," said Robbie. "The farmers are screaming for water."

"And they couldn't get it because the Indians said no. And they're still saying no!"

"Well, I guess what it comes down to is paying. The River's on the Reserve."

"Yeah, but paying how much? And what were they doing with the water? They weren't even using it."

"Maybe they think it's their property though."

"Well, we gave it to them in the first place. And they could get water from the dam for irrigation just as well as we can. And now there's this Native hiring thing. Everyone knows the Indians are all just a bunch of drunks. Never did a day's work in their lives. Can't train 'em, can't do anything with 'em."

Emma had been standing beside Dominique, chafing a little because Harry was still on his lap and he was listening to the others.

She said now: "You're prejudiced, Howie."

"You don't know anything about being prejudiced. I've known Indians all my life. Grew up right beside the Reserve—"

"So did I! Who do you think you're talking to!"

Robbie was listening to the argument with a heavy frown.

Harry put the toy truck confidentially into Dominique's hand. Then he began to climb down off his lap. He ran across the floor to Robbie and climbed up.

"Think you can say—!"

"—just because you're—!"

"What do you think about it, Dominique?" said Howie. He stood in front of the electric stove, four-square, but his hand trembled, holding the bottle. He was bright red with anger.

"Now you just leave Dominique—" Robbie spoke warningly.

"Well, he got some of that money they've been throwing at the Reserve," mumbled Howie. "He must have."

"Maybe Ma did. I wasn't here."

"You could have got it," said Howie, sticking to his guns.

"Let's go outside for a while, Howie," suggested Dominique. He went to the door.

There was an electric silence. Robbie was looking keenly at both of them, his arms around Harry, who was still on his knee.

Howie put down his empty beer bottle on the ledge. The grown-up air he had been assuming had departed suddenly, leaving him looking young and vulnerable.

"Stay here, Emma," said Robbie, as she made a move to follow.

They went out into the yard, beyond the circle of light from the porch. Dominique did not turn around until they had reached the perimeter of the ploughed field. Howie came up to stand beside him and they stared together out into the night over the cooling sweet-smelling earth.

"Shit, Dominique," said Howie. "I'm sorry for those things I said."

"It doesn't matter. Not between you and me."

"It's just—" Howie pounded his fist into his palm. "She gets me so mad!"

"I guess you know I'm in love with her."

Howie was paralysed with embarassment.

There was a quiet movement on the grass behind them. Robbie said, "I went and got a couple more of your beers, Howie."

He passed them each a bottle. "Everything okay?"

[129]

They drank. Dominique drank all of his in long cool draughts, enjoying the bitterish, sickly taste for the first time. It was delicious and it created a warm tingle in his belly, a liberation of the brain that made him not care about anything any more. He found this the most frightening thing that had happened that night.

Everyone was in the kitchen when they returned. It had been a four-alarm fire.

"Girls, off to bed," said Sonya instantly. "Harry, I don't know what you're doing here at all!"

Emma stood a little behind her, guilty, half-delighted eyes raised to see what Dominique had done to Howie. Mollie was looking as if she wanted to slap somebody, her mouth set.

"I'm taking Harry," Dominique announced.

"Yeah, Harry's too little," agreed Harry. "Can't go by himself." He grabbed Robbie's knees, putting his face up for a good-night kiss. Robbie lifted him up high, then put him into Dominique's arms.

"I like Howie," Harry murmured as Dominique tucked him in. "And there's tons of cement. Tons and tons of it."

"Yeah, that's all right, Harry," said Dominique. "I like him too."

The only person left in the kitchen when he got downstairs again was Emma. Dominique sat down at the table with elbows out flat, chin resting on his hands. He had sat this way so many times at this table, doing his homework, waiting for supper.

"You were mad at Howie. Were you going to fight him, Dominique? Robbie went out there to stop you, didn't he?"

"I'm not fighting with your brother."

"Why'd you make him go outside with you then?" she asked. She did not understand at all.

"I wanted to get him away. You were hurting his feelings," said Dominique, drawing on his last reserves of patience. Somehow she was incapable of looking under the surface of things.

"Me!" Emma was astounded. "But he was—! He said—!"

"So what?" Dominique got up and walked restlessly to the door. "He's your brother."

"What's that got to do with it? What'd you say to him out there, anyway?"

"I said that I love you."

"You did?" Emma was electrified. Her hand flew to her mouth.

"Yeah. Emmy, don't you understand? Someday we're going to get married and they've got to agree. They've got to want that too."

⊄ SEEDING BEGAN. ON SUNDAY DOMINIQUE WENT OVER TO BITTER Root to get Emma. She was talking on the phone, but she put it down, hardly even saying goodbye to the person on the other end when Dominique entered the kitchen. He got the feeling it was Dick, and he felt disquietude, not jealousy exactly. There was something else out there that she wanted; what was here apparently was not enough.

He wanted to ask her what she had been doing all day. She looked very discontented at the moment.

There was no time to play around when they were seeding. He had been working all day long, then going home to the Reserve to sleep. It was not just Emma he had been neglecting. He had hardly even seen Vicky since he got home. "Come on," he said suddenly. He took Emma's hand.

"What? Where are we going?"

She was still seated and he tugged on the hand till she rose to her feet.

She was wearing shorts, a brief top, and Dominique had a moment of doubt. He could just take her over to Roseland to see Poppalushka; they could eat in a country café. But his mother wasn't drinking.

"Going to the Reserve. To see Ma."

"Do we have to go there?" Emma was saying now.

"Sure," said Dominique. "She's my mother. She's got to see you."

"Oh yeah." Emma looked happier. She enjoyed showing off.

They were driving now in the direction of the uplands around the River. Trucks with enormous wheels were carrying quarried gravel to the dam site beyond the Reserve. It looked like they really were intending to build it now.

Emma looked out the window without comment, but Dominique was horrified. The last time he had passed this way, none of this had been happening. The go-ahead had been given for the dam now, he supposed. Another battle that the Reserve had finally lost.

"Who was Vicky's father?" Emma asked suddenly.

"Some guy who lived with Ma for a while."

"Didn't he even have a name? You're all Bouchers."

"They didn't get married, that's why."

"I just don't get it about you and Vicky," she said. "Why does she have to stay with you all the time? You're hardly even related."

"What? Vicky's my sister!"

"Well, I don't see what difference that makes. I'd hate having to live with Howie."

Dominique reminded himself that she didn't know what it would be like to have Eliza for a mother. She didn't know about the Reserve either. It was the reason he had to take her out there. She had to know.

Their way parted from the huge lumbering trucks as they turned onto the Reserve. Dominique had a momentary self-punishing desire to go look at the dam site. But then he decided not to. It would make him sad. It would make him sick. It might make him angry. He resolved to look at it from the air someday instead.

His mother wasn't drinking. But there was something wrong right from the start. He had been expecting that Emma wouldn't like Eliza right away, that she might be shocked. He had forgotten that his mother might not like Emma.

Dominique boiled the kettle and they had tea.

Eliza said nothing. She sat in the chrome chair by the kitchen table, as she always sat, saying nothing.

To Emma, Eliza must look like an old woman, he realized, a hundred years older than Robbie. For some reason she had elected to wear braids and leggings, instead of her usual jeans, her hair in a clip—even though he had telephoned, he had stopped at the gas station in Bitter Root to phone up and say he was bringing Emma.

"Where's Vicky?"

His mother shrugged.

"Emma and me and Vick'll probably get that house in Steamboat again this summer, Ma."

"Won't make no difference to me." They were never home anyway, she meant.

Emma said, "Where's your room, Dominique? I want to see your room."

He took her down the hall and showed her the room, his barren bed, just a mattress on the floor with Robbie's sleeping bag. He hadn't really lived in the house except to sleep there, for almost ten years.

"You live here?" she said, incredulous.

Coming back to the kitchen she caught sight of Vicky's room through the partly-open door. She pushed it open and went in.

Sitting on the ruffled comforter she looked around. A little white-painted desk and chair. A bureau. No poster or boyfriend photograph. But Dominique felt that the furniture must seem familiar to her at least.

Vicky entered by the front door and saw them at once, Emma sitting on the edge of her bed, Dominique standing in the doorway. Vicky looked at her, surprised, reserved.

"What's she doing here?" she asked Dominique.

Once again, he was not prepared for the hostility of his own family.

"I was just looking at your bedroom." Emma had not really noticed.

Vicky passed on down the hall and poured herself a cup of tea in the kitchen. When he and Emma got back there she was sitting silently beside her mother. There was something entrenched about them, something resistant. Vicky's face was blank. Emma at Poppalushka's in Steamboat was one thing; here, she was another.

"What're we going to do now?" Emma asked Dominique. She was bored. Silent Vicky, the old woman, nothing to speak of in the house.

She couldn't just sit with them. She was too impatient.

Dominique would have spent the afternoon fixing the furnace, or at least, trying to find out what was wrong with it. Looking at something Vicky showed him; a picture or a book she was reading. Watching TV. He was actually longing to just hang around at home. He never had time for that now.

"Dominique says we're going to get Poppalushka's again," Emma said to Vicky.

For the first time a trace of animation crossed Vicky's face. "I saw him again," she said. "The magician."

"The magician? Oh—! Do you mean Tim?" Emma laughed.

"He's here," said Vicky softly. "On the Reserve."

Dominique felt cold fear for a moment. The tone of her voice, the way Vicky's eyes were now shining, her skin a little flushed. She was looking so stunningly beautiful; it had to reflect some interior state. He didn't want her to feel that way—the way it looked as though she felt—about any man.

"That guy is crazy," said Emma. "I used to like him when I was a kid. But boy!—Now he's stoned all the time. Not just some of it."

"He was your mother's boyfriend, wasn't he?" Dominique knew Vicky wouldn't like this.

"Yeah. One summer. She never has 'em any more. I guess she got too old."

The other two had gone blank again. Eliza had not done anything more than look up anyway.

"She likes Indians," Emma continued, cheerful, certain of herself. "Maybe that's why she likes you, Dominique."

Mollie did like him, he realized, horrified. Was that why?

"The only good thing about that is that you don't like her!"

He took Emma away a short while later. They used the rest of the time together to go and look at the dam site, upriver from the Reserve, ugly and busy, even on Sunday afternoon. It did make him angry, as he had been afraid it would.

❡ IN THE WEEK THAT FOLLOWED, HE BECAME WORRIED ABOUT Emma. He had no time to see her because of seeding, but he had talked to her on the phone. Somehow she was never at Robbie and Sonya's any longer, only over in Bitter Root. The phone would be busy for hours. He would call at suppertime, again at nine or ten, during a tea break, and it would still be busy.

Dominique had not taken the idea of Dick as a rival seriously. Now he was seriously jealous. He was afraid for her too. He thought Dick was a kook; he had long hair. Perhaps he was one of those crazy people who smoked pot. Besides that, he was married—his life was all mixed up. Dominique had Robbie's horror of that kind of thing. He had had enough of it as a child, with Eliza.

What he was doing right now wasn't romantic and daring, like flying. He was working as a farmhand and his clothes were dirty. He lived at home on the Reserve—which bored and dismayed her. He knew all this—but what could he do about it?

The following week he took some time off. They were almost finished seeding. He and Emma went to Poppalushka for the key to the house.

Poppalushka was sentimentally delighted to see Emma again. "You grew your hair, Emmy." It hung loose down her back; in jeans, a fringed vest, she looked like a hippy, even to Dominique.

She gave Poppa a hug.

"Still got the same feller, I see. Going to work for me again? Won't be much till after seeding's done, of course."

They moved into the house. Vicky wouldn't come this time, though. Eliza started drinking again—a little. And every time he got over there, Vicky seemed to be out.

Dominique had begun working for Poppalushka as a mechanic. Relentless work—it was Robbie's example, heckled in by a thousand teachers, textbooks, ministers, and the country neighbours, who said that he wouldn't be able to get a job—or to keep it when he got one.

Emma was in Edmonton for a week. Then the next. She didn't make it home for the weekend.

There was nothing to grasp hold of here, nothing he could change. Her clothes, her hair, whatever was represented by Dick; it was another world, and apparently she wanted to be in it.

She came home on Saturday. She came to Robbie's in her mother's car, collected him and drove to Poppalushka's. It was almost the way it had been the very first time. Dick had been abolished. They ate pizza and Emma strutted naked through the high-ceilinged upper rooms of the house.

On Sunday she went home—while he was working for Robbie. He called, but the line was busy. He drove over there after he had finished work.

"Come in." Only Mollie was there.

"Did Emma go to Edmonton or something?"

She nodded. She was sorry for him, he saw.

"Well, then—"

"Sit down for a minute, Dominique. Maybe you need to talk to somebody."

"She just didn't tell me she was going, that was all."

"I think she's not telling you much of anything these days."

He had sat down, but only because he hardly knew what he was doing.

"She only came home to pick up her clothes. She's gone to Vancouver."

"What?"

"Yeah. I didn't think you'd know," said Mollie dryly.

"Did she go with—with Dick?"

Mollie shrugged. "Probably. Who's Dick?"

It was like a punch in the stomach. After the way it had been the previous night at Poppalushka's. Perhaps she had meant it to be farewell. But she hadn't said that. She had merely left the following morning in her mother's car.

"Look, maybe it doesn't help all that much if I say it now, but this has nothing to do with you, Dominique. It's because of what's going on in that contriving little head of hers. Her ambition. What she wants in her life. Her career!"

Her career—he had thought of this in the same way as Howie, as Mollie obviously did. Women didn't have careers. Did they?

Mollie wanted to detain him; to talk to him some more. To comfort him. But after what Emma had said about her attraction, he could no longer even sit with her. She repelled him; the idea that she might really like him in the way Emma had suggested made him sick.

❦ WHEN THE CUB CRASHED HE WAS LOW AND SLOW, AND IT was a downdraft that caught him, a draft that lurked in the shadows of a windbreak, caused by a ditch with a trickle of water in it. His wheels caught in the feathery mass of the pale green poplar leaves, held for a moment, then pitched the plane downwards, and for a second he was suspended forward with his head in the windshield. Then there was release and the plane fell right wing down onto the fence below and tipped forward. The dashboard smashed into his chest, but he was safe from the propeller, stuck fast in the soft earth underneath.

It was his test flight on the machine.

Dominique switched off the ignition and climbed out through the door, which he still could open. He felt curiously indifferent as he walked towards the farmhouse to call.

Poppalushka came out to look at the wreck. "Well, it ain't the end of the world," he said. He looked at Dominique. "Weren't drinking or nothing?"

"Nope." He had been the night before and he was going to be again tonight, though.

Poppalushka chewed his toothpick. "You want to start taking this thing apart? Maybe we can get her up and running again before the season starts."

"You could just collect on the insurance."

"Sounds like you don't care."

"No." Dominique considered. "No, I don't care."

Poppalushka seated himself laboriously upon one heel and stared up into the sky, squinting.

Dominique stood in front of him, his arms hanging loosely down. His chest and rib cage had begun to ache from the bruises left by the dashboard.

"You know, I kind of hate to see it all go down the drain," said Poppa, chewing and squinting. "You were doing pretty well for yourself. But you ain't got your heart in it no more. Not like you did."

"No."

"Want to go up North again and work for a while? I could probably find you something to do."

"No," said Dominique exhaustedly. "Don't worry about me, Poppa. I've got to stay here."

Dominique moved back to the Reserve that night. He was a little drunk already, on beer that had been left over from last year's party, in the kitchen at Poppalushka's. He had drunk it up as he was packing. Eliza was out, but he knew where she sometimes stashed a bottle. He poured himself a cupful.

Vicky entered the room and watched him do this in silence.

"What are you doing here?" She eyed the bottle.

"I came home."

"Really?" There was a flicker of animation in her voice. "Where's Emma?" she demanded. "You can't bring her here."

"I'm not going to."

Vicky sat down and they regarded one another. Then her eyes dropped as he took a swig out of the cup.

"Broke the plane," he said. He took up the bottle again. "Maybe I broke a few ribs too. Feels like fuckin' shit."

"I could get you that stuff, you know that stuff Ma put on her knee when—"

"Forget it, Vick."

He remained drunk for a week. Eliza drank with him, helping him out. Then her welfare cheque ran out and they had nothing more to buy whiskey. The boys on the Reserve bothered them, but not so much now that Dominique was back. They didn't like him; they were afraid of him.

Sonya came to visit one afternoon. Dominique was lying on the kitchen sofa. Eliza was housecleaning, washing all the accumulated dishes of their long silent binge.

"Hello, Dominique." She sat down at the rickety table.

Eliza poured her a cup of tea.

Sonya's figure had come back after the baby and she looked pretty and cool in a light cotton print dress, her hair tied back in a ponytail. She was incongruous here; her cheerfulness seemed false.

"All these eggs?" Eliza glanced at the flat of eggs Sonya had put on the table.

"The girls are doing hens for 4-H. We can't eat them all."

Vicky emerged from the hall, shot Sonya a hostile glance, hung in the doorway for a moment, then went to sit on the sofa arm at Dominique's feet, her knees drawn up.

"Hello, Vicky. Still in school?"

Vicky did not reply.

"She's still in school," Eliza said.

Sonya was glancing at Dominique. He knew she wanted to talk to him, but she did not quite dare, in front of the other two. She began to chatter about the children and the farm. Why did she bother? Eliza listened, now putting away the clean dishes. Sometimes she smiled slightly. She probably liked hearing about Sonya's life in that odd dry way of hers. Vicky hunched her shoulders even more, and clasped her knees with her small narrow hands.

"Come outside with me, Dominique." Sonya had got up to leave. "There's something funny about the truck these days. It doesn't always start."

Dominique followed her out. If he did not talk to her, she would send Robbie. Suddenly she seemed terrible to him. She was trying to get him back, to take him away from his family again.

"Dominique," she said, "you are frightening everybody. Poppalushka was almost crying when he talked to Robbie. What are you doing to yourself?"

"Nothing."

"Was it Emma? We tried—everybody tried to warn you."

He stared at her. There were tears in her eyes.

"Why are you here like this?"

"It's my place. My home," he said. "Maybe they need me here."

"Maybe they do, but not like this! Dominique, you've got to—!"

"I haven't got to do anything, Sonya. This is just none of your business." It was like swearing in front of Vicky to say something like this to Sonya.

"What about Robbie?" she said after a moment. "Would you talk to him?"

"I'd tell him it was none of his fuckin' business either. Go home, Sonya," he said shortly, turning away from the shock on her face.

❡ THE NEXT WEEK, DOMINIQUE GOT A JOB WORKING AS A labourer on Ochre River dam.

He was indifferent to the politics of the situation. His job was off-loading the heavy bundles of steel rods that reinforced the

[139]

cement, using a forklift, but also doing some of the carrying, with a few others. The carrying was bad; it was heavy and there was the chance of dropping a bundle—or having the mate at the other end drop it. A misstep could result in somebody getting hurt. He came home exhausted every night to sleep under a ragged blanket on the kitchen sofa.

He saw Howie a few times, working on the cranes, but they had no chance to talk. Dominique thought that Howie would have the guts to talk to him, even in front of his mates, but they had no time. It did not come up.

Nobody bothered him. It had never taken him long to win the reputation of being a good worker.

He gave his paycheque to Eliza who bought beer and whiskey with it. But the work was too hard for him to stay up at night with her and drink.

Nobody came to the house now. Eliza went out and sometimes stayed out all night. Vicky ignored this and so did he. He had the impression that Vicky was happy they were alone together. She liked to make soup out of a can and sit watching him eat it. Then she would wash the few little dishes while he went to sleep on the sofa. He always found himself covered with a blanket when he woke up.

Then Tim, the same magician of their party the previous fall, came to the work site. He did no tricks. He had come to talk about the dam. He talked at lunchtime to the small knot of men from the Reserve, eating their sandwiches or the pop and hotdogs from the lunch wagon. He was telling old stories of their people, about the River, the buffalo, the grizzlies. But they weren't like the stories Dominique had heard as a child; he must have read them somewhere, or made them up. It was crazy and Dominique didn't listen.

All Dominique could think of, as he sat at a little distance watching, was how he had seen this guy once before, in the backyard of Poppalushka's, under tall cool cottonwoods. He had been talking to Vicky.

The gang boss went to get him, looking for a fight, but Tim didn't fight.

"Want me to go?" he said coolly. "You know, this place is ours. I own the ground." He walked away, but very slowly.

Some of the Native men looked up and others looked down or away. There was a long silence as the magician drove off in his van.

"Were you listening to that crap?" Dominique's foreman, Milo, was standing beside him, folding his arms to make the muscles stand up.

"Nope."

"Well, there's going to be trouble if he comes back. Maybe you can tell them that." The foreman jerked his thumb at the Natives, now trailing slowly back to their various job sites.

"I'm not telling nobody nothing," said Dominique.

"Yeah? Okay. Maybe you're not." The young foreman frowned.

"I just work here. Got any complaints about that?"

"Nope. As long as you don't join the union." Milo grinned at him. There were no unionized workers, although the unions were constantly trying to get in. It was another issue, like the Native quotas.

That evening he began to drink with Eliza again.

Dominique had now passed the stage where he drank for the fire in his belly and the liberation of his brain. His ten-day drunk when he had moved to the Reserve had taught him to drink for the obliteration of sensibility. To achieve the point where consciousness was fuzzy, where his tongue was too thick for speech. This was the objective. He lay down on the sofa with the bottle, and continued to drink, summoning his own nothingness.

When he woke up the next morning, he had a hangover. But he went to work.

What the bosses said about the magician had frightened the other Native workers away. Dominique had forgotten that this might happen. He was the last one from the Reserve to go.

The man on the back of the bundle of rods they were carrying plunged forward, then jumped aside, leaving Dominique to fall forward with the crushing weight coming down on his back. But he was still quick enough to dodge aside. He fell and the bundle of rods glanced off his back, then scattered like toothpicks, all over the work site.

Dominique got up slowly.

"He dropped them on me," he said. "He threw them down." He was still too stunned, amazed really, to consider the consequences of saying it out loud like this.

The mate stood by, shouting angrily: "He fuckin' dropped them himself!"

The young foreman, Milo, took him by the elbow. "You're fuckin' drunk!"

Dominique wrenched his arm away. He had been drunk the night before, but he knew that he was sober now.

They were all in a circle around him now and they were ready to fight. Looking into their tight, hostile faces, Dominique saw that he was going to get hurt.

Then two of them were on him, taking him down, and the rest took their time over smashing him in the face, kicking in his ribs. Finally someone kicked him in the groin and he blacked out.

He was in the hospital for two weeks with a collapsed lung, some broken ribs, internal bleeding. While he was there, he was visited by a big man in a ten gallon hat who said he was a lawyer; but Dominique wouldn't speak to him. He wouldn't let Sonya take him home either. When he was well enough to get up and shuffle down the hospital corridor, he went back to the Reserve, where he was treated, for the moment at least, like a hero and a symbol of resistance.

In the wake of the publicity that surrounded his getting beaten up, and the collapse of the Native hiring program, the government had been forced to slow down its preparations for the dam. Thereafter, the tedious legal arguments against its being built at all began in the courts and in a series of Federal environmental hearings. This process took up the remainder of the decade and went on into the next.

5

1976 · The Magician

◀ VICKY SAW THE MAGICIAN. SHE SAW HIM FROM A DISTANCE
two or three times, driving through the village, once buying
cigarette papers in the store. Then he started giving magic shows
out of his van for the little kids.

She went to see one of his shows after school. He did some
tricks with handkerchiefs, then he pulled a rabbit out of a top hat.
But after a while he seemed just to get bored and disappeared with
a flash and a crack of powder.

He was charging admission in a half-hearted way. They were
supposed to pay as they went out, putting money into the top hat.
Most of the kids didn't bother to pay.

Vicky stayed where she was after they all left. He had some kind
of canopy set up off the back door of the van, a little stage, with
chairs from the community hall. She was curled up on a chair in
the back row. After a long time she moved up to the front row and
sat in the middle.

Tim came out of the van onto the stage, a cloud of marijuana
smoke wafting from the open door behind him. He shaded his
eyes, looking down at her. He seemed quite surprised to see her
there.

"Hello, Vicky," he said. It turned out he remembered things, in
spite of the dope. "How did you like my show?"

"You didn't make much," she said. "Most of them didn't pay."

"Well—who cares? People should only pay for real magic."

She was looking at him attentively. He was very handsome
to her, tall and brown, with his long nose, his dark eyes, his

hair in braids. He descended the steps and slouched in the chair beside her.

"Do you think there is any real magic?" she asked.

"Yes," he replied. He had had to think about it for a moment.

"They say there isn't. There's only science. And—you know—religion."

"Whatever that is." Tim shrugged. "You've never seen any magic, I guess," he continued.

She was feeling the same sense of connection, the same spellbound attention as she had felt last summer when she talked to him at Dominique's party.

"Can you do it?"

He looked at her for a moment, then got up and went back into his van. A moment later he came out carrying an artist's sketch pad and a piece of purple chalk. He sat down in front of her on the bottom step and began to draw.

He tore off the page and started again. "I'm all doped up."

"Are you trying to draw me?" She craned her neck to look.

"Just a minute. Hold still."

Vicky had seen quick sketch artists at fairs. They took longer than this, however. Tim passed her the sketch pad and she looked at herself. The long wavering line of her hair. One hand with slim fingers under her chin. The knee with the elbow resting on it briefly indicated.

"It's me?"

"Yeah. How could that be you?"

How could it be her? It was not like the neat, laborious drawings of the quick sketch artists. But it was, assuredly, her.

"I'm an artist," he said. "You know—Leonardo da Vinci, Michelangelo?"

"Why don't you do this to make money?"

He laughed. "Boy, you really thought my show was no good!"

Vicky made a protesting gesture with her hand.

He took back the sketch pad and drew her again, making that gesture. He passed the sketch pad and Vicky bent over it, pushing her hair back on her shoulders, fascinated. It was only five or six lines.

"If you knew anything about real magic, you'd say this was a trick."

"But you're good at it."

"Maybe I don't like doing tricks," he said. "This kind of tricks."

"People sell art."

"Black velvet paintings." He was drawing her again. This time he took a little longer and Vicky saw her face beginning to emerge.

"Probably I could do a better show if I had an assistant," he said, passing her the paper.

Vicky held the pad on her lap and gazed at him.

"Me?" she said. "Could I?"

"Why not? Let's. It sounds like a money-making proposition." He went into the van for a moment and came out smoking a joint. "What do you think we should do to make it better?"

"I think we should charge admission when they come in," said Vicky.

Tim laughed. "Okay."

"Could I disappear too?"

"It's easy."

"Well, I want to."

"Let's do some real magic too," he suggested. "We'll only charge for the bullshit."

"What will you do?"

He lay back in his metal chair, smoking and crossing one booted foot over the other. Vicky looked down at the face on the page in front of her. No one had told her she was beautiful before, and she looked at it shyly. It was so simple it could not be an exaggeration.

He saw her looking and smiled lazily.

"I'd like to paint you."

"But I couldn't—I mean I wouldn't—"

"Take off your clothes?" He was laughing. "How about if I just paint your arm then. It's naked."

Vicky looked at her arm, then folded it in her other arm. She unfolded them and then tucked them both, folded, under her jacket.

"It's okay, Vick. I couldn't paint you now anyway. I'm way too far gone. Besides, I don't have any paint."

"Oh." She looked up. "We could get some, though. If we made some money."

"Well—all right." He was very surprised.

They began doing shows together. Vicky quit school; she went over there first thing after she got up in the morning. He made her up and dressed her in different strange costumes made out of the stuff he had in the van, old blankets, drop cloths and tarpaulins. Sometimes he disappeared in a puff of smoke at the end, or else she did.

Vicky went home later on. Her mother had been drinking.

"There's no dinner." Eliza's voice was hoarse.

"That's okay, Ma. I ate something." It was not entirely true. She had had two pieces of bread in Tim's van at the end of the second show. It was the only thing she had had to eat. Tim had been smoking so he hadn't bothered to eat.

"Where's Dominique?"

"I don't know."

"Weren't you with him?"

Vicky sometimes thought her mother lived in her memory. When they were kids she had always been with Dominique.

"I don't know where he went, Ma."

"Oh yeah, he's drinkin'."

Dominique came in later. He was very drunk, hardly able to walk or see, but still on his feet. He and Eliza started an argument about something that had happened at a party. She was railing at him about money—and he was making an accusation about sex. Vicky could hardly listen.

She went to her room. Presently Dominique stumbled in there and fell down on her bed. He was snoring or else she would have lain down beside him. But from the sounds he was making she was afraid he would puke. She went out and walked down to the village.

Tim's van was always parked right beside the Catholic mission. For some reason he always wanted to park there. He felt that it had some kind of significance.

Vicky went into the tent and curled up miserably on a chair

beside the steps. She thought he must be asleep inside and she did not want to wake him, to explain. But she couldn't go home.

That afternoon he had made her up as an antelope. He had drawn her picture afterwards. "You tend to look best as one of the deer tribe, Vick."

She had been staring at the picture with shy pleasure.

"It's good." He considered it too, looking down, his head cocked. "I guess that's how men like women to look. Sort of vulnerable."

Vicky could not sleep at first. She was uncomfortable on the chair. After a while, she lay down on the ground and slept. When she woke up she was still curled up on the ground beside the steps. Tim was sitting on them, looking down at her sideways.

"What are you doing here, Vick? Were you here all night?"

Vicky nodded, looking up at him wordlessly.

"Won't your mother be worried?" He changed this. "Where's Dominique?"

"Dominique's drinking."

Vicky uncurled herself stiffly and went to sit on the steps beside him. After a moment he put his arm around her. She moved away a bit, but it was just a friendly arm, a gentle arm.

"What happened to Dominique? I didn't know he drank."

She began to tell him, speaking in a monotone. "Emma took off on him. Because of her career—you know, like, she thinks she's going to be on TV? That's all she really cares about anyway.

"And then he went to work on the dam. I don't know why he did that. It was after he crashed the plane."

He nodded. Apparently he knew that Dominique had been working on the dam. He was looking at her sombrely, seriously.

"He got beat up then. I don't know why it happened. They beat him up. Really bad. He had broken ribs, a collapsed lung. They kicked him in the face, between the legs. He was in the hospital for a while. Then when he got out—he began drinking." She hated telling this story. Her voice went on and on in a dreary monotone, all by itself.

"There was a lawyer—they wanted him to go to court over it. But Dominique just took the cheque. He wanted it—the cheque. He drinks all the time now."

[147]

Tim was making faces. He pounded his fist into his palm.

It was strange to see him reacting to her story with the body language of a whiteman. Sometimes he didn't seem like one of her people at all. "Why isn't there a revolution? Why is Dominique becoming a drunk? Why am I wasting time doing shows for children? Why aren't we doing something?"

"But what can we do about it?"

"What can we do about it? We can say it's there. We're just letting it happen to us and we don't even say it is happening. Not even to ourselves."

"You mean, like the dam?"

"Yeah, the dam. And Dominique thinking he could get himself a white girl and a white job. And you too," he exclaimed. "Look at you! Why are you hanging out here all the time? Don't you know this is the road to fucking ruin? You should be in school!"

She lifted up her chin and stared at him blankly.

"Yeah, I know you look like the Madonna now, but how is that going to turn out anyway? You're just going to get pregnant. Then you'll end up as a drunk like Eliza and your brother."

Vicky felt the tears rising into her eyes. If he was going to cast her out she would have no one, no one at all.

"Well, isn't it true?" he demanded.

"No." She spoke thickly, because of the tears.

He came over and took her chin, looking down into her face. "It is true. Tell the truth, at least!"

"Why don't you tell the truth about yourself?" she shouted, tearing herself away from him. "Why are you picking on me?"

He spun away from her and walked rapidly around the tent, clasping one hand in the other.

"Okay," he said. "Maybe I can do that. Maybe I'm the only person in this place who can!"

Vicky was crying. She put her hand up to wipe the tears off her cheeks with her trembling fingers.

Tim stood still, watching her from across the tent. "I'm sorry, Vick," he said, after a while.

She went over and sat down on the steps again, resting her

forehead on her folded arms. After a moment he brushed past her. He was going into the van to get a joint; she heard him strike a match. He came out and sat down behind her on the top step.

Vicky breathed in the thick, acrid smoke, trying to calm down, hoping it would help. If someone had given her a glass of whiskey right now she would have drunk it down, even though she hated the taste. There had to be some cure for this bitterness.

"I didn't mean to hurt you, Vicky."

Vicky didn't move.

"I mean it isn't you I wanted to hurt."

"Why should you want to hurt anyone?" she asked dully. She could tell that the marijuana was making him feel good and this made her angry. But she was trying to suppress all her feelings. It seemed the only way to cope.

He was smoking another joint right on top of the first one.

"Are you going to stick around? Want to do a show this afternoon?" he asked.

She nodded. "I'm hungry," she said.

He seemed surprised.

She continued to sit crouched on the steps.

"I don't think there's any food left."

"We could get breakfast from Joshua Joe."

"But I'm not—" He stopped. "Oh—okay."

They took the van and drove over the hill to Joshua Joe's garage on the highway outside the Reserve.

Joshua gave them breakfast. Mrs. Joshua kept chickens, so they had eggs. Vicky drank a lot of milk with her fried egg; they tended not to have it at home because it was a long way to carry it from the store.

"How's your brother?" Joshua asked.

"He's okay."

"A lot of guys are sayin' that was pretty damn bad luck. Me, I'm sayin' it wasn't any kind of luck at all." He patted Vicky's hand. He was being unusually talkative.

"My grandchildren always over at your show," he said to Tim.

"Yeah." Tim seemed abstracted. He was eating breakfast, however.

[149]

"Some guys say you're sellin' that stuff." Joshua sniffed. A smell of dope always hung about Tim, in his clothes and in his hair.

Tim shrugged.

"Better not sell any to my kids."

"Sure."

"And her. You smokin' that?" he demanded.

"No," said Vicky.

"He trouble for you. Just trouble," said Joshua. "Better go back to school."

"I told her that too."

"What are you doin' here anyway?" Joshua was staring at Tim, a long cool, thoughtful stare. The stare went on and on.

Tim shrugged. "Come on, Vick. Thanks for breakfast. You want money for that?"

"Don't want money," growled Joshua, as Vicky preceded Tim out the door, hurrying in her embarrassment. Tim followed her, stuffing a five dollar bill back into his wallet.

Vicky was thinking that Joshua must be right. Tim was selling the stuff, or he had been. She knew exactly how much they had made in the shows. None of it had come in the shape of a five dollar bill.

"There was a lot of truth in what he said. You know that?" They were outside the Reserve, driving eastward.

"Where are we going?"

"I don't know. Do you want to do another show?"

"Yes."

"Maybe it'll be the last one, though."

Vicky didn't say anything. The last show. Her heart was empty. She felt dead already.

"We need sound for this," he said. "We'll go see some friends of mine."

His friends lived in a ramshackle farmhouse behind a country junkyard. There were some pastures with broken fences, then the prairie began. They had a marijuana garden, beginning to sprout among the wrecked cars.

"Hey, Murray! It's the Old Dope Peddler!" The man in the yard

[150]

wore a plaid shirt and a sarong, no socks in his tennis shoes, dark glasses, long hair with bushy sideburns.

"I need drums, Brian," said Tim

"Who's this?" said the man.

"This is Vicky." Tim leaned on the fender of a Chevy truck with no wheels. "Vick, this is Brian. He's a musician."

"Where have you been all this time?" Another man, older than Tim and Brian, with a slight paunch, a balding head, a nervous manner, came jogging up the driveway. "You going to take this harvest to market?"

Tim shrugged. "We need Brian."

"Well, take him then! What'll you give me in exchange?" The fat man produced a falsetto crow of laughter.

"I can guarantee to get him back here alive," said Tim. "I think."

"Hey! What is it?"

"We're going to do a show on the Reserve."

"The Reserve!" Murray whistled. "Not too healthy this summer."

"I moved out there. So I guess I can do what I want. It's my home."

Vicky was surprised to hear him say this. The Reserve was not his home. She didn't know where he was from.

"You faking up some Indian stuff, man?" asked Brian.

"Yep."

"Adorable's in it too?"

"She is."

"Okay. You're on!"

They spent a long time collecting props. They never rehearsed, so Vicky was surprised that Tim was taking so much trouble over this show. He wanted all kinds of things: a cowhide, leather shoelaces, a Halloween mask of Dracula. Then they experimented all afternoon with music. Drums, recorder, flute, mouth organ, guitar, banjo, lute, harpsichord, piano; Brian could play everything.

"Here's something," he said. "Listen to this."

He tapped on the belly of his guitar with a fingernail. The guitar responded with a nervous hollow percussion, eccentric, deadpan, almost frightening.

"For God's sake! Not again!" Murray put his hands over his ears.

"Less is more," remarked Brian. "This is the way I play the guitar all the time these days."

Murray began to scream, his hands still over his ears.

Tim was making a headdress out of twigs. He laughed. "It's great."

They had dinner with Brian and Murray. Murray did the cooking. It was a large meal, pasta and sauce, salad, many vegetable dishes, including things like dark olives in oil and eggplant, which Vicky had never seen before. She was so hungry that she tasted everything that was put in front of her and all three men watched her eat with amazement. Afterwards, while they were cleaning up—Brian washed and Murray dried—she fell asleep in the sitting room.

Tim woke her up. "Time to go," he said, taking her gently by the shoulders.

"What time is it?" she asked.

"It's 10:00. We're going to do this after dark. But I need time to paint you first."

"Don't we need to advertise? They'll think you've gone. We weren't there all day."

"They'll see the fire."

"What is it going to be? You haven't told me."

"Something they'll think is real for a change."

TIM SPENT NEARLY TWO HOURS PAINTING HER. HE WRAPPED her up in the cowhide and then tied it on with leather shoelaces. Then he made her take off her jeans and he painted her legs and feet rusty red, with ochre. He painted her face like an antelope. Then he combed her hair down over her shoulders and put a headdress of twigs on her head.

"What am I going to do?" Vicky was trying to see herself in the reflection from the window of the van. But the windows were little and high; all she could see was a small, anxious-looking deer face.

"Be a deer. Just do your thing, Vick. You've been a deer before."

"What are you going to be?"

"I'm going to be a monster." He thought for a moment. "Don't be frightened, okay? I'm trying to frighten them, not you."

"Okay." She looked at him timidly. He had not painted himself at all. "Are we going to disappear?"

He laughed. "We may have to."

Murray had lit a fire in the field on the other side of the church. Brian was playing his guitar in the conventional way, and there was already a small crowd. Murray was driving them all back to one side of the fire when Vicky stepped out of the van. It was after midnight and quite dark.

She walked behind the church and through the graveyard, over to the fire, imagining how an antelope would walk, with small steady clops of her deer feet.

Brian started to tap his guitar and the crowd fell silent, watching Vicky moseying, dancing a little, her head swaying with the head-dress of twigs that was her antlers. She had never got into the part quite this well before. When he had painted her as a deer for their magic shows, it was just for decoration.

The crowd began to get bigger and Murray yelled at them to keep back. Vicky was dancing with the graveyard beside and behind her. The tapping of the guitar went on and on, and she danced, wondering whether this was all, surprised that she was holding their attention.

Suddenly the crowd made a noise of fear, the tapping stopped altogether, and Vicky turned around in shock, because a man had jumped out of the graveyard at her back. He was horrible, white-faced and naked except for his war paint, which was slathered in layers of red and yellow and turquoise on his body.

She had turned around to face him and he bore down upon her. Vicky backed away, her hands out to stop him, her mouth open to scream, terrified. His head was enormous, the mask topped by a huge headdress of branches, bigger than her own. And the mask, she saw, was the Dracula mask.

She knew he wanted her to continue to show terror. Perhaps he had not risked telling her what he was going to do beforehand because she might not have been able to act her fear. Now that she knew what was wanted, Vicky felt quite capable of it. She was not a bit afraid. But another part of her was at the same time going through the motions of stark terror. She backed away from him, feigned a stumble, then turned, screaming silently. The crowd surged backwards, trying to get away too.

When Tim seized her, she turned again in his arms, helping him to hoist her over his shoulder. A woman in the crowd screamed, a real, full-throated scream. Tim stood for a moment and Vicky hung limply down over his back, her hair streaming. She knew he was giving the crowd the full benefit of his pallid mask, his shocking nakedness. Then he turned and ran for the graveyard. As soon as they got behind the angel monument, he set Vicky down, panting, and took her hand.

"You know it's me?" he said.

"Yes."

"We've got to get out of here. Come on."

They ran for the van on the other side of the church.

"Get it all off, Vick." He was dressing fast, covering up the body paint. He gave her a bottle of baby oil and a towel.

A moment later, Vicky heard the sound of police sirens. The police had been hanging around the Reserve all through the spring, very quick to respond to any summons, real or imaginary. People thought they used the sirens as an excuse to get on the Reserve in the first place, then as intimidation when they were there.

Tim was looking quite normal now. He demolished his head-dress and hers by jumping on them and breaking up the twigs in his fingers. He put the Dracula mask in the garbage, torn in small pieces.

"Put the cowhide on the bed," he told Vicky. "Then come outside."

She continued to wipe off her face paint as he went out the door.

Outside she could hear Brian expostulating: "It was just a fire, man! We didn't know there was something illegal about making a fire."

When Vicky emerged from the van, there was a crowd standing all around, pressing up against its sides. The fire was out, but in the light streaming from the headlights of the police car, Tim stood talking to two big cops, both of them with their backs to her.

[154]

"We got a call."

"Well, I don't know what this is all about."

The crowd looked at the cops sullenly. Then somebody saw Vicky at the top of the steps and gave a slight cry, a mixture of fear and relief.

"Anyone here want to tell us what this is all about?" The cops were trying to discern who had made the noise.

But the people were beginning to go away. They faded into the darkness now and soon only the police, Tim and Brian were left. Vicky sat down on the steps of the van. Brian sat down too and began to play his guitar.

The cops left. There was nothing for them to do. The fire was out already, the people were gone.

"Shit, man, that was a bit much," said Murray, emerging quietly out of the darkness. "Maybe you could have told us what you were getting us into. Like, you know, just a hint?"

"I'll take you home," said Tim. "Come on, Vicky, I'll take you home too."

They all got into the front seat of the van. Murray sat on Brian's lap and Vicky was pressed tightly against Tim's side. Brian was humming mournfully and it shocked Vicky slightly to see that he had his arms around Murray's waist.

Tim stopped in front of Vicky's house and got out, then helped her out on his side. "Don't come looking for me tonight," he said. "I won't be here."

"Where are you going to be?"

"Oh, they'll probably put me up." He jerked his head at the two men in the van.

"Are you ever coming back?"

"I don't think I can resist. I'm not sure how that went. Not exactly the way I expected."

"You scared them."

"I didn't scare you?"

"No."

"That's good." He laughed. "You really got into that deer part, Vick. I didn't want to interrupt you. You were holding them all by yourself."

[155]

She knew that this was true. Whatever the significance of the abduction he had staged, for her the real meaning of the evening had been in her antelope dance. She was still amazed that she had been able to do that.

He had walked her up to the kitchen door, holding her arm, so that they were still pressed together, a secret source of joy. Now he let go of her abruptly and turned away. "Bye, Vick."

Vicky wanted to run after him. But she understood that he had not really noticed how she felt about him, or at least, was not taking it seriously.

❡ THINGS AT HOME WERE GOING FROM BAD TO WORSE. Dominique had got a compensation cheque and he used it to buy whiskey. There were parties at home now, not just the sullen sad figures of her mother and brother, drunk or arguing drunkenly. Now there was gaiety, card playing, dancing, but then later, puking, mindless sex going on in every room, then threats, screaming, punching, kicking, the fear of knives and guns. And there was never any food.

She could no longer afford to wait for Tim to come for her at home. She went down to the Band office and waited there. She sat on the steps. Then later, she got a little job, helping the secretary; she couldn't type as well as Vicky, who had done a general Grade 11 business course.

While she was working there, she heard a few things about Tim. She heard that the Band Council had invited him to a meeting. Some children told her he was a medicine man. But no one seemed to know exactly who he was.

Tim had said he was at home on the Reserve, but Vicky did not see how this was possible. He was considerably older than her, but she still would have known what family he came from, who his sisters were, his parents. He came out of nowhere as far as she was concerned.

Vicky was also watching the space beside the church. But when he came, he didn't park there again. He was going to the Band meeting. There were people from the government at this one, big shots from Ottawa too. And the Lovers of the Ochre River were present, the environmental activists who were the main opposition to the dam now, represented by oddly-dressed people with long hair, long skirts, pants belted with ties. But all of these whitemen had come to the meeting to screw the Reserve; she had heard this, as well.

She saw Tim going in, talking to a big whiteman. She was waiting for him when he came out, still with the same whiteman. Vicky went up to him anyway.

"Vick!" he said. He looked down at her with a smile.

The whiteman had paused and was looking at her too. Tim had taken both her hands, and the big man smiled and shrugged, then walked away.

"What were you doing at the meeting?" Vicky demanded.

Why was he here at all; why was he with that whiteman? The whole situation overwhelmed her.

"I just went to it. I was invited, Vick."

"But you mustn't! It's our river. We shouldn't let them talk about it!"

"Yeah, I see what you mean. Boy, it's hard not to sell out here."

They were walking together. Suddenly he stopped and looked at her.

"What are you doing here? Shouldn't you be home?" he said. "It's after midnight."

Vicky didn't know what to say. He turned her around gently but inexorably and began to walk her home.

"I'll tell you why they invited me."

Vicky had turned her head away, mute with misery. But there was a little bird of joy, perched upon her elbow. It was how he had turned her around, by the elbow.

"The Band Council thinks I might be a healer." He laughed.

Vicky began to laugh too.

There was something a little different about him. He was cleaner; he even smelled of soap. He had shaved and the sparse hairs of his beard and moustache were gone. He had not been willing to insult the people he was with tonight, and Vicky felt strangely disappointed by that.

"Our last show made the people who saw it—you know—a little

[157]

nervous." He laughed again. They had come up the hill now and were in front of Vicky's house.

"So that's why they think I might be a medicine man. A for-real medicine man. It's a sad thing they don't even know the difference," he added.

Dominique and Eliza were partying as usual. Every light in the house was on, even, Vicky saw, with fear and annoyance, her light, the one in her room. She was old enough and fast enough to get away from the fumbling drunks that infested her home. But she didn't know how she was going to hold out much longer. That feeling, the longing to become a corpse, almost overcame her.

Tim was looking attentively at the house now.

"Dominique got some money," Vicky explained.

"Who did he get it from?"

"Workers Compensation. It was a big cheque. That's all there is, though. He wanted it," she added.

Tim made a couple of gestures like a whiteman. He stamped. He growled. He hit his palm with his fist.

"Vicky, there's a criminal case in it! The fucking Labour Board! Where were they in all this?"

Vicky didn't like him momentarily. She didn't like his carrying on like this, and swearing. It was almost as bad as how cool he became after two joints in a row. She stood stiffly to one side.

"Okay. Let's go in," he said.

"You won't talk to him?" It would be impossible in any case, she knew, but she did not want him to try.

He was looking at her in surprise. "To Dominique? No," he said. "I won't talk to him. You should know me better than that. I don't do things that way."

They went into the house. Tim sat down at the kitchen table. The kitchen was momentarily empty. Vicky went to look in the fridge, but there was nothing there but beer and pop. She got out a can of pop.

"Want some?"

He shook his head. Then he took his rabbit out of the front of his jean jacket and put her on the table. She was not a large rabbit and she had become docile from being stoned most of the time.

She crouched on the table like a little brown bun, her nose twitching, while he scratched her ears.

Vicky was laughing because it was so unexpected.

"I took her along to the meeting. Just in case I needed her."

"But you didn't?"

"Not this time. They want me to do a show in the auditorium. For the kids. The subject is supposed to be Staying in School."

"Are you going to?"

"Sure. Why not? I'm a living example of where school gets you." He looked at her lazily. "I went to university."

Who are you? she wanted to ask. Where do you come from? Do you always hang around with whitemen when you go away?

"A bunch of other people are doing presentations. Slide shows—stuff like that. And the companies are going to give out a bunch of promotional stuff about jobs, apprenticeship. I guess the Band invited me to do the Native side of the story—whatever that is."

"What are you going to do?"

Tim shrugged. "I don't know."

Dominique had stumbled into the kitchen. He looked at them blearily for a moment, sitting across a corner of the table with the rabbit between them. Then he lurched to the fridge and got out a beer, knocking several bottles over in the process.

The party in the other room was becoming louder.

Dominique went to lie down on the sofa in the kitchen and passed out, half-lying on it, the open beer in his hand. Tim was watching him.

Vicky also watched him and she felt that her eyes were slowly being covered with dust, that her mouth was full of clay.

There were several other drunken people in the kitchen now.

"Where do you sleep?" asked Tim. "Do you have a bedroom?"

She stood up, wanting him to see it. He hesitated, then picked up the rabbit and followed her.

Her room was pretty. It had curtains with frills and a matching bedspread. Dominique had got her a dressing table with a mirror. There were posters on the walls. But at the moment there was a couple lying on the bed having sex. And one of them, the one

[159]

underneath, was her mother. They were both so drunk that they were hardly able to do it. The woman had actually taken off her pants; the man had simply pulled his down to the tops of his boots.

Vicky had backed up into Tim, who was standing stock-still behind her. The couple on the bed were disturbed. They began to disengage themselves.

Tim pushed Vicky down onto the bench of her dressing table. He pressed the rabbit, wrapped up in his jean jacket, firmly into her arms. Then he grabbed the drunken man, who was staggering towards him aggressively, spun him around and pushed him out the door into the hall. Then he picked up Eliza by the arms, and with slightly more ceremony, helped her through the door too.

Eliza was screaming abuse at both of them from the hall as he closed the door and put his back against it.

"It's Ma," said Vicky. The corpse-like feeling crept into her very bones. She could be dead. Why did this matter? It would not matter if she were dead.

The abuse in the hall was getting louder. There was no lock on the door.

"Maybe I should go?" He looked at her inquiringly.

Vicky started to cry. He was going to go.

"I'll go out the window, I think. They're getting up a posse."

"Could I be your assistant?" she asked. "In the show?"

"What show?" said Tim. He was examining the window. It would be easy: the screen popped out and it was only a short drop to the ground.

"The one you were telling me about. On Staying in School?"

He was almost out the window, an arm and a leg over the sill. "Staying in School? Oh, yeah. Sure. You could be." He was gone.

A moment later she heard him saying, "Take care of my rabbit, okay, Vick?" But when she looked out the window he was no longer there.

A whole lot of drunks were in her room now and Vicky began screaming at them to get out.

❡ A WEEK WENT BY, THEN ANOTHER ONE, AND VICKY WAS LIVING in hell. The only thing that comforted her was the rabbit. Tim had told her to take care of the rabbit, which meant he was probably coming back. She went down to the Band hall every day and hung around just to find out when the Staying in School show was to be.

The afternoon of the day it was to happen, she came home and found Eliza alone in the kitchen. There was no sign of Dominique and no party.

Eliza had been sobering up lately, trying to pull things back together. Dominique had taken his money elsewhere for a time. She was making a pizza from a mix when Vicky came in.

"Do the dishes," she said gruffly.

Vicky went to the sink. She felt as if she were trying to swim through sand these days. She just went through the motions of living. Eliza looked at the slow movements of her hands in the dishpan and grunted, then added dish soap.

"Rinse them good," she said. "I don't like soap in the coffee."

The pizza was beginning to smell good and Vicky felt hungry. Someone knocked on the kitchen door.

"Hi," said Tim.

"You, eh?" Eliza seemed to know him. Vicky didn't think she remembered the incident where she had been having sex with a man in Vicky's bed.

Tim was inside, past Eliza, and Vicky had turned around to look at him, her hands covered in soap bubbles. He was looking beautiful, as though he had been eating, showering, living in a house; he was shaved, his hair smoothly braided.

"Hey, Vick, have you still got my rabbit?"

"That bunny's been shitting all over her room," remarked Eliza. She looked into the oven.

Vicky felt like crying with relief. But she also felt angry with him. She could have gone over and hit him in the face. There was a change in her, however; an enormous restless energy had replaced that dead feeling.

What was actually going on was rather normal. Tim was eating a slice of pizza Eliza carved for him. Vicky was eating one herself, fresh and hot. While all the time she wanted to yell at him and pound on his chest with her fists: Why did you leave me? Where did you go for so long?

"I'm doing a show tonight," he was explaining.

"I heard about that."

"It's about staying in school, Ma," said Vicky.

Eliza looked at her sharply. "You been going, haven't you?"

"Yes, Ma," she lied. School was over now anyway, although her mother wouldn't know that either.

Eliza cut her another piece of pizza. She knew how hungry Vicky usually was when she came home from school.

"I want Vicky to be in my show."

"You do?"

The Reserve did not think Tim's show was going to be about Staying in School at all. They remembered or had heard about his last show. They were hoping, praying really, that it would be something like that, something magical, something to drive the government away from their River.

Vicky knew it would be something like that.

Tim also had another piece of pizza. He never ate like this; dope took the place of food for him usually.

"Come on, Vick."

"Take that bunny too, okay?"

As they were going down the hill he said, "Let's set her free."

"Will she be able to make it?"

Vicky was worried about Tim's doped-up rabbit. Could she manage to find some others, hop and nibble over the hills like a wild animal?

They looked up at the hills together. There had been a tiny bit of rain lately. The thin grass had begun to grow again and the land was covered with a skim of verdant green. The sky above, too, was green in the sunset, with one brilliant star just beginning to glimmer, low over the mountains.

"It's Venus," he remarked. "A planet."

It was the star of their people, but he could hardly be expected to know that. According to whitemen, Venus was the goddess of love, Vicky recalled. An irrelevant fact she had learned at school, out of someone else's world.

Tim set his jacket on the ground and let the rabbit hop out of it. To Vicky's surprise, she kept on going up the hill, making for freedom. It was a long hop for a small animal. Perhaps she would be dead by nightfall in the jaws of a coyote or the claws of a hawk. They watched until she disappeared, blending into the buff-coloured thatch on the hills.

"What are we going to do tonight?" asked Vicky.

"I've got Brian and Murray for this one too. It's a bit more complicated, doing it in an auditorium. Brian's doing the sound and I've got Murray on the lights."

"Will it be the same?"

He shook his head.

She wondered whether he knew yet what they would do.

"You'll just walk across the stage, okay?"

She was sure this was not all. As with the night she had played the antelope, she would have to wait until she was doing it to find out what it was he wanted. But she was alive again, after having been dead for two weeks.

They made her walk over and over again across the stage. Sometimes they just made her walk. Sometimes Tim told her she was a deer, a rabbit.

Vicky was getting tired. He still had not explained what it was all about. He was going to do something dull for once; or he did not know what he was going to do.

He must have gained ten pounds, she thought, although he was still thin. Where had he been? Why didn't he remember that he had left her in hell?

The evening's events, once they began, were unbelievably boring to Vicky. The presentation of the environmental group, Lovers of the Ochre, was given by a pale young whiteman—one of those with a tie holding up his pants in place of a belt—who talked for hours. There was not much of a slide show. The same big whiteman in the three piece suit, the ten gallon hat, who had been walking out of the last meeting with Tim, talked about the court case of the Reserve. The companies who were building the dam did an hour of propaganda on jobs.

At last they pulled the curtains on the stage. It was time for Tim's thing. Everyone else had left, by van, bus, Chevrolet and Jaguar. All the whitemen had had their say. Only the Band was still there.

[163]

It was dark now in the auditorium, dark and almost silent, except for the cries of the babies and young children. The restless eccentric flick of Brian's fingernail on the guitar brought a collective indrawn breath from the audience. They had not forgotten Tim's previous performance.

Vicky was standing in the wings. But she thought he really would not be able to pull this off. The audience wanted the antelope dance again; they wanted to feel terror. Vicky Boucher, in jeans and a T-shirt, would not be able to provide them with that.

Tim now appeared beside her. He was laughing, and although she could not smell smoke on him, it was the type of laughter produced by dope.

He began undressing her. "Take your time getting across, and wait for me on the other side," he said.

"What is it supposed to be?" she demanded. She was too shocked to stop him.

"This is about you, Vick. You, without clothes on." His hands were quite impersonal, unhooking her bra, drawing down her pants. He gave her a slight push when he was done.

"You know what to do," he said. "Just walk across."

She knew what to do. She walked out onto the stage, a corpse. But she took her time.

Again, she felt the long indrawn breath of the Reserve. She was completely unprotected from them, and the spotlight played hotly upon her naked body. But none of this mattered, as she was already dead.

There was a sound now, like the roar of the sea. It was the audience, starting from the back, beginning to catcall and scream. She heard the wild laughter of the children. She threw back her hair and stepped forward. They were jeering at her; someone might throw something. And the air was heavy with—what was it? Lust. Lust and fear. By the time she had reached the other side, she knew she was not dead. She was terrified.

How they hated her. How she hated herself. How they hated themselves.

She had gotten off the stage and Tim was there suddenly,

hurriedly dressing her, holding things out in order so she could pull them on.

"You were really great, Vick," he whispered. "Now, run!" He took her hand. They ran.

They ran out the fire door of the backstage and up the hill—but up the hill like a rabbit, not taking the road.

He put her into the house by her window, giving her a lift up onto the sill on his shoulder.

"Get into bed. Be asleep. Wear something, okay?"

Vicky got into bed fully dressed, even wearing her canvas shoes. She seemed actually to fall asleep briefly, but there were sirens in her sleep.

She heard Eliza saying, "I don't know. I don't know where she is. I'll look in her room."

The door opened. Vicky lay there with her eyes closed, breathing evenly. Eliza shut the door.

"Yeah. She's there."

The voices went further away. She heard Eliza saying:

"Well, I don't know when she came in. She's asleep."

Vicky remained where she was.

The door opened again and Dominique came in. She could smell the stale whiskey scent of his breath. He was drunk; she could tell that from the way he was walking. He came to the side of the bed and stood looking down at her. Vicky stirred and rolled to one side, wrinkling her nose, hunching under the blanket. Dominique stood there for a few seconds longer, then went out again, shutting the door quietly behind him.

Vicky waited awhile longer, but it seemed that the fuss was over. It was exactly like the last time; part of the illusion came from the appearance of normalcy afterwards. Both times Tim had made her into the victim of a terrible indecency and then transformed her back into an ordinary Native girl, leaving no one any cause for complaint.

No one except her had any cause for complaint. For she felt that the last time had been very different. Then they had both been dancers, both of them acting, she as the innocent antelope girl, he as the fearsome white demon who came to rape her. But it had been he who came, she had known he was there all the time, and she was safe.

This time though, he had exposed her to her own people and they had been her attackers. She still felt the little propelling push he had given her in the small of her back, sending her out onto the stage. He didn't care how she felt about it. He didn't care how she felt, who she was, or even whether she continued to exist now.

Vicky got up quietly and went out the window.

She was not sure she would be able to find him. He would not be on the Reserve. But she would not be able to go on living here now and there was nowhere for her to go but to him, if only just to tell him, to try to hurt him—as badly as she had been hurt.

She knew how to get to Brian and Murray's place. It took her the rest of the night, because she did not dare hitchhike. She walked in the ditch when the cars slowed down as they passed, ready to flee into the grain fields.

His van was not in the yard when she got there. She sat down on the doorstep and fell asleep.

"Hey, Murray," said Brian. "Look who's here!"

"Adorable!" said Murray, in surprise.

They hauled her inside and made her eat breakfast. Neither of them bothered to ask any questions. They both had been there too, after all.

She heard them talking together in the kitchen as they did the dishes. She was lying on the sofa in the living room with a blanket over her, pretending to sleep.

"Where d'you think he went?"

"Who knows?"

"Well, what are we going to do about Adorable?"

"Let her decide. Maybe she'll go home."

"Who the fuck does he think he is anyway?"

"That was a frightening scene there the other night. I didn't like it much."

"I guess Adorable didn't like it either."

Vicky slept through the afternoon. In the evening she got Murray to drive her back to Joshua's on the edge of the Reserve.

She could stay there and borrow some money. She did not feel like asking Brian and Murray for money. They were kind, but they were not her own people.

Joshua's wife gave her something to eat. She did not ask any questions. Even if she had not actually been present in the auditorium, she would have heard about it. When Joshua came in from the gas pumps he gave Vicky a long look of disapproval.

"I need money," she said.

"Where you going, my girl?"

She looked at him blankly. Joshua would help her, she knew that. He sat down, sighing, in a chair by the table. He was a big fat man and his feet hurt him. Like his wife, he had probably not been present at her performance. The Reserve was not accepting of Joshua because of his gas station, his white blood; and he didn't often go inside.

"Don't go," he said.

Vicky sat stolidly on the kitchen sofa, the sandwich in her hand.

"It isn't so good at home, I know. But at least you got people."

Vicky put the sandwich down on the plate on the sofa. She was not hungry, but she had eaten half of it out of politeness.

"That guy is here," said Joshua. He spoke reluctantly, clearing his throat.

Vicky felt herself become absolutely frozen—even her heart had stopped.

"Where?" she said, after a moment.

"He came asking about you this morning. Thought you might have been here for breakfast. I guess you wasn't home."

"Where is he?" she repeated.

"I let him camp in the old gravel pit over the hill there," said Joshua. She saw the sadness in his eyes, heard the heaviness with which he spoke. He didn't want to tell her where Tim was. He was only telling her to prevent her running away.

"I guess he's still there now."

Vicky got up. Joshua was giving her another long look. But he knew all the various evils that had befallen Vicky.

She went over the hill and saw the van parked in the quarry. There was no one in sight. She ran down the hill and stood for a moment at the bottom of the steps. Then she opened the door and went in.

Tim was lying on his bed, smoking. A thick fog of marijuana smoke went swirling out the door behind Vicky on the fresh evening breeze.

"Hi, Vick," he said in surprise. He got up on his elbow. "Where've you been? I've been looking for you."

Vicky advanced a little way into the van, looking down at him, her sense of the apocalyptic driving her forward. Since yesterday, she had run away from home; she had slept on the sofa of strange whitemen and tried to borrow a stake from Joshua. She was still more terrified of the Reserve than the outside world, in spite of the fact that it was her home. And in the meantime, Tim had just assumed she was there the way she always was.

"That was quite a bad scene the other night after you left." He laughed. "Brian and Murray thought they were going to get killed."

Vicky was looking at him in shock. He didn't think anything awful had happened to her at all.

"You were great, Vick. I don't know where you get it," he added.

"They were all yelling at me," she said slowly.

"Yeah. It was symbolic rape, that was what it was. I didn't really know what I was trying to get until I got it."

Vicky covered her trembling mouth with her hands. He was right. It had been a rape. Only she had been its victim. It was not as symbolic as he thought.

"I still can't quite explain what happened there." He sat up straight and swung his bare feet to the floor. "It was an experiment, really. That antelope thing first—but it was too much of an act, too laden with metaphorical shit. So then I thought I'd show them something they have that's good. That's pure. Show them how they hate it, I guess."

Vicky was crying now, the tears running slowly down her cheeks, over her down-turned lips.

The whole world was infected with filth. The Reserve, chanting and yelling at the sight of her naked body. Vicky thought of it with disgust, with fear. He thought of it in those terms too, but it seemed to make some point to him that was obscure to her. But then, it had only been an experiment to him. Interesting.

"Pure?" she asked.

Tim was looking at her now in surprise. She was crying openly.

"Pure," he repeated.

The air came in fresh out of the gathering darkness, through the open door. Venus was out there. Vicky saw it a little above the horizon, like a jewel in the sunset light. She looked out at it, turning away from Tim, rocking her body back and forth as the tears ran down her face.

Tim stood up and went past her. He threw open both doors and the last of the smoke in the van rose in a cloud and went out over their heads, dissipating in the cool air. Joshua Joe's horses grazed on the edge of the horizon under the green sky and the star the whitemen had named for the goddess of love.

Vicky wiped her eyes with her fingers, sniffing a little.

"Look," he said, turning around. "You know where it's at, Vicky. You aren't a virgin or anything. You live here. You must've had a few guys."

"My brother Dominique would kill you for saying that."

Vicky remembered, ashamed, how Dominique had been when Tim had seen him last, how he had seen Eliza. But it was all she could think of to say, to make him understand.

There was a long silence. They both stared, unseeing now, out into the green light, fading now to purple, to velvety blackness.

"Well, I guess that was what made you so effective," he said at last. "I just never thought of—that angle."

She had been dead. If she had not been dead she would never have started out across the stage. Then she had been terrified. And in retrospect, she was still terrified—by how they had yelled at her and stamped; her own people.

"But you were great, Vick. You were beautiful. You are beautiful," he added, almost in surprise. "It doesn't affect what you are, in yourself—whatever they thought. Don't you understand?"

He was standing right beside her, and he might have put his arm around her, the way he sometimes did, but she had the insight that he was afraid to touch her now. He was no longer indifferent to her beauty, her purity, the way he had been before.

"It's a good thing, a fine thing. The naked body—of—of a young girl." He stumbled slightly on these words.

Vicky turned her head to look at him curiously. He was very beautiful to her, even though he was so much older, a full-grown man. But he still had the slimness and quickness of a young person. And his face too, was beautiful, his long nose and dark eyes, his thin, clear-cut lips.

Which continued to move as he went on speaking fluently; something about how pornography worked. But there was an undercurrent of fear in his voice that had not been there before. He was scared. He thought he had injured her. He had finally noticed that she was a real person.

"Their reaction really had nothing to do with you. It came from inside them. Their lust, their fear. The hundred and one ways they are screwing themselves and being screwed. Your body just showed that to them. But your body is lovely. It's a beautiful thing, an adorable body." He had to turn his head away to say this. Vicky did not reply.

"Jesus, Vick. Say something. I'll never forgive myself if I really hurt you."

Vicky now realized that she had not been hurt. She had not been harmed at all. Not by his show, whatever it had meant. Not by anything he had done.

He was, in fact, her salvation, her only hope, just as she was his. This fleeting moment he was filling up with talk was the only time she had to make him see it.

"I ran away last night," she said. "I went to Brian and Murray's. Murray brought me back to Joshua's this afternoon. I tried to borrow some money from Joshua. That's when he told me you were here."

"You were running away from home?"

"I was trying to find you," she said. "I didn't think you'd dare to come back here."

"You were running away—to me?"

She nodded.

[170]

"Vick—You should have a young guy to go to," he said. "Some-one you're in love with."

Vicky looked at him stubbornly. He couldn't escape her now. She was inexorable.

He wanted to kiss her. She saw it in his face, in the way he was standing, a little irresolute, half turned her way. But he was still trapped by the belief that he had harmed her.

He did kiss her now, briefly, holding her by the shoulders, kissing her lips lightly. "You're scaring the shit out of me, Vicky," he said. "I've just been messing around, playing games here."

The cool pressure of his skin against hers, his closed lips on her closed lips, was almost unbearably delicious. Vicky pushed against the hands holding her shoulders, holding her away from him.

"Stop that, okay?" he said.

Vicky started to cry again. He sighed and drew her in against him.

She leaned on him, crying, and he embraced her, resting his cheek against her temple.

"What if you fell in love with me? We wouldn't just be playing with each other any more."

"I haven't been playing with you."

"No," said Tim. "I guess you haven't. Maybe you haven't had much of a chance to play with anybody yet," he went on.

He was putting up her purity as an obstacle now. When really, he was afraid of it. She couldn't let him get away with this. It seemed almost as though he was trying to trick her.

But Vicky understood quite fully how another one of his tricks had worked. She had noticed something during the antelope dance. It was one of the things that had made him so appalling to the audience; it was not just his nudity, but his arousal that had shocked them so.

She jumped back suddenly and stamped her foot. "You're frightened. You really think I'm dirty—like all those people in the audience! You're afraid of me!"

She ran down the steps, then turned, screaming at him: "Your lust! Your fear! The hundred and one ways you are screwing yourself and being screwed! That's all I am to you too!"

She turned and flung herself up the steep side of the gravel pit, running blindly, running uphill so he could catch her easily.

She knew he was coming behind her even before she heard him.

He caught up with her, grabbing her shoulder and turning her around so that when they fell, they fell in each other's arms and lay panting together on the hard gravelly ground. Without hesitation he kissed her now and she lay half underneath him, pinned against the ground, sobbing triumphantly. As they struggled together, under the starry sky, to undo her virginity.

At last they lay still. She thought he might even be asleep, he was so quiet and heavy on her, but after a moment he rolled away and began, more clumsily than usual, trying to dress her. It was getting cold.

He was buttoning up her blouse. Vicky had already gingerly pulled on her jeans.

He was getting dressed himself now. A moment later he stood up and gave her his hand to help her to her feet. Timidly, she put up her lips to be kissed and he took her in his arms.

"I hurt you, didn't I?"

"No." She was lying.

"Do you want to go home now?"

"No!" Her breath caught in her throat. "I want to stay with you!"

"Okay." He laughed.

"Not just for tonight."

"Yeah. I thought you were going to say that." He put his arm around her and they went down the hill, the joy and triumph in Vicky's heart rising almost to choke her, causing her to cry again, but silently, happily.

In the van, he made his bed and put her into it, for she was dropping with exhaustion. It had been a long frightening day, and only now, for the first time in almost twenty-four hours, did she feel completely safe. She was aware of him sitting opposite her in a chair, watching her go to sleep and she knew that she had finally succeeded in getting his full attention.

She slept profoundly all night, unafraid at last.

❡ WHEN SHE WOKE UP IT WAS DAYLIGHT ALREADY, ALTHOUGH
still very early. A bird was singing outside, a complex spring song
about mating and making nests. She sat up. Tim was asleep on the
bench on the other side of the van behind the table.

She climbed cautiously out of the bed, not wanting to wake him.
She still felt stiff and sore from their lovemaking. But she thought
of it with joy as she went outside. She had managed to accomplish
this all by herself, shy and prudish Vicky, Dominique Boucher's
overprotected little sister.

Tim woke up as she came in again. He groaned, then jackknifed
himself up from behind the confining table. Then as Vicky went
through the cupboard looking for food, he stood up, unselfconsciously shedding his clothes, and threw himself down on the bed
with a sigh of pleasure, lying across it face downwards.

As she began pumping up the Coleman stove, he turned over on
his back.

"Would you like tea?" she asked.

"Sure."

There was not much to eat. Half a jar of jam. Stale bread. Dry
cereal. No milk.

He was smoking a joint reflectively, lying in bed with an arm
behind his head.

When she took him a mug of tea he grasped her hand and
pulled her down to sit beside him on the bed. He was naked, slim
and brown and strong-looking, the thin blanket only covering him
from the waist down.

She looked at him over the rim of her mug. She was shy, but she
was still feeling very pleased with herself. She had captured him.

"This is sort of unbelievable," he said. "I think I want to paint
you."

"With no clothes on?" Vicky remembered every word of their
conversation about this the first day he had drawn her.

He nodded, smiling.

In her life up until now, nakedness had been something that
hardly occurred. There was her own nakedness in the shower
or sometimes in the privacy of her own room at night—but she

[173]

had never seen other people completely naked even when she had come across them having sex together. But she saw now that nakedness—his own and that of other people, of her—was an important part of how he saw the world, and she had already begun getting used to this.

She was still looking at him with shy pleasure as he reached forward to take the cup out of her hand. He knelt in front of her on the bed to unbutton her blouse and undo her bra, then to slide off her pants. He seemed not to be in any kind of hurry.

Vicky was still growing, and she sometimes felt that she was all arms and legs. Her belly, deprived of regular meals lately, declined into a cave over her navel and her breasts were still small and hard. Tim merely seemed to want to feel her all over as though he were blind. Vicky lay in his arms and let him touch her and run his fingers smoothly across the planes and hollows of her skin.

Finally, having achieved no particular object that she could see, besides her happiness, he got up and went outside, still naked. After a moment's thought, she put on some of her clothes and began to tidy up the van, which was a mess, and also exceedingly, unremittingly filthy, from the grey bedclothes to the blackened floor.

When he came in he smiled at her efforts with the broom and, pulling on his jeans, sat down to drink some more tea.

"So you're going to come with me?" he asked.

She nodded, looking at him, willing him to accept this answer as final.

"Where are we going?" she asked after a moment.

"I was going to go into Steamboat to see if I could set up a sideshow at the rodeo," he said.

"I'm going to be in it too."

"Do you want to? After that thing we did here?" he asked.

Vicky realized what he meant. It seemed so far away, so long gone to her now. "That thing we did here"—when had that happened?

"I want to."

"Really? Look, Vick, none of this stuff is art. It's all more or less bullshit."

"What is art?" she asked.

He was looking out the open back door of the van. "I'm not sure." He spoke vaguely. "I didn't meet any art for a long time."

Vicky laughed.

"Yeah." He laughed too. "Now I've got some, I don't know what to do with it."

"You've got some?"

"I mean you," he said. "I guess what I'm going to do is paint you. I mean paint on you. Then if it's no good, you can just wash it off."

"Paint on me? You mean, like when I was an antelope?"

"It was good, wasn't it?"

Vicky nodded. What she remembered was not the paint, but the clicking of her little hoofs, the weight of the twigs on her brow.

Tim was looking at her intently.

"Paint," he said. "Baby oil, sponges, maybe brushes, charcoal—we need to make a lot out of this thing we do in Steamboat. What could we do that would make a lot of money?"

6

1976 · The Human Paintbrush

THE HUMAN PAINTBRUSH SHOW AT THE RODEO WAS A GREAT
success; they were making money. They even had trouble with the
police. According to Tim, this was the final compliment.

Vicky was wearing sky blue paint the day of the police raid. They
had quite a large crowd standing around the enclosure. Tim was
urging people not to throw pop cans and peanut shells down onto
the canvas, actually the back of a large sheet of linoleum. Vicky
slithered around the edges, making a wave design she had lately
invented.

She saw a big whiteman in a ten gallon hat watching her from
the front corner. The reason he caught her attention at first was
that he wasn't making any noise; he was merely looking at her.
When she glanced at him he smiled. It was not a salacious smile;
he merely seemed amused.

Then the cops arrived. One of them began shoving away the
people while the other hopped over the barricade and grabbed
her arm. Tim was arguing with the one who was kicking out the
customers, but when he saw the other cop holding Vicky with her
arm twisted behind her he came right over.

"Hey!"

"She your daughter?"

"Nope. She's his lawfully wedded wife," the other one called over.

"Stop twisting her arm."

"Don't get excited, Jack. We're just going to take her and book
her, but you could find yourself in a lot more trouble if—"

"I said, stop twisting her—!"

The big whiteman seemed to have negotiated something with

[177]

the other cop, for he now came over to the one who was holding Vicky.

"Dad! What the fuck are you doing here?" said Tim, catching sight of him.

The cop who was holding Vicky loosened his grip a little, although he continued to grasp her by the upper arm. The whiteman looked as if he meant business, even though he was still smiling.

"I heard about your show down at the courthouse this morning, Tim. I'm Tim Steen," he remarked evenly to the cop who was holding Vicky. "I'm his father—and incidentally, I'm a lawyer."

The cop let go of her upper arm altogether and Vicky rubbed it. She was going to get a bruise.

"Look here, sir," said the number one cop. "She's in the nude; that's in clear violation of the Act. Looks to me as though she's underage, got no license such as the Act specifies, and continued the performance after a warning—"

The big whiteman continued to smile at Vicky and at the policeman who was now standing a few feet away from her, getting the blue paint off his hand with a crumpled Kleenex.

Tim folded his arms. His hair was ruffled; he didn't look cool.

"Okay. We were going to book her. But we'll call this the last warning."

"I would regard that as a favour." This was a very cool person.

"Now wait a minute," said Tim. "I'm not running a striptease joint. This is art, even if you think that's a nickname."

"Better talk to your kid here, sir," said cop number one. "Tell him the facts of life."

"Yes, and also the way you did your thing here, I think that should get an airing! She's going to get a bruise on her arm. Do you get off on that or something?"

"Look, do you really want to go for a ride?" said the cop shrugging. "Let's get out of here," he said to the other one.

"See you again, then!" said Tim.

"You know, he could get into real trouble if that girl is jailbait."

The two police started back across the rodeo to their patrol car, leather holsters clacking. The big whiteman looked at Tim, still smiling. Tim glared at him. Then, after a moment, he smiled back. "Hope you liked the show, Dad."

"Sure." He laughed.

Vicky was pulling on the paint-stained shirt she used as a dressing gown.

"This is Vicky. Vicky Boucher."

"A Boucher from the Reserve?"

Tim shrugged. "Vick's a girl, Dad."

"A lovely girl," he agreed. "Nice to meet you, Vicky."

Vicky went to stand beside Tim and he put his arm around her. She was shivering. "Were you scared?" he murmured.

She nodded. Tim's dad was looking at his watch.

"I've got to go," he said. "I'm supposed to be in court this morning. Valerie's giving her garden party the day after tomorrow. How about bringing Vicky?"

Tim seemed to hesitate and the big man continued smoothly:

"We'd like to see a bit more of you, you know that? Valerie's always telling me to do something about it. But I've had one hell of a schedule this summer because of the dam."

"Me too," said Tim. His father looked at him sharply, then laughed.

"I heard," he said. "I heard about that show you did on the Reserve. I guess we're on the same side of this—are we?"

"Oh yeah," said Tim. "We are."

◁ TIM WAS PAINTING VICKY WITH WHITE PAINT. HE USED A palette knife or his fingers, sometimes the chewed end of a twig. This time he was using a fine brush. She had to stand up for hours.

"Why is your dad a whiteman?" Vicky was puzzled.

"He's not really my dad. He adopted me when I was a baby."

"So you were brought up a whiteman?"

"He's been working for the Band as long as I can remember. I always knew I was, you know, from here."

"What about your mother?"

"Dad got a divorce the same year he adopted me. He had a lot of girlfriends, but the last few years he's been hanging out with Valerie. Looks pretty permanent—with Valerie."

"Is she a whiteman?"

"Yeah." Tim shifted Vicky into the sunlight coming through the open back doors of the van. The pattern he was painting was a kind of filigree, very intricate. It was taking him a long time to do a tiny motif over her breasts. "She went to art school—has a bunch of degrees, but she's not much of an artist. She's into fashion, really. I get along with Valerie," he added.

This explained a lot about Tim, Vicky thought. He had been brought up as a whiteman. She thought of how he had nearly lost his temper with the cops, when they were twisting her arm, how he had lost his temper over what happened to Dominique.

They had left the rodeo and gone out on the prairie for the afternoon. Tim had smoked a lot of dope. That was when he had decided to paint her for the garden party.

"I can't go to that without my clothes," said Vicky in dismay.

"Oh, it'll be okay," said Tim. "You'll be wearing something. Although I guess Dad wouldn't mind. At the rodeo he thought you were great. But I'm doing this for Valerie. You'll make her flip when I'm finished with you."

In the end he took Vicky's curtains down from the window of the van—they were white sheers she had got at a flea market in town—and wound them tightly around her waist and legs. After he finished the painting of her arms and chest in white filigree lace, he combed her hair and wound string in it with intricate knots and lacings. Finally, he made up her face and knotted the last curtain into her hair.

"What about shoes?" Vicky was looking at her reflection in the windowpane, trying to see herself—a bride.

Tim had already knelt to draw shoes on her feet, with white painted ribbons that went up her legs under the long tight skirt. "Perfect," he said. "Valerie'll love it."

Valerie loved it.

She came streaming towards them, a tall middle-aged white-woman, overdressed, too much makeup. She shrieked, hugged Tim, then looked at Vicky, shrieked again, and hugged Tim. Tim was laughing, but Vicky could tell that he didn't like being shrieked at and hugged. She began to relax. Tim's dressing her up for Valerie was to make up for something, something he didn't like about his dad's girlfriend. Vicky was no longer afraid of Valerie now that she knew.

"Tim! Tim!" Valerie was calling, and the big whiteman came through the crowd in the garden towards them.

"Look at this, darling! Look what your gorgeous intelligent son has done!"

"I've been painting her a lot lately. Different ways. But this is for you, Valerie," said Tim.

"For me? Really? Oh, I see. Well I love it anyway. Even if it isn't art."

"The last time I saw Vicky, she was completely covered in sky blue poster paint," said Tim's dad, smiling at Vicky.

"That's the kind of stuff you can sell," agreed Tim.

"But she's gorgeous!" exclaimed Valerie. "My God, darling, don't you think she's wonderful? Wherever did you find her, Tim?"

"This is Vicky Boucher," said the big man dryly. "As a matter of fact, I know your brother, Vicky. He's the one that got hurt on the dam?"

Vicky nodded.

"Oh!" Valerie had been listening alertly. "You're from the Reserve?—But that's wonderful! Oh, darling, Tim has a wonderful girlfriend, you even know her family—!" She put out her arms and hugged Vicky for a moment, but very cleverly, doing nothing to mess up the paint.

Deftly she separated Vicky from Tim and led her through the crowded garden of her upper class Mount Royal home, introducing her to all her guests as Tim's girlfriend and showing her off with shrieks and cries of admiration. When they had finished their promenade she took Vicky to a table inside laden with bottles and gave her a glass of sour fizzy champagne and some rather surprising whiteman's food.

"We were so delighted when we heard about you, darling," Valerie was telling her. "Tim and his father get along very well except over this marijuana business. So it's wonderful he has a girlfriend, he's painting—! What wonderful news!"

Vicky was feeling quite safe with Valerie. She didn't need

[181]

to talk; Valerie didn't expect her to or want her to. And she was completely sincere in saying—over and over—that Vicky was the crowning decoration of her party.

The party itself was terrifying. Vicky had never been to a party like this before; hundreds of people, some of them dressed to the teeth; nearly all of them whitemen except some even more frightening ones who were Native. The Band Chief from the Reserve was there, dressed as he never dressed at home, in a suit.

Someone came up behind her and put his arms around her waist. It was Tim. He had been drinking whiskey; she could smell it on his breath. But he wasn't drunk. After a moment she realized that he was holding her because he thought she might be frightened of Valerie or Valerie's party. Vicky leaned back against him and Valerie gave a tiny cry of admiration.

"So wonderful! So romantic! Dressed as a bride! A virgin bride! Tim, I'm going to cry! And Vicky, darling, you are so beautiful! Such deep, dark eyes, a face like a shy woodland creature, so solemn, so still, high cheekbones, beautiful wide mouth, lovely little nose. Oh, there's someone here, a fashion editor for the paper. You must meet him! Tim, don't you think she could make her fortune? Imagine her on a magazine cover! Oh, I must introduce—!"

"Come on, Valerie, this is Vicky. She's really a lot more interesting than her dress—her face!"

Oh, I know that, but her dress makes me cry, that's all." Valerie began to laugh instead. Tim was laughing too, just a little.

"We're going to stay the night, I guess. We'll need a shower to wash Vick off."

"Oh, please do. You can have your usual room."

Tim undressed her and unknotted her hair, then washed the paint off her in a large sunken marble tub with a whirlpool in the adjoining bathroom.

"Is this really your room?" They were lying on the bed and Tim was smoking a joint, gazing at the ceiling. The party was still going on outside.

"The whole place is Valerie's. She's some kind of interior

decorator. Dad doesn't really go for this kind of thing, but he puts up with it for Valerie. We used to just live in apartments."

"I like it," said Vicky.

"Do you?" Tim rolled over on his elbow and smiled at her.

"It's like being inside a magazine."

"Yeah. The whole place has been in *Chatelaine*. Would you like to be in a magazine yourself?"

"Me?"

"Well, you heard what she said."

He didn't want her to say yes, she knew.

"Valerie knows hordes of people like that fashion editor she showed you to. And you've got the looks for photography." He inspected her critically.

When he looked at her like this Vicky felt she could faint with joy. It seemed as though she had just come to life, as though the Vicky Boucher of last year was like a shell she had discarded and left behind. And it seemed she could do all kinds of things, live in houses that were in magazines, be on the covers of other magazines.

"Yeah, but don't fall for it," said Tim. "You were made for better things."

"I was?"

"You're a work of art, Vick. God's art. That's why I'm painting you all the time. I'm trying to find out how God did it."

"I loved my dress." She was shy.

"It was good," he admitted. "I didn't really know how good it was myself till I got you here among all these Mau Maus. It said something about you—even if Valerie did like it."

"But isn't that what those fashion magazines are all about? Getting dressed up and painted?"

"Yeah—but that doesn't have anything to do with God's art— or with who you are, either, Vick. With fashion you just stand there and get decorated however some screwball decides to do it, because it's being done that way."

Vicky secretly felt that this was exactly like Tim painting her. He never bothered to try to explain what he was doing.

It was uncomfortable and she got cold and cramped and hungry. Whatever he said about God's art, that was not like being adored. And being adored was what she liked, being adored by him and by other people too.

They slept in the bed for a while, then awakened late at night. Tim was hungry. He put on some clothes and went out of the room, returning a short while later with some of the party food on a large platter. The party was still going on. She could hear it when he opened the door.

"I went to the van too and got my paints. I had a pretty fantastic idea, what I could do, when I was out there."

Vicky ate some of the strange food, which she now found delicious: pineapple wedges and grapes, strong-smelling cheese with crackers, tiny bites of meat on toothpicks.

"It's pretty wild out there." Valerie's shrieks could still occasionally be heard. "But she's not as high as she sounds."

The room was lovely and warm. She just wanted to be sure she wasn't going to get hungry, if he was going to start painting her.

Tim was smoking a joint. But he put it out decisively and began to eat as well. He had apparently had the same thought.

He began to paint her in white and blue in the same wavy designs she had made as the human paintbrush. He used his fingers for the most part, but also a sponge from the bathroom, and one of the candlesticks from the mantle piece in the room. Vicky stood in front of a huge wall mirror beside the bed. Tim had spread a sheet over the carpet.

At last he seemed to be almost finished. He was smoking the second half of his joint, looking at her, his eyes half-closed against the smoke. He didn't know what to do with her face.

There was a knock on the door.

"Who is it?" asked Tim absently.

"Dad."

The big whiteman came into the room, carrying a whiskey bottle and three glasses. He was wearing a bathrobe and his hair was wet. It looked as though he had just taken a shower.

"I wasn't sure you'd still be awake." He glanced at Vicky. "Am I interrupting your painting?"

Tim nodded his head, then shook it.

"It's okay. I think I lost it, whatever it was."

"Then please give the child something to wear."

"Oh yeah." Tim looked around vaguely, then took off his shirt and gave it to Vicky.

His father sat down on the bed. Grizzled hair on his chest poked through the vee of the dressing gown. It occurred to Vicky with mild disgust that he slept with Valerie; he might even have been doing that before he took the shower. The sounds of the party had stopped.

The big man was sniffing the air. He cocked his eyebrow at Tim. "Want some whiskey?"

"Sure. Why not?"

"What about you, Vicky?"

"Better have some," said Tim. "You've been standing up a long time."

Vicky sat down on a chair and took her glass from Tim. It was a large heavy glass with a diamond pattern in the crystal, just a little whiskey in the bottom. She held it on her knee.

"Are you old enough to drink, Vicky?"

"I'm eighteen."

"Well, maybe she's not old enough to drink, but she's old enough to screw."

"Don't get defensive."

"Okay. It was just because of what those cops said the other day, I guess."

"I thought I could save you a little trouble, coming down there. I guess I saved Vicky a little trouble too."

Tim took a swig of his drink. "Okay. Thanks," he said.

"You've got a beautiful girl here. You're painting. I'm happy for you." He sniffed the air again. "I guess you can't give that up altogether?"

"I'm not doing so much of it these days."

"I'm glad. It was the mindless lying on your back all day that kind of got to me."

"Yeah, well, lately, I've been busy."

"I heard about your show on the Reserve."

[185]

"Oh yeah?"

"What did I hear? Let's see." The big man put the tips of his fingers to his forehead. "Well, first of all it was inexpressibly obscene."

Tim smiled at Vicky. "We did it, Vick!"

"Yes. If you ever did it again, you'd certainly find yourself in a cell overnight. Booking, handcuffs, the works. Four squad cars, with dogs probably. Not like that little scene at the rodeo."

"Cops've got no jurisdiction on the Reserve."

"They do if the Chief and Council call them in."

"So it got to them too, did it?"

Tim's father laughed. "That was the point, was it?"

"All great art is obscene, Dad."

"I guess so. Still, from a lawyer's point of view, I don't know that there'd have been much I could do for you."

Tim laughed. So did Vicky.

His father looked at her in a friendly way. "How is your brother getting along?" he asked.

She looked up at him timidly, not sure what to say.

"He's a real symbol of resistance, you know."

"Yeah. Looks like Dominique stopped the dam," said Tim.

"Well, I wouldn't count on it. But in some quarters he's a hero. Is he okay?"

"He got better from being beaten up," she said. "But—he's drinking."

The man nodded.

"Well, it was a great thing he did. This Native hiring business was pulling the wool over a lot of people's eyes. If there were jobs for Natives ... then the Natives could get jobs. I guess Dominique Boucher proved to a lot of people that an Indian from this Reserve can't get a job building the Ochre River dam."

Vicky looked down at her hands curved around her untouched glass.

The big man stood up and gurgled more whiskey into his glass and Tim's.

"Dominique fits into some whiteman's story that goes like that," said Tim. Vicky could feel both of them looking at her.

[186]

"That's not the whiteman's story you read in the newspapers, my son," said his father sharply.

"Oh yeah. The newspapers. Money. Jobs. That's whiteman's language for Ochre River."

"And what is Indian's language for Ochre River? You tell me."

"Maybe they've forgotten it. Something about a River, I think." Tim lay back on the bottom of the bed lazily.

"I'm not discounting the environmental side of the issue. I've been working on this for a long time, don't forget."

"Yeah. I only started working on it this summer," said Tim. "After I met Vick."

"Well, why don't you tell me your perspective?"

Tim was silent, lying there, his glass perched upon his chest.

"I mean, what do you think is the position of the Natives?"

Tim got up and went over to Vicky. He took her hand and she stood up beside him. Then he pushed the open cuff of his shirt sleeve till it slid nearly as far as her shoulder, wiping off the paint. He was showing his father the bruise on her arm.

"Think this is just what one white cop did to one Native girl, Dad?"

His father stared at the bruise for a moment.

"Damn it," he said. He came over and looked down into Vicky's eyes. "I'm so sorry," he said.

"But what can you make of that?" he said to Tim a moment later.

"I don't know. Here's how you see it though. You see it as noise, static. There's the political process, the courts, justice. Then there's this social violence getting in the way, making a shambles out of something neat, orderly, sensible. All I'm saying is: the pain is real. It's like the River, a real thing. Maybe you've got to start with that. Start with your pain. Feel it. Understand it. The pain itself."

His father looked into his glass thoughtfully.

"But we're all hurting somehow," he said. "I don't see how feeling your pain is going to help. That's mysticism. And maybe it leads to more violence in the end."

"Maybe it does."

"I'm not getting on board then. Violence is bad no matter who's responsible. White cops or whoever. And it leads to more atrocities like that." He looked again at Vicky's bruise. Tim let the shirt sleeve slide down her arm again.

Vicky's heart was beating fast and anxiously. She was following their conversation closely. She thought she understood Tim; she agreed with him. What was killing Dominique was not as simple as the politics of jobs at the dam, after all. But Tim's father really cared about Tim, she could see that. He was afraid for him.

"The pain is really there."

"So let's do something to prevent it."

"You have to know it's there first. Otherwise whatever you do makes no sense."

"I know it's there. But what is needed is justice, not the kind of introspection that leads to worse things. Like what happened to Vicky's brother. It should never have happened. He should sue the shit out of the employer. That's the only way it's going to change."

"Yeah, but only Dominique knows who Dominique is. Besides, he's not drinking because he lost his job and some rednecks kicked the crap out of him. You should hear what Vick thinks. Why is Dominique drinking, Vick?"

"Because Emma took off," she said.

"Emma was his girlfriend. A white girl, incidentally. Not that it's that simple."

"Pain," said the big whiteman meditatively. He swirled the whiskey in his glass. "I suppose that's where art comes into it."

"Yeah," said Tim. "Art comes into it."

"You know, it's interesting to talk to you." His father finished his drink. "I guess a person can get sewed into his own perspective on something. I didn't see what you were up to till now."

"Yeah. But this is what I'm really up to," said Tim. He put his arm around Vicky and she could feel the stripes of blue and white paint smearing the inside of his shirt. It was all right; he was through with that painting.

"The dress," said his father. "Valerie thought it was brilliant." He smiled at Vicky again. "You liked it too, didn't you?" he said. "You turned the whole party inside out."

Tim laughed. "That was just art school stuff," he said. "Vick was made for the big canvas. She doesn't know it yet. She needs an artist, maybe a better one than me."

"You'd have to be a pretty generous man to let another artist have her," said his dad. "Even if he was a better one."

"What does Valerie think?" Tim sounded sarcastic.

"You want to know what Valerie thinks? She's in love with both of you. She'd give you the house, the pool, her Jaguar, anything you want. She has really got a generous heart, Tim."

"She introduced Vick to all of those friends of hers."

"Artists in their way."

"Yeah, but I don't want Vick photographed as an ad. They'd take her as a bottle of toilet cleaner if they thought there was any money in it."

"Look, do you know what Valerie really wants? She wants a whole family and unfortunately I couldn't provide one. This big house is pretty empty after a party, when all the guests and the photographers are gone."

"Well, at least we really messed up the spare room for her," said Tim. He looked around at the paints, the sponge, the candlestick, the spattered sheet on the rug.

"Just be gentle with her, okay?" The father got up to go. He picked up the whiskey bottle. "Do you want me to leave this?"

"No," said Tim. "Vick doesn't drink. See?" He gave Vicky's glass to his father who looked at it for a moment, then swirled the whiskey around and gulped it down. Then he went over to Vicky and took her hands.

"Look, if you see your brother, remind him I exist, okay? I do a lot of work for nothing. And I'd go to court for him. I'd like to take that one to court." He laughed.

Vicky looked up at him, liking him, thinking how much Tim liked him. Dominique would like him too—but he would never go to court.

"God! I wish I could paint," he said. With a certain solemnity, that derived, she thought, from the whiskey he had been drinking, he

[189]

bent down and kissed her on the forehead, then went out the door, touching Tim on the shoulder as he went past.

Tim washed her again and they went to bed.

❧ VICKY WOKE UP. THERE HAD BEEN A KNOCK ON THE DOOR.
The large clean room was shining with sunlight; sunlight on the mirrors, on the polished wood surfaces of the furniture, on the crystal vase of roses on the mantel, and on the white sheet strewn with painting things on the rug. Valerie came in with a tray.

"I brought you breakfast in bed. Oh, I want you to think this is just like a honeymoon! After the lovely wedding you made for my party!"

Tim sat up and took the tray on his knees.

"Thanks, Valerie," he said. He stretched and yawned. "Have some of this food, Vick. Vick's always hungry when she wakes up," he explained.

Valerie sat down on the foot of the bed. She was casually dressed in fawn-coloured slacks and a sweater, but already fully made up. She watched Tim buttering a roll for Vicky with luminous eyes.

"Coffee in bowls. Apricot jam. Is this supposed to be a honeymoon in Paris, Valerie?"

"What could be more wonderful! Young and in love with each other! Oh, I remember my own honeymoon! That was not with your father of course. The first one—my first husband."

"Was it in Paris?"

"No, it was Niagara Falls. We were very poor, very young and poor, but it was very, very wonderful!"

Tim began to butter a roll for himself. Vicky was enjoying the food, the milky coffee in a painted bowl and the delicious flaky texture of the roll.

It was very easy to be with these people, as they seemed to expect absolutely nothing of her but her mere existence. They did want something from Tim; his father expected something from him, he expected a lot, and Valerie was begging for his love and compassion. But it was completely unnecessary for her to talk or indeed, do anything; they seemed to love her already just because she was with Tim.

[190]

Vicky finished her coffee and her roll and put the bowl down on the tray. Then she moved a little towards Tim. He glanced at her, crinkling his brow slightly, then put his arm around her and she nestled against him. Valerie gave a small ecstatic cry.

"Oh, Tim, darling, will you please do something for me? Please, will you? Will you please dress the darling up again and let me have her photographed? Please? Just for the paper. Because it was the crowning glory of my party and you came so late, after the photographers from the paper had gone. Oh, please!"

Tim sighed.

"She wants to, don't you, darling? You were so lovely, it was breathtaking. And you loved being dressed up in that wonder-ful—!"

Vicky nodded. Valerie crowed joyously.

"I'm not sure I could do the same thing again."

"Well, that doesn't matter! The lace, you wouldn't have to do it exactly—It was the effect. You could get the effect again, I'm sure."

"Oh yeah," he said disgustedly. "But do you really want to, Vick? It's hours of standing, all just to get a picture in the Calgary paper."

"No, no, she must start a portfolio! We'll get copies, we could send them—"

Tim was looking at Vicky. She nodded again. It would be fun. Almost worth the hours of standing, for a change. He laughed. "Okay," he said.

"And you too, Tim. With her. Dressed just the way you were last night. Without the shirt perhaps. Just a dark jacket. And perhaps a tie, a bolo, a string one, we'll have to see how it looks on your bare—" She put her clasped hands up prayerfully under her chin. "Oh please, please, will you be in the picture too?"

"Jesus, Valerie!"

"Well, we'll talk about it. But you would like him to be in the picture too, wouldn't you, darling? When he took you in his arms last night I nearly swooned, it was so romantic, so wonderful!"

They spent the morning on the painting. Tim made Valerie get him some more paint; she seemed to have a lot of paint herself, but not the right kind. At first he was annoyed and impatient, but after he began working on the lace he became absorbed.

"I'm doing it entirely differently," he remarked, standing back to look. "But she'll never even notice."

"Is it better?"

"I don't know yet. It would be interesting to do a whole body painting this way. You'd have to hold still for about three days, though. I'm not sure you could take it."

Valerie brought them lunch. Tim had to feed her because the lace painting was still drying on her arms. Lunch was more bizarre food like the things at the party, only in larger pieces. Vicky was becoming accustomed to luxury. It was easy to become accustomed to it.

VALERIE WANTED TO MAKE UP VICKY'S FACE BUT TIM WOULDN'T let her. He did it himself, using some of Valerie's makeup. He was getting annoyed again because they had to wait for the photographer. But when the photographer arrived, Valerie made him dress up too.

"This isn't anything real," he said to Vicky.

She thought he was looking very handsome. Valerie's taste was very good in matters of male dress. Tim, with his spare, Plains face, his long nose; even slouching in a chair, he looked wonderful in the shirtless jacket, the bolo tie that she made him wear.

Valerie didn't want either of them to stop playing the fairy tale she had invented for them. She parted reluctantly with the photographer. "But you are going to stay for dinner? And another night at least? Oh please, please don't take off your wonderful party clothes!"

But Tim had already begun to remove Vicky's face paint.

Valerie wanted him to use the jars and bottles of pink and peach-coloured creams she brought out from her bedroom. "Water? You'll ruin her skin!"

"Come on, Valerie." He took Valerie by the shoulders and turned her around towards the door of the room. "Out you go."

"Oh! I see! But you will stay for dinner?"

Tim washed her. He was abstracted; he even seemed a little depressed. He lay smoking a joint and staring at the ceiling. Vicky turned her head to look at them reflected in the wall mirror.

[192]

The mirror was almost like the camera. They both took you in and then showed you back to yourself. With the camera, it had been strangely as if she had already known what it was registering about her. It was like making love with Tim; the camera came and got her, it took her with it and then she showed it things she didn't know she had in her, she revealed herself to it completely.

The photographer had been astounded. He was only a fashion and wedding photographer for a small city paper, but even he had known that Vicky was exceptional.

"I need canvas," said Tim. "I guess we're going to stay for dinner. I need real paint too. We haven't got the money."

"We could do another show," suggested Vicky.

"No. I don't have time right now. I'll have to get the stuff off Valerie. She'll give it to me if we stay for dinner."

"I wonder what we're going to have to eat?"

"Oh, something," he said absently. "You see, I had an idea about you, Vick. But I was wrong. It isn't just in the way you're made. It's something you do too. I could get that on canvas. In fact, I'm going to draw you the way you are right now."

She looked at him wonderingly. He was bending over her.

"Go on staring at yourself like that in the mirror." He had taken up his sketch pad and was drawing on it using his finger dipped in some black paint.

About three hours later someone banged on the door.

"Who is it?"

"Are you asleep? It's Dad."

"I'm drawing Vicky."

"Well, put some clothes on and come to dinner, okay?"

"Oh yeah. Clothes."

Vicky laughed. "We don't have any clothes, Tim."

His shirt was smeared with paint. Vicky's jeans and blouse were in the van. In the end, Vicky wore the curtain tied around her like a sarong. Tim wore jeans and the jacket Valerie had given him.

The dinner was cooked by Valerie, long and elaborate. Vicky ate everything. Everyone seemed to enjoy watching her eat. Tim liked it as well. "Vick's always hungry at night," he said.

"You should have seen the darling in front of the camera," Valerie said to Tim's father. "She knew exactly what to do. Poor Tom Steger, he'll never be the same again. He fell in love, I think."

Tim frowned. "It wasn't real," he said. "But I ought to thank you, Valerie. You showed me something."

"Oh, darling! Me? What was it? I'm so pleased!"

"I thought I'd given up working with canvas. But now I see it. Vick is perfect for canvas. I didn't know till this afternoon."

"Canvas? You mean paintings on canvas?"

"That's what I thought he meant too," said Tim's dad dryly. "It's something quite new, I believe. Tim thought of it this afternoon."

"I've been drawing her all along, of course. But you see how she is."

"I can see that she likes good hot food."

"The way she was with the camera," said Valerie thoughtfully.

"But I need paint. All I've got is junk. And I need the cloth."

"But darling! You can have anything you want! You can have all of mine! You'll have to come and see after dinner. And you will stay the night, won't you?"

"Oh sure," said Tim.

❧ THEY SPENT THE NEXT THREE WEEKS ON THE PRAIRIE. TIM was painting her. He had all of Valerie's canvas and lots of paint. And he was working very fast. She posed from morning till dark. Sometimes he was working on two or three pictures at once. He had almost given up smoking.

He was trying to get something from her. She wasn't sure what it was, but she was doing all she could to give it to him. It was not like the human paintbrush or the body paintings; he wanted to capture something. Something she was. Or did.

But they were running out of money. They would have to give a show, some kind of a show, Vicky thought.

Tim had put her in a very formal pose, standing on the steps of the van, wearing a long full skirt made out of a yellow canvas drop cloth, a wide leather belt belonging to him, and a sheer white blouse made out of the curtain, artfully draped and folded. A black-eyed Susan plant bloomed in dusty profusion beside her knee and she held a drooping bouquet of it in her hands.

[194]

"Oh, the gorgeous darling! She's Victoria of the Plains! You must call it that, Tim."

Valerie had come out on the prairie in her black Jaguar. She had found them somehow.

"What do you want, Valerie? I'm pretty busy."

"Oh, it's nothing really, darling. I've just been looking for you because I've got photographers calling me up every day begging to meet you and Vicky. I could get you about half a dozen little assignments. And they'd really make you a lot of money, you know, darling. You and Vicky."

"Assignments? Like doing what?" said Tim. He took his eyes off Vicky and put down his brush. She seated herself carefully on the steps.

"Just getting your picture taken. And you are a genius, darling. This scene here. A photograph of this would—"

"Sell a lot of perfume," agreed Tim.

"Well, but she could have a perfume named for her someday. You know that. She is a great beauty, Tim."

"How much money could we make?" asked Vicky. "Suppose we did just one of those things."

"We can do a show, Vick."

"But you don't have time. And you need more canvas. And we don't have anything to eat."

"Would it really be worse than doing a show, darling? Your father was telling me about that thing you did at the rodeo—"

"Do you want to?" Tim asked Vicky. But he already knew she did.

It was the camera she wanted. She knew what she had done with it before, even though she had never seen the pictures. She wanted to do that again.

Valerie was now getting the photographs out of her purse.

"Look at this, darling." She brought them over to show Vicky.

It was a stunning sequence. Vicky could hardly take her eyes off it. Tim was looking at them too.

"Poor little Tom is panting to sell it to somebody. But of course the paper owns the rights, so it'll probably go to something dull like Travel Alberta."

"All right," said Tim. He folded his arms. "With him. At least two hundred dollars per pose. That's all."

"And come to dinner! Please?"

"Jesus, Valerie. We don't have time!"

"I'm hungry," said Vicky.

Valerie laughed triumphantly.

After a moment Tim laughed too. "Okay. You can't argue with that."

When they were driving into town she asked him, "Can you take pictures, Tim? Pictures with a camera?"

"I fooled around with cameras in art school. That was a long time ago. But I thought I was a painter. That was a long time ago too."

He wasn't satisfied with what he was getting. She knew that. He was driving himself and her, but it was not coming the way he wanted it to.

"Look, Vick," he said. "I'm not trying to keep you from doing what you want. And you probably could make money doing it. Maybe a lot. Maybe even really a lot. That's what Valerie thinks. But you belong to God, not to some slimy photographer. The best thing I can do now is make you know that for yourself."

"I just thought that—you know—those pictures were nice."

"Yeah. The first time that guy ever met God's art, I guess." He laughed. "This is going to be hell for me, Vick. I had you to myself up till now."

Vicky moved over to sit close beside him on the bench seat of the van. They were getting into Calgary.

"Let's do a show," she said. "With real magic. After this."

"Yeah. I'm thinking about that. I think we're going to do something like that next."

❡ THEY DID THE PHOTOGRAPH IN VALERIE'S GARDEN USING A climbing pink rose to stand in for the black-eyed Susan. Valerie wanted to give Vicky a real blouse and skirt but even the photographer was adamant that they had to use the drop cloth and Tim's belt.

It was a Sunday and Tim's dad was prowling around the

sunny garden. But Tim was kept busy. He had made Vicky up, arranged her skirt, invented the folds of her blouse. But then it came to the moment when she stood alone by the rose trellis and looked into the camera. In spite of her joy and triumph, she knew that she was making him unhappy. He had invented this, but he couldn't turn it into art for himself. He had tried and failed. He wanted to try again, but she knew that she, not he, was the artist when she looked into the camera.

"How did you think of it?" said the big whiteman.

He had a whiskey bottle in his hand, and he sat down at the round white table in the garden and poured out two glasses, for himself and Tim.

Vicky came over and Tim pulled her down on his lap, drop cloth and all. "What did it say to you, Dad?"

"It reminded me of a picture of my mother. A photograph. What do they call that colour?" He snapped his fingers. "Sepia. The settlers. Something about the pioneers, that's what it says. My mother was a pioneer, after all. She came to Alberta as a baby on the back of a wagon. Her dad and her brothers walked their cows and horses into the country here in the spring, when the snow was still up to a man's thigh in places."

"Yeah, but look at Vick. She's not a settler."

"Old pictures, then. Chiefs wearing parlour clothes. Children at the mission schools in pinafore dresses."

"All photographs," said Tim thoughtfully.

"The camera loves her."

Tim was drinking whiskey, holding Vicky against him, hugging her.

Vicky was hugging herself. She loved the camera. There was something about it; it didn't tell her what to do. It didn't set her up and demand that she pose for hours at a time. It asked her to do something for it, something she was good at, something that came naturally to her.

"Those old pictures," said Tim's dad. "They carry a lot of political baggage. Genocide. The slaughter of the buffalo. Assimilation. The mission schools. Are you still talking about knowing your pain?"

"Yeah. But yesterday's sepia photograph is tomorrow's cigarette ad," Tim said. "I'm trying for something better than that. I've just been on the wrong track, that's all."

"I don't know that you're right about that. Those photographs speak to me. They say something about all I've been fighting for for years. Social justice. Maybe a recognition that something that couldn't happen here did happen here, about seventy years ago, when my uncles were fencing in their land."

He looked like a settler to Vicky, a big man, silvering hair, western shirt and boots—what his uncles and his father had looked like years before, probably. He expressed that background in everything about him, in his appearance, the self-confidence of his gestures, the slow drawl of his voice, the very whiskey in his glass, and it was therefore strange to her that he had taken up the cause of her people, that he could even conceive of that as his business.

"The tide is turning. The environmental movement is growing in this country, even in this part of the country. The Lovers of Ochre River may not be able to kill this dam. But maybe that kind of protest will work against the next one. Personally though, I can't see the issue of simple justice subordinated to anything else, and that's the issue here."

"Do you really think man is that important?" Tim asked. "Justice seems like kind of a petty thing when we're up against the suicide of the whole species."

"Justice is the only thing we've got. Sure, it's an approximation in practise. But without it we haven't got anything."

"But what have we got with it? Power? Money? Government? Is that what I want? I don't want all that."

Valerie came over to them, carrying two glasses and a bottle of mineral water. She set them on the table and the big man looked up at her with a smile. She put her hand, heavy with rings, on his shoulder.

"I think it's going to make a wonderful picture," she said. "Darling Vicky! Tim, you clever, clever boy! And it is so wonderful, that it could all have happened here in our garden, darling!"

Tim's dad took Valerie's hand and pulled her down onto his lap too. Tim made a slight movement of his whole body and Vicky knew he didn't like seeing Valerie as his father's lover.

"Let go of me, darling. I'm making dinner," said Valerie, laughing. "But you will stay?" she went on.

"Yes," said Vicky. They had had a delicious lunch, but she was hungry again.

"What do you think he'll do with that photograph?" Tim's dad asked. Valerie had got off his lap quickly. She knew Tim didn't like it.

"He's going to try to make his fortune," she said. "But he's not good enough. Next time you should hold out for much more money and a better photographer. A wonderful photographer."

"Next time?" said Tim.

"You can't stop now. You're on a roll! And Vicky is going to be famous. Darling Vicky! Victoria of the Plains!" Valerie held up her glass of water.

"Vick is just Vick. That's who she is. Herself."

"Of course," said Valerie. "Of course she is." She was trying to seem submissive. "But darling, she's got it in her to be famous. You have got it, Vicky. I know the real thing when I see it."

"Yeah. She's a real thing, Valerie."

Valerie was silent for a moment. "You mustn't stop her," she said.

"I'm not stopping her." Tim was rigid. Vicky continued to sit heavily on his lap. She had felt this confrontation taking shape all along. But it was all right. Among these kind people, in this beautiful house, nothing bad was going to happen. And Tim had had a new idea. She had noticed him thinking about it all afternoon, developing it. He was really invulnerable to Valerie right now.

"I need a video camera," he said abruptly.

"Well, why didn't you say so?" Valerie laughed, delighted.

"We might even have one," said the big whiteman. "Don't we have one?"

"Darling, of course we have one! We have two! Tim can have mine. And lots and lots of tape! Darling, what a wonderful idea!"

Vicky watched the big whiteman and Valerie together all evening. It was quite fascinating to see them together. Valerie was the most forceful woman Vicky had ever met. When she wanted something she went straight to it and got it. But what she wanted was often too complicated or delicate for that approach to work.

[199]

It was that lack of tact, that clumsiness, that made Tim recoil from her—for he was one of the things she wanted. She wanted his liking; she wanted his respect.

They went to her studio to get the camera. Her studio was an enormous, well-lit room, overflowing with things—fabrics, a desk covered with letters and drawings. Pictures on all the walls. Easels, several of them. It was what Tim should have, what any artist would want, but at the same time, Vicky knew that it was not the studio of a real artist. Valerie turned from the flower painting on her easel to the telephone on her mahogany table. She went out to lunch and discussed a wall hanging with a client. But she had never been like Tim, when he was driving himself to create, grappling with his vision, single-minded, failing repeatedly to capture the vision, but relentlessly trying again.

They played with the camera all night.

"You love it, don't you, Vick?"

"Yes," she said drowsily.

"What makes you feel like that? What are you responding to?"

"It's almost like making love," she said hesitantly.

"I touch you." He touched her delicately, running his fingers across her belly. "And you let me. You open yourself up to it?"

"Yes. Not just to the camera though. To everything."

"Not to the camera?"

"It's like being touched by everything."

Tim lay down beside her and she pulled the sheet over them. He put his arm under her head. He was still thinking.

"I don't know anything about this, Vick," he said at last. "But Valerie's right. You could make your fortune at it. And before that happens, we've got to find out what it's all about. So you'll know."

"I don't care about making a lot of money," she said. "But we've been living on bread and jam lately."

"I keep forgetting. And you're probably still growing."

"You said you were going to do a show."

"Yeah. We are. We'll do it with the camera. I just hope I can do it myself. We need a whole lot of things. A studio. Sound. Music, maybe. A client. Selling it might not be such a problem, though, if only I can do it, what I have in mind."

❡ THEY HAD THE CAMERA WITH THEM CONSTANTLY OVER THE next week. They ate with it. They slept with it. They both played with it.

In the meantime Tim sold one of his pictures of Vicky, one of the nudes, and they had a little more money for food.

"But it isn't your thing, paint," he said. "And that's too bad, because it's mine."

"I liked being the human paintbrush," she said.

He laughed. "You're an actress, I think."

"Am I?"

They were sitting on the steps of the van. Tim was making a daisy chain and Vicky had turned the camera on his hands, slim and brown, busy with the stems.

"Yeah. You are. The thing is to remember where it's at. I've had a hard time with that all my life. Maybe it's why I never did anything till now. With painting, it's the way the paint goes onto the canvas. That's all. It doesn't matter how it makes you feel, or what the creep that bought it is going to do with it. It's only the paint."

"And what is it with acting?"

He shrugged. "I think it's the moment when you look into the camera and do it. What happens to the image after that is nothing: when your face goes up on a billboard or they show you on TV every eight minutes, putting on your deodorant."

"But isn't a photograph or a film sort of like a painting?"

"No. Maybe. Maybe that's why I don't usually use canvas. I like it to go away after I do it. No one can take it and turn it into a deodorant ad. It doesn't lose its reality."

"Like a flower," said Vicky.

"Like a person," said Tim. "Like you, Vick. See, what Valerie and Tom wanted out of that Victoria thing was a certain kind of image—something they could hold onto and sell. But what did you get out of it?"

"I don't know. Being that girl, I guess. The one in the photograph."

"Yeah. You even reminded my dad of his mother. It was great. I didn't see what it was when I was still thinking of it as paint."

The next day they went out on the Reserve and down a narrow

rutted road to a spot by the Ochre River where the raspberries grew in thick abundance. Vicky didn't know the place. It was far away from the village. But Tim had been there. He had camped all over the River valley, on and off the Reserve.

"Maybe we need paint in this," he said.

"Are you going to paint me?" He was holding the camera.

"No. But you are. Using raspberry juice."

"It doesn't work," she said, somewhat later. She had been walking shoulder high in the raspberry canes, trying to stain her arms with the juice.

"It's great," said Tim.

Vicky looked into the camera. "Am I going to take off my clothes?" She was wearing her ordinary clothes, jeans and a blouse, her old canvas shoes, hair loose over her shoulders.

"If you want to. Maybe not."

"Just tell me a little. I need to know something."

"Okay, Vick. Here's the River. You see this River?"

Vicky left the canes and went out to the riverbank. The cliffs of the Ochre loomed above her in three wide shelving benches. There was a point on a bend, with some river stones forming a little beach. It was a brilliant Alberta day. The mountains shimmered like a mirage as Vicky perched on a boulder.

Vicky looked at the water, purling along. This was a river, a real thing. They all talked about it all the time; the very name, Ochre River, was shorthand for so many other things: Dominique getting hurt, Tim's dad wanting to take that one to court, irrigation, aboriginal rights, compensation, what was happening to the environment, ancient wrongs, an ancient river.

What had it, what had she, Vicky Boucher, got to do with all that? She thought of Tim's dad. To him, the river, Dominique, herself, they were all symbols of injustice. When he thought about them he thought about things that weren't real. On the other hand, when he had spoken of his mother and his uncles, Vicky had seen them making fences, killing off the last of the buffalo, driving the elk out of their fields. And she herself had had a grandmother who was alive then, and who had walked on the banks of this river, who had certainly been here …

"Go for it, Vick," said Tim. He was holding up the camera and Vicky walked into it, walking into the sun with the mountains and the river at her back.

He went on shooting till they ran out of tape.

They were both tired. Tim made a fire and they drank some tea and ate bread and jam on the steps of the van.

When she woke up her skin was stiff from raspberry juice. The brilliant sun poured in through the windows, lighting up the clean shabby interior of the van.

Tim groaned, then woke up too. He lay there, arms behind his head, watching her wash. "Know what? You're great. Pretty soon everybody's going to know that. But you're already great."

"You must have a mile of tape."

"Yeah. I've got to get some help with this. We have to cut it down to about half a minute's worth of good shots."

"What are we going to do with it?"

"Give it to the Lovers of Ochre River. They can call it something. Spirit of the Ochre or some stupid thing like that. And that'll be you, Vick. Before Tom and Valerie can turn you into Miss Travel Alberta."

"But why would the Lovers of Ochre River want it?" she asked.

"You know what it's about. You did it."

"It's about me."

"You. A Native girl walking in a raspberry patch. Putting juice on your arms, standing on a boulder in the River."

"A symbol of something?"

"Yeah, but you've got a lot of reality too. It fights with the symbolic side. It comes through."

"But what will they do with it?"

"Put it on TV probably. It'll grab people better than a clip of Dad talking about Native hiring don't you think?" He was laughing.

◖ THEY WENT TO SEE BRIAN AND MURRAY THAT NIGHT.

"It's the Old Dope Peddler," said Murray lazily.

"Yeah, but I'm not buying any of your stuff. For one thing, it's parsley, and for another thing, I'm not smoking much these days."

"Parsley! What are you talking about, man? Hey Brian, you ever cut dope with parsley?"

"Nope, I use only Canada number one grade A oregano when I cut dope, which I never do, never do cut dope."

"Come on in, man. We'll give you some oregano. You're still travelling with Adorable here?"

"We've been doing some stuff with video tape."

"Jesus, you sold out, eh? Where'd you get the camera? That's a good camera."

"My dad's girlfriend." Tim put the camera down carefully on the kitchen table. "You'd better see it, Murray. It's good."

"Oh fuck, do you have to do this to my head? I don't want film. I gave all of that up after I found alfalfa. Please, please, don't show me any pictures!"

"Yeah, but you're the only guy I've got who knows how to use the knife."

He turned on the finder and Murray watched the tiny image of Vicky. Presently he began to scream. He put both hands up over his ears and shrieked. Tim turned off the finder.

"You got too much there," commented Brian, who had been watching over Murray's shoulder.

"I know," said Tim. "I need electronic scissors."

"Oh, fuck! fuck! fuck! Why me?"

"It's great, though," said Brian. "Hey, Murray, you could maybe produce it and take a percent. Who'd you get a commission from anyway, man? How much? We could use the bread."

Tim turned on the finder again and Murray watched eagerly, his hands still over his ears, elbows out at the sides of his head. He watched it through to the end. Then he put his head down on his arms and began to sob.

"Why'd you sell out?" he mumbled. "I thought you were a painter."

"Vick's not right for paint. She's an artist herself."

"She's Adorable. But is it Art?" asked Brian.

"It's art," said Tim. "But is he up to it?"

"Do you think he can do it?" Vicky echoed.

They all looked at Murray. He was still sobbing, his head down on the table.

"Well, he knows how. He used to be a TV producer before he became a dopehead. He's got all the contacts. He can get a studio. He knows how to cut."

"Yeah, but he'll have to put on a dress and go into the city," said Brian. "I'm not sure he is up to it."

They went in to Calgary the next night. Murray had been on the phone all the previous afternoon. He had lined up a studio, a sound man, and all the trimmings.

"Who's this?"

"This is Adorable."

It was a very long and boring evening for Vicky. Tim, too, was looking bored, although she felt that he was really annoyed rather than bored. This was another case where it was hell for him; whatever they were doing to the tape was something he had no control over. It had passed out of his hands and out of hers as well.

Vicky didn't care. She merely wanted now to do another one.

"Hey! Who're you going to sell this thing to?" asked the producer who came with the studio.

Murray jerked his thumb at Tim. "Ask him."

"The Lovers of Ochre River," said Tim. "But we're going to give it to them. They haven't got any dough anyway."

"Really? Maybe I could get you something better than that for a thing like this."

"We're going to do some other stuff. Probably give that away too, though."

"Yeah. He used to be a painter," said Murray. "Now he's an Indian, did you notice?"

Vicky went to sleep on Tim's jacket spread on the clean slippery floor outside the studio. When she woke up he was sitting beside her, his back against the wall. It was long after midnight.

"Do you want to see it?"

She shook her head.

"You really don't?"

"No. You were right. It's all done already."

"When was it all done?" he asked curiously. "Just when you did it?"

"No. When the camera took it."

"It's only about half a minute long now."

"Let's do something else."

"We're out of tape."

"Let's do something different then."

THEY WENT BACK TO CAMP AT THE SAME SPOT ON OCHRE RIVER after Tim had given the tape to the Lovers. He seemed disinclined to do much now. He went on drawing her but he did not paint. They made love and ate raspberries for a week.

Tim's dad found them this time. He was driving a 4x4 pickup and he came rattling and jerking down the stony road.

"I knew where you were," he said. "After we saw the TV clip."

"It's on, Vick," said Tim. "They used it."

"Are you kidding? It's been on quite a lot. This environmental protest is getting big, you know. Valerie and I sit there on the sofa and see it a couple of times every evening."

"We need some more tape," said Tim.

"Valerie sent tape." The big man had eased himself into a crouch, one knee up, in front of where they were sitting on the van steps. He was wearing the common working clothes of the West: the ten gallon hat, the jeans, the western shirt, the pointed boots. "She sent some food too. What have you been living on? Raspberries?"

"Vick made some into jam."

"Well, Valerie gave me a whole bunch of stuff: cold chicken, ham, pickles, cheese, fruit, rolls, rye bread, a couple of bottles of wine."

He got to his feet again, sighing, and went to the back of his 4x4 to lift out a huge cardboard box. Vicky led him inside the van, which was relatively cool, standing in the shadow of the cotton-wood trees on the second bench of the riverbank.

"This is nice," said Tim's dad. "You cleaned it up." He smiled at the curtains, which she had washed and put up again. Then he sat down on the bed.

Vicky was looking through the food. Since it was all fresh stuff, they would have to eat most of it right away. Perhaps they could hang some things in the river, but the smell would attract bears.

She was hungry. She felt that she could eat all of the meat herself.

"Mind if I open a bottle of wine?" Tim's dad asked. "Vicky, just go ahead and eat, okay?"

Tim stowed the tapes with the camera under a bench.

"How did you do it?" the big whiteman asked. He was asking her, Vicky realized after a moment.

"Tim told me to think about the river," she said.

"Well, I guess there are some people in this province who never thought about Ochre River before at all—till they saw you thinking about it."

Tim laughed.

Vicky began eating a ham sandwich. She passed him a chicken wing. His dad poured wine into a clean jam jar and took a sip.

"How did you know the road?" she asked. "Do you know this place?"

"My dad used to come hunting out here. It was legal then if you hired a guide from the Reserve. He shot a grizzly bear on this River once."

"We used to go berry picking. But never very far up. Because of the bears," she said, feeling shy.

"The Reserve doesn't know the River valley the way they used to in the old days. I climbed all over this ravine here and even farther back. With a gun—that was when I was too young to know better."

He loved this place. Vicky was arrested by the thought. She had thought all whitemen lived in the glass high-rises of downtown Calgary, in the ugly spreading subdivisions. They had no land of their own, no river.

But for her too, the River had only been a word, until she met Tim.

"You know—" he said. "If only the clock could be turned back. If I could be my grandfather, or even my dad, knowing what I know now, how things turned out—"

"Think it would have made a difference?" said Tim. He was

slowly eating his chicken wing. Vicky's sandwich was gone and she was buttering another piece of bread.

"My ancestors didn't want this any more than the Natives do," he replied. "The development. Suburbs spreading as far as the eye can see. Agro-business."

"Yeah," said Tim. "They wouldn't have wanted what happened to you, I guess."

"You?—Oh, I see. You whitemen, you mean?"

Tim nodded.

"We're in a mess, aren't we?" He sighed. "Tell me the answer."

"I don't know," said Tim. "It kind of depressed me for a while."

They both looked at Vicky eating grapes.

"You know you've got yourself some kind of a reputation?" said his father.

"For what?"

"You've done a couple of things this summer that people didn't expect."

"Didn't understand, you mean."

"Yes. Probably. But I've been working on this for a long time, remember, and it's the first time that I've felt any hope. There's opposition to the dam; there's opposition on this Reserve, of course, but it's a kind of entrenched resistance, a passive thing. I see the forces massed against this poor place, the people who live here, and I want to meet someone who feels—something about that. Some lively emotion."

Vicky remembered herself in the spring as he spoke, that dead feeling, her robot-like behaviour. Then Tim had come. He had saved her.

He was lying back on the bench with his boots up on the one opposite, eating the bunch of grapes she had given him.

"There's a fellow who wants to do a film," said the big whiteman. "Actually he wanted to do a documentary about me." He seemed hesitant, a little embarrassed. "Then he called me up and said he'd heard that something new was going on out here. So I told him about you."

"Well?" said Tim lazily.

"He wants to meet you."

[208]

"Why don't you just show him the Band Council?"

"A bunch of old men?—And me, too. We're not very photogenic."

Tim laughed. "But we are, are we?"

Vicky smiled too. Tim was looking at her. But he already knew she wanted to do another film.

"By God! Yes, you are! Both of you." His father laughed. "What are you doing these days, anyhow?"

"We're kind of broke," said Vicky. "Tim has been drawing."

"I'm glad to hear that," said his dad. "Defending an artist for obscenity is so much more interesting than drug charges. Could I see that?" Vicky had got out Tim's sketchbook and he held out his hand for it.

"Sure," said Tim. "You were wondering whether anyone in this place felt a lively emotion," he went on, looking over his father's shoulder.

"You can't imagine how happy I feel for you. Just to look at these," said his father quietly, turning the pages.

Vicky was looking at them too. They were all of her. Some of them were quick sketches, some more elaborate drawings. The happiness she felt, the joy of being alive, shone in these drawings the way it had not come through in his paintings.

"They're good," said the big whiteman. "They're very good. Surely you could sell these?" he asked, looking up at Tim.

"Yeah. But I'd rather sell the stuff that turns out to be junk, though."

"Why?" asked his father. "The emotion. You don't need to be ashamed of that."

"Yeah. But it's mine—and hers. No one else can have it, I guess."

"But I thought the meaning of the image was in its universality."

"No! The more universal it gets the less meaning it has. It just becomes some kind of weird, abstract symbol. A peace sign. A Mercedes star. A logo."

"But doesn't a picture express human constants? Look at this." His father held up a drawing of Vicky cautiously putting her foot out, toe extended, to test the coldness of the river. "That gesture. The young girl. Happiness. What do you think? Someone on the other side of the earth wouldn't get what you were saying?"

"Yeah, but it says less and less as it gets further out. Vick's beauty. What I did with the pencil to get it. That doesn't have anything to do with generalizations, human constants, all that bullshit."

"I thought that was just what great art is: telling us about man and nature."

"No, it's about individual things. And look, Dad, all that the picture is—really—is just those marks on the paper." Tim pointed to the simple fluid line that was Vicky's foot and pointing toe. "It's a thing too."

The big man gazed down at the paper in his hands.

"But can't there be art for the mass market?" he asked after a moment. "What about those images that we see over and over again?"

"When you make a thing you have to be careful. About what happens when it gets out there."

"You seem to be saying that you should keep your art to yourself."

"Maybe not just to myself." Tim was thinking about this. So was Vicky. She was sure this idea was wrong, even though the other one sounded wrong as well. But one did not do such things for no one to see. And the fact that someone was going to see it made it better.

"You don't do it just for yourself," she said firmly.

"Maybe you do it for your own tribe, then," suggested the big whiteman. He was looking at her with interest.

"But even the tribe wants to make it a symbol," said Tim.

"You said that the reality comes through the symbol. It fights with it," she said to Tim.

"Yeah. That's true. That's what made that clip we did for the Lovers kind of interesting," Tim said to his father.

The man nodded. He was still looking thoughtfully at Vicky and she knew that he was surprised that she had made a contribution.

The big man poured the last of the wine into his glass. Then he stood up and went to the door of the van with it, looking out.

He turned back. "I never thought I'd be having a conversation like this with you."

"Well—that's okay," said Tim awkwardly.

"It's a lot better than okay. For years it seemed as though you weren't even there. Just a shell we all called Tim."

"Well, I still smoke." But he wasn't smoking. Vicky too regarded smoke as the enemy and she kept count. He had not had a joint for days now. They had run out and he had not thought it worthwhile to leave their camp and go get any more.

Her mind had turned to something else, something she had been wondering about in the spring, that was still on her mind. "What is your tribe?" she asked Tim.

"The same one as yours," he replied. He was smiling.

"But who are you then? Why doesn't anyone know who you are?"

She was staring at him, but for a moment he did not return her glance. His father too, remained silent.

"It's not because I'm ashamed of it," said Tim. "It doesn't come up."

The eyes of the big man were on Tim, sombre and a little anxious.

"My name is Medicine Bear," said Tim. "And everyone knows who I am. They just don't like to think of it, that's all."

"Why not?"

"My father murdered my mother when I was a baby. He was one of the last ones hanged in Prince Albert—in the early fifties."

"It was one of my first cases," said the big whiteman. "If only I had known what I know now. But then again, those were different times, worse times—much worse. He wasn't guilty," he went on, looking at Vicky. "I never believed he was guilty."

Vicky remembered Joshua Joe looking at Tim with that clear stare, so long ago when they were at his place for breakfast.

"But why did you go to him?" she asked after a moment, gesturing at the older man. There must have been a grandmother or an aunt. Surely someone else on the Reserve could have taken Tim when he was a baby.

"That was the way it was done back then," said the big whiteman. "Tim was a ward of the province. No one cared about cultural survival in those days. I had an unhappy wife and a childless marriage. It seemed like a good scenario for adoption."

Vicky did not see how he could bear it. To be deprived of his family, his own people. And to come back here years later as an outcast, as though he were a whiteman or someone from another Reserve.

"I told your father I was going to take you. I went to see him in Prince Albert. I don't know whether he was glad. He just nodded his head. That was all."

Although Vicky had not seen her mother or Dominique since the night she ran away, they were still there, they were hers and she was theirs, and if like Dominique, she came home someday to lie drunk on the sofa in the kitchen, they would never cast her out or deny that it was her place and they were her people. But Tim, she realized, had no one; no one to whom his right was unquestionable.

"I always hoped you would come back here sometime," said the big man. He was still looking sombrely at Tim.

"Well, I didn't really intend to, but then—" Tim stretched out his arm to Vicky and she came to stand beside him gladly, understanding that she was not just his only love but all of his people.

"I know you had kind of a different scenario written for me, Dad, like law school, partnership, all that."

"Well, I don't really mind. Perhaps this is the best way after all," said his father.

Tim shrugged. "It seems to be the only way."

Again she felt that they didn't think she was following their conversation. And Tim was even trying to indicate that it did not matter very much. But she understood very well just how much it did matter, and that she was even more important to him than he knew.

7

1977 · Mollie Hallouran

HE WAS AWARE OF A VOICE, A VOICE HE KNEW, FAMILIAR,
and yet so strange that he could not be sure that he was hearing it.

"Get up, Dominique," it was saying. "Get up."

Hands were pulling at him. He realized that he was cold; he was
in fact freezing, and parts of his body, his legs and arms, were so
numb that he felt nothing. But the euphoria of drink had left him,
and the voice prodded him into fright.

He was in a car. Then he was in a house. Then he was in a bath,
and the water gradually grew warmer. It became warmer and
warmer and somebody who was holding his head continued to
speak.

"Damn fool," she was saying. "Damn stupid fool! Why am I
bothering? What the hell is it to me, anyway? Go and get dead,
Dominique! You aren't my boy!"

"Mollie," mumbled Dominique. It was Emma's mother, but why
was she here?

"Oh, you're there, are you? Well, get out and walk!"

Gentle insistent hands helped him out of the bathtub and dried
him off. His feet and hands were now burning with pain. He
stumbled with her guidance into the downstairs bedroom, and lay
down, for the first time in many months, on a bed with sheets and
blankets on it.

Somewhat later, he woke up. It was light. He was almost
clear-headed but the pain was terrible. He felt his hands under the
coverlet, touched his feet together, trying to understand, by the
induction of graver pain, that they were indeed still there.

Mollie was talking to someone, and after a while, in the torrent of her words, he made out that she must be on the telephone.

"Yeah? Well, that's my business. You can just stay out of that. I'm asking for your medical advice, Robbie, not your entire world view. No, I would not like you to. I said, I found him on the road to Bitter Root. All right, I'll do that, but it won't make any difference."

She hung up, saying "Bye!" as a kind of afterthought, and he heard her advancing feet.

She sat down on the bed and regarded him with a slight cynical smile. "Awake, eh?"

"Yeah." Dominique tried to raise himself on his elbow, then decided against it.

"I was just talking to my brother on the telephone, in case you heard that. He suggests I tell you this ought to be a lesson."

Dominique lay fully back down with a gasp and stared at the ceiling.

On the road to Bitter Root. He couldn't remember what he had been doing there. They got liquor in Bitter Root with his money, from the store or the bootlegger. But normally someone would have taken him in a car. Perhaps they had dumped him and stolen it.

"Could you eat some soup or would it make you puke again?"

"Again?"

"Don't you know? I found you lying in it," she said.

Dominique slept and ate all day. At intervals he threw up, then she fed him again. He floated in an in-between state of consciousness, in pain all the time but not sure whether he was asleep or awake. By nightfall he was well enough to start getting the horrors.

"Yeah. Just shut up," Mollie ordered, introducing a spoonful of straight whiskey into his mouth. "How's that?"

"More."

"A little more."

At times he could hear himself crying. But he was not crying because of the pain in his feet and hands. Was it really he who was crying?

"Boy, this is not what the doctor ordered," said Mollie, chuckling.

She sat on the bottom of the bed in her nightgown with the whiskey bottle in her arms. "Better?"

"More."

"No. Later." She took a swig herself, then put the cap on.

"Now."

"Want your feet to fall off, kiddo? Later, I said."

Interminably that night passed and day broke. She was off in some other part of the house sleeping. He was enough himself to realize that. His eyes felt enormous, swollen. Sometimes he could not close them. At other times, the images becoming fearsome, gross, unendurable, he strove to open them, and then realized they were open. He awoke to the sound of his screaming.

"Tell you what, Robbie." Mollie addressed the whiskey bottle, setting it up like a mannequin on her knee. "You make him do this cold turkey."

He wanted to snatch the bottle from her hands but his own hands were gone.

Eons passed while he struggled with his daydreams. When the dreams passed there was always the pain. It seemed as though the pain was dragging him back, pulling him away from some kind of cliff inside his mind.

❧ IT WAS LATE AT NIGHT AND THERE WAS A FIRE DOWN BY THE graveyard. He could hear the odd syncopation of a drum. He stumbled nearer and he thought he was hallucinating. It was hard to tell what was going on these days.

There was a dancer in the space in front of the fire and it seemed to be Vicky, yet Vicky as he had never seen her before. She had a power about her, almost as though it was drawn over and around her in lines in the air. The crowd swayed, mesmerized, watching her. And yet she seemed unconscious they were there; he had the impression the dance she was doing was for her own pleasure. Why was she dressed so strangely, as some kind of deer, an antelope?

Then suddenly, out from behind the church leaped a demonic figure. It was painted in horrible colours, with war paint. But the face of the figure was white, dead white, with a trail of blood coming down over the chin out of one corner of the mouth.

The figure jumped in front of the antelope girl and Vicky backed suddenly, screaming. She turned her face around and screamed silently. If he had not been in the power of the dance, Dominique would have thrown himself through the crowd to save her. As it was, he drew in his breath with the others in a vast collective moan. A woman cried aloud.

For the white monster had picked Vicky up and thrown her over his back. He stood there motionless for just a moment, letting the crowd view the front of his naked body, his horrible arousal, then turned and dashed off with the helpless girl, who now hung limply down his back, her hair streaming over his buttocks.

The fire went out abruptly. And in the darkness there was the sound of sirens.

❡ "I'LL TELL YOU SOMETHING," SAID MOLLIE CONVERSATIONALLY, changing the fouled pillow slip, the fat white pillow tucked under her chin. "You're a lot worse than my old man ever got. I used to think he was faking a lot of it."

"How—how long—?"

"Three days. Cheer up. The worst is over."

"Awful. Too stiff. Can't—"

"Oh yeah." She put the pillow under his neck and shoulders and removed the other one. "You're going to be in bed awhile with those feet."

Finally it was just pain that he felt. And shame.

Mollie came and sat in a chair beside the bed. Sometimes she read a book or the newspaper. Sometimes she just sat and stared at him thoughtfully. Dominique lay in silence, gazing at the ceiling, sleeping fitfully.

Mollie's family doctor came and looked at his feet.

"You're pretty lucky, young man," he said severely. "You could have lost those. From what I hear, you could have frozen to death."

"Sure," said Dominique, turning his head away.

"Well, you better be grateful to her."

"I am." He wasn't.

Mollie did not seem to care. She came and went, feeding him, carrying away the bed bottle or helping him to stagger to the bathroom, chatting in her cynical way. When he was able to stay up for a while, she made him sit in an armchair in the kitchen.

"You can watch me. It'll give your eyes something to do," she explained.

Gradually he did begin to watch her.

He had always seen Mollie through Robbie's eyes, as a hard woman with a bitter tongue. A promiscuous woman as well, with a tendency to wear embarrassing and revealing clothes. Her farm was small and poor, crumbling away, and she would accept no help.

Now he watched her day by day, struggling into ancient work clothes and rubber boots to feed the cattle she owned, cleaning the floors of the house on her hands and knees, cooking almost continuously for no other purpose than to feed herself and him and the cavernous maw of the freezer, and he saw this was not really a true picture. She was a compulsive worker.

"I'll tell you what," she said. "I'd be a drunk too. But there's something inside of me that just won't lie down. I guess you don't know what I mean."

"Maybe I do."

"Well, you sure weren't acting that way when I looked last."

The sharpness of her tongue did not hurt or annoy him now. Her cynicism was so universal that it did not imply any criticism of him in particular.

"Tell me," she said. "What was it, anyway? What sent you over the edge like that? Was it Emma?"

Dominique didn't know. Something had happened to him. It seemed such a short time ago that he had been planning to set up housekeeping at Poppalushka's with his true love and his little sister. He had had all sorts of plans. And then one day all that had vanished into whiskey.

"You don't even know why, do you?"

Again he reflected. It was surprising. Was it the whiskey itself? It was not the whiskey he wanted, but the obliteration of himself.

Yet the sick form of life he had been living for months, barely conscious most of the time, was repulsive to him now. Why had he wanted that?

"I got a letter from Emma. She writes sometimes."

"Where is she?" He found that he could ask this. Mollie's sarcastic tongue was a shield and a refuge to him.

"She's in Vancouver still. Working in a TV station. Doing something for now, like receptionist. She says she's going to be a producer, maybe even a host. I'll believe that when I see it."

"Is she still with Dick?"

Mollie shrugged. "How should I know? Don't break your heart over it. Oh yeah, I forgot—! You already did."

He met her eyes, which finally wavered, then fell.

◖ ANOTHER DAY. ANOTHER NIGHT. INTERMINABLY, TIME CREPT forward. In the kitchen, after supper. The bandages had come off his hands, but were still on his feet. The skin of his arms and legs was strange: patchy, bluish, and peeling.

"All right," she said. "Let's talk about me if you don't want to talk about you."

"Go ahead."

"Well, to start with, I've had a pretty lousy life. Know what I was thinking about when I was giving you whiskey by the teaspoon and cleaning up the puke? My husband. I told you that a couple of times—maybe you don't remember. The only way that you were different was that you couldn't get up and clobber me when the cobras were biting."

"What happened to him?"

"He died—oh, about ten years ago—just before Sonya went out to the Reserve and got you. Leaving me with this farm, which was mine already, as a matter of fact, and two lovely children."

"How did he die?"

"He drank a bottle of methyl alcohol. He lived a couple of hours. Just long enough to wake up and die in my arms. Boy, was that touching. Everybody wondered why I didn't cry."

"You did cry," he said.

"Okay, that's true. I did." Mollie leaned her forehead on the back of her wrist.

The story must be a shameful family secret. He wondered why she wanted to tell him so badly.

"Why did you marry him?"

She shrugged. "I often wonder. Dad was Irish and he drank too much. But I found a man who really knew how to drink! And boy! He'd give me the back of his hand if he knew what I was doing now!" she went on.

"Why? You're not doing anything wrong."

"Maybe not. But you know what's at the heart of a relationship between a man and a woman? I think I finally figured this out. She wants to get hurt."

"That isn't true."

"Oh yeah. So you think it isn't, do you?"

"I don't hurt women," he said.

"You don't, eh? Well, that's what you think."

Dominique found himself hating the conversation. He hated what she was telling him; and he hated the way she was telling it.

"Do you want me to change the bandage?"

"No."

"Want an Aspirin?"

"No. I want to go to bed." It was 11:00 by the wall clock in the kitchen.

"Christ! Well, all right!" She got up to help him as usual and they began the slow shuffle to the room at the back of the house.

◖ "SHE WAS LOVELY AND FAIR AS THE ROSE OF THE SUMMER, BUT 'twas not her beauty alone that won me!" sang Mollie, washing dishes, and making a few ironic gestures to go with her Irish vocables. She had a nice voice. He often heard her singing, working in other parts of the house.

"Oh no, 'twas the truth in her eyes ever shining, That made me love Mary, the Rose of Tralee!

"Irish songs. Dad used to sing them in the evenings sometimes. They're the only kind I like," she remarked, rinsing the dish towel.

"Want to hear a bedtime story?" She sat down opposite him, bright-eyed. "I could tell you about Two Crows. Your uncle."

"Okay." No one but Mollie had ever told him about these people.

"Sometimes we called him One Crow. It was a joke. You know—'One crow sorrow, two crows joy'?—He turned up again. With Eliza's father. After that winter when they dumped Eliza on us. They got back to the Reserve the next summer; they worked on our harvest that year. Then they caught that crazy guy and sent him to residential school. His dad couldn't get him away to the U.S. again quick enough."

"Why was he crazy?"

"He just was," she replied. "He was completely crazy, not just partly, the way you are. The only thing he gave a damn about was his own courage. Horses, that was where they showed their stuff back in those days, roping and daredevil riding in the cattle drives. This was the wild West, you know. I don't know what they had to do to him in residential school to make him sit down. But when he was about sixteen, he started going to the school of me." She looked complacently at her hands folded in her lap.

"He already could read and write. So what was left for me to teach him? Oh yeah, the history of the world. For me, that meant Ireland. And kissing.

"We'd sit under a haystack and play poker. Just him and me. He was crazy for gambling—I figured it was good for his arithmetic. Of course, neither of us had a red cent. We called it kiss poker.

"The rules were that when you lost your stake you got kissed by the winner. The object of the game was not to get kissed. Kids, you know. Except pretty soon the object of the game was to get kissed. Then we finally noticed it didn't matter who won. It was just him and me anyway." She chuckled.

"All right. So you want to know what happened, don't you? It's a short story, actually. My mother noticed something was going on between me and him. She sent me back east to school. I had an aunt in Winnipeg. I could cry my eyes out, but it didn't make any difference. There was no money to come home. I was away for four years."

Dominique was thinking of Sonya's plans to send Emma to college. But they had not needed to do that, in Emma's case.

"What happened to him then?"

"Yeah, well. I was afraid you were going to ask." Mollie leaned her forehead on the back of her hand.

"He died, I guess." He thought of the tears pouring down Eliza's face.

"Yeah. He died."

"How? Of some disease?"

"TB. It happened while I was away. And there wasn't a damn thing I could have done about that, even if I'd been here," she went on. "But if only I'd been here anyway. I've spent my life, wishing I'd been around to see somebody die." She had begun to cry.

"Shit!" she said a moment later. "It was that damn haystack, I guess. I never told anyone that before. Want some tea?"

"No."

"Going to bed?"

He had got to his feet.

"I guess so."

She didn't really need to help him any longer. But she got up anyway. As she stood in front of him, waiting to take his arm and begin helping him walk to the back bedroom, it finally dawned on him that all this was leading somewhere.

She raised her head and he saw that her eyes were wide, her hard mouth vulnerable. Perhaps she had not known where it was going until now either. It was one of those things that was just going to happen.

They stared at each other for a long moment, and he realized that she was waiting, waiting for him. She would not be the one to make the first move. Even though she had, in effect, already made it.

He kissed her and she responded instantly. He lifted his head, bothered by her eagerness, and she sighed and leaned her forehead against his shoulder.

Dominique examined his feelings in curiosity. He had really disliked her so recently. Now what he felt for her was pity, apparently—and a kind of respect, even liking. And he knew she wanted him.

"Aren't you—going to bed?" she inquired.

"Yeah. With you."

"Well, then—" She laughed abruptly. "Let's go. Get it over with."

He had been sleeping in her bed all this time but he had been in such a disconnected state he had hardly noticed that until now. He sat down on the edge of the bed, relieving his aching feet. His hands, unbandaged now, were still peeling, numb in patches. He doubted himself. Could he manage this?

Mollie, ignoring him, was taking off her clothes.

Painfully, slowly, Dominique unbuttoned his shirt and unbuckled his belt. She had been doing this for him as recently as yesterday, before the bandages came off.

Her skin was pale, freckled here and there with dark moles. Her breasts, large and heavy for her slight build, sagged a little from childbearing. She did not remind him of Emma, which was good.

"Do you think you can still screw?" asked Mollie, putting it into words, as usual.

"Maybe not."

She got in between the sheets from the other side of the bed. Dominique shed the rest of his clothes and sat still for a moment, gathering himself together.

"Want to forget it?" She gave a shaky laugh. "I've got some second thoughts about this myself."

Dominique slid in beside her. The sheets were cool and smooth, and she felt very warm. She lifted her head and he put his arm under her neck. They lay side by side for a few moments. Then Mollie made a movement under the covers.

"Just wait," said Dominique.

"I could probably help you out."

"I don't want you to."

She sighed again, a sigh of mock resignation. He could feel her heartbeat faintly, against the arm under her neck. It was beating fast.

Things that moved and excited her, his resemblance to Eliza's brother, the fact that she was his father's sister—the badness of it; these things did not excite him the way they did her. What did move him was that a smaller and weaker creature wanted him for something. All the others had been lost to him, and now there was only this one.

◀ MOLLIE ALWAYS GOT UP WITH THE FIRST CRY OF THE ROOSTER, more than an hour before first light at this time of the year. He was aware of her waking, her stealthy withdrawal. When he next awoke, it was broad daylight and she was standing beside the bed in muddy jeans and a thick sweater, a bowl of porridge in her hand.

"Here." She handed it to him, and while he sat up, reached automatically behind to fluff the pillows.

"Well." She perched on the bottom of the bed, carefully tenting the bedclothes over his feet, and regarded him with bright, Hallouran-blue eyes.

Dominique smiled at her and began to eat.

"Great sex, eh?" she said satirically.

"Yeah." He continued to smile.

Mollie smiled too. Then she laughed.

"Last night I probably said a lot of things—when we were doing it. Forget all that, will you? Do me a favour."

Dominique licked the spoon, watching her. He was not going to forget all that.

"D'you want more breakfast?"

"Nope. Maybe later." He stretched and the sheet dropped into his lap. She widened her eyes at him mockingly. But it was not all mockery. She had stopped smiling.

"Come here." He sat forward and pulled her down straight on top of him. She was remarkably small and light.

"You take them off. I can't."

She was already doing so, kicking off the jeans and shedding the sweater, a flannel shirt underneath.

She was something for him to protect. To protect against herself. That was where she needed the protection most of all.

Dominique lay still letting sadness wash over him, knowing that it would go away in a moment; in a few minutes it would be gone. He bent to kiss the small shining knob of her shoulder.

It was too sweet a gesture for her, apparently, for she grimaced and sat up, her hand over the bone. She looked down at him, bending a little, so that her soft, pear-shaped breasts swung free.

"You want to know something?"

"Maybe."

"I was jealous. Of Sonya, first of all. I always wondered—"

"What are you saying?" Dominique shot upright, furious. "Jesus Christ! How can you say that?"

"All right! Okay! I didn't really think you slept with her." Mollie eyed him for a moment and he saw how even this little violence excited her. She shivered and pulled her flannel shirt around her shoulders.

Dominique lay down again, allowing his fury to die. There was no reason why he should care.

"You were in love with her," she said.

"So what?" said Dominique. "Maybe it's even true. Forget it."

"Oh no. There's a bit more to this. When you came back—I was jealous of Emma too. My own daughter. Bad, isn't it?"

"Yeah," he said shortly.

"So now you know." She smiled, hesitant, a little embarrassed. "That's my confession for this morning. Now I have to go out again and shove my arm up poor old Buttercup's vagina. She's due to calve this month. Do you want anything more to eat?"

"I can get up and get it myself."

"No. You just stay put until I come in again." She began to dress herself unselfconsciously. "Stay off those feet."

Fully dressed, she came around the bed to pick up the porridge bowl. Dominique, ahead of her, picked it up himself, and grabbed the extended hand.

"Hey! What's this?"

"You talk too much, but I like you anyway," he said, retaining the hand.

"Do you?"

Her laugh was false and grated upon his ears. But as he nodded, she stopped laughing and Dominique rejoiced in the flood of affection that had arisen in his barren heart.

◖ DOMINIQUE AND MOLLIE WERE PLAYING RUMMY AT THE kitchen table. It was a windy March night and they had just both come from the barn.

They often played cards in the evening. Now that Dominique's feet were better, he could help with the farm work; but Mollie was not an easy person to help. Things were good because they were done the way she did them; she would not do them in a particular way because it was good. It had taken him awhile to get a grip on this general principle. She would not let him go near the calving cow; although he knew he would be much more patient with it than she was. She took no suggestions. He could only do the heavy work and not all of that without interference.

But he was content to let her have her way. In the two months he had stayed there they had been surprisingly happy together. They both needed each other for something as simple as company; for this thing they had now, with cards and hot chocolate in the draughty kitchen.

Mollie had given up trying to show off and wore her glasses to play cards. She preferred winning to vanity. In addition to the glasses, she was wearing a horse blanket over her shoulders to protect her back from the shrill draft of the chinook around the door. Dominique had already suggested weatherstripping, and now she made him sit beside the oil stove. Hot in his steaming, sweaty clothes, for he had been shovelling snow, he had stripped to jeans and bare feet.

"You see this card?" She held up the remaining card in her hand. "I'm going to pick up the pile and—"

She sorted through it and produced three kings, an eight to add to his three eights, added a ten and a six to her run of clubs, put down the two of hearts to his three-four-five and found a nine-ten combination to add to a royal flush. She still had one card.

"Jesus," said Dominique, turning up and discarding a useless six.

"You must have put your brains away out there and brought in the snow shovel," she said, triumphantly, pouncing upon it to add to the run of hearts, and discarding her last card.

If it had been kiss rummy, he would always have been the one getting kissed.

Someone was stamping his feet on the doorstep and Mollie shouted carelessly, "Come in!"

It was Robbie.

He looked at Dominique in surprise, and then turned his eyes away quickly, his nostrils expanded. Dominique knew his state of mind exactly. He was trying not to know something that he did know, that he had instantly seen.

"I came over to see how your cow was doing," he said to Mollie, his voice rough.

"She's okay. I just checked."

"This is the kind of night they have 'em."

"Sit down, Robbie. Since you're here."

Robbie had been hovering by the door. He approached the table reluctantly, still not taking off his boots, and sat down. Dominique got up and set about making him a cup of cocoa.

"How are the feet?"

"Just about healed."

"There's a place that isn't. You might as well show it to Robbie, so he won't have to think he came over here for nothing."

There was a moment's awkwardness, while Robbie bent down as though to look at Dominique's foot while he was still standing on it. Dominique put his foot up on a chair.

"I didn't know you were still here, Dominique," said Robbie, prodding the oozing sore gently.

"Where'd you expect him to go on those feet? Back to the bar?"

Dominique said, "She can use the help."

"The hell I can!" Mollie was indignant.

"That's going to be okay if you stay off it," said Robbie to Dominique, putting the foot down.

"I told him that!"

"You quit drinking?" Robbie was ignoring his sister. He looked down at the table, involuntarily smiling at the disposition of the cards.

"Yeah."

"Going to keep away from it now?"

"I guess so."

"Jesus Christ, Robbie! Who do you think you are? First my cow needs your expert assistance, and now you sit here and give Dominique the third degree. Keep your big fat nose out of this!"

"Where's Howie these days?" asked Robbie, with a certain flash in his eyes.

"Up north. Now that there's nothing doing on the dam again. He wrote me a letter, as a matter of fact. Want to see it?" Mollie put her glasses back on her nose and went rummaging in her purse.

Dominique and Robbie watched her, not looking at each other.

She wanted Robbie to know something and she might even try to tell him. Dominique felt that he had to prevent this, if he could. He did not want to do anything bad to Robbie.

Robbie was reading the letter slowly, moving his lips.

"As you see, he's not coming back to work on the farm. Never thinks of me." She looked at Dominique. "So it's kind of nice to have Dominique here. Not that it's for the help I want him."

Robbie had stopped reading but he was still looking down at the letter. She liked to frighten herself. But she could hurt Robbie, she could hurt them all.

Dominique stood up. "Want to have a look at that cow, Robbie? I'd like to have your opinion."

Mollie's mouth dropped open in outrage.

"Sure," said Robbie, standing up too. He drank down his cocoa and walked to the door.

"Damn you and damn you!" shouted Mollie. "That is my cow! I just looked at her!"

Robbie went out, allowing the door to bang gently.

Dominique didn't move. There was a long moment of furious silence, during which Mollie was hastily pulling on her boots, her jacket.

Dominique sat down.

She turned around at the door to glare at him, and suddenly broke into a laugh.

"Very funny!" She went out, slamming the door.

After about fifteen minutes, during which he picked up the cards and washed the soup bowls from their supper, and the cocoa cups as well, Dominique realized that they were not coming back.

By one of those odd flukes of fortune, the cow was having her calf, just as Robbie had predicted, on the wildest night of the month—and by Mollie's calculations, four days early.

They were all very busy in the next couple of hours. All of Mollie's energy was taken up with telling them what to do and trying to prevent them from doing anything.

Standing in the dark yard, the wild wind of early spring blowing in their faces, Mollie invited Robbie back into the house.

He glanced at his watch. "Sonya'll be waiting up for me. She'll sure be glad to hear you quit drinking, Dominique."

Dominique and Mollie went into the house together as Robbie started his truck and began to splash out the driveway.

Mollie turned on him. "Jesus!" she shouted. "The poor thing could have had her calf in peace if you hadn't—!"

Dominique put his arms around her.

"And another thing!" She struggled half-heartedly. "Sonya's got nothing to do with you giving up drinking. If I thought she did, I'd buy you a forty ounce bottle of rye right now!"

Dominique laughed. After a moment, she began to laugh herself, looking up into his face.

"Want more cocoa now? Or shall we just go to bed?" They were already halfway down the hall to the bedroom.

"And here's another thing," she murmured into his neck. "Stay off your feet!"

Dominique woke up in the night, sweating. His feet were hurting, but it was the dream that woke him. He seemed to be in a dark cave of some kind, and all around him were people. There was that hush, the expectant pause of an audience, a desiring, collective silence. The odd sound of the drum, whimsical, tickling, was coming at them from all sides. Then a lighted place appeared, high up in front of him, and a moment later his sister came into it from one side, naked. She was walking lightly on her bare feet, with her long bare legs, her breasts high and small, hair streaming.

She looked neither to the right nor to the left; it was very quick. The lights went out suddenly, and the screaming, catcalling audience all about him suddenly fell back into a shocked silence.

A shameful thing to dream about. Or had it really happened?

◀ HE LAY WIDE AWAKE, KNOWING THAT HE WOULD NEVER BE through with this now, although it occurred less and less frequently. First there was the shocking imagery, which he could not suppress. Then the awful sweats and chills. And the terrible consciousness that it would all be over—he could take care of it completely— if he could only have a drink.

He looked at the bedside alarm clock. It was three hours before Mollie would wake up. He had three hours, three hours, three hours to go. He knew he could take it for three hours. He would wait, wait for Mollie, wait for Mollie to …

"Dominique," said Mollie. She sat up in bed. Then she switched on the light. "Bad, eh?"

"Yeah." There was no point denying it. He was shaking with the fever.

She hopped out of bed and returned, chastely dressed in her shabby bathrobe, with a glass of water.

"Drink it in sips." She took his hand. "Shall I tell you a story?"

He nodded, barely able to attend.

Mollie pulled her horse blanket up over her knees and smoothed it with her other hand. She began to sing instead.

"'Twas the last rose of summer, Left blooming, alone …"

She was tender, almost sweet, as unlike her fierce prickly day-to-day self as she could possibly be. He listened, trying hard. The song was a sad one, one of her Irish songs.

He was going to win. The pointlessness of it all was over. There was somebody, somebody in his universe on whom he could turn his full attention, who needed that.

"All her lovely companions, Are withered, and gone."

His being here made a difference. It made a difference to her. The shaking fit was over. The bedsheet was soaked with the drops of his sweat.

"Oh God!" he cried, grinding his teeth.

It was almost over. It was nearly over. It would only last a little longer. It was over, over, over. The pointlessness of it all—was over.

"Sorry," he said, lying back, weak and limp. He put one arm over his eyes. She was still holding the other hand.

"I'm going to change the sheet," she said. "It's soaking wet."

"Don't bother."

"Don't be silly. I said I'm going to change the sheet."

He grinned. She was going to change the sheet. He struggled to stay awake while she went to get another. She needed to do that; it was why he was here.

◖ SPRING CAME SLOWLY THAT YEAR, WITH CHINOOKS, FOLLOWED by bitter unseasonable weather. Howie came home for Easter and brought the girl he was engaged to. She was pretty, white-skinned, short-haired, not very tall. Howie exhibited an infatuated dominance that made Mollie's lips twitch.

Dominique had been exiled to the hired man's room in the barn for this visit. Even Mollie was not inclined to push this point with Howie. The embarrassment he felt on finding Dominique there at all infected them like a disease.

They were eating breakfast. Dominique had just come in and was beating the snow off his boots and trousers in preparation for making his way to the bathroom. Howie looked mutely into his plate.

Muffin, his girlfriend, said, "Morning, Dominique." She spoke with a self-conscious trill in her voice.

Dominique returned, wet-haired from the shower, and found only Muffin and Mollie in place at the table. Mollie put a fried egg in front of him, while Muffin assiduously buttered his toast.

"I already watered 'em," said Dominique, noticing Howard's absence.

"He wanted to go out," said Mollie, raising her eyebrows.

"Today is Howie's birthday," Muffin announced.

"I remember that." Mollie spoke dryly.

"Aren't we going to have a—you know, a little party?"

So many years marked by so many parties. The innocent

sentimentality of the request reminded Dominique: Sonya and Robbie had always had birthday parties every year, for all the children, for him too.

"Who do you want to invite?" Mollie asked.

They had to invite everyone in the family. Muffin was well-informed.

By afternoon the air was so charged with Mollie's boredom that it was almost a relief to see the Hallouran family car turning up the driveway. Howie and Dominique had been exiled together to a cold and miserable coexistence in the farmyard while the birthday preparations were going forth. They were perched side by side on the fence like storm-driven ravens, tolerant of each other, but wary.

The Hallouran children swarmed out of the car and across the yard. "Lizzie won the egg hunt!"

"Yeah, but that was because Dad helped her!"

Imperious Marian led Lizzie into the house. Howie jumped down to follow. Robbie paused, raised a hand to Dominique, and tramped inside. Sonya lingered and presently drifted with diffident Harry, towards the fence.

"Hi, Dominique," she said.

Harry, her echo, said, "Hi, Dominique."

Dominique knew that his appearance shocked her. It shocked him too sometimes. He had become painfully thin, his face no longer the smooth brown of youth, but seamed and dry like an old man's face.

"I'm glad—" she said, and stopped. She smiled a little, tentative, fearful smile as she saw the limitations on what she could say.

"Go in, Mother. You're shivering," said Harry, and gave her a little push towards the door. He jumped up on the fence beside Dominique.

Sonya went, looking over her shoulder at them, reassuring herself at the sight of them sitting there, side by side, her adopted son and her real one.

Harry produced a chocolate egg from his pocket and put it in Dominique's hand. "Dad thinks Lizzie has to win everything now."

"Do you mind if I eat it later?"

"Nope," said Harry. He continued, "They said you were sick."

"I was sick, but I'm going to be okay."

"Well, that's good." Harry sighed like Robbie.

He moved on to his own preoccupation now. "Is Howie going to marry that girl?"

"I guess so."

"Does he sleep in her bed?"

Dominique considered. "I think he does," he said.

"Dad told me something. Then Marian said it was a lie."

"That's because she doesn't know."

"Oh." Harry looked at him slantwise. "I thought she just wanted me to shut up."

Dominique laughed.

"Is she nice?" Harry asked.

"No."

Harry jumped off the fence. "I'm going to go see. Coming?"

Dominique followed him into the house.

Mollie was moving through the little house like a tornado, her eyes glittering with suppressed fury. Howie was pouring drinks for everyone out of some bottles he had been keeping in the trunk of his car. Muffin was boring Sonya with snapshots of her sister's wedding. They looked very much alike, plump, white-skinned, curly-haired, passing the pictures back and forth. Robbie, comforted by the resemblance, was looking over at them with approval and relief.

The adept Hallourans could master any social occasion even when it turned out to be as dull and uneasy as this one. The girls gently detached their bewildered mother from tedious Muffin. Howie glowed with proprietorial pride and they treated him with respect and tender pity. Even Mollie began to enjoy herself after they had eaten the cake and ice cream. Lizzie had been encouraged to put forty-eight candles on the cake while Muffin was looking for her camera.

"Doing okay?" Robbie asked Dominique privately.

"Oh yeah." He was already looking forward to a grim night in the barn room.

Mollie glared, seeing them talking together, and Harry gravitated idly in their direction.

"I don't think Muffin knows either," he remarked to Dominique, frowning.

"Oh yeah. She does. She's just pretending not to."

"What are you talking about, Harry?" said Robbie.

"I asked Dominique, and he said Muffin's sleeping in Howie's bed," whispered Harry.

A cloud passed across Robbie's forehead and then he broke into a shout of laughter in spite of himself.

At last they all went home. Dominique helped Muffin wash all the dishes. Mollie sat reading a newspaper beside the oil stove, the remains of somebody's drink in her hand and the horse blanket on her knees.

"Thanks for the party, Mother," said exuberant Howie, and Mollie put out a gentle absent hand to touch his arm.

Dominique knew that he would not be able to sleep, but it helped to pretend for a while. When the fever hit him, he stripped and walked naked about the cold room, muttering and whining to himself. At least out here he couldn't wake anyone up.

The bottles were in the trunk of the car. The bottles were locked in the trunk. The bottles were locked up and Howie's keys were in his trousers. Howie was in his room and the keys were in his jeans.

Dominique wiped the tears off his face and got back into bed. He was cold. He was very cold. He got up again and turned on the light to drive away the naked girl and the masked demon, and the dreadful tedious hollow sound of the finger drum. He was freezing.

Hell was cold. Where had he heard that? Hell froze. Mollie said it sometimes. He was not going to make it if he could not get warm. He could not put on his clothes because the keys, the keys were in Howie's trousers and he might go outside to the car and smash the lock.

He was standing at the top of the steps when there was a light footstep on the ladder and Mollie emerged in her shabby dressing gown, her black hair ruffled and showing streaks of grey.

She led him back to bed and Dominique lay down obediently, his teeth chattering.

"God damn him. Just when you were getting over it."

[233]

"I have to—have to get used to it."

"Yeah, but to top it all, he's pretty mean with his booze," said Mollie. "It's not as if the rest of us were having such a good time."

"Just sit there. I'm okay. But just sit there."

"I was thinking of asking him if I could have another drink after everyone left. But what the hell, Sonya gave me hers."

"Yeah. Go on talking."

"And as for that lollipop he's going to marry—Well, go ahead! Maybe the two of them deserve each other!"

Dominique gripped her hands tightly. It was nearly over. It was going to be over soon. The chill meant it was going to be over.

"And all the time—" Mollie put her forehead down upon their joined hands, "all I was thinking was that I'd have to sleep alone one more of these hellish nights. What kind of a mother am I?"

"Oh, Christ, I'm cold!"

There was a loud noise below. Still grasping each other's hands Dominique and Mollie stared at one another. Someone had tripped over the boxes beside the bottom of the ladder.

Now there was a footstep. Howie swore. "Goddamn mess in here!" His voice was thick. He was coming up the ladder.

"For God's sake, Howie, what is it?" Mollie went irritably to the door.

"What are you doing here? What are you doing here?" Howie grabbed her shoulders and shook her two or three times. Mollie's mouth fell open in astonishment. The bathrobe came open, revealing her decent flannelette nightgown, her carpet-slippered feet.

"I saw the light!" he shouted, thrusting her away and moving towards Dominique, still convulsed with his chill in the sleeping bag. "And you know what? I dream about it, this light. Mother's out means she's up here with one of those men. Doing it with the light on!"

"Do you do it with the light off?" inquired Mollie coldly.

Howie turned around and hit her on the mouth with the heel of his open hand.

Dominique leapt naked out of the sleeping bag and they stood there for a moment. Then Howie began to cry. Blubbering, he advanced on Dominique, who remained stock-still, not knowing what to do.

"If you touch him, Howie, you and I are going to be finished. Even more finished than we are now." Mollie wiped the blood off her lip with the back of her hand.

Dominique's teeth began to chatter again as he relaxed.

"Get back into bed," she ordered him.

"You wrecked my childhood," wept Howie. "Now you're still wrecking my life. I bring home my bride. Home? What kind of home is it where—"

"Shut your dirty mouth, my boy," said Mollie over her shoulder, forcing Dominique back into the sleeping bag.

"I told her—I had to tell her where I was going! Jesus! What kind of thing is that to tell your wife about your mother!" Howie stood there, helplessly crying, his fists clenching and unclenching at his sides.

Mollie sat down on the edge of the bed. "How could you tell her," she said, "when you don't know anything? Dominique has the DT's because of that stinking party she threw," she went on.

"I don't believe that! What are you doing here? What are you doing here?"

Dominique groaned, clenching his teeth. The shivering fit was over, but Howie's passion moved him horribly.

Mollie clapped her hands. "That's enough! Take your wife and your booze and get out of here!"

"No!" cried Dominique.

"Are you sick?" Howie moved to see him. "Is she telling the truth?"

"Yeah," said Dominique hoarsely.

"She came out here because you were sick? How did she know?"

"Christ!" said Mollie. "I knew. Now shut up and get out!"

Howie fell forward on his knees and buried his face in his mother's dressing gown. He wept unrestrainedly, begging her pardon. Suddenly he was one of the passionate Hallourans, not his own stolid, bullish self.

After a moment Mollie stroked his hair, murmuring softly.

With her other hand she reached gropingly behind her. Dominique took it and felt the nails bite in.

Howie stumbled to his feet. Mollie looked up at him.

"Muffin will be worrying." Howie turned his face childishly aside. "Will you make hot milk, Mama?"

"She can make it," said Mollie sharply.

"Please come, Mama!"

"Do you want me to show her my swollen lip?"

"Just come!" He was desperate now that things should seem to be all right.

"Dominique?" Mollie turned around, not bothering to hide their clasped hands any longer.

"Go on," he said.

"In a minute."

Howie blundered out the door.

Her hand went up to cover her lip. Dominique, sitting forward, pushed the hand gently aside and brushed the place with his finger. There was only a small cut; a swelling that would become a bruise tomorrow.

"First the father. Then the son," said Mollie, her tears falling over his hand.

❧ IT WAS A HOT SUMMER AND THE HEAT CAME EARLY.

Dominique worked on the seeding with Robbie. He and Mollie were farming; they had a very large garden.

Howie had been married up north in the Swan Hills, and Mollie went away to the wedding. It was the first time she had been away and Dominique enjoyed the peace her absence left him in. He spent the evenings making unobtrusive alterations to various little things she would not let him set his hand to when she was around. The door was weatherstripped, and Mollie would not notice till next winter when it would be too late to argue.

He missed her while she was away. It was never easy to get along with Mollie, but he missed being the beneficiary of the secret, unsatisfied tenderness of her heart. He felt none of the fever he had known for Emma, but he was looking forward to her coming home.

When she drove up the driveway he was all ready for her. Tea was setting, dinner in the oven, a large bunch of daisies in a glass jar in the middle of the table. He looked forward to the torrent of scorn she was going to pour on his domesticity.

Mollie got out of the truck, still wearing her corsage from the wedding reception on the lapel of her blue suit. Dominique lurked inside the back door. She looked around warily for a moment, and then walked very fast towards the house. It occurred to him that she was frightened.

Her lips were grimly set. Going away to the wedding had cost her something. Mollie often slept less well than Dominique, and she had had a bad dream before she left. He guessed now what it had been about.

"Boo!" he said quietly, pushing open the screen and drawing her into his embrace.

She could not hide her pleasure; she was actually blushing. For a moment she clung to him.

Then, disregarding the daisies, she walked over to the oven, looked inside, and turned the heat off. "Did you boil the tea?"

"No."

"Good. I hate it that way."

She took off her hat, a felt fedora that went with the suit.

"Shit! That was awful," she said, throwing it into the porch, and simultaneously discarding her high-heeled shoes.

"What happened?"

"They got married, stupid! I could almost take the rest. Damn! I'm still nervous," she said, walking around the room.

"Come on. The bride was lovely."

"Emma was there. No one told me that was going to happen."

Dominique sat down.

"Don't give me that blank stare! She was there, that's all! And no, she is not coming here."

"Well, that's good."

"Yes, it is, isn't it?" She was too jittery even to look at him, he noticed.

"Tell me, then."

"Tell you?" She stood in front of him now, arms akimbo.

"What is there to tell? She had some horrible man in tow, who thought the whole thing was too funny for words. She weighs about ninety-eight pounds and looks twenty years older. That's it."

"What did she think of Muffin?"

"She's not my daughter for nothing! Though—God!—I used to think Howie was the one with taste."

"But everything went okay?"

"I suppose you might say so," replied Mollie coldly. "I don't want this tea!" She pushed it away. She got up again and walked restlessly around the room. "Do you think this is wrong?" she asked, her back to him.

"No. Who says?"

"No one says. Howie minds, that's all."

"He doesn't know anything about it." Or she had made him believe that he didn't.

"Oh yeah? Well, his wife does. Your name was on her lips— several times. 'And how is Dominique? He was sick, remember? I do hope he's better now.' 'Mum, I was just asking after Howie's cousin, Dominique.' See what I mean?"

"Well, so what?"

"You're right, I guess. I just don't like the idea of her putting the screws on Howie with all that."

"Maybe it gives her a thrill."

"He's all confused about—well, about sex. As well as marriage— love. It's my fault, I know that. You remember that stuff he was saying about me. Well, it's true, I kind of went crazy in there for a while. After Otto died." Mollie pondered. "Do you think he and Muffin ever actually—? Before?"

"Yeah." Dominique thought of Harry with a smile.

"Well, you sure couldn't tell from the way they were acting. I know they shared a room when they stayed here, but—"

"Come on, Mollie. The bride's supposed to be a virgin at a wedding."

"Mm. I just hope she wasn't really."

"Are you hungry?"

"No. I had too much lunch."

"Want to go for a walk?"

"Are you crazy?"

"Well then—want to come and lie down with me?"

She began to laugh as Dominique started to push her through the living room doorway on the way to the bedroom at the back of the house. "Lie down?"

HIS EXPERIENCE OF DAILY EVENTS AND COMMONPLACE THINGS was more intense that summer since he seemed to have been so far away from them for so long. Taste and smell came back; so did the simple kinaesthetic relationship, intimate and familiar, with his own muscles.

To eat a tomato in the garden: the satin skin, warm with sun and faintly dusty, sun on his shoulders and bare forearms, juice squirting into his mouth, oozing over his lips and chin, the hot heavy toes of his boots buried in crumbly soil.

Mollie, living in her own, largely verbal universe, regarded the renewal of his relationship with the sensible world, with fond— if critical—pride.

They went to Abercrombie to buy spark plugs, a new rake handle, a box of grass seed. This ended with an orgy of window shopping in the supermarket.

"Eggplant," said Mollie. "California. Probably bitter."

"Pretty," he said, admiring the mirror-like sheen of rich purple-black skin.

"I bet those turnips are wormy." Pinkish white globes like spinning tops, a sprout of green leaf above.

"Asparagus. Too late. Where'd it come from anyway? Some place where they have spring in July?" Sharp, scaly, acid-green spears ending in a tight afro of curls.

"This broccoli is in flower. Look, it's American. Can't we grow better broccoli right here?" Dark, dark green, dusted with mustard yellow.

"How they have the face to go on selling BC apples at this time of year, I—" Pink, greyish-green stripes.

"Let's go home and have something to eat."

"Well, we're not buying any of this junk."

"C'mon," said Dominique, thinking of his tomato of that morning.

"Let me have a look at the meat. Ugh. Plastic." The meat lay before them, wine red, glistening under its icy wrappings.

"Not so fast. Jesus, it's disgusting what they do to chickens nowadays!"

"I'm starving."

"All right, all right!—God! Lobster in Alberta! Why bother?"

They got into the car and Mollie pulled out of the parking lot, driving with her usual irritability, a little too fast. Dominique's stomach growled.

"You'd think you didn't eat all the time, from the sound of it!"

"Well, I'm hungry!"

She put her hand on his knee by way of reply.

Dominique felt the hand, even after she had removed it, a light touch that sent a tingle along the skin under the rough denim of his jeans, a tiny electric current. Warmth spread upwards into his belly.

"Looks like it might rain," said Mollie absently. "Hey! What are you staring at?"

"You."

"What?" She was pleased. "I thought you were hungry?"

"I can be more than one thing at a time."

Her tanned neck glistened under a shimmer of perspiration from the heat. Inside the open lapel of her sleeveless white cotton blouse, he could see the heave of her breast, pushed up by her brassiere. A mole on her cheek that Mollie herself was unaware of enhanced the high curve of her cheekbone. Hair restrained by a comb exposed the innocent bloom of the earlobe. The clear globe of her eyeball extended out beyond the flat coloured substance behind it, and the eye itself, in a delicate hollow, was framed by the sooty curling lashes of the Hallouran family.

She paused by the mail box at the bottom of the driveway and Dominique leaned over to collect the letters. Mollie took them away from him, sorting, her lips pursed. "Shit! The gas bill. Well, they'll just have to wait. What's this garbage? More of it! Tool

[240]

catalogue; do you want it? Oh hell! Here's a letter from my darling daughter." She slit it open with an impatient forefinger.

"'I am fine. Send more money.'" She made a face. She read the letter, frowning, then put it in her purse.

Dominique looked out at the pearly mass of rain clouds piling up on the mountains. They were due for a summer storm and the crops could use it. He looked down over Mollie's land, feeling in anticipation its relief when the rain would fall.

"Well, no point just sitting here," said Mollie crossly, starting the truck. "I thought you were hungry?"

Coming to himself he realized that she had been sitting there for some moments on the crest of the hill above the driveway, the mail lying in her lap.

"Go get some lettuce!" she commanded, stopping the truck in the dooryard.

She continued to be cross and preoccupied throughout their supper preparations. Used to this, Dominique went out afterwards and did the chores, battening down for the rain.

They had now established what part of the outdoor work was his. The patient day-to-day work of farming was not a strong point with Mollie. She tended to allow the tasks to accumulate and then attempt them all in one large burst of energy. The tedious hours of repair and conservation that Robbie put into his farm, hours of mending machinery, fence-posting, pitching straw and manure, fixing the catch on the chicken coop door—with all this, Mollie simply could not be bothered. She looked after the animals with patience and tenderness, watered the garden, and did the weeding and hoeing in furious bursts. Her relentless cleanliness inside the house had been taught her as a child, then forced upon her by husband and necessity.

Dominique stood for a while, looking into the darkening sky, as the clouds rose in a roiling mass above the plains. It was not going to be a soft rain, but one of those summer downpours where the sky lets loose its burden all at once. The air was heavy, brooding, ominous.

He went inside. Mollie was standing in the dark sitting room, her arms wrapped around her chest. He thought perhaps the weather was oppressing her and went to stand in front, letting her lean on him, their foreheads touching.

"Want to beat me at rummy?"

"No. Too easy."

"What do you want to do?"

"I thought you had something in mind." She spoke wryly.

"Maybe you're not feeling like it."

"You would have made somebody a good husband."

The first gentle drops of rain came pattering down upon the roof.

"Nice," said Dominique, tightening his arms around her.

"Damn," said Mollie, and sat down on the sofa abruptly. He knelt in front of her and she began to cry.

"What is it?"

"The hell with it. It's in my purse. Go get it."

He went into the kitchen and found the letter from Emma in the labyrinth of her purse. He brought it back out to Mollie, then remembered her glasses, left behind on the kitchen table.

"No. You read it."

"What's going on?"

"She's coming home. Can I tell her not to? I'm her mother."

He opened the stiff, crackling paper of the letter, and read it in the light streaming from the kitchen doorway.

> Dear Mother,
> Things have not worked out in this new place. Maybe I'm
> having a nervous breakdown or something. The point is that I
> have to get out of here right away. Could you put some money
> in my account? $200. would be enough. To tell you the truth
> it is urgent, as I am pregnant. P.S. Say hi to Dominique for me.
> Howie said that he is working for you or something.

"How do you like the punch line?" said Mollie bitterly.

The rain was now beating on the asphalt shingles of the roof like a pair of hands on a drumhead.

Dominique folded up the letter and fitted it back into the carelessly torn envelope, then tried to marshal his own slow thoughts.

It seemed to him that Emma was back there in the darkness where he had been; in the ecstasy of his recovery, he had not thought of her, left behind there.

"Listen, whatever, poor old Howie said she got an earful from that bitch of his. So you can just discard the idea that she doesn't know." Mollie smiled maliciously. "If you were comforting yourself with that."

"I never thought about it," said Dominique, still wondering at himself.

"She's pregnant. What all that other stuff means, we don't know. Where the hell am I going to get two hundred dollars?"

"Maybe Robbie would—"

"Oh yes. But you stay out of this!" she said. "And you're going to have to go too. That's the whole point, isn't it?"

She was right and he knew it. This was not really his home; she could not be his woman. The rain made a cold and lonely sound out there as it came hissing and spattering down.

"Shit." Mollie blew her nose. "I wish you'd had a little more time."

"More time?" He had been living outside time, floating in a bubble on the sea of time.

"You just crawled out of the gutter."

"I'm okay now."

"No, you're not. Where are you going to go?"

"I'll find something somewhere."

Mollie now began to cry unrestrainedly. "Do you think I'm a fool? I knew there was no way this was going to last."

She wanted him to deny it. But he couldn't forbid Emma to come home. Especially when he even wanted her to come home.

"Don't cry." Dominique sat down beside her and she turned away. He put his hands on her shoulders and she shook them off.

"I'll cry if I want to! I'm crying for me, not for you."

In the end, he went to bed in the room upstairs. Lying still, up there, he could hear Mollie walking about the house down below, sometimes swearing in a low voice at the walls. After a while, merely out of the well-being of fatigue, he fell into a dreamless sleep.

8

1993 · A Thousand Voices Crying

◀ VICKY WENT BACK. SHE PUT ON HER JEANS AND A PAIR OF
sunglasses and took the bus to Steamboat.

"Oh, I'm going to be a country girl again!" sang her friend, who
had produced her last film. But she wouldn't let him come with
her; she left him behind in Calgary.

Steamboat had become smaller, the café and the movie theatre
closed. Many farms were uninhabited, Canola in the fields, planted
by agro-business; others lay deserted—they didn't look fallow.

Her perception of the place amazed her. In France or England,
a farm was just a farm and perhaps represented a holiday: a rustic
bed and breakfast where the milk came from the cow. Here, a farm
was a form of alien occupation. Cultivated fields evoked in her not
just indifference, but hostility. If Donovan had been with her, she
knew she would not have seen this, not even this much, and there
was more to discover.

Dominique got out of a farm truck and came towards her.
She ran into his arms and he was pleased, though, she could tell,
surprised. The logo on the door of the truck said "Hallouran
Family Farms."

"Farms? With an 's'?"

"Mollie's place too." Dominique was looking straight ahead,
driving.

"Did you actually marry Emma?"

"Yep."

"Where is she now?" said Vicky. "Or do you know?"

"Oh yeah. I know. She lives in Calgary. She did some stuff for a

TV station there for a while. She got married again. I think she sells real estate."

"Oh." They never talked about his life, her life. A postcard. A phone call. One of Dominique's letters. The love between them didn't require talk. "But you have the kid? So you must have a place?"

"Poppalushka's."

The house was now very different—no longer the crumbling, half-derelict town mansion of before, but neat and tidy, painted, the tiny lawn in front mowed. There were two boys on the porch, one about fourteen. The older one was Robbie and Sonya's; she didn't even have to ask. He looked like both of them. The fourteen-year-old was Dominique's boy, blond, bright-looking. He was not really Dominique's boy, of course.

"Harry. Tony. This is Vicky. Your aunt."

"Tony's aunt," said the older boy. "My mother is always looking for your picture," he went on, half shy. "In the magazines."

"I'm an actress, now," said Vicky. "I came back to Canada to be an actress."

"My mother used to be on TV," said Tony, boasting.

"Did you get some parts?" inquired Dominique, heaving her suitcase up the steps of the porch.

"I did. The film industry's small. But I think I'm getting somewhere."

The boys were looking at her in awe and Vicky saw that she was a legend to them, someone in magazines and on TV, someone their elders told them had got out of Steamboat—off the Reserve, for God's sake!—and become a supermodel.

Over lunch they talked and told stories. About the old days, when Dominique had worked for Poppa as a spray pilot, about the summer they had had the house and how they had given a garden party, and how all the Ukrainians had begun singing.

Vicky had begun to feel happier and happier. Dominique was well, he was fine; he had grown up and turned out okay. It had disturbed her at first to see that he had chosen to become a Hallouran, that he lived in Steamboat. But he was himself again, the real Dominique, not the wreck of a man, convalescing and drinking himself to death on the sofa in Eliza's kitchen, and not the half-healed ghost she had seen once or twice that last summer with Tim, the one Mollie Hallouran was screwing.

It was a relief, a joy to see that Dominique had achieved this security, this happiness. He even had someone to love. The boy, Tony, whom as she had instantly perceived, the house, the whole establishment in Steamboat was really all about. And the other boy, who plainly regarded him as a hero.

The three of them piled in the truck and went over to the farm after lunch, going to work. It was seeding time. "Coming?"

"No," said Vicky.

Dominique regarded her for a moment, unsmiling. But the Hallourans were none of hers. The only one of them she really even knew was Emma.

Vicky took a taxi to visit her mother on the Reserve. Eliza's house, too, was neater, painted, refurbished. The whole Reserve seemed neater. It now had a high school of its own. And the big Band hall complex, which had been built when Vicky was a girl, was crumbling to decay in the centre.

Eliza was beginning to get old. She was smaller, bent and wrinkled, the interminable cigarette stuck in her mouth, except when she was coughing. She was expecting Vicky, who had both written and called. But she refused to accept any money.

Although the place was Spartan, empty as ever of furnishings and decoration, it was not completely barren. It was not the way it had been when Eliza was drinking. There was a certain amount of food in the cupboard, milk in the fridge for tea. Eliza's clothes, knit pants, a blouse, a sweater, looked warm enough, looked good. Probably Dominique was taking care of her; the money was coming from him.

Eliza surprised Vicky by taking some pride in her achievements. She had a collection of magazines. "Sonya brought 'em over. We used to look at 'em together."

"I'm trying to get a new career, Ma. I did some things for TV."

"Like that whore that married your brother?"

Vicky began making tea while Eliza lay on the sofa, coughing.

"Dominique lives in that house with his boy now." His boy, she said, although she obviously knew that Tony wasn't really his. "Want to stay with me?"

"I don't know. I'll see what Dominique wants."

Vicky had already glimpsed her old room through its open door. One could see into every room from the hall of this flimsy plywood house. Her room was the way it always had been. The pathetic girlish furniture Dominique had given her.

Could she ask about Tim? Eliza probably wouldn't know, anyway.

Dominique picked her up without comment and took her back to Poppalushka's for supper.

"She wants me to stay with her."

"Want to?"

"I don't know."

After supper, he went back to work. They were seeding. The days were long and they would work late, with the lights on the machines these days. The boys came and went with Dominique. The older one was driving the truck; he would probably be a farmer. He was Robbie Hallouran's boy, after all.

The younger one was a natural entertainer, an actor. Fun to be with in another setting; in this one he seemed forced, almost feverish, against the stolidity, the embarrassment of the other two. She thought he was probably gay, although none of them seemed aware of it.

Dominique came home sometime during the night, she knew, because he was there in the kitchen when she got up. They ate toast in silence.

The phone rang. It was Donovan, getting impatient in his hotel room in Calgary.

"Well, maybe you should go to Banff for the weekend." She already knew that she would never bring him here.

"Was that your boyfriend?" asked Tony excitedly.

Dominique was silently frying Tony an egg. His affection for the boy touched her. There was true love for him after all.

Was it the only love he had now? But then why had he stayed out nearly all night?

"Maybe I'll go stay with Ma, Dominique."

[248]

"Well, okay." He didn't want her to go.

"You could come see her. You could bring Tony." She remembered how Eliza had called Tony 'his boy'.

She still loved him more than anyone else here—more than anyone who was here now. And he loved her too, not her myth, but her real self—the Vicky who had been his little sister.

"How long are you planning to stay?"

"Oh, I don't know. Maybe all summer if you and Ma can put up with me."

"You'd better tell that guy to go see Jasper too."

Vicky laughed.

Dominique drove her out to the Reserve. "Joshua died of lung cancer."

"Joshua. I might have run away from home. But for him."

"Jesus, Vicky. Where was I?"

"It's okay, Dominique. You were my mother and father all those years. You know that," she said, her voice breaking.

Dominique put his hand over hers on the seat of the farm truck. "I was a drunk."

"There were reasons for that. And you pulled it back together. You've got it all together now, haven't you?"

"The drinking? Oh yeah. I haven't had a drink since—" He didn't finish the sentence, as she knew, because he would have had to mention Mollie. And Mollie was off-limits between them.

It was wrong to make anything off limits and she realized that this, more than anything else, was why she had wanted to come back—to break through those barriers. But she found that many of them were still up; the people themselves wanted them. Maybe even she wanted them. And then there was the Reserve, too. Just going there the other day had nearly choked her.

"The person who really got me through those years was Tim." She was trying to break one of those taboos. "Where is he now, Dominique? Do you know?"

She turned her head. Dominique had said nothing, and she was surprised to see that he was glancing at her, not staring straight ahead. "You don't?" he asked.

"No."

He gave an incredulous laugh. "I thought you must've seen him the other day. Didn't Ma tell you he's the Chief?"

"He is? But—he's almost a whiteman. I mean—"

"It's all different now, Vicky, the kind of guy who gets to be Chief."

He meant, she supposed, that the men who became chiefs nowadays could use computers and fax machines and write their own letters. But still, it seemed impossible. Tim with his backwards and upside-down view of the world. The dope-smoking artist-dreamer. Those long conversations he had had with his father about art and politics. She could still remember all of that. It had changed her whole world.

"He came to see me one time. Asked me to run for Band Council. That was—oh—ten years ago. He wasn't the Chief then. Told him I'm a half-breed."

"That's not even a word any longer, is it? So how long—? He's been the Chief for ten years?" They had pulled into Eliza's yard by now and were just sitting in the truck.

"I guess you'll see him." He didn't smile and neither did she.

She found that just sitting with Eliza, drinking tea, suffocated her. She went out into the landscape and walked around. It was an early summer night, with Venus low on the horizon. She went down the road to the slope where they had let the rabbit go.

She was remembering the last scene between them when Tim had pushed her, slapped her. He had actually driven her out of his life. She remembered him yelling—that, in itself, so untypical of Tim, "I can't stand it! I can't paint! I can't even think! Take your career out of my face!"

"I thought I'd find you here again sometime."

She turned around in shock. She had been staring up the hill for—how long? It seemed almost as though she had raised a ghost.

If so, it was a middle-aged ghost she had raised, a man in his mid-forties, no longer so slim, lacking the starvation of drugs and the leanness of youth, but still with the same long-nosed, fine-lipped, clever face, the same smile, even the braids.

"Tim!" But she did not rush to embrace him. The slap and the push were still there.

They stared at one another.

He must have known that she was here, Vicky thought, pulling herself together. He would have heard. There were no secrets on the Reserve. Everyone would have known she had visited Eliza the other day.

"Do you think the rabbit lived?" she asked.

"Maybe. Maybe not. Either way, it was better off—out of the cage. Don't you think? There's nothing to be afraid of," he went on. "I haven't done any painting in years."

She was not the only one who remembered the last scene between them.

"Dominique told me you're the Chief here. I didn't know."

His lips twisted into a wry smile. "Yeah. I'm the Chief that let them build the Ochre River dam."

"I never dreamed that—I mean, I didn't expect that you'd be here at all."

"Valerie didn't tell you?"

"We lost touch. I've been meaning to see her, though. Now that I've come back."

"You've come back?"

"I mean—I came back to visit." She felt they were still struggling to communicate.

"I'm sorry," she said. "So much has happened. Did you get married, Tim?"

"No."

"Me neither." She smiled.

"As a matter of fact, I already knew that. Let's go uphill, shall we? I don't really know what's up here."

He reached out to take her hand. It was Tim, she had to remind herself, even though he did not seem the same. The timidity and aggressiveness on his side of the conversation dismayed her. He seemed to be expecting her to snub him.

They reached the top of the hill and stared out over a horizon of other hills rising beyond it, into the foothills of the mountains. The sky had changed from grass green to turquoise to sapphire, and other stars twinkled dimly above Venus.

"Have you ever bought *Vogue* magazine in a tax-free tobacco store on an Indian Reserve?" he asked abruptly.

Vicky began to laugh. "Did you?"

He had let go of her hand briefly while they were scrambling up to the top. Now he put his arms around her and they began to kiss. But this too was different, the kiss of an older man and an experienced woman. In the past they had not kissed much; they had had an intimacy much more extreme than kissing. They came apart spontaneously.

"Let's just sit down and talk first," she suggested.

"First?" He gave an astonished laugh.

They sat down on the rough, stony ground in the thin harsh grass, gazing westward into the last of the sunlight. It was getting late, well after 10:00.

"Why did you come back?" he asked.

"To see Dominique. And Ma. But it was really for me that I came back."

"For you, eh?"

"Yes. To find out—something about me. I'm not sure what."

He was silent, staring into the lucid emptiness above the next hill.

"I'm an actress, Tim. I tried to make it in the U.S. first. But I realized that if it was going to mean anything I had to do it here. I've been in Toronto over a year now."

"Toronto's just about as far away as California—from this," he said, gesturing at the empty landscape.

"Well, but I'm not sure if this has anything to do with it."

"How could it not have something to do with it?"

They sat in silence and she had the impression again that this was a conversation with which they both were wrestling.

"Well, I guess I'm not part of that equation any longer," he said after a moment. "This damn place has been my life for fifteen years. The thing you run hardest to get away from is what you're really heading for. Know that, Vick?"

"I suppose so." She laughed.

"It's been fifteen years I've regretted that slap," he said suddenly.

"Well—it started me running," she said.

"Yeah? Well, it pretty well finished me off. I thought I was kind of far gone to be slapping models around."

In a way he was trying to apologize, but he was getting the facts wrong. She had not just been a model to him. His defensiveness startled and dismayed her. He had lit a cigarette and sat there, hunched, in profile, smoking it.

"Tell me about yourself," she suggested. "How did you get to be Chief?"

"Oh yeah, well—" He flicked the long ash off his cigarette, looking away. "I moved onto the Reserve. I stayed with Eliza, believe it or not. I guess she didn't tell you. I was a paying guest only, however, not like Mollie Hallouran and your brother," he added and she felt he wanted to make this sting as much as possible.

"And then—?"

"And then?" He made a wide gesture with his left hand, which she now saw had a cheap silver and turquoise ring on the fourth finger. "I ran for Band Council. Got elected. Ran for Chief. Since then, it's been one long meeting with the whiteman."

"Your adopted father must be happy."

"Oh yeah. But, you know, we don't look at things the same way. The dam. He always saw that as a matter of negotiation—for compensation." He put out the cigarette and slumped upon the ground. "Well, they're getting old, you know, him and Valerie." He sat up straight suddenly. "They always have a shindig at this time of year. Want to go?"

He grinned, glancing at her. Vicky laughed.

"Jesus, what will Valerie say?" He mimicked her with popping eyes, the elegant swooping gestures of her hands—and again Vicky noticed that cheap ring.

A moment later he had placed a heavy hand on her arm and she realized that the memory of that party excited him in some secret place, just as it did her.

"I don't think I'm ready for this, Tim." He was going to kiss her again and she remembered his tobacco-smelling breath, the heaviness of his middle-aged body.

She stood up. "Let's go back now. I need time—time to digest all this, I guess."

"Whatever you want." You won't digest me, said his voice.

He stood up and extended his hand to help her to her feet. They stood for a moment, face to face, looking at one another, not smiling. Vicky felt a deep tremor pass through her. Whatever was going to happen now would happen.

In silence still, they began to scramble down the slope. The moon was full up now, casting long shadows over the ground, grass and stone shadows. They parted without a kiss, without even a touch, in the darkness in front of Eliza's, the moonless side of the house.

"Till tomorrow then," he said. "I'll come get you."

She was silent, thinking of the unspoken assumption that was between them. He reconfirmed this by saying abruptly: "Maybe you're right. We'd better start slow. I've got some excess baggage in my life too."

It was presumptuous of him, she thought, restlessly rolling over and banging the pillow flat for the third time. Who was he anyway? Just some Chief.

Her baggage turned up the next morning in the form of a phone call from Donovan. "Look, am I unpresentable or something? I'm a well-known Canadian filmmaker, for Christ's sake! Maybe your mother would even like to meet me."

She could not tell him that she had not even mentioned him to Eliza.

"And here's another thing. I talked to your brother last night. He gave me the number. But when I called she wouldn't tell me where you were. She even hung up on me. Where were you?"

Eliza knew where she was, Vicky reflected, and she had obviously made the wrong assumption about that. But Eliza wouldn't have told Donovan anything anyway. The silence of the Reserve was not really silence; it was the sound of a thousand voices—the ghost voices of women—crying.

"Look, I don't care, Vicky, whoever it was. But you're hanging me up here. I've got better things to do, while you're—well, whatever you're doing."

"Look, Donovan, I told you, I can't—"

"Well, never mind. I'll wait." His voice had softened.

"That's good. But—"

"I'll wait, I said. Bye, darling." He even sounded good-humoured all of a sudden.

Vicky put on a long white muslin dress for the party. She knew Tim wanted to put on a show, but they were going to do that just by being there.

Tim arrived in a pickup truck, clad in a bearskin and a loin cloth. Vicky thought of their Band Chief at that garden party so long ago, in a suit.

"Not bad, Vick," he remarked. "It even reminds me of the curtain."

She laughed.

"You came back at a bad time," he went on, lighting a cigarette as he began to drive off. "I'm trying to quit smoking."

"Dominique told me you'd given up smoking dope."

"Oh, you asked about it, did you?" Once again she was insulting him, she wasn't sure exactly how. Perhaps he didn't think she was taking him seriously enough.

"I just wanted to know how you are."

"Well, he wouldn't really know. He's pretty out of it. Apolitical. Like a whiteman. They're all apolitical. Hey, Vick, listen to this!"

He was fumbling with the cassette deck. Then he began to play her a speech he had made. There was a lot of stuff in it she had never heard before about the Ochre River dam, which had been built, but never opened because of the environmental movement, the fight that was continuing in the courts. It had become a very complicated question; it wasn't problematic just because the Indians owned the River.

However, this was what the speech said was problematic. Aboriginal rights versus the Ochre River dam. According to the speech, it was Tim versus everybody.

Finally he snapped it off, although it was not over. They were coming into the outskirts of Calgary. "What do you think?"

"I think I'm pretty out of it," she said, laughing. "It was a good speech, though. Wonderful. Where did you make that?" Surely not on the Reserve, she was thinking.

"In Brussels." He shrugged. "I was invited by the European Parliament. I just played it so you'd get into your role, really."

He was looking at her critically, the old Tim, inspecting her to make sure she was a finished creation of his. "Ready to Mau Mau?" They were rolling along beside the river towards the expensive street where his father lived.

"Vicky! Oh my God! Oh my God! Vicky!" Valerie's piercing shriek could be heard all over the garden. Heads turned, faces craned forward.

Tim still had her by the arm and Valerie was embracing both of them: soap-and-shampoo-scented Vicky, and the smelly bearskin in one huge hug. Valerie didn't mind however. Laughing and crying she kissed them both.

"By God, I think I've seen this before," remarked the big white-man, coming over and removing a cigar from his mouth. He gave the heaving hug that was Valerie, Vicky and Medicine Bear a few pats with his freckled old hand.

"Oh Vicky! Vicky!" Valerie was hanging on Vicky's arm now, simultaneously making quick deft adjustments to her clothes, her hair, patting her cheeks dry.

"So you decided to come after all?" The old man spoke dryly to Tim.

"Had to bring Vick."

"Well, I'll never forget—" He was nodding, smiling at Vicky, his eyes examining her curiously at the same time. "But you aren't the same girl—woman—are you? You're famous now."

"Famous? Darling, that doesn't say it!" cried Valerie. "And I always think—Well, when I think that it started here at this very garden party, it makes me cry!" She was still crying. Crying and patting her cheeks dry. Vicky also had tears in her eyes.

"Yeah, well, but it didn't start here, you know, Valerie. It started over on the Reserve." Tim spoke evenly.

Valerie looked up, obedient, instantly contrite. "When you— oh, I know, you discovered her really, darling, but—"

"No. I mean, when she was born."

So he was still inside there somewhere, the magician, inside this brown middle-aged, unsmiling man.

"Oh, darling, there's someone here you must meet! You absolutely must! He's very famous here in Canada! Naturally, that's not—! Actually he made a name for himself working with Native—!" She was trying to lead, or rather, propel, the cumbrous cluster formed by Tim, Vicky and her own husband, further into the garden.

At the next instant, Vicky found herself face to face with Donovan. He was staring at her, already white with fury. He had a furious temper, an Irish temper. The blue veins were standing out on his temples, his nostrils were expanded.

"Donovan! You simply must meet Vicky Boucher! Vicky, Donovan is so well-known in Canada—! And oh! Donovan, it was right here in this garden that—!"

"How do you do?" said Donovan between his teeth. "It's so lucky I decided to come to this party, isn't it? We might not have met."

Vicky, who had seen him make scenes before, although never with her as their focus, shrank back, and was surprised to find bearskin beside her and around her.

"Who is your escort?" he went on.

"Oh, darling!" cried Valerie, bewildered, still not in the picture. "This is Chief Medicine Bear. But of course we don't call him that, because he's my—he's our—"

"Well, I'm pleased to meet you too," said Donovan. "Valerie, your party is so—"

"So much fun, darling!"

"Enlightening," he continued.

"You know this guy?" Tim said to Vicky. He was—incredibly—grinning.

"Yes, I came to Alberta with him. I told you to go to Banff," she said to Donovan.

"Oh, you know each other—!" Valerie was prepared to be excited about that too, although obviously it was a disappointment to her.

Donovan had picked up a potted begonia from a little table nearby. Gritting his teeth, and still staring straight at Vicky, he threw it down upon the patio stones at his feet, where it shattered, exploding earth and leaves all over the gowns and trouser legs of the people standing nearby. A hush fell upon the party.

"Go for it," remarked Tim. "Break the place up. Valerie'll love you for it!"

"Yes, well, I did want to meet you. That's why I came, really." Donovan's nostrils were white. "But now—I could break your sweet little neck, Vicky," he went on.

"Maybe you're one of those whitemen who likes hitting women, are you?"

"For heaven's sake, Tim! Donovan—!"

"Please, darling," said Valerie, interposing herself between Donovan and Tim, taking the lapels of the whiteman's tuxedo coaxingly in her long white fingers.

"I'm going, Valerie," he said abruptly. "Sorry about the plant. I'll buy another one. I'll buy you two. Sorry about the party."

"No, we're going, Valerie," said Tim.

She swung around. "Oh no! Must you?"

"Well, I didn't plan to stay long anyway. Don't worry," he added. "You'll see Vick again." Tim had turned the enormous bulk of the bearskin plus Vicky around 180 degrees by this time and he spoke to Valerie over his shoulder. Then they were out of the garden, walking rapidly down the street to the parked truck.

They took off in a hurry, with some jerks as Tim squealed his tires, got into the wrong gear, stalled, got into the right one. He was not as cool as he wanted to seem.

"Boy! We got out of there fast." He sighed, then glanced over his shoulder as he pulled out into traffic. "Is that the man, Vick?"

"Not really," she said. She felt cold now—from shock, probably.

"Not really. Well, I'm glad to hear that. I guess he thinks he is, though."

"I guess he does." She had had a glimpse of Donovan through Valerie's eyes. He hadn't followed her to Alberta just to hang around.

"You didn't set me up for that?" Tim glanced at her.

"Of course not!"

"Okay. I guess not. I wanted to meet the guy anyway. That was

before you showed up. I didn't know you were going to show up."
He smiled at her and—suddenly lighthearted—she smiled back.

"Of course there had to be a man in the piece," he remarked.

He swung the wheel and they were suddenly in under the arcade of a fancy downtown hotel. "Sure hope whatsisname isn't staying here."

She shook her head, smiling. Donovan would not have the money for a room in a place like this, although apparently Tim did.

The doorman let her out and Tim came around the truck to take her arm.

"Any luggage, sir?"

"Nope."

There was a hush all around them as deep as the hush in Valerie's garden after Donovan broke the plant. Vicky felt as though she were in a play. Maybe it was for this even more than for the garden party that he had worn the bearskin.

He shed his heavy garment on the bed and in moccasins and a loincloth went to the mini bar. But he only took out a pop and pulled the tab, then offered it to her. Vicky had sat down on a straight chair. She shook her head.

"You okay?"

She nodded.

"Speak."

"I see that you are the same, Tim. I see that now. The perform-ance artist."

He shrugged.

"Don't you remember? You told me once that performance is all there is to art. The further it gets away from that the closer it is to being a perfume ad."

"Oh yeah. But that's what you decided to do anyway, Vick."

"Well, but ten years or so of being a perfume ad was enough. I came back to Canada because I wanted to do something that was more—more—"

"Real? Meaningful? Worthwhile?"

"More personal. I met Donovan about six months ago. He's a man who has something to say. He was interested in me too."

[259]

"I noticed."

"Then, this spring—I wanted to get back here. To see where I came from."

"Collecting material for your career?"

She shook her head. "I wouldn't mind just being an actress. Getting some small parts. It doesn't have to be about this. I just wanted to do this trip for me."

"He decided to come, huh?"

"Yes. I thought it was okay. But when we got close—I couldn't even take him to Steamboat. And not to the Reserve!"

"Maybe he'd have been collecting material."

"It would have interfered with my seeing it. It wouldn't have been Vicky seeing it, somehow, but all him. He's got—he's kind of powerful. The way you were."

"The way I was, eh?"

She laughed. "All right. The way you still are, Tim. Last night, I wasn't sure I knew you any longer. Today—"

"Today?" He came over and drew her to her feet. They began to kiss, cool kisses, exploratory, looking deep into each other's eyes.

"So, you weren't looking for me at all?" They were on the bed now.

"No." She gasped. "Yes. I was. I've been looking for you everywhere, Tim. For years."

She was till searching for him, bewildered. The Tim she knew must be there somewhere.

Her dress was becoming crumpled and smeared with some kind of body paint, ochre, that he had all over his upper arms, his chest. He was moving in on her too fast.

"What's this?" Her fingers had found a massive scar on his back. She had not seen it because of the bearskin, the body paint.

"Oh—I got shot about ten years ago. Some woman shot me."

"Just some woman, Tim?" She laughed. It was a terrible scar.

"Look, I'll tell you about that—some other time."

But she had had time to grasp now that he did this—he took women to hotel rooms. In Calgary. In Brussels. Women he could get by snapping his fingers.

"Not here!" she said. "Let's not do this here!"

"Why not? It's a bed."

She sat up, smoothing her dress. "You're treating me like an object. A trophy! As though you'd gotten me away from another man."

"Well, I did. And who made you an object but yourself? I didn't put you on a magazine cover. I never would have done that!"

"I have to want you."

"You do want me." He folded his arms.

"Yes, but I want the one that's inside. The real one. Not the Tim that stages shows. The one that feels pain."

"I'm here," he said. "How can you doubt that? Jesus, Vicky, I felt pain after you left. After I hit you. I pushed you down. Don't you think I regretted it? Talk about pain!"

She began to cry, staring at him. Surely it shouldn't have had to turn out this way. That they should meet as strangers in a hotel room.

"Oh, for Christ's sake! Let's go back to the Reserve!"

"I'm sorry, Tim. I feel like a tease."

"Yeah, but you aren't one, are you? You just don't like fancy hotel rooms with king-sized beds in them. You'd rather have it off with me on a mattress on the floor—in a dirty broken-down old government rental on the Reserve!"

"I would!" She stopped crying and began to laugh.

TIM'S HOUSE TURNED OUT TO BE FAR CRY FROM HIS description. It was a much newer model than Eliza's. It looked like an ordinary suburban middle-class home; it also looked as though he hardly lived there at all.

They had gotten back late. They had gone to his office and she had gone in with him while he collected a pile of reading matter that now littered the bedroom floor. It had been Saturday evening, so no one else was there, but she noticed that he even had a secretary. The office was panelled with teak.

Then they drove over to the house and went in by the front door. Tim shed his skin robe on the sofa, sighing. Vicky had stopped, arrested by the sight of the unfinished picture of Victoria of the Plains over the false mantel.

"Good, isn't it?" he said, pausing beside her to look.

The fact that it wasn't finished made it better, in a way. It reminded her of the photograph which had been the beginning of her career.

"There's a drawing in the Art Gallery of Alberta," he said. "One of the ones of you in the River. No one knows who did it. It's signed Tim Steen. I don't use that any more."

They were standing side by side and she noticed that in high heels they were nearly the same height. He had always seemed bigger than he really was. And now he was filled with a kind of cynical power that made her almost afraid of him.

He turned to embrace her, determined, this time, business-like, almost brisk, and then it was like going to bed with any man for the first time, a kind of transaction that had its own rules, its own power play. When it was over and he lay smoking beside her, she was feeling a pang of disappointment. What did he mean to her anyway? Whatever it was, it was not captured in the grossness and simplicity of the physical act they had just performed, which was like all the other times she had done this with men, not worse, but no more sublime.

He turned to put the cigarette out in the empty package that lay there on the floor beside the mattress, then rolled over, suddenly, urgently, and began to touch her. It was a sensation she well remembered. It didn't have much to do with pleasure of the physical kind. She had stood for hours while he painted her, and if there was pleasure in that, it was his, not hers.

He had never been grateful for anything, she remembered. He had seemed unaware that he was taking. The idea of giving and taking had been entirely hers, not his: she the giver, he the taker. What made her understand that the dynamic between them was different now was that he had tears in his eyes.

"I never thought I'd get a chance to tell you," he said. "Back then. It was a mistake I made. I thought I was the artist."

"You were."

"Whatever I had there, Vick. I was gettimg it from you."

"But Tim, what you told me, what I learned from you, I'll never forget it. Remember God's art? Remember the Spirit of the Ochre?"

She rolled over, interrupting the nervous stroking of his fingers. "You saved my life."

"I know. But, God!—Did we ever talk? I'd forgotten."

She was embracing him and the tears were in her eyes now. "I'll always love you. The only reason I never said it was because I wasn't allowed to."

"So—let's try this deal again," he said. "I'm out of not allowing you to do things."

TIM LEFT RATHER EARLY IN THE MORNING WITH THE REMARK that he had to see someone. The fact that it was Sunday struck Vicky when she finally got up. She looked over at the Band Hall, but did not see his truck. The things he had to do were obviously somewhere else.

She then looked through the kitchen cupboards and found some tea, part of a loaf of bread. Butter in the refrigerator. That was about all that was in there, though. A container half full of milk. Presently she was eating a piece of toast, something she never ate normally. Toast with butter on it.

That was nice, but a moment later, the phone rang and she found herself having a conversation with Donovan. How had he got the number?

"Why the hell couldn't you at least have told me?"

"Told you what? I didn't know that I was going to Valerie's party till I met him. That was last night. No, the night before. I didn't know he was here, Donovan."

"How come I did and you didn't? And why wouldn't you take me there?"

"I just—I couldn't."

"See what I mean? You're not telling me anything."

"I'm sorry, Donovan. I didn't plan this. You have to take my word for that."

"And what is *this*? What is it? Tell me that!"

"Okay. I'm not sure. I slept with him. But I think you already know that. So now—I'll see what happens, I guess."

"Well, thanks for telling me. But what a waste!"

"It's not a waste."

"Yes it is. A waste of my time, totally, of course. We were going to do things together, remember?"

It was true that they had intended to do something. Now they never would. The future she was in now was completely discontinuous with that future. Thinking this she asked:

"Why did you want to meet Tim anyway? You said you wanted to meet him."

"Who's Tim?"

"Medicine Bear."

"Tim, eh?"

"Where are you staying?"

"With Valerie. But I won't be here much longer."

She got away from him then. One of them had hung up. She sat looking at the phone for a little while, wondering at herself. For this was not like her at all. She was decent, she was kind; and she felt that she had hurt him.

Vicky then looked vaguely around the house and noticing for the first time how dirty it was, decided that she would have to get it cleaned. She was efficient about things like this. She had hired housekeepers in many different parts of the world, as well as plumbers, chauffeurs, accountants. And once, in Thailand, some kind of snake charmer, to take care of the cobras in the bathroom.

It was not comfortable to sit there in the messy, empty kitchen, so she put on some clothes, her jeans, a sweater, and walked over to see her mother.

Sunday afternoon at home with Eliza. Ironic silence. No, "Where were you last night?" from her mother. She got up to return home. As she was now thinking of it.

Eliza stood up too. She stood beside the table, little and wizened, and it looked as though her eyes were closed—maybe it was just because of the wrinkles on her eyelids, though. "Just go back," she said suddenly. "Go back where you came from."

"It's okay, Ma."

"You're a famous model. Don't mess around with Medicine Bear. That guy poison. He like poison to you!"

Vicky went back into the house with a certain grim purpose. But it was evident—she did not have to look farther than the empty front room, the lack of all comfort—that there was no woman living here. Whatever her mother had meant, it wasn't that.

But it had not escaped her attention that sometime between yesterday and today the cheap silver and turquoise ring had gone from the fourth finger of his left hand. It was almost inconceivable that there was no one at all.

❡ SOMEHOW IT HAD BECOME LATE IN THE DAY, AND VICKY WAS doing yoga in the dimness of the front room.

"What the hell do you think you're doing in a place like this?" Donovan had come through the front door. Outside, Vicky now heard the hole-in-the-muffler-sound of Tim's truck driving off.

She was, just for a moment, terrified. But it was an irrational thought. Donovan was not going to attack her.

He looked around the room, nostrils expanded still, but his breathing was beginning to even out, the pulsating veins sinking back into the white skin of his temples.

"All right," he said. "We've only got a moment. He had the decency to let me have it. I love you, don't you know that? I've got to have you back!"

"Back?" she said.

"Well, it was like that, wasn't it? Before we came here. Before this came up. We were moving towards—towards—"

"We weren't living together."

"We weren't. I give you that. I give you everything! There was no commitment. That's why I'm here. To tell you—tell you—! Vicky, I'm in love with you! Don't you understand?"

The tears had sprung to her eyes. But only because she was sorry.

"I came out here only to—And then I find you in a hole like this! Oh, this is ridiculous! I should just pick you up and leave. We can sort all this out on the way to the airport. See yourself, Vicky! You can't stay here!"

Tim now entered the room, coming in by the back door. He was wearing the clothes he had put on that morning: clean jeans, clean shirt, headband—he had even brushed his boots—and she now understood why he had taken such care over what he was wearing. He had gone to Calgary, to make amends to Valerie.

But she realized that there was a plan behind it too. She glanced at his face. He liked the way this was working out, it was clear. He was smiling.

The anger she felt was on Donovan's behalf. He shouldn't have been tricked into this. Unsatisfactory as it was, their phone call should have been enough.

"Why did you bring him here?" she demanded.

"I wanted to show him something, Vicky."

The other two watched him now, open-mouthed, as he took a video from the pocket of a parka hanging in the front porch. "Sit," he said, sliding it into the machine.

Vicky sat down and after a moment, Donovan sat down as well.

It was—she should have been expecting this—the Spirit of the Ochre. The uncut version before Murray had spliced and edited it and turned it into a TV clip. The sound was only the flicking of the finger drum on the guitar, relentless, simple.

Did he play this over to himself, over and over, reliving that time? It made her relive it. Watching the girl on the screen, Vicky was inside her once again—the excitement in that ecstatic body, the joy expressed by the toe pointed into cold water.

Tim leaned against the wall, folding his arms. She saw the tenderness with which he was watching her in the set of his thin lips. He was watching Donovan too.

Without consulting them, but undoubtedly in response to their transfixed faces, Tim rewound the tape and played it again.

"Okay," he said at last. "You saw it."

"That was you, wasn't it?" said Donovan to Vicky.

"You'd better believe it!" said Tim. "That was the face that burned a thousand boats, my friend. And it was already a hot summer. They started building the dam that year."

"It became a TV clip. For the Lovers of Ochre River," Vicky explained.

"You made it with him?"

"Political art," said Tim. "But we did it—for love."

Donovan got up and walked around the room, frowning. He paused in front of the mantelpiece and stared into the serious face of the picture, the young girl and her black-eyed Susans.

"Who are you?" he said, turning to Tim. "They said you were the Chief here. I went to that damn party—"

"I am the Chief here."

"But you seem to be some kind of an artist."

Tim shook his head. "I've given up all that visual shit."

"Visual shit?" Donovan's voice was full of sarcasm.

"Look, I need somebody to make a film."

"Well, I don't hire out my services. Not any more. I don't have to."

"I'm not buying you. If you're not interested, that's fine with me. But it just occurred to me—with the actress I've got here—"

"What? Tim, what is this all about? Why didn't you tell me—? Did you plan this?"

Staring into their two hostile faces, Tim began to laugh.

"Jesus, Vick, how can you ask? You turning up—was that because of anything I did? And this guy. I already wanted to get him in here somehow. But as for plan—you might as well say Valerie planned it. Or you did."

Donovan here on the Reserve was something she could never have planned.

"In fact, it was sprung on me," he continued. "No one told me I was going to have to fight for you at a garden party. I was just doing my thing there as usual when this guy began acting like Tarzan."

"Tarzan!" To her amazement, Donovan seemed to be both amused and complimented. He laughed suddenly. "Okay. What kind of film do you want to make? The least I can do is hear about it and say no."

"I told you. I don't want to make it. I can't make it. I just want to have my input. The rest is—well, it's really up to you and her."

"But what would it be about?" Donovan turned away, frowning, but Vicky too had heard the cunning lure laid down by "you and her."

"I guess if you stick around you'll find out."

"You want me to say something for you? I don't do propaganda."

"Oh yeah. I know that. Speak for yourself. Or say it for her."

"What makes you think you would like what I had to say?"

"I've heard of you. A long time ago—remember?—you wanted to do something on us. Then you made that thing on the Lubicon—"

"I don't do documentaries any longer."

"Call it what you will. 'Beauty is truth, truth beauty.'"

"Will you get a load of this guy?" said Donovan.

"All right. I'll give you a scenario. You don't have to use it. And believe me, it just came up. A woman who's a world-class model comes back to her Reserve in Canada to visit her mother. She meets the Chief of her Band—that's me—who was someone she used to know, and hey, presto! she falls for him again. What she doesn't know, though, that he has troubles of his own. He was away, giving a speech in Brussels last spring, and ever since then—The fact is, his political enemies both inside and outside the Reserve are trying to—" He drew a finger across his throat.

"Oh, I see. You want me to help save your neck, is that right?"

Tim shrugged. "I'm not telling you what to do."

Donovan walked over to the stairs. Then he turned around and walked back the whole length of the room to the mantel, glancing at the picture with a frown.

"Ask her what she wants," said Tim.

"All right. Do you want to do a film, Vicky? On something right here—not necessarily that," he added.

Vicky was staring at Tim instead, angry, amazed. He may not have been telling Donovan what to do, but he was certainly telling her. Ordinarily, she wouldn't have let it go on happening this way, but this was Tim.

"She'll do it," said Tim. "She knows this is the place, too."

"Do you have any idea what's involved? How much money we'd have to raise?"

Tim snapped his fingers. "Money's no problem. Hundreds of thousands out there in blood money and bribes. This is the Reserve they screwed by building a dam, my friend. The whiteman will throw the money at you as long as all you're going to do is make a movie!"

Donovan had an unpleasant habit of nibbling, almost eating the ends of his fingers when he was thinking hard about something. He was doing this now.

"You don't think she's got it?" demanded Tim. "You saw the Spirit of the Ochre, man. What else is there to say?"

"I know she's got it." Donovan spoke crossly. "I already knew that!"

"Want to get started right away? I'd say you've got five weeks, maybe six, if I can put off that election."

"Six weeks! Hardly!"

"I haven't got a lot of time to go on being Chief in this place. And *après moi*—" Tim shrugged.

"I thought you said this was going to be about Vicky. Not about you."

"Yeah, but you've got nothing after I'm gone. I'm letting you in."

Donovan returned to his fingers. But Vicky could see that he was hooked. It was what had attracted him to her in the first place, that this Reserve was in the background. He had tried to talk to her before about the politics of Ochre River and she had evaded him. He knew that this was right at the centre. And he wouldn't leave if there was a chance to stay here with her.

And in a way, she was hooked too. She needed to know how this was going to turn out.

Tim had a hateful kind of genius to know how to take advantage of that.

"All right," said Donovan suddenly. "I'll do it. On one condition, Vicky."

"What?" said Tim alertly.

"I want to meet your mother."

9

1993 · My Mother Spoke to Me

TIM DIDN'T BOTHER TO GO TO HIS OFFICE DURING THE NEXT few days. Sometimes he spoke to people on the phone. They got some more groceries—bacon, eggs, bread—at the little store that now belonged to Joshua's son Eddie, and they spent most of their time sleeping and eating. She had not yet bothered to try finding a housekeeping service. Together, they cleaned the bathroom.

"Well, what do you expect?" he said. "I haven't been home for ten years."

"You must have had a girlfriend—or two?"

"Oh, yeah. Women."

They left it at that. Although there was more to it, she knew. He had not got around yet to telling her about the big scar that covered nearly half his back.

The rest of the night he spent talking to her about politics. They lay on the mattress and he described the ins and outs of the fight he was having with everyone. She couldn't figure out what it was really all about. These abstractions: the Reserve system, aboriginal rights, status and assimilation—these were characteristics of Tim's mind, not of tribal politics as she remembered it.

"You see, they've got us in the coop. And as long as there's blood money pouring in none of us chickens is going to squawk. You can have it either way, actually. Keep the Natives too poor and demoralized to have any influence on what happens or else bribe them, keep them fattened up. Either way, they're in the coop."

"Well, but at least the Reserve makes us safe. Out there, we're not anything. We're not even Indians."

"Yeah. I guess you'd know. You spent years being—something. Some kind of exotic plant, I guess."

"In Paris," she remarked, "a Native from a Canadian Reserve is on the runway right after a girl from the Sudan or Fiji."

"Paris. Yeah. I've been there," he said frowning, tapping his fingers on the mattress. He had given up smoking again, which made him nervous and irritable.

"The point is," he resumed, "that the whole place really belongs to us. That's the thing they know and it scares them. We should start with that as a premise. It's the whiteman who should be out on the Reserves."

"What are you going to do? Start a war? They'd kill us all, this time."

"Sure. There are plenty of people who want to see us dead. But you might as well say what you think. Then they hear you."

Vicky lifted up a slender leg and began to get into a yoga position. He watched, fascinated and annoyed.

"You're doing this to get thin?"

"I am thin. I'm doing this because the idea of you talking to a bunch of whitemen who want you dead is making me nervous."

"I don't know. I kind of like it. It makes the moral reality just that much clearer, you know? Who's right, who isn't."

"The fact that they want you dead makes you right?"

"There are some people right here who want me dead too. Dead or in jail."

"Why?"

He shrugged. "I talk too much. This isn't a democracy."

"You were elected, weren't you?"

"Sure. And I'm going to get unelected, like I told you. But a Chief's a Chief. I'm Medicine Bear."

"But don't you represent people? You're not saying what they think?"

"They didn't think at all till I said it. Now they're thinking it too. It kind of scares them. Will you come down out of that! It's making my neck hurt."

Vicky descended from the hoop she had constructed.

"I'm going to lie on you till you stay flat."

ON THE THIRD DAY TIM TOOK HER OVER TO THE BAND OFFICE. It was full of people, some of them with cameras. "How did you get to know each other?"

Tim was grinning. "Just go ahead. I've got work to do. Got a little behind."

The Native press was there, a reporter from the Calgary paper. Someone had called them. If it was Tim, she had not heard him doing it. But once again, he knew, and she didn't, that this was going to happen.

"So are you going to stay here now?"

"What do you see this as doing to your career?"

"Do you think of yourself as a role model?"

"I just came home to see my mother. I didn't think anyone would notice."

"Are you kidding? In Alberta, Victoria Boucher is huge news."

Even Eliza had seen pictures of her, knew she was famous. So there must be something in what they said.

"Are you going to do a film?"

"You were in Calgary with Donovan, right? C'mon. Give us the scoop."

She didn't know what to say.

"Okay, okay. This guy you're with now sure makes a lot of people mad."

"Hey, where are you going?"

She had set out on foot.

"To see my mother."

Dominique was there. Vicky saw the Hallouran farm truck in the yard and hesitated. But she went in. Eliza was not at home.

"Ma said you haven't been home for three nights."

She shook her head, smiling.

"Don't you think you're behaving like a Reserve girl in the bar in Steamboat?"

"It's Tim, Dominique. Just Tim."

"Why should that make me feel any better?"

Eliza came in with a bag of groceries. Dominique must have given her some money. She looked from one to the other of them and then began making tea.

[273]

"Don't you know he's corrupt? The money here is all in the Chief's pocket."

"I don't see how you know that. You refused to run for Band Council." She astounded herself. She would never have answered him back like this long ago.

"What am I going to tell Tony? You come in with one man and start sleeping with another one right away. That's not right; not something he needs to know."

"Where do you go at night, Dominique? When his cousin stays over?"

Dominique's eyes were wide open like a stallion's. He might slap her. But he would never slap her.

"That guy phoning here again last night. This morning too," interposed Eliza.

"What did you say?" Vicky was alarmed.

"I hang up. I got nothing to say."

Eliza had the tea ready now. She made them sit down by setting cups around the table. There was a bag of cookies too. They had been her favourite kind as a child, Vicky remembered. Now she didn't eat cookies. Except with Tim. At midnight. After the bacon and eggs.

She heard the sound of Tim's pickup outside.

She could take the initiative and just get up and leave. Now—before he came in. But it was already too late. Tim stood in the doorway. He lifted his hand to Dominique, who regarded him expressionlessly. Then he moved out of the doorway and into the room and Vicky saw, with shock, that Donovan was behind him.

She stood up in consternation.

Everything about this was wrong. Her mother, unprepared; her brother—that he was even present.

Tim was already making the introductions. "Eliza. This is Donovan. And Vicky's brother, Dominique."

"How did you get here?" Vicky demanded, still staring at Donovan.

"I took a taxi. I phoned here first," he said, looking pointedly at the wall phone.

"He didn't know where to go, so I brought him over," Tim added.

"He's been staying with Valerie. Buying her a new plant every day. Hey, Dominique! This guy threw a plant pot at a party when he saw me there with Vick!"

Dominique's eyes flickered and he looked away. He hated violence.

"Oh God. Of course! You're Dominique Boucher," said Donovan suddenly. He wasn't asking; he stated it. He sat down beside Vicky, still staring at Dominique.

"You've heard of Dominique?" asked Tim, surprised.

"You're the guy that nearly got killed, beaten up by that crew, when they were building the first phase of the dam—back in the seventies?"

"Holy Saint Valerie," said Tim complacently.

"How are you these days, Dominique?" Donovan spoke gently, sweetly. It was his Irish sweetness; he could charm the birds down off the trees. Vicky was not sure about his effect on her brother, however.

Eliza put a cup of tea in front of him. Tim had already been helping himself. Donovan looked up at Eliza and a kind of reverential light shone from his eyes.

"You're Vicky's mother? God! I'm happy—I'm so happy to be here!"

"Yeah. I guess this brings it all together for you, doesn't it? It's all here," said Tim.

Donovan looked up sharply. He said, "Just remember, I'm not committed to any project of yours. I've just always wanted to meet these people. Vicky's family."

Dominique was finishing up his tea. Eliza looked at him and there was a flicker of emotion in her eyes. She didn't want Dominique to leave. He stood up.

"Please don't go," said Donovan in a low voice. He seemed to think that dealing with Dominique was like taming an animal.

Dominique sighed and Vicky suddenly saw Robbie Hallouran in him. "Come to Poppalushka's whenever you want, Vicky," he said. "Tony's always home."

"But he's going to school. And you're working," she reminded him.

"Yeah, that's why I have to go now. The seeder's broke again."

"Poppalushka's?" Donovan was looking at Vicky, bewildered.

"It's his house in Steamboat." Tim shrugged. "Why it's called that? It's a long story. But hey! Here's an idea. Why don't you stay with Dominique? He's got a ton of room. And it's not too far away from here."

Vicky was staring at Tim, aghast. But Dominique had paused. He too was staring at Tim, with a hard dislike in his eyes. Then for the first time, he looked at Donovan.

"It would be great if I could," Donovan murmured. "One of those trips by taxi is enough to break the bank."

"Sure," said Dominique.

"You really mean this? I could pay room and board, of course."

"But Dominique—" Vicky could see what Dominique's reasoning was. It was almost because she had jilted Donovan that he felt he had to be generous.

Donovan was drinking in the silent exchange between them, his face luminous with understanding.

"Maybe you can get over there yourself later? Tony'll be home. I've got to—" Dominique was going out the door already, his boot heels cracking on the ancient linoleum tiles.

Vicky put her hands over her face momentarily. Donovan was a clever man. He was already wondering all kinds of things, peripheral things like who Tony was, and vital, central things like why Dominique didn't live on the Reserve. Tim had him hooked like a fish. The only way she could get out of this was by leaving, herself. And she would not be able to do that.

Donovan had transferred all of his charm to Eliza now that Dominique was gone.

"Eliza here is one of the few people I'd trust in this whole place, if I were you," Tim was telling him.

Vicky thought of Eliza warning her the other day: "That guy poison. He like poison to you."

"So we'll take you over to Poppalushka's and you can—settle in." Tim wasn't as calm as he was pretending, however. Vicky saw him make one of those convulsive gestures of his, that came from a desire to smoke.

"And now—" he went on, some time later, shepherding them up the front walk at Poppalushka's. "You're kind of on your own, man. You've got a place to stay, you met the people—this is Tony, by the way. Hello, Tony. So you can wander around here and on the Reserve and find out what kind of a shit I am."

Donovan had taken his suitcase off the back of Tim's truck. He put it down on the porch, looking kindly at Tony. Now he swung around, addressing Vicky, "Where are you going?"

"Sorry, but she's coming home with me, my friend. But—oh yeah—come to the Band meeting tomorrow night. It'll be in the hall. A lot of people there. Major revelations about the mismanagement of my expense account. They're going to hold my feet to the fire. Don't miss it!"

"You okay?" he said to her a moment later in the truck. She had her arms wrapped around her upper body. "It'll be all right, you know."

"What about this Band meeting?"

"Oh yeah. That's next. Got to get through that." He frowned and again she saw his hand groping for a cigarette. Perhaps he thought the Band meeting was not going to be as easy for him to manage as Vicky and her family.

◖ TIM TOOK HER OVER TO A RESTAURANT IN ABERCROMBIE before the Band meeting. The truck had a tire problem now, as well as an exhaust problem, and they drove along, thumpity-thump all the way.

Abercrombie had a small town jewellery store on the main street, between the hotel and the Chinese restaurant. They gazed at the display in the window.

"Want a diamond, Vick?"

"Bought out of your expense account? No," she replied.

He laughed.

"I'm going to buy you a ring instead."

She had plenty of money. And although it was a conventional gesture that was hardly needed between them, she wanted to do it. The cheap silver and turquoise ring had left a slight sting—the way he had removed it without any explanation.

[277]

They purchased a gold band, wide enough to be exciting.

"Gonna buy me a bracelet too? So I'll look like the premier?"

They each had a fried steak with mashed potatoes, canned vegetables, an anaemic slice of tomato. Tim had pumpkin pie too.

"We should get the tire fixed," she pointed out.

"Oh yeah," he said. "I'll pay for that one." She had not let him buy her meal.

The Band meeting was being held in the Band hall, with the Band Council at a table in the middle, microphones in front of them all. Nearly the entire population of the Reserve was in attendance; Vicky had never seen such a meeting, not even in the old days, when the whiteman was trying to get the dam started.

Donovan had been waiting for her; he was already there, lurking beside the door when she entered.

"Did you have a good meal?" he whispered, sitting down in one of the grey metal chairs beside her in the back of the hall. "He took you to Abercrombie?"

There was some kind of espionage going on. "Where did you eat," she demanded.

"Poppalushka's. Tony was there. Dominique's still seeding, so he wasn't in. "

Vicky's heart sank. Yet she was not sure why his being here was such an invasion. She trusted and liked this man, had even begun to love him. He was a kind person, an intelligent man. He wouldn't hurt her deliberately. He was desperate, really, to know her—and he had found out now, how much there was to know.

Throughout the meeting he stirred and twisted, shifting his weight. It was an uncomfortable chair, but she felt also that he was embarrassed. He had expected something different, probably, something more political, less downright. Tim's feet were being held to the fire.

Tim hardly spoke throughout the evening except as chairman of the meeting, trying to move them through the agenda. This did not happen. They got stuck right at the beginning, on the monthly financial statement.

There were two years' worth of expense accounts—not accounted for. The credit card interest had begun to invade the whole accounting system. The Band manager announced her resignation. The whole staff resigned in protest.

"Why doesn't that guy just resign?" whispered Donovan.

"Maybe it's because you're here," she replied bitterly.

"No. Because you're here," he corrected her.

Donovan wanted to go at midnight. "Maybe Dominique'll be home by now," he whispered. "Want to come?"

She shook her head. And Donovan stayed.

The meeting was finally over at 2:00 AM. It broke up only because most of the audience and finally the councillors began to straggle home. There was no official adjournment. Tim merely looked around the table and then at the dwindling audience, shrugged, and stood up.

Vicky went out of the hall and into the darkness outside, feeling exhaustion and relief. For some reason he had wanted to put himself through this. There was so much opposition to him as Chief that it was amazing that they had not simply made a motion to depose him.

When all of this was over they would just go. She was not exactly sure where, because Tim would never be willing to share the lifestyle she had established for herself up to now. But they would go somewhere and be together. She could support them; she never had to worry about money.

In the press of people she had been parted from Donovan. Tim was still inside, he would probably be the last one out. A woman was suddenly standing in front of her, hands on her hips. Her face was contorted—Vicky thought it was grief at first, because of the tears on her cheeks, then realized it was fury. Her face was heavily handsome, her figure stocky and middle-aged. Her long black hair swung to her waist, clung messily around her shoulders and to her swollen features. She just stood there.

There was a little hush in the crowd, which parted, still streaming past them, people looking over their shoulders at slim Vicky and her four-square opponent.

Tim was pushing through the people, trying to get to the woman.

She swung around and grabbed him, his hands. She lifted up

[279]

his left hand and examined the ring closely, the gold ring that Vicky had just bought for him. Then she threw the hand away from her, making a noise like the snarl of an animal.

She turned and ran out of the lighted space in front of the doorway. Someone else was running after her, a young girl. Tim shaded his eyes, looking after them. Then he came forward and taking Vicky's arm, swept her off into the darkness.

They walked in silence. The gravel road crackled under their feet. Seeking some sort of solace, Vicky looked up at the summer sky, brilliant with stars.

"You should have told me," she said. "You set these things up. With my lover. Now with your—"

"I didn't set that up."

"But you should have talked to her! You should have told me!—It was her ring, wasn't it?" But she had to take some kind of responsibility for that, she realized.

"Oh yeah. The ring. The turquoise. You saw that, did you?" There was the ghost of a smile in his voice.

"I just wanted to give you something," she said. "It wasn't to— It had nothing to do with her. Who is she anyway? I've never seen her before."

"She's my half-sister. Marina is her name." He spoke quietly into the dark.

"Oh." It was all she could say.

"She's mad—jealous, probably," he went on. "I took her to Arizona last year. She bought the ring from the Navajos and gave it to me. I only took it off because—because I thought it might confuse things there in the beginning."

"You have a sister? But Tim, I thought all of your people—were dead?"

"So did I. She just showed up here one day—with her kids. About a year after I became the Chief. She made me take her in actually, her and the kids. They didn't have anything and some guy was after her. It was how I got shot. I told you about that."

"No, you didn't! You said a woman shot you!"

"Well—God! I can't do everything at once! She shot me because she thought I was the guy who was stalking her. I nearly died. She nearly died."

"The way you keep me informed is really amazing."

"Well, okay. There really was someone stalking her. She was lying in wait for him at home, and when I opened the door—What else do you want to know?"

The darkness had begun to fade, the eastern edge of the horizon glowed pale beyond the broken land. They were walking, hand in hand, in the wrong direction.

"Where are we going, Tim?"

"We're going to her place. She probably won't talk to me though."

"She doesn't know anything about me. Is that right?"

"Oh yeah. She knows. She hadn't been living in the house more than a week before she knew all about you."

Vicky was marvelling. So he had a family. He had hidden it from her; he wanted her to think he was exactly the same.

They began to ascend the porch steps of a house that was about the same age as Eliza's. Porch railings missing. Metal siding. The door, one of those old thin hollow doors that had been on the houses years before. Tim went in without knocking. A young girl whom Vicky could only compare to herself—the way she had been years ago—stood in the front hall. She smiled shyly.

"Jasmine. Where's Rose?" said Tim.

The girl who was Rose appeared in the doorway of the living room. Rose looked to be about seventeen, but she had a more competent expression than Jasmine. She was the one who had gone running after Marina.

"We're giving William tea," said Rose.

"This is Vicky."

"I know."

"They named the baby Tim," he went on, pointing out a small boy on the sofa, already asleep.

Marina was sitting at the table with a strange-looking old man who turned around and smiled, a big toothless smile, at Tim. She had her face averted.

"Vicky. This is my sister, Marina. Her kids. The most important people in my life." Marina merely turned her face further away. "And look, this is Rose. Where would we be without Rose?"

Rose smiled at him and put a little more tea in the old man's cup. He was sitting in a wheelchair, Vicky saw.

"William Hogan," said Tim. "He was nearly killed in that thing I was telling you about."

"Hello, William," said Vicky timidly. The whole party, including William, had apparently been at the Band meeting. It was 3:00 in the morning.

"You see—Marina had been driving William's car," he went on.

"Then she went home. Because she was scared," said Rose.

"Yeah, and he went home too. In his car, unfortunately. And that guy—"

"Lionel—" put in Marina, not turning her head back.

"He made William go into his house. And then he killed William's mum. He kept William a hostage—"

"William managed to call somebody, while he was asleep for a few minutes. While the guy—"

"Lionel—" repeated Marina, turning her head around this time.

"—while he was asleep." Rose had taken charge of the story, Vicky noticed.

"William tried to call Mom. But she was scared, and didn't answer. Then he called Tim. At his office."

"And I called the cops. But then I went home," said Tim.

"And she shot Tim," said Rose. "She didn't mean to. William got shot too," she added. "That's why he's crippled." The old guy was nodding his head and smiling.

"Marina," said Tim. "I didn't throw your ring away or anything." He dug it out of his pocket and put it on his other hand. Marina turned her head away again abruptly. But in the meantime, she had been looking at Vicky with shrewd, curious eyes.

"Okay, now you see Vicky," Tim said. "So, Rose, what are you going to do with your life? Not going to be a fashion model, right?"

"I'm going to be a lawyer," said Rose. "But—" She was gazing at Vicky with a very intense expression, like a fan, like an autograph-seeker. "My sister and I—"

[282]

"What?" Tim was crisp. He didn't like this at all.

"We've been trying to do French braiding," said Rose. "I can do it on her and she can sort of do it on me. But how do you do it on yourself?"

"Oh! Well—I could show you! It isn't very hard."

"For God's sake!" said Tim.

"Well, but the way she does her hair—!"

"Oh yeah. The way she does her hair! All right, you guys! Want me to help you put William to bed, Rose?"

"Tim—" said Rose, standing up, and then balancing on one hip. Her hair, like her sister's, was very long and thick. But Rose was merely pretty, Vicky noticed, unlike Jasmine. "We were all at the meeting," she said. "What's going to happen?"

"They're going to throw me out. And elect someone else."

"But Tim," Rose thought for a moment. "Can't we do something? I mean, about those expense accounts? Oh!" She twisted her hands together. "If only I could help. I wish I were already in Law School."

"Well, look," he said. "I don't care what's going to happen. You'll go to Law School. Now—William? Oh, Marina, you're going to do it with me, are you? Okay Rose. Stay here. Vicky! Show them your hair! I'll be back before dawn."

◀ THE FOLLOWING AFTERNOON, THEY WERE BOTH IN TIM'S office with Rose. Rose was the only person—Vicky had grasped this last night—who could make Tim do anything.

There was no office staff. Everyone had resigned at the meeting. Tim began doing the work of the social worker, as it was the day welfare was issued. Rose was sitting behind the big desk in his office, looking hopelessly at a pile—a heap covering the whole desk—of unlabelled folders, with Visa bills, Mastercard statements, cash register receipts falling out of them. There was even a shoe-box, lacking a top, which seemed to contain nothing but receipts.

"I don't even know where to begin!" But she was beginning, Vicky noticed.

"I always hire an accountant," said Vicky.

"Oh! Do you think—?" Rose raised her head. "But who would do it? In this situation, I mean—on a Reserve."

"You just pay them," Vicky pointed out.

"I'm going to call Grandpa."

"Grandpa?"

"Tim Steen. He's—you know, he's Tim's—"

"Well, that's a good idea. He's a lawyer, isn't he? He'll know an accountant."

The big whiteman arrived later that afternoon in a Cadillac, with the accountant. Tim was infuriated. But he couldn't argue with Rose. And he was too busy, anyway. The social worker's position was a full-time job.

Donovan came in the following morning. Rose and the accountant were closeted in the Chief's office with the paperwork. Tim was still dealing with welfare, using the desk of his secretary. Vicky was sitting cross-legged in a corner, practising a mantra someone had given her a few years ago in Katmandu.

Tim looked up. "So now you've got the dirt on me," he remarked.

Donovan nodded.

"You're going to tell me that the money I spent on talking to the whiteman could have gone into housing and infrastructure, better services—repairing this crummy Band hall. You were going to tell me that, right?"

"I didn't say anything, actually."

"Yeah, but that's what you were thinking. It's what a lot of people right here are thinking. Tell me about it!"

Donovan nodded, frowning.

"See, that money is given to us by the Feds, by whoever—so we'll stay in here. It's a concentration camp but the food is supposed to be good!"

"Frankly, I don't see what you're trying to persuade me of. You mishandled your expense accounts. This is a red herring."

"I'm not trying to persuade you of—!"

"And furthermore, it isn't just mismanagement. From what they're all saying, you just do whatever you want. You're a dictator!"

"Oh yeah. Well, way to go!" replied Tim. He waved his hands

above his head. The phone on his desk was ringing. The social worker position was a full-time job.

Donovan turned right around to look at Vicky. "How are you?" he said.

"I'm okay."

"I was worried about you. So was your brother."

Vicky stared at him. It was unbearable to think that Dominique had been talking to him; that he had been talking to Dominique.

Donovan said, "Well, but if we are really going to do something here, Dominique's right at the centre of that, don't you think? He's—I don't know—kind of an icon. He doesn't say much," he added.

Vicky watched out the window as he got into his little car. He must be renting that. He had some equipment with him too, a video camera, a tape recorder.

Whatever Donovan was going to do, she didn't want it to be about Dominique. It was not just she who wouldn't like that.

❧ AS THE DAYS PASSED, TIM AND VICKY REALLY BEGAN TO LIVE together. Vicky made Tim take her to the farmers' market in Abercrombie, to the health food store. The muffler was replaced on his truck. She still had not managed to hire a housekeeping service. Getting Tim to swallow the accountant was hard enough. But the house had begun to seem friendlier and cosier just because they were living in it.

Rose came over one evening and washed the kitchen floor. She was obviously very bright. The whole family in the little brown house depended upon her. She was the one who did the most for William, getting him in and out of his wheelchair, feeding him. Tim was now doing whatever she told him to do, unearthing more boxes of receipts, recalling where he had been in what month of what year.

The old man came out to the Reserve every day now too, and sat in the office. He actually seemed to be coming so that he could play with Timmy, Rose's little brother, who was also at the office every day, hanging around. He gave him things, unexpected things like milk bottles, and then told him what they were. He provided pencils and paper, and then mesmerized Timmy, who loved to draw, by drawing difficult things himself: a man riding a bicycle, a grove of poplars, complete with the underground root system, showing how they were really all one tree. These children were the closest thing to grandchildren that he had, of course.

As for Rose, the old man obviously worshipped the ground she trod on.

Roses bloomed, then re-bloomed in the hot dry ditches of the Reserve. The grasses rose, knee-high, then waist high. It was the beginning of July. For several weeks now there had been no sign of Donovan.

Somehow when she thought about it later, it seemed like a time out of time to Vicky. She had been caught, not against her will at all, in an eddy of history, living from day to day, making love, eating whatever she wanted, usually with her fingers, and walking barefoot on the dusty roads. The Reserve no longer suffocated her. She merely ignored it. Time slowed, almost stopped.

But Tim was tense. She knew that now. Despite everything he said about his job, warring within him was the desire to pick up the pieces.

She told him stories about her years away. They seemed like fairy tales to him, she realized, or at least, she could tell them that way. Possibly at one time he had seen himself in that world; he had been on the fringes of it, at art school, in university. But she had—or had she?—once owned a flat in Paris, had done shoots in Rome, in Thailand.

Welfare was with him constantly now, invading the office, usually in the form of distraught women. Men were unemployed, went to detox, or to jail. Women went on welfare. Were unmarried with children on welfare. Were old and unsupported except by welfare. All of this was administered out of the Band office.

"This is what we call Native self-government," Tim remarked disgustedly.

However, he treated these women with respect and kindness, filling out their forms for them, getting on the phone to find them things they needed: baby formula, insulin, a new lock on the back door. Then he would go home and lie in bed, sleepless, getting up after midnight to go outside and smoke the small cigars he had taken up. Vicky would go out too and sit on the porch rail, staring into the sky above the hill, which at different hours of the night, at different temperatures and atmospheric pressures, was many shades of green including chartreuse, or lemon yellow; violent orange in the dawn, or purple, blending into the dense velvety blackness of the night.

"I never knew there were so many of these women." He gestured with the cigar.

"Well, at least you're making a difference."

"No, I'm not. It just keeps coming."

"But that's why you're making a difference."

"Marina," he said. "When she got here—she was in a mess. On the run. No milk for the baby. No money. She spent the last of it on the bus ticket."

"You really made a difference to her. And the kids."

"I did. At least I did that."

She wanted him to come in with her. He had just lit another cigar.

"When I was in New York one time—" It was the first time she had ever told stories to anyone.

"Did you go to the Met? I used to want to see the Picassos in the Met."

"No, we did a shoot on Ellis Island—the place where the European immigrants were processed."

"You ever think about that, Vick? European immigrants? Hallourans."

"That was the whole point of the shoot. They had me and a girl from Wyoming, and someone else; she said she was a Dene from up North—"

"Oh yeah? Just some Native women and the Statue of Liberty? What'd they make you do? Bow down?"

"The Statue was just in the background. It was for some kind of catalogue clothing. We didn't wear much. The photographer made us put makeup on our nipples, some kind of dark-coloured greasepaint. We ate pretzels afterwards. Did you ever have one of those big hot pretzels?"

He shook his head. But he was putting out the cigar.

"Come inside."

If she could just awaken his interest, however briefly—maybe it was the nipples that had done it, or else the Picassos in the Met—he would come inside, and later he could sleep.

"They kicked me out before, you know. It was about ten years ago. The faction that wants to negotiate got me out."

"They thought they could get something better?"

"Yeah. Sometimes I think it would be great if I just didn't have to deal with the people here. Consensus—that's what happens when nobody can agree on anything."

"So what came of it?"

"Nothing." He shrugged. "There wasn't anything to negotiate. I kept telling them that. The government decided to build the dam off-Reserve so we wouldn't have anything to sell."

"You got re-elected?"

"Yeah, but they tried to get rid of me again about two years ago. There was a little trouble. Maybe you heard about that."

"Was there violence?"

"Not exactly. There were arrests. Mostly it was a bunch of young braves running around with cans of spray paint. Sometimes I think I'm running a daycare."

"I think you're trying to do something that's too hard. It would be too hard for anyone. Even for someone who was born here."

He looked at her oddly. "I was born here."

She never really thought of him as a product of this place. Because of his background, growing up in Calgary, because of his whiteman's education. But really, it was not because of that, she realized. It was because he was unique. He was like a star that had fallen to earth. He had always seemed like that to her.

"In Thailand once we were taken to see a cockfight."

"A cockfight!"

"They raise the roosters to fight. They fight to the death with silver spurs on their legs. There's some guy down there in the pit, covered with blood, wearing a huge grin. His teeth are made of stainless steel and he's hugging a chicken."

"You saw that? Who were you with?"

"Well, there was the photographer. He kept saying he should be working for the National-fucking-Geographic. Then there was a girl from Ethiopia, me—I forget."

"Fashion photographers—they're like some kind of pashas."

"What's that?"

"A guy who has a harem."

"Are you kidding? He was gay."

The sky, on that evening, was an evil uneven grey. Later it began to rain.

Lying there in the rain, they both woke up. It was such an unusual sound in that part of the world. The plopping of the big drops on the roof, on the ground outside, their long viscous slide down windowpanes and metal doors.

Ever after, she would remember the way they lay there together in the rain. It only happened once. Water falling from the sky was so rare in this country. The water they were used to, that they depended on, came from the high mountains, carried down to them by their River.

He was gone when she woke up and she was aware that he must have left early, perhaps without sleeping again. The idea that Tim was manipulating her was long gone. He was tense; he was miserable. He could barely stay abreast of his own life. The only way out for him that she could see was the wormhole in space she would be able to create, that would get him out of here and into her life. She had shown up just in time.

How had Tim become the Chief? It still seemed to her so unlikely. He was by no means a natural politician; he really cared nothing for the things that concerned most other people. It must have been because he was Medicine Bear, and she still didn't understand the significance of that. But the older people on the

Reserve knew what it was all about. Her mother knew too; Vicky recalled how Eliza had seemed to know who Tim was right from the start, years ago.

She walked slowly, pondering, going over to sit with her mother. Then she saw the little car. Donovan was there.

He was sitting at Eliza's table and she was sitting across from him, unsmiling. There were no teacups between them. But they had been talking. She had heard the murmur of his voice at the same time it was registering on her that it was his car.

"You came back."

He swung around at once. "Vicky! Oh God!—I'm so glad—"

Vicky smiled at him She couldn't actually help it. Even though it had been a shock to find him here, interviewing—or trying to interview—her mother, she had suddenly remembered, upon seeing him, his natural sweetness, his goodness.

She began making tea. But Eliza stood up.

"I'm going to bingo," she announced.

"Oh, for heaven's sake. Bingo—at two o'clock in the afternoon! You haven't had the tea yet!"

They sat, saying nothing, all three drinking tea. But after she had consumed a cupful, Eliza got up and went out. She didn't bother to say it was bingo again.

"She's kind of a hard nut to crack, your mother." Donovan was looking at Vicky beseechingly, a crooked smile appearing on his lips. "Darling—"

"Donovan, please."

"I was only going to say how much I wanted to know your mother."

"Why?"

"Because I wanted to undestand why—You were keeping it hidden. There's all this stuff inside you. I suppose there's a lot of stuff inside everyone, of course," he said thoughtfully. "But this happens to interest me. Deeply."

It seemed to her that all this must seem so foreign to him as to be almost meaningless. She had met his mother. A sweet old whitewoman, an Irish Canadian. His father lived in Ireland and to some extent, the whole family, his sister and brother, lived and breathed Ireland.

"Where are you staying now?"

"Oh—Poppalushka's. I have a standing invitation. I told you I'm not so unpresentable," he went on, smiling at her, coaxing her to smile back.

"You've been away for a while." But she had known he was coming back.

"I needed to think—Vicky, I've got a scenario."

"Is it about Dominique?" she asked, her heart sinking.

"It is! Jesus, the guy's a hero, Vicky. When you consider the whole history of the building of the dam, it's the only, the only … I don't know. It seems to epitomize the injustice of the whole thing for me."

"What? Dominique getting beaten up?" But Vicky was remembering everything else. The long ugly duration of Dominique's convalescence. The compensation cheque. That time when she had begun to die.

"And now he just gets along, living there with the boy—looking after the kid by himself after the mother took off. Working as a farm labourer."

"Maybe you don't know. The guy he works for—Robbie Hallouran—is his father."

"Well, that even adds to the ironies, doesn't it?"

"I think you don't know—about the ironies."

"Okay. I heard he became a drunk. He told me so himself, actually. He isn't ashamed of it, Vicky. You don't need to be either. It happens."

"You don't understand."

They stared at one another. He knew what had happened to Dominique, maybe he even thought he knew all of it. But any attempt he made to dramatize this story would be like ripping her heart out. And Dominique: the fragile peace he had achieved in the world … Donovan could capsize that forever with his film.

"There's a reason why you don't want me to do this, isn't there?"

"Because I want him to—I just want you to leave him alone!"

He still was looking at her, queerly, penetratingly. The whole of his family believed that they had second sight. He said, "Who is Mollie, Vicky?"

❦ THEY WERE DRIVING TOWARDS BITTER ROOT.

"It's okay, Vicky. I was going to come over here by myself. It might have been today even."

"How did you find out about her?" Vicky felt as though she was involved in some horrible kind of betrayal.

"I've heard Tony and the Hallouran boy talking. That Harry's got a head on his shoulders, you know. And as for Tony—" He chuckled.

"What did they say?"

"Dominique was late. Tony said he was probably having tea with Mollie."

"That was all?"

"I don't know. Maybe it was the way he pronounced the word 'tea'. People are always having tea around here, aren't they?" he went on. "It reminds me of Ireland."

Vicky was thinking desperately. There was no reason why he should know any more about it, then. Emma was long gone. He had never met Robbie Hallouran.

But she realized that he would get it in the end. He would dig and dig, finding out about Dominique and finally he would ferret this out too. She didn't want him to bother Dominique at all. And when he found out—it would bother Dominique.

The only way was to tell him now. Then he would see he needed to leave it alone. He was a kind person. The trouble was, she didn't even know where to start.

"I'm going to shoot this," said Donovan. He stopped the car and stepping out onto the verge of the ditch with his video camera, began to shoot Dominique driving a tractor across Mollie's fields towards the house.

Small fields. It was a small farm. Once again, Vicky experienced that feeling of distaste—it could be an even stronger feeling than that—for farming.

"I'm keeping a visual diary," he said. "I didn't dare ask your mother."

"No," agreed Vicky.

"I'm going to get you talking about him on tape. You're in this too, you know."

"Oh God. No, I'm not."

They descended the short steep driveway and then they were in Mollie's yard. Vicky had never actually been here.

"Well?" said Donovan. They were still sitting in the car. The tractor was coming towards them now.

Dominique had already spotted them. But there was still a little time. She began now, feebly, to explain the relationships.

"Mollie Hallouran is Tony's grandmother, Donovan. His mother is Mollie's daughter, Emma. But Tony's not really Dominique's son."

"Really? What a fantastic guy he is!" said Donovan enthusiastically.

"Mollie—Mollie is Robbie Hallouran's sister." She was still trying. It was too late, however. Dominique had got off the tractor and bent over the little car, looking at Vicky in surprise. Donovan was already getting out on the other side.

"Come in," Dominique said to Vicky. Then he smiled at Donovan. He liked him, Vicky saw. The idea that this might be some kind of terrible invasion had never crossed his mind.

They followed Dominique through the screen door. Donovan was shooting again. The little house would be in his film, with all those quaint country features. He put the camera down as they went in. Dominique was running water into the kettle.

"Oh my God! Vicky!—I was wondering who was here." Mollie came into the room. She stood in the middle of the little room, a small ugly woman, getting to be an old woman, bright eyes, wattled skin, her hair black with dye.

She looked much older than Dominique and Vicky stared at her in dislike. She had been with Tim once upon a time too. It seemed almost perverse that she had this attraction, this secret passion, for Native people—like her brother Robbie.

Mollie was staring back at Vicky and then suddenly, embarrassingly, tears began to roll down her cheeks.

Vicky stood still, on her side of the room. She would not hug Mollie.

Mollie sat down, trying to cope with her mascara, still gazing at Vicky. "Who's this?" she said sharply, noticing Donovan.

"I'm Donovan." Donovan spoke eagerly. "I've been staying at Poppalushka's."

Mollie looked at Dominique.

"Vicky's friend," he explained, smiling.

"But—you're with Tim again, aren't you, Vicky? Medicine Bear?" Mollie's lips twisted wryly. It was another one of the ironies. A minor one.

"Donovan is a filmmaker," said Vicky. "We've—we were thinking of doing something together."

"Really? Making a movie?"

She had not noticed that it was a warning.

"That's why I got Vicky to bring me over here. I really wanted to meet you," Donovan was saying eagerly.

"Meet me!" Mollie laughed. Then she looked at Dominique. She had got it now.

She was a dangerous person. Vicky had only ever seen her once or twice. But she reminded her of Emma. She was a person who liked to arouse fear, in other people, but even more, in herself.

"Let's get this straight. She told you—told you about me?"

"Mollie—" said Dominique.

"The boys. I heard them talking about you," said Donovan. "Vicky said you're Tony's grandma. I just think it's fantastic that Dominique's providing a home for Tony," he went on irrelevantly.

"Oh, I see. Have you met my brother Robbie yet?—God! I love family trees!" Mollie suddenly went off into a peal of laughter.

"Mollie—" repeated Dominique.

She looked at him and stopped laughing.

Vicky found this fascinating. Even in the turmoil of her emotions, she caught a glimpse of what was between them.

Donovan had seen enough now to catch on, quick as he was.

He was staring at Vicky; he was finally working out the relationship.

"You see?" said Mollie, speaking quietly now, to Dominique. "The kids know. I told you they did."

He nodded. He didn't like it, Vicky thought. But nothing was going to stop this, whatever was between these two people now. Maybe it wasn't sex any more. But it was love, she could see that.

"So let's see," Mollie turned to Vicky. "He's doing a film with you, is that right? And you introduced him to Dominique. Now you brought him over here?"

Donovan intervened. "She's innocent," he said. "She didn't even want to come."

Mollie looked at Vicky, a hard look. Then she nodded. "I can see she didn't."

"Yeah, but I wanted Vicky to come over," Dominique said quietly. "I wanted to bring her here a month ago." He put his hand gently over Mollie's where it was clenched on the edge of the table. "Just talk to her, okay, Mollie?"

"All right," said Mollie, after a moment. "It's just that it isn't often that you meet a supermodel in your kitchen."

Dominique smiled.

"It's strange that you and I only met once before," said Mollie. "It was at that party Dominique and Emma gave in Steamboat. And I brought Tim. Do you remember that?"

"Of course! It was when I first saw him."

"You must have been—what? Sixteen or seventeen? Did you talk to him?"

"I talked to him. It was the first time I ever heard of—of Medicine Bear."

"Oh yeah. Hocus pocus," said Mollie. She laughed. Then she looked at Donovan. "Irish?" she said.

He nodded. She tilted her head and they smiled at one another. "You're just a friend of hers?"

"Yes," he replied.

"Hard to believe. You're making a film? Is it about her?"

"I don't make documentaries any longer. Vicky's an actress."

"Oh! I see! So none of us are in any danger? I thought for a moment you might be intending to screw up my life story."

Donovan shook his head, smiling. "I'm a friend of his too," he remarked, and Dominique smiled back at him.

"I want to go home now," said Vicky, rather piteously. "Donovan, could you take me home?"

"Of course." He got up immediately.

"Goodbye, Vicky. You'll come again?" Mollie even sounded gentle.

"I'll bring her over," said Dominique. He followed them out through the screen door to the car. He opened the car door for Vicky. They stood there for a moment facing one another.

Vicky hugged him, beginning to cry. Then she got into the car.

It was overwhelming and she cried for a long time, careless of where they were going.

"Could you just tell me—some of this?" said Donovan helplessly. "I promise never to use it."

"It was because I—I couldn't save him. I could barely save myself. I couldn't save myself! That year he began to drink I started to die!"

Donovan pulled over onto a grass verge beside a windbreak. They were on a section road. He turned in his seat and put his arms around her.

"The person who saved me was Tim! The person who saved him was her! I've always hated her! She's a Hallouran."

"They're bad, the Hallourans? Dominique's dad—"

"They took him away from us. Robbie and Sonya made him go with them. So he could go to high school. And now he's—he's still with them. With the farmers!"

"Vicky. You ought to understand now. You're a grown-up. That woman isn't bad for Dominique. And it's his choice."

Vicky drew in a long breath and began wiping her nose with her palm. Donovan produced a white cambric handkerchief and they sat for a while on the edge of the road. He still had his arm around her.

"So now I don't have a scenario, right?" He laughed.

"No."

"Well, it's been worth it. Even though I have to tell everybody

that it's all off. At least I got to know Dominique. And you too—
a little better, I think."

"I'm sorry, Donovan."

"Don't be." He gave her a gentle kiss. He was being very careful.
Now that he had got inside her life, he didn't want her to notice he
was there.

"Well, where to now, sister?" he remarked, starting the car. "Over
the state line?"

"Just take me home."

"And where is home?"

"The Reserve. Tim's house."

He began to turn around, using a crossroads to do a 360
degree turn.

"I hope I can find my way back. Or do I hope that?"

Her heart, which she felt had been almost breaking up to this
point, seemed to slow in its fast, relentless beating. She entered a
quiet place, lulled by the steady purring of the engine of the little
car. Donovan seemed to have no idea where he was going, but this
didn't bother her. They drove. And she fell asleep.

When she woke up it had ceased being late afternoon and
somehow become evening. They were in Tim's dooryard and there
were lights on in the house.

"Look," he said. "Are you sure you want to go in there? There's
still time to make a break for it. I could get you home—to my
place. My place in Toronto. And I have a place in Galway too.
That's a long, long way away from here."

"I'm going in."

"Okay. I'm coming in too," he said, getting out on his side and
coming around to open her door.

There was warmth and light inside. They went up the front
steps and in through the front door. Tim came rapidly out through
the kitchen door, a strangely disturbed expression on his face. He
looked frightened and angry. It was not at all characteristic of him.
He removed Vicky from Donovan, who was holding her elbow,
and led her inside.

"Vicky! Are you okay?—What's the story?" he demanded of
Donovan. "Did you try to run away with her?"

"I did, actually," replied Donovan. "But she wouldn't go."

"Where have you been?" murmured Tim. He sat down on the sofa, pulling her down beside him.

"She took me to see Mollie Hallouran," said Donovan. "And it blew my script to hell and smithereens," he added.

"Oh yeah? Her, eh?" Tim laughed.

"He was going to write a film about Dominique. I just couldn't let him," said Vicky. She was empty of emotion now. She knew that she looked woebegone, but nothing bad was going to happen. Donovan would go home to Toronto—or Galway. And she would take Tim out of here too, when the time came.

"Well, that was never what you were going to do your film on anyway, my friend," Tim was saying.

"Oh yeah. Your problems. Still looking for a way to save your neck, are you?"

"No," said Tim. "I'm going to introduce you to my sister."

She was there, Vicky saw, suddenly. Marina was standing in the kitchen doorway, with her long hair, her heavy, brooding face.

"Marina. This is Donovan."

Marina ignored Donovan. She was looking straight at Vicky. "You really love him?" she demanded, jerking her head at Tim.

Vicky was slightly breathless. The kind of toughness she had cultivated in her life, what she would put up with, what she would not put up with, didn't help her here.

"Yes," she said.

"But he never told you about the trial."

"The trial?" Vicky was looking at her in surprise. She had heard the story of how Marina shot Tim. But no one had mentioned a trial.

"I was going crazy without my mother. They put me in a foster home. I didn't even know where my baby brother was. Then they started coming, with the briefcases. They asked me, What did you see? Who was it killed your mother? Was it your father? Who was it?"

"Oh, my God!" There had been a trial, she realized. The trial of Tim's father. For the murder of his mother. This was what she was talking about.

"It wasn't my father that did it. That was all I knew. I knew it wasn't him."

"Marina—" Tim had stepped forward to intervene. Vicky saw that his face was contorted. Marina was making him cry. She had never seen Tim cry.

"That old man, he cross-examined me." Marina stepped away from Tim's embrace. She was still talking strictly to Vicky.

She meant Tim Steen, the old man, Vicky guessed, who was now like a kind of saint to her.

"Said I'm a liar."

Vicky thought about how the old man came to see Marina's children, especially the little boy. How he loved Rose.

"Well, but you know, he had to defend Tim's—"

"I know!" exclaimed Marina. "Now I know. You think I don't know? Tim told me that guy says he's sorry. I'm the one who's sorry. I'll always be sorry."

She was crying now, but she didn't put her hands up to cover her face. She looked at Vicky and the big tears fell straight out of her eyes to the floor. "I let them say it was Joe," she said. "I couldn't tell them it was my father."

It was the story Tim had never told her: what had happened to his parents. Vicky had begun to cry as well. Behind her stood Donovan, drinking it in. Like a sponge. A sponge that soaked up pain and used it to make art. She could almost hate him for it.

"I forgot about Joe all those years. After Tim came, I saw Joe in him. I saw Joe and then I knew what I did."

THEY WERE WAY UP BEYOND THE BOUNDARIES OF THE RESERVE. He drove the truck as far as he could, leaving gravel road for track, and finally leaving track for a kind of trace left on the buckskin hills by centuries of travel. Finally they came to a halt beside a coulee down which huge boulders rolled in the rare sudden flash floods.

"We'll pack in from here." He collected a packsack from the back of the truck and gave Vicky another, nearly as large and heavy.

It could not be the same place, she thought. The place where they had filmed the Spirit of the Ochre. They had got the van all the way in there.

"No one ever comes out this far any more," he remarked over his shoulder.

Once beyond the coulee the walking became easier. The Ochre was hidden hereabouts somewhere in the folds of the hills. The place they had been in before was in a deep valley, she remembered, with steep sides, a little track leading down beside a crack in the cliff to the second bench of the River, where they had camped. But they were way out beyond that. They were in the wild—what was left of it.

The place on the Ochre that they came to, after what seemed like a wearisome walk to Vicky, unused to packing, was high in the hills, much closer to its source. The deep gorge it had carved down below in the plains had not yet emerged. It flowed almost straight downhill, leaping and bounding over the obstacles, spreading out in a silver veil in places. This place was flatter, with a wide beach of fine gravel, a little point that stuck out creating a bend, matched on the other side by a cliff, perhaps twenty or thirty feet high.

"Aren't there bears up here?" asked Vicky, shivering.

He shrugged.

There was no tent. What equipment they had he must have bought for this trip: a stainless steel cook set, still in the plastic bag, high-tech down hikers' sleeping bags, some freeze-dried grub. Neither of them had warm clothes. Vicky was wearing a leather jacket of Tim's she had found in the truck.

He had not bothered to ask her—or tell her anything. They had just got up and started out in the late morning. It was now getting late in the afternoon, a dull day, with the lowering cloudiness of a chinook.

"Why are we out here?" she demanded, standing over him, shivering. He had started to make a fire of driftwood on the bare ground, three river stones holding it together.

"Why didn't you tell me about—about that stuff Marina told Donovan last night. You haven't ever told me anything. And before that—you made him meet my brother, my mother."

"Okay but, you can't just hand a guy like that a slice. You can't come up to somebody you meet at a party and say, I want you to make a film about my pain. First there was the pain you felt,

Vicky—just getting back here. Maybe he had to see some of that to understand."

"To understand! I didn't want him to understand!"

"Well, he had to think this thing was about you too. And it is about you. You just don't know that yet."

"I don't know—anything at all!" But she couldn't really feel angry at him. What he had felt last night was pain too. He had not gone to bed till well after dawn. He had stayed with Marina; eventually he must have taken her home, but by that time Vicky had been asleep downstairs.

"If you hadn't come back … I don't know. I wasn't expecting you or anything. To tell you the truth, I'd almost given up. They built the dam. They're going to open it. I can't stop that. So I didn't even know what I was doing here any longer. That's why I'd let things get so—"

"But why did we come out here? What is it all about, Tim? I have to know now."

"I'm going to tell you," he said.

The little tent of tinder was alight by now, and he began adding some larger pieces. It was still warm enough not to need this fire. It was for comfort, to keep away the bears, a little flag or signal that they were out here in the wild, dry landscape.

"Couldn't we just—be together," she said piteously.

"We are."

But it had come to her finally that he didn't think they were going to be. He wasn't coming away with her. Whatever he intended to do, it was here, on the Reserve. Whether he actually succeeded in surmounting the obstacles to being re-elected as Chief—and he certainly seemed to be making a big effort to do that—he didn't see, he wouldn't see, that there was anything in it for him, to simply follow her out of here. There was no wormhole.

There were the others too. He wasn't going to leave Marina, and Rose and William Hogan, Jasmine and little Tim. They were his family. He had one of those too.

And she? She couldn't live here. She remembered her mother's warning: he's like poison to you. Eliza must have thought he meant to keep her here. But he wasn't intending to keep her.

[301]

He was going to make her go. Again, the way he had done before, less cruelly this time. Or would it be less cruel? She wrapped her arms around herself, pressing the flaps of the leather jacket closed over her throat.

"Don't be scared, Vick."

"I'm not used to—this." She indicated the sweep of country all around them.

"This is your roots, Vicky. Most people aren't used to thinking about it—even seeing it—any longer. They sit in their houses and watch Westerns on TV."

She remembered that. People did watch Westerns on the Reserve. When she was a child they had gone to see movie Westerns in the place that had preceded the Rec Centre—one night a week. It was on Tuesday nights, she thought.

He was looking up at her from his crouch there on the ground and suddenly, spontaneously, they both began to laugh.

The fire was crackling, rising higher, and Vicky began to feel its comfort. She crouched beside Tim and he put his arm across her shoulders. The sky lowered darkly overhead. It looked like it was going to rain. But it never rained.

"Listen, Vicky. I want to do this the right way this time."

She knew what he was talking about and bent her head obstinately.

"You said you want to be an actress. To do something real. That guy's your ticket."

She shook her head. "I'm not sure I could work with Donovan anyway. It's too complicated. After this."

"Sure, it's complicated. But you know he's a guy who can do something big."

"Yes, but—I can't—he can't—"

"And then, in spite of that, you weren't going to show him anything. He wouldn't have come here. He'd never even have seen Eliza if I hadn't brought him over."

"But you got what you wanted! A film about the trial of your father. Maybe he'll do that now. I don't have anything to do with it."

Tim shook his head. "That's not what he's going to do," he said.

"He's going to do something else. And it can't be done without you."

"What?" She was looking at him in shock. So many false trails.

"That's why I brought you here. To tell you what it is."

❡ IT WAS LATE AND VICKY, HER BACK TO THE FIRE, WAS LOOKING out across the shelter of Tim's shoulder, at the great darkness that lay on the hills. The earth was black under the luminous sky.

She knew she was afraid out here. The lonely swishing of the wind over the thin grasses and the murmur of the River were in her ears now, once Tim had ceased to speak.

"Do you come out here like this often?" she asked.

"Sometimes," he replied. "I used to."

"Were you trying to find out—when you came out here—"

"I was looking for my father," he said. "Because of the name, you know? I thought that it might come—whatever it was—in the form of a bear."

"Did it come?" She shivered, trying once more to see out into the earthly darkness that was all around them.

"No."

"But how do you know?" she asked. "How can you know—that it happened—that way?"

"It wasn't my father who came. It was my mother. My mother spoke to me."

IO

1947 · Joe Bear

◖ JOE BEAR WAS DIGGING A GRAVE. IT WAS MARCH AND THE ground had not yet come unfrozen; the digging could not be done with axe and shovel alone. They lit fires in long trenches; then when the fire burned down, they scraped aside the ashes and debris and dug again.

The little graveyard was the scene of a mass grave. They were creating a long scar down through the lines of little neat graves with their white crosses. It reminded him of the graves they had made after the D-Day landing; for he had fought at Caen. He had never expected to see such a sight at home.

The Reserve had been hit by a flu epidemic that winter. TB cases were usually taken away to the sanatoriums or the hospitals and buried or cremated. But these flu victims died at home; hospitals wouldn't take them or were already full. He thought he had buried dozens of children since Christmas. Children and old people.

Joe's wife had died of flu—she had been pregnant with their second child. His baby daughter, Bella, had died. His mother too. His father was already dead. He had died in the early years of the war, after they had got the news about his brother John.

Now his sister, Sarah, had died, and he and his brother-in-law were digging her grave in the long line or trench of other graves that were being dug that day. His brother-in-law was crying as he dug, and a hum or chant of mourning hung in the air above the sobbing gasps of the men wielding the axes.

Joe was alone now. First his brothers had been killed. They were both old enough to sign up right away in 1939. Fred was buried somewhere in North Africa; his brother John had disappeared after a troop transport was torpedoed by a submarine, somewhere in the Atlantic.

He himself had not really expected to get through. When D-Day came and he realized what it was and where he was going, he had thought: "Well, this is it for me too." And he had been glad—in a way, at least—that he had not been married like the other two— that he would be leaving only his mother and his sister to grieve for him. But as it now turned out, he was the one left to grieve.

He was actually doing his best to get sick himself. Every day he handled the dead. When the doctor came to the Reserve to make his useless infrequent rounds, Joe went with him, and then went back to check, to make sure instructions were being carried out: the fluids, the Aspirin, the thin blankets. Which had to be kept on the sweating, feverish patients, who would sometimes go outside and throw themselves down in the snow.

Joe had been trained as a medic. He had signed up for it while still waiting in Canada, in all the various boot camps and holding locations, waiting and waiting with the other men to throw himself away on the battlefields of Europe. And so he had seen death before, the hideous deaths of men who were blown apart, torn apart, fractured, had holes blown through them, were broken, burned, mutilated; the flayed, armless, legless, faceless, speechless victims of the battlefield.

He had nevertheless not been prepared to meet death here—not so much death, so suddenly and mysteriously delivered; delivered so personally, just when he was home, beginning to be aware of his safety, his security, his happiness.

There is a picture of Joe as a corporal in the Canadian army. A tall, slim young man (he was twenty-three when it was taken) with the short, short hair of the army not hiding its straightness and blackness as it rose in a brush above his forehead. He had laughing eyes and a mouth that teased the French girls; for he learned quite a bit of French.

But of his wife and the one living child, there are no photographs. She had been a Bear too, a second cousin, a teenage sweetheart; and she waited for him, receiving three letters in all the time he was away. One from a boot camp in Ontario when he was nineteen and still deeply, unutterably lonely and homesick; one from France, to tell her that he had survived the D-Day landing and the battle of Caen; and one from Halifax, on his disembarking, to tell her he was taking the train.

He had gotten off the train in Abercrombie and taken the bus to Bitter Root, then walked home to the Reserve with his pack, his suitcase, marvelling all the way at the clean blue sky, the sight of the towering high mountains projected at him through the clear air, the dusty road lined with the pink roses of Alberta. He was home. And the next week he hitchhiked into Abercrombie again to get a marriage license.

The child, Bella, was born almost nine months to the day after the wedding. Joe delivered her himself. His mother had given up her bed for Marie to lie on in her labour. Ordinarily, Joe and Marie slept on the floor of the outer and main room of his parents' little house, his mother sleeping in the inner room on the only bed.

The labour had been easy. But everything seemed easy to Joe in those days. Marie was fine; it had been short and straightforward and she was only in pain for about twenty minutes. She was not scared at all because he was with her, holding her hand under the ragged blanket, talking to her all the time, telling stories, anything that came into his head—about guiding bear hunters with his father when he was a boy, about men he had known in camps all over Canada, about France, and memories of their childhood and school days together, because they were the same age, twenty-seven.

Bella was a quick child, early to walk, already beginning to talk before she was two. She had been the first to die of flu, but Marie's grief was not prolonged. She was already sick and by the time their Bella was dead, she was dying.

The winter wore itself out, and somehow, with the spring, the epidemic sickness grew slowly less virulent. The long fires in the graveyard flickered out and the last few people who died were buried in soft earth under grass and dandelions.

Joe now lived alone in the little house. He snared rabbits for stew, went out with the other men and shot ducks along the banks of the river; but he did not join the outfitters escorting the American tourists into the grizzly killing grounds of the Rockies, because his mother had sold the family's horses. Long ago, after his father died.

The heart had gone out of him and it seemed as though it had gone out of all the people. There were no big gatherings that summer, no dances, no days of games. The epidemic had swept away hundreds of people, including the Chief and most of the elders—those who had not already been killed by tuberculosis. When Joe looked back on his homecoming now, his short and rapturous marriage, his wife, his baby daughter, and the unborn child, it seemed like just a flash of sunlight under the lowering clouds of the chinook, which had been his life so far.

He had gained something of a reputation on the Reserve as a healer and people began to call on him as though he were a doctor. A doctor and a midwife. It had been an unusual thing to deliver his own wife in the village when there were still many old women with experience as midwives. Now they were all gone, killed by the flu. There was no doctor in Bitter Root any longer and the only doctor in Abercrombie who would come to the Reserve was slow and old.

At the usual time of the summer festival the Indian agent called a Band meeting. Joe and three others showed up.

"Who's the Chief now?" he said. "You've got to have a Chief. I need him to distribute the annuities."

The other three looked at Joe.

"What's your name?" said the Indian agent briskly.

Joe Bear was considerably surprised and startled as the man began to write his name down in the space beside "Chief" at the top of the Band list.

"He's a medicine man," said one of the others. It was a sly remark.

The Indian agent looked up sharply at Joe, over his rimless glasses. Medicine, in the sense of old-time shamanism, was utterly proscribed by the Church. They no longer were allowed to hold any of their old ceremonies. The old people who still held onto the talismans of the past were persecuted by the government agents, who confused Native medicine with European witchcraft.

"I was a medic," Joe explained. "47th Alberta Rifle Brigade."

The Indian agent nodded and wrote "Medic" in brackets after Joe's name as the three others, all unable to read his writing, gravely looked on.

From then on he lost his first name and was known to everyone as Medicine Bear. In any case, there was no one left alive to want to call him Joe.

As the Chief he received a small gratuity when he was required to stay at home and talk to the whiteman; there were a number of meetings that fall about the River. The farmers wanted water. Medicine Bear was in town going to meetings while all the men were gone with the outfitters or off hunting for elk.

They regarded his job as senseless and easy, not the work of a real Chief at all, who would have been hunting with them at this time of year, rather than staying at home with pregnant women. But the women liked him and many of them were attracted to him—for his teasing face, the sadness in his eyes, his kindness to anyone helpless or in pain. This did not make him very popular with the men either.

Medicine Bear carried a big bunch of black-eyed Susans of the late summer prairie out to the graveyard and placed it on the graves of his wife and daughter. Then he went to a meeting held in the Indian agent's house, with the agent himself, two farmers from a county association, a civil engineer sent down from Edmonton, and the local MLA. They had drawn up a paper called "Agreement in Principle." It was not given to Medicine Bear to read, but he was asked to sign it, the place indicated kindly by the Indian agent, on a line immediately below his own signature.

He refused to sign and they cajoled him. Water diversion was essential to agriculture. No one could claim to own water, and therefore the River was a resource that everybody owned. All that was required was cooperation so that it could be divided up and used fairly.

He still refused to sign and they threatened him then. The Indian agent said that his election as Chief had been improperly carried out and that there had been accusations of fraudulence in the vote count. He said that he would certainly insist upon a new election as soon as the men returned from fall hunting.

Joe went out of the Indian agent's house and into the blissful cool of the evening, already dusk—which began to fall earlier and earlier at this time of year after the seemingly endless days of summer.

An old woman had sent for him to come after the meeting. This woman lived alone in a little house by the road out of the village leading to the River, on the edge of a patch of scrub. She had an unhealing sore on her leg and he thought that she probably had a chronic disease. It was surprising that she had lived through the flu epidemic; perhaps it was because of her isolation—and her leg bothered her enough to keep her from visiting other people.

After he had looked at her sore and applied some compresses and showed her how to wash it with salt water, he made them both a cup of tea. There was actually no tea in the house because she was so poor; they merely sat there drinking the hot water in silence.

They were not at all uncomfortable to be sitting there like that, each busy with his own thoughts. It reminded Joe of his parents sitting beside the River for hours at a time: his father squatting on one heel or standing, his mother sitting upright with her legs straight out in front of her, her skirt pulled down neatly over her leggings.

He got up to go. It was after midnight. But the old woman detained him, reaching out her knobbly old hand to his arm, her eyes bright under the folds of skin on her eyelids.

"They made you Chief, my son," she began.

He thought he was not going to be Chief much longer. But he could hardly explain this to her. The story was too long and complicated. Besides, she wanted to say something.

"It was because you are a healer."

He nodded, even though this was not true. She was still holding him down, bent over her, with her arthritic hand crooked upon his forearm. She was old, probably over sixty, but he felt he was actually older than she was. He had seen so many more people die.

"Will you heal my daughter?" she said, her cracked voice hardly above a whisper.

"Where is she?" He looked around the room, thinking at the same time that of course there was no one there. The old woman had been alone when he came in. Except that, as he now noticed, beyond the stove on a pallet stuffed with straw, a child lay sleeping, a thin red blanket covering her. He had not noticed this before, owing to the general disorder in the room and the dim light. This child, however, could not be the old woman's daughter.

"Wait!" she said. She let go of his arm quite suddenly and he almost felt as though she had pushed him away, the current of excitement and agitation coming from her had been so strong. She was still looking at him with piercing eyes, but gradually, as she assured herself that he was going to stay, that he had sat down, they grew duller, and her face became bland again.

The daughter must be coming tonight, perhaps to pick up the little girl, he surmised. He had seen from the fall of black hair over the end of the pallet that the child was female.

It was late and he felt a little like a sleepwalker, stunned, or in another, dream-like state. First there had been the meeting, and he was still realizing what a trap he was in, perhaps even placed there by his own people. No one had wanted to be Chief; they had seen this coming. Perhaps it had happened before, while he was away. His naïveté, and his prestige, had pushed him forward into the position and he now saw no way to retreat.

Now there was this. The long silence between him and the old woman, which he had interpreted as merely companionable, was a preface to her demand that he heal someone, someone who might very well have an incurable disease.

He knew that he had no experience as a leader. He had never even made a speech. And he was not a healer in the sense that the old woman meant. His medical knowledge came from courses he had taken in the army and from battlefield triage. The only medicine he had ever practised unsupported by doctors and a field hospital was at the birth of his daughter; and that had been an entirely normal thing; it had not required his intervention at all.

He was sitting there, brooding—grieving, really, when he

thought of his child being born in the spring of the previous year—when the door of the little hut was flung open and a woman came in. She seemed to be in a great hurry, for he saw only the flash of her eyes as she went to the pallet and lifted the child up in her arms.

For a moment she stood there, holding the child, with the blanket falling down between them, murmuring something in another language, words he could not understand. The little girl opened her eyes, yawned, and said: "Mama!" Then she clasped her arms around the woman's neck, and the woman seemed to be preparing to take her out. She was enfolding the child in the blanket.

The old woman asked her something, speaking softly in that other language.

"He's gone with the pack train," said the younger woman, turning around to look at her mother with her eyes flashing again as they caught the light of the lamp. And Joe was considerably startled to see that her face was decorated with—could it be?—tattoos, of a most startling and original kind, abstract designs of curling lines that encircled her lips, her eyes, and met in flourishes and dots on her forehead and chin.

She smiled to see the surprise and doubt on his face; it was a fierce smile, almost a smile of triumph.

"You know who this is?" asked the old woman, indicating Joe.

The younger one nodded, and then once again began to swaddle the child against the cold of the night outside, paying no more attention to Joe.

But how did she know who he was? For he did not know her—nor this old woman—even though he had been born here and lived here till he went into the army, and then had come back and been home for nearly two years. He was still standing there, dumb as an ox, staring at the younger woman as she wrapped up the child, and wondering what he was being called upon to do. For there was something wrong, there was certainly something wrong with her.

The old woman said coaxingly: "Selene, Selena."

"There is nothing, Ma. There is just nothing he can do!" She went out just as suddenly and swiftly as she had arrived, taking the child with her, sleeping again in her arms.

He went home himself then, for it was very late by this time. But the following evening he went back to attend to the compresses on the old woman's leg and he heard her story.

Her name was Rachel, and she had come to this Reserve from another one further north, about five years ago, with her daughter, who had married a man from here. This man's name was Thomas Mountain. The Mountains were a family Joe knew; the Chief had been a Mountain when he was a boy. Thomas was some years older than Joe, and he often worked on the pack trains for the white big-game hunters. A big man, tough, strong, competent with his horses, respected as a guide.

Their child had been born, the girl that Joe had seen, but for some reason Thomas had taken against her. He had attempted to starve the baby by refusing to allow his wife to feed her from the breast. He would only permit her to give the child a little flour mixed with water. At the same time he became tremendously jealous of Selene herself and would scarcely let her out of his sight when he was in town; but things were much worse than that when he came back from a guiding expedition, for then his jealous suspicions reached a pitch and he delivered fearful beatings upon Selene, and also upon anyone else who attempted to intervene.

At this point Rachel had taken the child and moved into this hut on the edge of the village by herself, where she was able to make a small living cleaning in the church and for the priest, and as a washer of the dead. The hut had belonged to the man who had performed the office of washing the dead before, and had lain empty for a while; no one had wanted to live in it because of a kind of superstitious horror. She and her daughter had no way of returning to Rachel's reserve; and there was nothing better where they had come from, the old woman made this clear. Her family was dead—of TB, probably—and this daughter was the only one she had left.

For a while things had gone better. Then Selene had had another child, a son, who died in infancy, of a fever. This had happened about two years ago and since then things had been getting worse again. Thomas Mountain was an industrious man, a good worker, but he became a monster when he was drunk, and the baby's death had pitched him into despair and alcoholism. He had returned to beating Selene regularly and he could not be trusted near his daughter, whose mere name caused him to erupt into violence.

In the meantime, Selene had responded in a way that her mother found almost as frightening as the irrational rages of Thomas. She had developed an entirely delusional life, and she told her child stories about the wonderful father that she had, who cared for her more than anything, and who bought (or sent) wonderful gifts, although these were often such things as a piece of wood painted like a doll by the mother, or a stone shaped like a cat or rabbit.

The child believed utterly in this father since she was kept away from the real one, and was carefully watched, kept separate from other children and not allowed to wander in the village for fear that Thomas might catch her and beat or kill her. And lately, Rachel continued, she had come to think that Selene herself believed in this fictional man, this wonderful lover and provider, who met her sometimes in the woods, when she was driven out there to sleep shivering under the cottonwoods, and who moved in with her and the child when Thomas was gone with the pack trains.

Selene had also developed an eccentricity of dress and manner. Since she too kept away from other people out of fear of Thomas's jealous reprisals, she entertained herself by painting her face and body with colours and designs, decorating her hair oddly with things she picked up in the woods, and dressing in coloured rags.

Rachel told him all this as he dressed her wound, and he realized that she did not so much expect something of him, as merely hope for something. It was a last hope really, because although she was completely lucid, she was weak and getting weaker. The wound on her leg was gravely infected, but worse than that, her underlying disease raged out of control. Since his first visit she had been forced to retire to bed.

He brought the doctor on the third day, but there was not much that could be done. The doctor offered Rachel the hospital in Edmonton and she refused.

Joe did not see Selene during this time and he realized that he had never seen her before because she was obliged to stay away from all men.

In the meantime, the Indian agent had called another Band meeting. Surprisingly—or at least Joe was surprised—a lot of people came to this meeting.

The Indian agent said that it was necessary for the Band to have a good Chief now, one who was honest and reliable. He said that the Chief they had elected had proven to be unreliable. He had not distributed the annuities and the shells and other things that were to be given out in the summer in accordance with the treaty. These things were no longer in the warehouse, but had been taken by him for his own use.

The agent then led the men from his own house to Joe's house and exhibited the pouch containing the money and the boxes of shells which had been thrown down on the floor there while the meeting was going on. He called for another election on the spot.

However, the people looked at him blankly and in silence, and then began drifting away.

After they were gone, the agent showed Joe his name in the book where he had written it before: Chief Joe Bear (Medic). Slowly he took his fountain pen out of his breast pocket and scrawled over the entry, so that it was unreadable, it was entirely rubbed out.

Joe found an old man, who was one of the last living in his family, named Antoine Bear, who helped him to remember the names of all the families, and they divided up the shells as fairly as they could. The money was also distributed, and then the festival that was usually held in the summer was held in October instead, because of the lateness of the Indian agent in getting these things to the people.

At this festival, Joe made his first speech as Chief. He explained in the barest terms how it was that he had been selected as Chief, and about the meeting where he refused to sign the paper. Then he told how the shells and money had been dumped down in his house during the second meeting of the Band called by the agent. The agent, who was attending the party, looked at him blandly as he said all this. So then Joe, who was feeling indignation at that bland glance, said that he would never sign any paper that gave away the River or the water of the River.

At this there was a murmur of assent from everybody present.

Somewhat emboldened by that, he went on to say that a proper Chief election would be held before Christmas, when everyone was back from guiding, and that he himself would stand, and that any other candidate was free to announce himself between now and then, and stand as well.

And again there was that murmur of agreement. The Indian agent left the place on the riverbank where they were holding the feast, and his face was no longer so bland.

Joe was very busy in November and December because of the women giving birth. The flu epidemic had killed many people but the baby boom continued. The men who had been suspicious and jealous before, when he apparently did nothing, turned to him in panic as their wives went into labour; and the women now treated him as a sexless being, an angel, who had come from heaven to save them.

At the Christmas feast he was acclaimed as Chief. No one had stood against him, and Joe was glad. He hadn't wanted the job when it had been thrust upon him, and he had had the sense that he was a dupe, even in the eyes of his own people. But now, thanks to the trick of the Indian agent, all of that had been clarified. If he had ever been a dupe he was not one any longer, and everyone knew that.

Antoine Bear made a speech in their own language at the feast. In it he stated the ancient belief of the people, that water was a living thing and should be treated with respect. Water must be drunk of course, but it should be handled in the same spirit of honour with which an animal is taken and killed, according to taboo, according to need. Joe himself had seen the rivers of Europe, flowing with sewage, their banks cased in stonework. He knew how the whiteman mistreated water. Antoine had not once mentioned the dam the whiteman was proposing, but everyone knew that the speech was against the dam.

In the very cold days of January, Rachel died. She had been

growing more and more feeble, and the wound had become larger and larger, so that her leg was now one huge suppurating sore. Joe brought the doctor to see her again, but she would not go to hospital and it was wise of her, as they all three knew that she would go there only to die. Even if her leg could still be amputated, the disease was consuming her; she was vague and weak, and sometimes Joe would find her unconscious on the floor, or the child would.

The cause of her death was apparently pneumonia, although by now the infection in her wound would have been enough to kill anyone with a weaker spirit. Joe sat with her during the three days it took her to die of the lung disease, only going out one night to help a woman through a short successful labour to the birth of a baby boy.

Rachel died during the night. Joe was with her and awake. When the child woke up next morning, he tried to explain about the death of the grandmother, realizing at the same time what a disaster this might be for Marina. But he found her calm. She told him that her father had visited the previous night, when he had been away, looking after the birth of the baby boy, and had explained about the forthcoming death of her grandmother and promised to take her afterwards and care for her.

Joe was surprised and relieved to hear this, and for a short while he believed it. But Thomas Mountain did not come for Marina, and at the funeral he saw Selene with her face bruised all down one side.

He guessed then that Selene had come to visit her mother for one last time, and to talk to Marina, and that they had entered together into their strange delusion. Since Thomas Mountain was at home now, as there was no work for the guides during the deep winter, Selene had not been able to come again, and she had apparently been fearfully punished for the time she did come. He now guessed that it was the delusional father who had promised to take Marina, not the real one.

This strange and horrible marriage was not the way things usually went among these people and it surprised and horrified Joe. He was aware that women sometimes got beaten, especially when their husbands drank, and there was a code of silence among the men and of subservience among the women that preserved such marriages. But this was not the normal way. His own parents, for example, had never openly fought in his presence. Joe could not have dreamed of hitting his wife. The brutality of Thomas and Selene's marriage was stunning; it amazed him that the other women tolerated it. He thought it was because Rachel and Selene were strangers, from another Reserve, and therefore helpless.

He wondered if in telling her that her delusional father was going to take her, Selene had been trying to prepare Marina for death. For she now had no one but Selene; and Selene could not defend her from Thomas.

Joe had been living in Rachel's cottage for the past week or so. He now continued to do so while he pondered what, if anything, he could do in this strange case.

It would not have been the role, even of an old-time Chief, to interfere directly between a man and his wife. When the priests had come into the country it had surprised and affronted the people that the whitemen involved themselves in such private matters. On the other hand, whitemen had introduced the idea of marriage as an indissoluble union; it was only because of this that a man and a woman could be locked into lifelong misery together.

Joe and the child had now begun to keep house and she accepted him as matter-of-factly as she had accepted her grandmother. The night of the funeral she cried for a while, lying on her straw bed, and Joe crouched beside her, holding her hand. But she went to sleep and the next morning she was calm.

He did not see what he could do except to go on looking after Marina. There was no other grandmother he could give her to; Thomas Mountain lived with his parents, and there was no one else but Selene, who never came, now that he was staying here. But he understood that this was because she feared for her own life, and even more for Marina's.

The Indian agent sent for him to come to his house one evening. Joe took his old uncle, Antoine Bear, with him to be a witness. Antoine rarely spoke English in the presence of a whiteman, but he understood it perfectly well and he would see and know things that Joe felt he might not see and know.

"It was a misunderstanding—about the annuities," the agent began. "You are supposed to distribute those in summer."

Joe said, "I didn't know that you expected me to come for them."

"I thought that you did not intend to do your duty as the Chief."

Joe did not reply, although he felt that the accusation that the agent had made against him in the fall was between them. The agent had sent the shells and the money pouch to be thrown down in his house, making it look as though he had intended to steal them. Also, Joe still felt indignation at the way the agent had scratched out his name on the Band list.

The agent then went on to say that the damming or diversion of the River was a plan that was being talked about and that it would require cooperation and agreement from the Reserve. He said that the government in Edmonton wanted to talk to Joe and that there would be a meeting there, to which he would take him.

Joe and Antoine discussed this later.

"He is not to be trusted," said Antoine.

"I know. But I think I have to go to this meeting to find out their plans."

"But what if they try to make you sign things using trickery."

"I won't sign anything. I'll say I have to talk to the people."

Antoine was a small man, thin and wizened, with a face like a pine cone, seamed with age and smoke. He looked wise; in some ways he was wise. He knew far more than Joe about old times and the way things should be done.

He said apprehensively, "Maybe they will keep you there until you sign."

Joe laughed. "I'll wear my uniform," he said. "That will make it hard for them."

He knew that Antoine was right. They might try to trick him by telling lies and they might even try to keep him there, thinking that he would be dependent upon the Indian agent in the big city, like an old-time Chief. But his uniform, he felt, would make them ashamed of their lies, and there was no way they could keep him,

[319]

for he had been in much bigger cities than Edmonton during the war and had always managed to find his way around.

He went home to get out his uniform and brush it and to find the decorations he had won for being at the D-Day landing and being in the battle of Caen. His house seemed dusty and unused, he had not lived there for so long. Then he went back to spend the night as usual in Rachel's house with Marina, and for the first time he wondered what he would do about her while he was away.

He thought of leaving her with Antoine, but Antoine's wife had died long ago of TB and so had all his children. He could leave her with the priest, Father François, but he did not like Father François; in any case, it did not strike him as suitable to leave her with a man. He forgot that he himself was a man.

In many ways he did not regard himself as a man at all any longer. He thought that part of his life was over, buried in the graveyard with Marie and Bella and the unborn baby.

When he showed up the next morning at the agent's house he was in uniform and he was holding Marina's hand. In her other hand she held a small carpet bag containing her wooden doll and a few rocks.

"The child can't come," said the agent, frowning.

"Then I can't go," said Joe.

"Whose is the child?" demanded the agent. "It isn't yours. Your child died in the epidemic."

It seemed to Joe that this whiteman had been watching him for some time.

"The child belonged to Rachel Pelletier," he said. "When she died she left the child in my care."

"Can't you leave the child with someone else?"

They stared at one another and then the agent's eyes dropped to the medals on Joe's chest.

"We will have to stay in a hotel for two nights. There will be no place for the child."

"She will stay with me," said Joe, somewhat surprised. She was staying with him already.

"Very well. But you may have to pay extra for the room."

"I have no money."

Again they stared at one another like buffaloes, and again the agent's eyes were the first to drop.

The trip to Edmonton was made by train from Abercrombie and took much of the day. Joe had been on many trains before and this one seemed comparatively luxurious. Marina was very matter-of-fact, although she had never seen a train before. After one startled glance, she followed Joe down the platform, her hand in his hand, her other hand clutching the carpet bag. And on the train she was good; she played quietly with the things in the carpet bag or looked out the window.

The Indian agent contemplated her with a moody stare for a few minutes and then went to sleep. Joe thought that Marina would be a witness in a way, to whatever happened. Whatever the whitemen were planning—whether it was as devious as Antoine thought—they would not have expected him to bring a little girl.

In the hotel that night Marina ate whiteman's food for the first time: bread, not bannock, corn scallop, which she seemed to like well enough, and canned fruit, which Joe got her a second helping of. At night he made her a bed in the corner, using two pillows and the extra blanket from his bed.

He was becoming aware of something he had not had an opportunity to notice about her at home, because he was so often out of the house, hunting, or seeing his patients. Marina was living another life that went on all the time, even when she was apparently sitting quietly doing nothing. The things inside the carpet bag were not just toys—they were real to her and she talked to them constantly, about the life that she and they lived together in a quite different world with her mother and father.

Joe had begun to listen while they were on the train. He now listened more while they were in the hotel room before she went to sleep and began to feel alarmed and disturbed. Somehow, he realized, he was going to have to wean her away from her imaginary world. And yet, when that was gone, what would Marina have left?

The following morning the meeting took place in a grand room in the legislature building. Joe met a couple of men whose names and titles were not clarified to him. He stood in front of them while they sat at a long oaken table. The MLA was there, but otherwise he did not recognize the men. Once again, they offered him the paper to sign.

"I have not read the paper," said Joe.

"Can you read?" asked the politician.

"Will you look at the man?" suggested one of the unnamed men and they all stared for a moment at Joe in his uniform with the corporal's insignia and the decorations from D-Day.

The paper was given to him and he began to read it. After he had finished he kept it in his hand.

"You have to sign it now," said the Indian agent in a low voice. He was directing Joe, almost as if Joe were blind or a child.

"I would like to take this and read it to the people."

The men at the table looked at one another. "It is only a preliminary document," said one of them. "It would not be an accurate reflection of the government's plans."

"It says we agree to let you dam our River," said Joe. "I couldn't sign that without reading it to the people first to see if they agree."

Again, they all looked at one another.

"You're the Chief," the Indian agent said to Joe. "This is your decision."

Joe looked at him with irony and shook his head.

"It is not your River," said one of the men, clearing his throat. "Water does not belong to anyone."

Again Joe felt the irony of the situation. "No," he said. "Water does not belong to anyone. So why are you trying to take it?"

"It would be for everyone's use."

"It would be for your use."

"Well, you aren't using it."

"May I take the paper?" Joe said.

There was a long silence. "Shall we meet again this afternoon?" said the first man. He held out his hand for the paper and Joe gave it to him.

"You are holding everybody up," said the Indian agent. "These are busy men."

"Will you give me another paper to sign this afternoon? Or will you give me this one again?" Joe asked.

[322]

The first man looked at the Indian agent with a frown. Joe could tell he thought the agent was a bungler.

"You said the Band would have a Chief who would be willing to come to an agreement."

"I'm sorry, sir. There's been a misunderstanding."

"Well, don't let this happen again." The men filed out, leaving Joe and the Indian agent in the large grand room of the legislature building. Marina played with her rocks and her wooden doll in the corner.

"I will tell these men you are willing to sign this afternoon. Or else you won't go home," said the agent. "I won't take you back unless you sign!"

Joe laughed. Antoine had been right. He went over to Marina and took her hand. Together they went out of the room, down the marble stairs and out onto 109th Street. They walked across the High Level Bridge and when they got to Strathcona, Joe began to hitchhike.

He had no problem getting rides in his uniform, holding Marina's hand. It took them the rest of the day and the night and part of the next day to get home, only because it was more than two hundred miles and the cars and trucks and farm vehicles that picked them up were slower than the train.

Joe put Marina to bed in Rachel's bed, because she was exhausted. He lay down upon the straw pallet himself—because he was exhausted too. They slept, even though they had not eaten much that day, and slowly it became dark outside, and snow, which had been in the air all day, began to fall in thick flakes. It was a blizzard. They had got home just in time.

It was quite dark in the cabin and both the man and the child were sleeping soundly. Suddenly the door flew open and a great gust of snow and wind blew in.

Joe woke up instantly and sprang to his feet. The wind was howling inside the cabin, whining and whistling as it drove the snow before it through the narrow door opening. He was struggling with the door now, as the wind threatened to blow it off its hinges. He got it shut somehow and the latch down, then turned around panting, with his back against it.

Marina's mother was in the room, crouching over the empty straw mattress. She stood up and he caught the wild flash of her eyes in the dimness. She stood facing him and he was afraid that she was going to fly at him and try to kill him.

"She's on the bed," he said.

The woman instantly turned around to the bed and bent over Marina, who still did not wake up. She lay down beside her and put her head beside Marina's on the pillow Joe had brought to Rachel before she died, and stroked and smoothed the bedclothes over the child.

Joe managed to find and light the lamp. Then he noticed that Selene was not wearing a winter coat or even a jacket, only a ragged dress and leggings like an old woman. At the same time he saw that her hands and arms were dyed to the elbow with ochre.

He stoked the stove with kindling wood and began to make tea. For there was tea in the house now that he was living here with Marina.

Selene had been murmuring, almost crooning to Marina, but when the child did not wake up, she gradually ceased. When Joe finished making the tea and turned back, she was sitting on the edge of the bed watching him with eyes that were still serious and alarmed.

He gave her the enamel cup and when their hands met, he was horrified by how cold her fingers were.

Thomas Mountain was at home; everyone was at home during this period of deep winter. Joe had heard that Thomas sometimes drove Selene out during the night and locked the door against her. In the past, of course, she had been able to come to Rachel. Although sometimes she had not come, Rachel said, because if Thomas followed her, he might kill the child.

Joe was remembering all these things, and also wondering at the man's monumental jealousy. It was really not safe for Selene to be here with him. And he began to ask himself if he was afraid of the big man.

In the meantime Selene was drinking the tea. It was scalding hot, but she drank it down greedily. She seemed careless of personal injury, coming through the raging blizzard with even her arms and her neck bare. She had been terrified about Marina, this was clear. She must have heard that Joe had taken her away.

"I went to Edmonton," he said. "We just got back."

She continued to look at him with that wild stare. Perhaps she thought there was some harm in the relationship, although Joe did not see what harm there could be. Marina was still very young.

"I had to take her," he said. "I—I don't have anybody."

He had meant to say that there was no woman he could leave her with, but it came out as this weak, sad utterance. He wished he had not said it the instant it was out of his mouth. It was like something a child might say.

However, her glare had softened. Then her eyes dropped to her empty cup. He turned away to get her some more tea.

"Why did you go to Edmonton?" she asked in a strange cracked voice. He thought she was not used to speaking at all.

"I went with the agent. To see the government. They tried to get me to sign the paper letting them have the River." He was glad to say all this. He had not yet had a chance to talk to anyone and he realized that he would be saying it over and over.

She did not seem to know what he was talking about. She raised one shoulder indifferently, then held out the teacup, which was empty again.

"We stayed in a hotel," he went on. "I made Marina a bed on the floor."

He wanted to say this especially, just in case she still thought there was something wrong. "On the way back, I—we had to hitchhike. So we didn't sleep."

"I saw a hotel once," she said. He looked at her in surprise.

"It was very long and all red inside, like an animal's belly," she went on. "I stayed inside for several months, moving from section to section, and then I came out."

What did she mean? It could not have been a hotel.

"I was warm the whole time. It was very warm in there."

Joe looked for something to put over her shoulders. The stove was roaring after he had made up the fire to boil the kettle, but it hardly competed with the wind, which was coming through every crack and chink in the walls. He took his army overcoat off a peg and offered it to her, and after a moment's hesitation she took it, but did not pull it around her, merely laid it carefully over her knees, fanned out on the floor like a long skirt. She seemed to admire its texture as well, for she smoothed it, looking down attentively at the watery pattern of the cloth as she pushed the wrinkles ahead of her hands.

While she did this, patiently, repetitively, he was looking at her. The craziness of what she had said and how she was behaving now had temporarily allayed the pity he felt for her, and he saw her again with the same clarity with which he had seen her when he first came to wash the sore on Rachel's leg.

Her hair hung in drabs around her face, tangled in clumps, showing patches where her scalp was almost bald; perhaps as the result of her husband dragging her by the hair. Her face, aside from the bruise on her cheek, was unmarked; the designs he had seen last time had evidently been made with paint or ink, for there was now no sign of them. She was older than he was by some years, like Thomas Mountain, but she did not look old. She had the appearance of a female wolf he had once seen after a hard winter: thin and wild, her silvery fur scruffy and shedding, but still full of grace and a kind of magic.

The tattoos were gone, and the only thing that was odd now was the ochre she had painted on her arms . She decorated herself. She had no nice clothing, no ribbon or pin; all she had was boot polish, and soot or ink, and the ochre from the River.

Marina now woke up as Joe stood there, watching her mother. She wrinkled up her face in a yawn, then her eyes flew open and in the next moment she had sat up and was embracing her mother in rapture, winding her arms around her neck.

They began talking together softly in Selene's language; it was a language he didn't know at all. They seemed to be talking about him, for he saw Marina's eyes on him, shy, but trusting, and the woman too was looking at him without any of her previous fierceness.

Marina said, "My mother is hungry, Joe."

Joe nodded. He hadn't thought of it before, but now that she had said it, he noticed that he was hungry too. They had had nothing to eat during their long journey and Marina had borne that with stoicism. But she was hungry too.

He found the flour bag and began to make bannock, mixing the flour with a little lard that he found in the can, then adding baking powder and water, shaping the flat cakes and laying them directly on the clean stove top. There was no meat. This was all they had.

It was in a way strange to be doing this himself with two women present, but Joe was accustomed by now to giving food to the child. He was reminded of a time when he was young, when the whole family had been on the trail, and his father had made just such flat cakes over the fire and given them to his children and his wife. There had been nothing to eat but flour that time too.

Joe gave a hot bannock to Marina.

She said: "Oh, it is good! It is as good as the ones my father makes!"

Turning to her mother, she broke the cake in half, juggling it carefully in her hands because it was hot.

"You did not eat anything this good in the hotel," her mother said.

"We ate a thing that was flat and a funny shape, like this." Marina drew the chef's hat shape of a slice of bread on the flat surface of Joe's overcoat, and her mother, munching, looked down at it seriously. "And then we ate a thing that was sweet and came in a sweet drink. It was yellow."

She meant the canned peaches, he guessed.

Selene said: "Did you have that thing they call manna?"

The little girl shook her head. "I don't think so."

"I have eaten manna sometimes when I am camping out. Your father gives it to me. It is as sweet as berries."

"These things were like that. Were they manna, Joe?"

"No, it was peaches," he replied.

He was stunned by the entrance of the father into the conversation. However, another bannock was brown and ready and he took it off the stove. This time he broke it into two pieces himself and gave one half to each of them.

"I wanted to bring you the peaches, Mama, but I could not have carried it," said Marina.

"They were yellow, you say?"

"In France," Joe remarked, "I ate figs. They are hard and green on the outside, but then they split open and when they do that they are purple inside."

They regarded him gravely, sitting side by side on the edge of the bed, both eating daintily, with his overcoat now spread out across both their laps like a ball gown.

"The purple means they are sweet and ripe," he said.

"Purple," repeated Selene. She seemed to like the word. She was quiet and receptive like Marina when she was interested.

"One time—" He was still cooking and he turned to adjust the draft on the stove. "One time our platoon came down a rocky hillside and there was a vineyard. The grapes were ripe and we picked whole bunches and stuffed them in our mouths. When I crunched my teeth down on them each one made a little pop in my mouth and then the sweet juice rushed out. They were purple too," he added.

Another bannock was ready now and he began to eat it, remembering.

"Some men lay on their backs under the vines and pulled down the grapes into their mouths," he went on. "The vineyard belonged to someone, but he must have run away; there had been so much fighting."

"Was it a whiteman that owned the purple fruit?"

"It must have been." It was odd to think of the French as whitemen. That category had hardly seemed to apply at the time. Besides, they weren't very white; they tended to be a brown colour, not far off his own. He thought of the brown bodies of various girls he had slept with; they had seemed to admire him more because of his colour.

"I will ask your father," Selene said to Marina. "But I think he does not own any purple fruit."

"Well, we don't own fruit," said Joe, once again, taken aback. "Only whitemen own things like that here."

Selene yawned suddenly. She lay back on the bed. Marina pulled the overcoat up around her—she, at least, seemed to know what he had intended it for. Tenderly she tucked her mother in and slipped the pillow under her head. Selene curled her legs up and went to sleep quite suddenly, her hand under her cheek. She looked as innocent as Marina in her sleep.

"You should sleep again too," said Joe to the child. "It is night and storming outside." He meant that there was nothing to fear from Marina's real father while the blizzard raged; but he was not quite sure she understood.

"I'm thirsty, Joe."

He gave her a drink from the dipper and then she lay down beside Selene on the bed, the button edge of the coat's long skirt turned down under her chin.

Joe had a hard time going back to sleep, although he lay down on the pallet. Talking of France had reminded him of many people dead or lost, and scenes long gone. When he did sleep, it was in a nightmarish way, mixing up things he had seen in the war with the pity he felt for the two forlorn female creatures on the bed.

He had once seen a prostitute brought out on the street with her head shaved, and the injustice of that scene had not escaped him.

When he woke up there was a little daylight, but the storm was still continuing. There were only three cold bannocks, which he had finished cooking the night before, and that was all the food they had. The water was still fine; since they had been home with the stove going for twelve hours or so, it had thawed, and now there was only an ice cake floating in the centre of the wooden butt. They could make tea.

The other two woke up then, and they ate and drank. Then, as usual, he gave Marina his comb so that she could comb her hair. Her hair was unusually thick and long and he had wondered what Rachel did to keep it in order before he came with his comb. It would take her hours and hours to comb and untangle hair like that with her fingers; but he thought that perhaps the people where they came from did not have combs, or else it was just that they were too poor ever to have owned one.

The two women spent the morning sitting on the bed, which Selene had straightened out as neatly as he would have done, and they combed each other's hair. After they finished, the mother's hair hung down straight enough, but it was ragged and uneven like

[329]

the fur of the timber wolf Joe had seen. Then Selene took some coloured threads out of the end of the blanket and began to make braids in Marina's hair with knots and wrappings done in the red yarn of the blanket. She braided her own hair then, taking some time over it, and using more red threads. After she had finished that she made a face painting on each of them, using soot from the stove, spitting into her hand and mixing up the soot to make paint.

Neither of them were even slightly bored. They chattered together as the decorations continued, sitting very close to each other. It was obviously a kind of holiday for them to be together like this.

In the afternoon, the wind began to die down and the snow did not seem so thick. Joe put on his overcoat and forced his way out the door, but it was hardly possible to get through it. The snow came up to the sill of the cabin's high little window. There was no way of going anywhere without snowshoes; but he realized that there was no point in any case. The snare lines were buried deep. They would have to starve another day until he could get out on top of the snow with his gun. When the snow stopped, the men of the village would be out combing the hillsides for their horses; at least Joe did not have horses to worry about.

The two women were completely unbothered by having to go without food. They had turned now to decorating Marina's wooden doll—and he guessed that Marina's imaginary father was in their play just as he was when Marina played alone.

Joe thought, as he watched them, that this strange delusion would probably pass if Marina stayed with him. As she came to realize that it was he she depended upon, he felt that the imaginary father would slowly go away.

But about Selene he was not so sure. He had originally believed that the father had been made up by her deliberately to comfort Marina, but it now seemed as though she herself believed in the reality of this person as well. She seemed quite mad to Joe, although he could well see how she had become this way.

He had not slept with Marie before he left for the army; they had just been boy and girl together, and the Church had told them that sleeping with a woman outside of marriage was a sin. When he got back, he found that she had waited for him and he was glad, although he would have married her anyway, even if she had had other men in the meantime.

He understood, however, how some men felt about this, Thomas Mountain, evidently, among them. When Thomas had found out that Marina might not be his child he had no doubt tried to put Selene away, but he had not been able to get her out of his mind, to remove his desires from her. And so, he had tried to destroy the child instead. But that had not been successful either, and he had had to go along still wanting his wife, with this third, undesired person whom she loved apparently more than she loved him. Then had come the death of his own child, for which he had perhaps blamed his wife, and he had tried hard then to drive her out.

Maybe it was this last thing that had finally unhinged him, for in driving her out of the house to spend nights and days crouching in the woods, he had exposed her to other men.

Joe knew this had happened. He had heard the boys talking about it. Even quite young boys would get together in gangs to catch and torment Selene. And he thought that probably Thomas Mountain did not believe that this stopped at harassment, as indeed, perhaps it did not.

It had come to him that now that he was the Chief he would have to try to put a stop to this. He continued to wonder whether he was afraid of Thomas Mountain, and whether he would be able to deal with him by reasoning alone, especially after Selene had spent two nights with him in her mother's cabin. However, this fact made it a certainty that he would have to deal with Thomas Mountain.

The snow finally let up the following day. Joe went out on snowshoes, but the only animal or bird he came across was a single partridge, which he shot.

He had not told Selene to stay at home, but it was hardly necessary to say it. The snow was so deep that it almost covered the little house in a gigantic curving drift that extended from the edge of the road to the trees behind.

Once again, he had to be glad that he had no horses. Those who did would be out frantically searching, for not many animals could have survived the intensity of the storm, and the ones which had were deeply mired, buried in some cases, in the drifted snow.

When he came home with the partridge, his mouth already watering in anticipation of the soup he would make, he found that Marina and her mother had been bathing and washing clothes in his absence. They had washed all of Marina's little things: her dress and underwear, and the long stockings that came up under her bloomers. She wore her grandmother's fringed shawl. They had also washed Selene's ragged dress and she wore the red blanket, which she had belted around her with Joe's army belt. The wet things hung steaming around the stove. All the water had been taken out of the butt.

Marina looked at Joe anxiously to see whether he was angry as he went outside with a pot to get some fresh snow for water to cook the partridge in.

When he came back, Marina said timidly, "She's just borrowing the belt for a little while."

"It's all right." He was even thinking it was good. He would not have known how to wash Marina's things.

He was also thinking that it was only by good luck that he and Marina had got back before the snow began. The cabin had been locked while they were away. He did not think Selene would have survived out of doors in the snowstorm.

Later that day he went out again, looking for food. He came upon a steer from the agency herd that had died in the storm, been buried by a drift, then partly uncovered again by the wind. He hesitated to take some of the meat, for it was not his steer; it belonged to the government herd. But there was no other food and so he cut off a leg and made his way back to the cabin. Later he learned that many others had done the same thing; the agency herd had been entirely wiped out and they were all still finding the frozen animals long into the winter.

When he came back in the evening from that second trip they were wearing their clean clothes and his belt had been neatly hung on its hook with his jacket. The water butt was half full of melted snow water. She might be mad, but he saw that she was able to keep house.

The following day was clear and the people began to come out of their houses and take stock of the strange new world in which they were living, and they also began to clear away the snow from the roads and in front of their houses, those who were not still out on the hills searching for the horses.

"Perhaps my father will come for my mother. Do you think he will come in all this snow?" Marina asked. She meant the imaginary father, but Joe was more concerned now about the real one.

Joe spent the day helping people to clear snow, but he went back to the cabin to make sure everything was all right there. Selene showed no disposition to leave now. She sat cross-legged on the floor and she had some things spread out in front of her that were like the contents of Marina's carpet bag: painted stones, horsehair braids with a few beads strung on them, feathers, animal bones with strange designs on them like the design in soot she had made on her face. She looked up at him apprehensively and began to gather the things together again.

It looked like a woman's bundle to Joe. Women were not allowed to make bundles any longer, but they did anyway, in secret. His mother's bundle, which he had seen even when she was alive, contained her marriage license, locks of hair from Joe and his brothers and sister when they were little, a decorated pipe she had inherited from her mother, and a little tobacco.

He said, "Selene, now that your mother is dead, this cabin is yours. I think you should stay here with Marina."

She was looking up at him while continuing to fold, more slowly now, the scrap of cloth around her pathetic treasures.

He went on, "I will move back to my parents' house, the house that was theirs when they were alive, but I will protect you. Today I will go around to all the people and get them to agree that it is your right to stay here."

She seemed to understand, because she nodded. Then she said, "My husband will not agree."

Joe said, "I will talk to Thomas Mountain."

It had been in his mind already that he would go around the village and tell everyone about how the agent had tried to trap him. But he had no idea how he was going to talk to Thomas Mountain.

He decided to begin that very evening, at the home of Thomas and his parents, because he now felt that if he could not resolve this he would not want to be Chief any longer. The old people were at home and although he must have been out all day looking for his horses, Thomas was there, cutting wood in the yard. When he saw that Joe had come to visit he put down his axe and came into the house which had two rooms like the home of Joe's parents. Joe supposed that when Selene was here, she and Thomas slept together in the outer room, just as he and Marie had slept in the outer room of his mother's cabin.

Joe said, "I think you know that since the death of Rachel, I have been looking after Marina."

Thomas raised his shoulder to indicate his indifference. He was a big man. His face was heavy like his body, and he frowned with concentration when Joe went on to explain how he had taken Marina with him to Edmonton and what the agent had tried to do there. Then Joe described how he and Marina had come home, and how they had just managed to arrive before the big snowstorm.

"Selene came just after the storm began. I think she was angry and afraid because I had taken Marina," he said.

Thomas Mountain was staring at him and he felt that he had the big man's full attention at last.

"She stayed in the house for three days and three nights because of the storm. I was there but I did not touch her. I think that Selene is not all there. But why was she out in the storm without even a jacket?"

Joe looked at Thomas, who said nothing. Then he looked at the old people and he saw that the mother was glad that he was saying these things and that she, at least, would agree with his request.

"In the past it was possible for a man and a woman to get un-married, I have heard," he continued. "This is not possible these days because of the priest, and I don't know how it was done among our people. But I think this is what you should do," he told Thomas.

The mother was nodding vigorously. Thomas continued to stare at him, but without the heaviness of suspicion. In his slow way, he was thinking.

"Selene has a cabin. She could stay there and look after the child. And as it is in an out-of-the-way place you would never have to walk past. This whole thing could simply be over for you," Joe suggested.

His mother was still nodding and the father nodded now too. Of course, this marriage had been their misery too, since they shared their cabin with it.

"But who will hunt for her?" asked Thomas. "Will they starve?"

"I will hunt for her," said Joe. "My parents and my wife are dead." He did not mention his dead children, although he thought of them. "I have no one to share my meat with. She will be under my protection, but I will live in my own house."

"This is a good way," said the father, and the mother was still nodding her head off. "You should agree to it, Thomas."

"But what if he is doing this because he sees Selene and wants to have her for himself?" demanded Thomas.

"I think Selene is mad," said Joe. "I do not want a madwoman."

"I have said this to you myself, that she is mad," interposed Thomas's mother.

"What if I see her sometimes? I might want to have her," he said.

"You could just think to yourself that you had been married to her before but now she is mad."

Joe realized how he was by implication validating Thomas's past behaviour, which he did not agree with or approve of at all. But it seemed necessary to do this in order to convince Thomas that he was not all bad, that he would be capable of making a good decision now. "I will tell Selene to stay away from you just as you will stay away from her," he said.

It seemed that agreement had been reached and he felt very good about this. He would be able to stay here and go on being the Chief. Otherwise he had contemplated that he might have to take Marina away, and Selene too, and he did not know where he could take them.

For the rest of the day he went from house to house telling

people about his trip to Edmonton. And he made sure to tell about how Selene had come to the cabin and spent the three days and three nights there with him and Marina, and how Thomas Mountain had now agreed to let her stay there and to leave her alone.

In the evening he went back to the cabin and found Marina playing outside in the snow. Selene was there, sleeping. But she woke up when he came in with the child. The whole top of the table had been decorated with an intricate design using soot and powdered ochre. It was probably what she had opened her bundle for, the bag of ochre. The dye on her hands and arms was renewed as well.

Marina said, "It is pretty, Mama! But how will we use the table?"

"Oh, we will sit on the floor! It is clean. I washed it," said Selene.

They both hung over the decorations on the tabletop, speaking to each other in their own language, which sounded like the cooing of doves in their soft voices.

"I spoke to Thomas Mountain," he said to Selene. "He has agreed to let you stay here and to leave you alone."

He felt he hardly had to tell her that she was to leave Thomas alone too.

"I told him he could get un-married to you, and I think he wanted that."

Selene said to Marina, "I was never married to him at all. I am married to your father."

Joe had heard that in the past, when there had been shortages of women, sometimes women did have two husbands. He thought he had better not confuse the issue, however. He began picking up his things, his uniform jacket and belt, the overcoat, the packsack he had taken to Edmonton. But he left many of the small things he had brought from home: a good bucket, the pot for boiling meat, boxes of matches, a towel. The comb he decided to leave as well. His hair was longer than it had been when he was in the army, but he could still comb it with his fingers.

Marina saw that he was going to leave and she was frightened. "What will we do at night?"

"She will be with you."

Selene was now looking at him with fear too.

Joe himself knew that it was a dilemma, but he could not stay with them without arousing the suspicions of Thomas Mountain.

There was a padlock, but the hasp was only on the outside. There was no way they could lock themselves in.

He took the heavy curved knife that Rachel had used for cutting meat and scraping hides from its place on the shelf and stuck it crosswise into the jamb of the door. "When you are here alone you should keep this knife here," he suggested.

"Can no one open it then?"

He went outside and called to Selene to stick the knife in the jamb. Then he demonstrated that the door could not be opened.

It was a sturdy door. No one could easily break it down unless he had an axe.

II

1947–9 · The Knife in the Door

◖ IN SPITE OF THE KNIFE IN THE DOOR, JOE WENT TO CHECK
on the cabin that night. The moon was up and there was light all
around it. No one had been there; the only tracks were his own,
going in and out during the previous day. It was hard for him to
reassure himself that the women were safe, however, and he had a
troubled sleep until morning. And in the nights after that, his sleep
was disturbed by dreams, not the dreams of the past, in which he
sometimes saw—as he longed to see—his loved ones, but strange
fearsome dreams which were connected to his worry about the
two helpless creatures alone in the cabin.

The following day the sun came out and a glaze of ice was on
the surface of the deep snow. Although it was still cold, there was
some indication that spring was coming now. It was almost Easter.

The Indian agent sent for Joe, telling him to come to the Mission
instead of the agent's house.

Joe went to the priest's house beside the church. Their priest had
been there a very long time. He was old and going blind, and the
people pitied him now and forgave him, at least a little, for some
of the things he had done with women when he was younger.

The priest and the agent were together with a strange whitewoman in the parlour of the house. Joe was not told the name
of the whitewoman, only that she was from the Children's Aid
Society and that she had come to take Marina.

"When we went to Edmonton, you took a child who was not
yours," said the agent. "That was how I became aware that you
have this girl. It is not healthy. It is not right."

"I didn't hurt Marina," said Joe. "I only took her to Edmonton with me because I had no one in my family I could leave her with."

"The child is an orphan?" asked the whitewoman, speaking briskly to the priest and the agent.

"She is not an orphan," said the priest slowly. He had his hand cupped behind his ear to catch what was said. Joe saw that he did not like the interference of this woman. He probably felt that she might blame him if she knew the whole story of Thomas Mountain and his mistreatment of Selene and Marina. For the priest himself had done nothing to stop it.

"Marina's mother is living in her house now, the one that became hers after Rachel died," Joe said. "Marina is there too. They are living together."

"The child is with the mother? Then what is the problem?" asked the woman.

The problem, Joe thought, is that the agent brought you here one day too late.

The priest was looking at Joe in surprise. "She is with the mother, you say?"

"I'll take you there," said Joe. "Then everyone will see that what I say is true."

He led the way, helping the priest along with a hand under his arm. They went down the road like a parade. Marina came running out of the cabin when she saw them coming.

"Put a cloth over the table for the tea," said Joe meaningfully. "Tell your mother we are all coming to see her."

Marina ran into the cabin while they waited outside. A moment later she came out with Selene and they stood hand in hand on the steps, looking at the visitors.

"Will they come in?" asked Selene, shading her eyes and looking at Joe.

It seemed to him that this was a perfectly reasonable thing to ask. But he was still nervous that she might exhibit her craziness.

"I think I had better see the inside of the house," said the whitewoman to the agent. "But I don't want tea."

When they got inside, the kettle was on the stove and in lieu of a cloth, Marina had put the fringed shawl over the table, covering up the designs in ochre and soot.

"It seems clean enough." The whitewoman wrinkled up her nose.

The priest too was peering around benignly, although he could hardly see. The little room was completely full with six people in it, and there was no place to sit down except on the bed or the bench behind the table. Marina took the kettle off the stove and put tea into the water.

"Why did you take the child to Edmonton?" asked the agent. "Did the mother agree to let her go?"

"Marina was living with her grandmother, who had just died," Joe replied.

"Where was the mother before?" asked the whitewoman. None of them was going to ask Selene anything, he saw, and he was relieved.

"She was with her husband who mistreated her and Marina. But now she has come to live here in her mother's house and I have got him to agree to leave them alone," said Joe.

"You have?" said the priest, astounded. He alone of the three whitemen knew the story and Joe thought that he should be ashamed; he had been their priest and he had not even tried to intervene.

"Is this the Chief?" the whitewoman asked the agent. He nodded, with a flash of dislike at Joe.

"Then I think you are probably doing a very good job," she said directly to Joe. "I would have taken the child if she had been in a bad place, but this is clean at least and she is with her mother. She is not an orphan."

The priest was smiling. The Indian agent was scowling. Joe wanted to laugh, but kept his features composed.

"Where would you have taken me?" asked Marina suddenly. She and Selene had been in eclipse while the others stood in the middle of the floor, debating their fate. She suddenly stood out again, the tea kettle in her hand.

"I would have taken you to a good place in Calgary called the orphanage, and then perhaps we would have gotten you a foster home with white people," answered the woman with assurance. She was used to talking to children crisply and decisively.

"But I want to stay here with my mother!" said Marina, and Joe, watching her hands, wondered whether she would throw the boiling tea and run for it if they tried to make her come with them.

"There!" said the woman, laughing. She turned around and marched out of the cabin, leading the two men, who followed after her meekly.

Joe decided not to go, because for one thing he liked the sight of the Indian agent now having to lead Father François on his arm, and for another thing he knew that if he went along to hear what the whitewoman said to the agent for bringing her from Calgary for nothing, it would awaken the agent's rancour against him even more. Instead he stayed and drank tea with Selene and Marina.

"Were you afraid?" he asked Marina.

"Yes," she said.

"I would not have brought them here if I had thought they would take you away."

"Your father would not have let them take you," said Selene.

Every night he got up and went down the road to check on the cabin in the clearing, and Joe began to feel rather light-headed from sleeplessness. Two pregnancies then came to term and he was up two nights in a row without any sleep. However, nothing worse happened than that he fell asleep when he was having tea with Selene and Marina, and slept the whole night on the floor. When he woke up he found that Selene had jammed the knife in the door although he was inside.

His home was very dusty and disorderly now because he spent almost no time there except when he was lying down at night. Since he ate with Selene and Marina and usually spent most of the day outside, he really did not need a home.

He decided to make the outer room of his house into a kind of office, like the Indian room of the agent's house. In future, he thought, it would be a good thing if he and his council could summon the agent and not the other way around. For he had a council now as well; they had been elected at Christmas. Antoine Bear was one of the councillors, as well as John Mountain,

Thomas Mountain's uncle. He cleaned up the outer room, and since he never cooked or ate there, this was easy. More things went to Selene's cabin: the long-handled ladle, a few plates and cups, things of that sort. Then he took things out of the inner room as well. The clothes of his wife and baby daughter he put into a box which he buried, but he found he could wear some of his father's clothing. His clothes from the army were becoming rather threadbare. His mother's bundle, with the marriage license and the locks of hair, he kept, without looking in it. Among his mother's other things he found two lengths of calico, a green one and a shorter piece which was blue, and he gave these to Selene.

Joe wondered when he gave her the cloth, whether Selene could sew. The next day he brought her his mother's sewing kit and he found that she had already started. Without needle and thread or scissors, there was not much she could do but tear the cloth, but she had constructed a skirt for Marina out of the blue piece, with a sash that tied. As soon as she got the sewing things she started in on the top of the dress, finishing it properly with a yoke and long sleeves.

Her own dress was already done, the skirt gathered with a sash, and the top roughly made out of one piece of cloth with a hole torn for her head.

They both seemed to love the dresses even before they were finished, and it gave him a peculiar pleasure to see Selene smoothing and minutely examining the pattern of tiny flowers on the cloth. He thought of taking her the mirror. The Band Council, he was sure, would not like to look in the mirror the way Selene would.

He brought it with him the following morning. It was just a small rectangle of glass, about the size of a cracker box. Marina looked into it for a moment, smiling at herself, then turned to Selene. "Look, Mama! Joe has a mirror!"

Selene approached very slowly, looking into it as the child held it up steadily in front of her. She stared and stared at herself, and then Joe was horrified to see that big tears had formed in her eyes and ran down her cheeks while she still went on staring.

He knew that she was crying over her lost beauty and he wished

[343]

that he had not brought it. Although her appearance had already improved greatly. She was not so pitifully thin and her eyes were no longer reddened and staring. Her hair was still patchy, and drabbled down at different lengths, but she had taken to putting it up in a bun at the back of her head and pinning it there with a peeled stick.

He suddenly could see that she once had been very lovely, with smooth skin, not roughened by exposure to the weather, a long neck, eyes dark and soft, a small straight nose, and hair as long and glossy and thick as Marina's. All of this demure traditional beauty had been taken and thrown away by Thomas Mountain, and now she was this thin, raddled creature.

"Don't cry, Mama," said Marina. "Look at our beautiful dresses."

They did that, both of them, for a few minutes, standing the mirror on the bench against the wall and smoothing and admiring, pulling their bodices straight, and twitching Rachel's shawl so that it hung down evenly over Selene's bare shoulders.

An old man died at Easter, and Joe took Selene to wash him. It had occurred to him that she could take over this office from her mother, and it would provide her with a tiny income.

He was a little afraid that she would not know what to do, although he thought that she might have helped her mother in the past. She seemed quite competent, however, and he left her after a few moments, to finish the job by herself, using a bucket of hot water and a soft cloth they had brought with them. But when he came back into the room, he found that she only had the corpse half into its clothes. The designs she had drawn on the old man's chest in ochre were disappearing as she buttoned his shirt.

She looked at Joe sideways. Then she gently painted a soft paste of ochre in each of the old man's hands, making a red spot on each palm. His hands would lie, of course, palm down, crossed upon his chest.

Joe knew that it had not been their custom until the coming of the mission to bury the dead underground. Instead, the corpse was decorated in a ceremonial fashion, then bound upon an elevated platform and left, high enough up and well-secured, so that it did not become ordinary carrion. The Church had forbidden this

custom and the places where the dead people had been left were
utterly proscribed and regarded with superstitious dread. Joe
now wondered how many old people had gone into the ground
decorated in this traditional fashion under their Sunday clothes.

Selene completed the dressing by tucking a white handkerchief,
folded and pressed by the old man's daughter, into the breast
pocket of his coat, then adding braided horsehair, threaded with
tiny beads and knotted around the small fluffy feather from a
grouse's foot. It was all she had. The other things that would go in
the coffin, perhaps a ring, or a prayer book, or a rosary, would all
be placed there under the eyes of the priest.

During the ceremony, as they sat and stood or knelt on opposite
sides of the church from one another, Joe and Selene were both
thinking of the decorations in the coffin, he knew.

For her service, Selene received a quarter from the old man's
daughter. She gave the money instantly to Joe with an air of
quiet confidence and the people standing around smiled slyly and
averted their eyes. They were making an assumption, he knew.
However, he could not help that.

He could have used the money to buy flour or sugar or tea.
But as they already had all of these things and were well-supplied
with meat, Joe walked to Bitter Root the following day and bought
a couple of lengths of satin ribbon in the general store. He was
aware by now of the craving of this woman for beautiful things,
and the ribbons were the only beautiful things he could buy there.

Selene took the ribbons with delight, treating them almost as if
they were alive, holding them in her hands and letting them spill
out and down onto the table in the lamplight. She did not seem to
realize that they were intended for her hair.

She had been finishing the bodice of her dress finally, trimming
it with the scissors and sewing the edges down. It was still not
the conventional style in which she had dressed Marina, but with
Rachel's shawl over her bare arms, it was decent enough. Noticing
this made him think again of his mother's scissors.

"I want you to cut my hair," he said. "It is getting as long as a
woman's."

Selene looked at the scissors on the table with the other sewing

[345]

things, but she did not pick them up. Instead she approached him, her eyes examining his hair. She went around to the back then, to look at the way it hung over his collar. Joe bunched it in his hand to show her.

A moment later she took the bunch away from him and began making it into a thick, short braid. Joe was surprised. He knew what she was doing because he could feel her thumbs and her knuckles pressing against his neck and the tug as she took up each bundle of hair in turn. But he could not act to stop her because he was suddenly overtaken by weakness. He had not been touched by a woman for more than a year, because his mother and his wife were dead. Feeling her cool deft fingers braiding his hair made him feel light-headed, with a yearning he interpreted as grief.

He could have taken his hair out of the braid immediately, or even just let it fall out while he was sleeping. It did fall out, but he renewed it himself the next morning.

There are no photographs of Medicine Bear with his hair in a braid. The only camera between Bitter Root and the mountains belonged to the Indian agent, who was not inclined to photograph the Chief.

The ice broke on the River. And then, almost instantly, it was summer. There was always this brief little time, between the ice and the arrival of the swarms of stinging flies and mosquitoes, when the people went to the River to bathe. The little boys, of course, went during the daylight hours, lit their small fires, tore off their clothes and danced up and down the beaches, in and out of the freezing cold water. Young men and women went as well, but after dark, and two by two. It was a time of tryst.

Joe woke up in the night, as he still usually did at least once, and went to check the place by the cabin. It had not occurred to him that this was an obsession, but he was driven to do it even now that the situation had apparently normalized itself and Selene and Marina slept safely inside, the door jammed with Rachel's knife. He was just in time to see Selene locking the door on the outside with the padlock and stealing away in the direction of the River.

Joe was overcome by a spasm of jealousy. This was an emotion he had never known. He believed she must be intending to meet one of the men other than her husband who had been with her. He believed suddenly, as he had never believed before, in her promiscuity—the notion that had driven Thomas Mountain into his jealous rages.

However, she did not go directly to the River by way of the road. Instead, she set off across country from behind her cabin, then mounted the bare hill beyond, and followed a long diagonal track towards the upper reaches of the River, some distance away.

It was not safe. This was bear country and Joe had not brought his gun. He had no idea that a woman would know how to reach the River this way and this thought aroused his jealousy even more. Although, if he had thought of it, he would have realized that she had lived for many years out on these bare hills and that the upper reaches of the River, distant from the village, were a place of refuge from her tormentors.

Their strange walk together took more than an hour. He had got behind for the sake of concealment, yet he was always able to follow her because she sang more or less constantly, humming or chanting in her own language. At last she came down to a flat bank on a curve of the River, a beach opposite a low cliff on the other side. Joe had been here many times before, hunting. It was a wild place.

He should have realized that she had come this far so as not to meet any of the younger people from the village, but he was still gripped by the idea that she was meeting someone.

He crouched on the bench above the River, watching her down there on the beach. She went to the edge of the water and, removing her slippers, she gingerly extended her bare toe, to test the temperature of the water. The way she bent over, removing the shoe, then putting out her toe, was wildly exciting to Joe. The shawl had slipped down and she had pulled it tightly around her waist so that the contour of her hips and legs was revealed; her arms and neck were bare.

She loosened the shawl and began to pull the dress off up over her head. Joe was clinging to a willow bush on the verge of the bank, shaking like a fever patient.

He saw her bare legs, her back, exposed in the moonlight. She

[347]

threw the dress behind her on the shingle and lifted her arms to the moon, chanting mournfully. Then she began to walk forwards into the swirling flooded River and he was suddenly terrified. The water was treacherous at this time of year, full of eddies and submerged logs and brush from the upper reaches. Also, as she was a woman, he believed she could not swim.

He no longer thought she was meeting anyone. His desire for her when she undressed had wiped that thought from his mind. He just knew that, intentionally or not, she might drown herself in the flooded River. He plunged down the bank in a shower of sand and arrived in time to grab her, nearly waist deep in the water, by her bare shoulders.

She twisted in his arms like a fish, but he held tight. A moment later she had turned around fully and was looking up into his face. Wet to the thigh, he began to draw her out of the water, grasping her by the upper arms, her breasts still pressed against his chest.

Even though he saw that her face was again decorated with one of her drawings in soot, it was an enchanted moment. As soon as she knew who he was, she had come willingly, and everything that happened after that she did willingly as well.

They were out there under the moon, alone together on the sand, and it seemed to them as though they had known it for some time, as though this were something that had already happened.

But then it was not like anything that had ever happened. Joe lay there on the sand, thinking that this woman whom he had just taken, perhaps was mad.

For one moment it seemed as though he looked over his shoulder at that sunlit flash that had been his life with Marie and their baby, between the mountains and the overarching cloud. But then it was gone.

"Joe," she whispered. "I want to go swimming!"

"But it isn't safe," he replied.

"Yes, it is. It's safe here. On this side of the bend, it's safe. The logs come up on the beach on the other side."

"Can you swim?"

"My brothers taught me."

By this time they were in the water again, arguing, waist deep.

He knew now that she was completely sane. She had been hiding it—to excuse her behaviour perhaps, or to save her life—for there were men, like Thomas Mountain, who would kill a woman who could swim.

They were both swimming, ducking under the water, coming up to splash each other and laugh. It was like being a child again. Joe caught a slender speeding foot, and reeled her in. She came, tumbling into his arms.

In the morning they went home, hand in hand. The soot marks were gone from her face, washed off in the River. But that was not the last time she decorated her face and body with soot or ochre. And she decorated him too. There are no pictures of that.

❦ THERE WAS A SURVEYING PARTY IN THE COUNTRY NOW. THEY came in from the northwest, over the mountains, and it seemed that they were avoiding the village and the Native people. At first there were rumours from people who had unexpectedly encountered them while pasturing horses. But then they got closer to the village, on lower reaches of the River, and they became less of a myth—the myth of an invading force of whitemen, or perhaps ghosts—and resolved themselves into a middle-aged whiteman, a civil engineer, and his younger assistant, going about their business, doing a survey of the elevations of the River.

Joe sent for the Indian agent to come to his parents' house. He and the Band Council sat on chairs in the front room while the agent stood in front of them.

"What are the men doing?" asked Joe. He knew the answer, as he had already talked to the older man that morning in their camp, while he was having breakfast.

"They were sent by the government to measure the River," replied the agent. There was actually a chair for him to sit in, but he was too proud, or else afraid.

"This Reserve belongs to us," said Joe. "The government should have sent to ask if we wanted the men to survey our River."

"Well, I am telling you that now." The agent was impatient. But when Joe had said the word "survey" he had been surprised. His eyebrows had gone up. He did not think Joe would know that word.

"Will we get a copy of their report?" asked Joe.

"No, their report is to the cabinet and the premier. Even I will not see the report," answered the agent. "I am an agent of the federal government. I have nothing to do with the premier."

Joe felt that this was false. The agent had taken him to Edmonton, after all. He seemed to be hand in glove with the provincial government.

"I am wondering what good it is to have you as an agent," he said. "You don't let us know what the government is doing and you refuse to tell the government what we want. Are you good for nothing but to pass out the money and the shells?"

The agent's face became very red, but he said nothing.

"I don't know whether you will see the premier. But I'm sure that you will see someone in the government after this meeting. Perhaps it will be those men you did not introduce me to in Edmonton. Tell them that we did not ask for our River to be surveyed and that we want to see the report."

The agent was bright red with fury. He burst out, "I will tell them nothing of the sort! But I will tell people who are powerful and important how insolent you are and they will send the Mounties to put you in jail!"

Joe said, "Well, perhaps the Mounties will come but I don't think they will put me in jail for asking you to do your job. And on the subject of the shells and the money; you delivered them very late last year when you threw them down in my house here. Please be more punctual this time!"

The Band Council was rather timid in the presence of the agent, but still they could not help laughing. The way Joe said this made it a tremendous joke on the agent and it tickled everybody's sense of humour. A tremendous shout of laughter went up after he had turned on his heel and gone out.

Joe was not so foolish as to think that by scoring off the Indian agent he would stop the government's plans and he went home after this meeting, considering.

Home was now Selene's cabin. He had given up any pretence

of staying in his parents' house, although since he was out all day walking about the village and talking to people, seeing the ones who considered themselves his patients, as well as checking his snare lines and hunting, it would have been hard for anyone to detect any difference in his habits. However, Selene and Marina knew.

They were delighted to see him so early in the evening. Marina ran to put the kettle on. Selene got up from where she had been sitting cross-legged on the floor making a complex arrangement of twigs and small animal bones.

Although he now knew she was not a madwoman, Joe still found her habits perplexing. Making these designs was part of her way of living, like the eccentricity of her dress and the elaborate face and body paintings that she made. She often would start as soon as she woke up in the morning and would sit for hours laying it out. He thought that perhaps it came from a dream. She put the things out this way, then that way; maybe she was trying to remember how it had been in the dream.

They sat for a while in silence, drinking tea. At first Joe was still thinking about the Indian agent, but gradually, as the peace of the moment began to soothe him, he started wondering whether Selene would go swimming with him that night, and picturing what it would be like. He thought of the way they would sometimes lie in the burbling shallows out of the mosquitoes, talking softly. For he was now telling the story of his life, which was really the story of his time in the war, but not as he had with Marie, leaving many things out. He was omitting nothing. For he knew that Selene had the passion and imagination to understand the tragedy that it all had been, and he was not afraid that he might hurt her by telling; she was not a naive young girl like Marie. Her life had contained as much tragedy as his, in its own way.

The disposition of things in the cabin was still that Marina and Selene shared Rachel's bed, while Joe slept on the straw pallet. They made love only late at night when they went to the River. This was partly so as not to shock or frighten Marina, who might wake up. But also it was because neither of them could afford to have it known that they were lovers. And because they felt that the way they had found one another was unique, and that they were coming to know things about one another in this secret life they were leading at night. Things that neither of them had ever been able to reveal before.

Later on, they stole out and made their way over the hills, leaving Marina locked in the little house. The brief spring was still with them and the stinging insects were very numerous, forming huge swarms all along the lowlands of the River. It was a relief to get out on the hills where the night breeze was blowing. For a while they were not alone, for there were other lovers, even married people, who took advantage of the warm nights to get out of their over-populated homes. But as they got further and further away from the village, the sound of hushed talk and stifled laughter died away. Once they were on their bend in the River again, Joe was fairly sure they would be alone.

The surveyors' camp was downstream about half a mile, and this was something else that would guarantee their solitude. The surveyors were regarded with superstitious dread, even though it was now known what they were doing. Whitemen never came to stay on the Reserve. People knew that they were afraid to come; so those few whitemen who ever set foot on the land, like the agent and the priest, were thought to possess special authority and protection, perhaps of a supernatural kind.

Once they reached the little shingle on the bend of the River opposite the cliff, they fell into each other's arms. Then talking quietly and laughing they made their way hand in hand into the freezing water of the River. It was not possible to stay long in the water, but staying out was equally impossible because of the swarms of biting insects. Somehow these difficulties were not bothersome because they were in each other's company.

Humans were not the only creatures beset by the mosquitoes on these early summer nights. Coming over the hills they would often meet small herds of elk or antelope running wildly, faces to the wind, trying to escape the torment of the stinging hordes around their eyes and tender noses. Other animals, the predators, were also driven mad by the clouds of mosquitoes, even though their thick coats protected them to some extent.

[352]

Joe and Selene crouched shivering in the shallows while he described in minute, painful detail, how after the battle of Caen, despite the incredible losses sustained by his battalion, the Canadians had pressed forward against the German tanks.

Suddenly out of the darkness up the bank a huge form appeared, coming straight towards them.

Joe stood up, naked, the water lapping around his knees, with Selene a little behind him.

For a moment he thought they were both doomed to die. The enormous creature was moving at the speed of a train. And it seemed that even if it wanted to avoid collision, it would not be able to stop.

It was a full-grown male mountain grizzly, its huge neck ruff silvery in the moonlight, its tiny eyes wild with the horror of the flies, its nose plastered with clay from the benches of the River in a desperate attempt to protect this tender exposed place.

At the last moment it swerved and plunged into the water so close beside them that the splash and spray broke over them like surf. It reached the current in the stream and began to swim strongly with it; then still visible, beaching again several hundred yards downstream, above the surveyors' camp. It climbed the riverbank there and then was gone from sight.

Joe turned around and took the woman in his arms, supposing that she would cry. She hugged him tightly, but did not do any of the hysterical things he was expecting. Instead she gave him a long rapturous kiss, her body melting against his.

It was Joe himself who seemed the more adversely affected by the incident. His heart was still beating crazily; he was out of breath and could not speak. For a short while he was barely aware of the woman in his arms and could only think of his gun, where it hung in the cabin at home. But then after a few moments he became aware again of the hushed peace all around them, and of the delicate body he was clasping so closely.

Somewhat later, crouching in the shallows, she said: "I think your protective spirit must be a bear, Joe."

"Well, it is my name, Bear," he said, wondering.

And it was true, he remembered, that when he had helped his

father as a boy, guiding the tourists, the rich whitemen who shot grizzlies as trophies, and had their heads stuffed and mounted to hang on the walls of their houses, he had never himself harmed a bear. He had shot plenty of other animals for meat or sport, but never a bear.

It was not until the following evening that he discovered what the bear had done in the camp of the surveyors.

He and Antoine and another older man, named Tall Grass, had gone out to see the surveyors—actually to ask them if they needed help in moving their camp, for this was something they had to do every couple of days. It was not in anyone's mind to harm these men, merely to help them, and perhaps find out more from them about the government's plans for the River. However, when they came to the surveyors' camp they found it torn to shreds and trampled. The tent was in rags, the flag thrown down on the ground and ripped, its pole broken in half. The food had been excavated from its burial place, and empty tins were strewn across the dead firepit and over the torn and broken body of the surveyor. His assistant lay about fifty yards away; he had apparently had time to run and climb a cottonwood while the crazed animal was mauling and tearing his boss, but the bear had then come after him and, rearing on its hind legs, had torn off branches of the tree and finally bent and snapped the top of the main trunk to which the terrified young man must have been clinging. The three men were appalled, standing on the edge of all this carnage.

"I'll go get the agent," said Joe.

"Perhaps he will have you arrested by the Mounties," suggested Antoine.

"The Mounties will have to come," agreed Joe. "Maybe I should get them first before I get the agent."

The other two looked at him in surprise.

"I'll go to Bitter Root and call them to come from Abercrombie," Joe said. "In the meantime, you will have to watch over this place. Don't touch anything."

Joe then walked and ran the ten miles into Bitter Root and used the telephone in the store there to call the Mounties. The police stopped on the way to pick him up and then they drove to the village and some distance on a trail toward that part of the River, being stopped in the end by the dry track of a stream. By the time they arrived at the surveyors' camp it was getting dark, but the moon was up.

The police looked around rather helplessly; then they took the shattered corpses of the two men and jolted back over the hills to the agent's house. From there the police corporal put through a call to his wife and to the coroner in Abercrombie while the other policeman took a deposition from Joe.

The agent broke in: "Why did this man walk to Bitter Root to call you? He knew there was a telephone in this house."

The policeman looked at Joe, who said calmly:

"I didn't want the camp to be disturbed. I left Antoine and Joseph Tall Grass to watch over it."

"To watch over it! Perhaps to change things."

"To change things?" asked the senior Mountie. "What do you mean by that?"

"Perhaps they set it up afterwards to look like a bear attack. But what if it was murder instead?"

The two policemen regarded the agent very seriously. Then they looked at Joe.

"Why didn't you use this telephone?" asked the older one.

"Because I wanted to have you see the camp first," said Joe. "I thought the agent might tell you to arrest me before you had seen it."

The agent looked at Joe and snarled: "I would certainly have done that!"

"Have you seen the camp yourself, sir?" asked the policeman.

"No. This is the first I've heard of it. I told you!"

"Why did you say that you thought there might be foul play then?"

"Because this man—this Chief—was against the survey of the River, which those men were carrying out under government seal."

"It is not true we were against the survey. We had only just heard about it. We went to the camp today to try to find out what it was about."

"We thought we could help them to move their camp too," said

Antoine, who had just come in, out of breath. It was a long walk, but there had been no room in the policemen's car.

"Well—" the corporal looked at the constable. "I thought it looked like a bear attack. Didn't you?"

They both stared at the Indian agent who was bright red with anger.

"The tree—it was actually broken off by the bear, sir," said the constable.

"A man might have done that."

"A man with claws," said the corporal.

"Who weighed nearly half a ton," added the constable.

When Joe got home it was nearly morning. He had gone back to the camp with the coroner, helped the police to shroud the two corpses, and then made a further deposition to the coroner's assistant.

Selene heard him knocking on the door and rushed to take out the knife. Then she flew into his arms. She was more terrified now than she had been when the bear was coming toward them. She had not been afraid to die. It must have happened often enough to her that she thought she was going to. But she was afraid for him.

They were embracing inside the cabin now with the door jammed again, and Marina woke up in the bed.

"Joe!" she said. She was yawning and stretching as they sprang apart.

"You see, it was all right, Mama," she remarked. "Joe came back."

They were both so relieved that they began to laugh. They all laughed and then Marina lay back down and went to sleep again, almost instantly.

The other two lay down together on the insufficient straw pallet, and Joe whispered to Selene what had happened during the night while she lay listening with eyes wide with alarm.

"The agent wants to get rid of you. Perhaps he wants to kill you," she said.

"Maybe. But how can he do it?" asked Joe. He was accustomed to the idea that someone wanted to kill him. A great many people had tried, although perhaps it was not so personal.

"He will try to make them think that you are bad. This time he failed, but perhaps he will do it next time something happens."

"I think I have embarrassed him so much before those policemen that he will not be able to do it."

She looked at him with a smile. "You are so smart, Joe."

"I didn't want to be flattered."

"You did want to be flattered. But now that I have done that, you are too smart for me."

"Maybe I am smart. But there is something I would like to know," he said. "What are you doing when you lay out the twigs and animal bones in your bundle?"

"I don't know," she said vaguely.

"Tell me just a little."

"Well, sometimes I see things," she said. "But it is not that simple."

"But do you see things in the future?" he asked. "Or only things in the past or made-up things?" He felt that he needed to know this. There had not been any seers among them for so long. He had never met one. "Do you ever see me in your vision?"

"I am trying to!"

"I would like to know what is going to happen."

"I only know that I love you!" she cried, embracing him with her long slim arms.

Their long flight together into the mosquitoes was now over. The imaginary father was still there, however. He showed up the next morning.

"Was my father here last night?" asked Marina.

"Yes, he was here," said Selene, looking at Joe. "You ought to remember."

"I only saw Joe." Marina also looked at Joe with a smile.

He felt it was all going to come together for her soon and that he would become Marina's father. He wondered if he would like that. He thought that he would.

The time when they collected the annuity was approaching again. Joe thought how naive he had been the previous summer when the agent had made him Chief. This year he sent some young men and boys to the agent's house with a note saying they had come for the things. The agent obviously considered it prudent to send them; then he would not have to appear at all, which was Joe's intention.

They had the midsummer feast as usual. The old priest was there and started the feast with a long prayer. He could hardly see at all any longer and had to be supported on either side by a young boy. Somehow, time had turned him into an angelic old man who was loved by all the people. Joe had heard many things about his behaviour as a younger man, however, and he could remember the catechistical instruction he had received from Father François, whereby it had seemed that his very thoughts were going to send him to hell. If this priest had not been present, if he had never come to live with them, the feast they were at would have been very different, and they would have been dancing dances that no one now could remember and singing songs and chants to which no living person now knew the words.

At this feast Thomas Mountain stood with another woman. The woman was a widow with a couple of children; her husband had died in the flu epidemic. She was tall and strong like Thomas, with thick hair and a broad face, like Thomas's face. Looking at them, Joe thought that they were well-matched. Thomas no longer had the brooding, unhinged look he had had before.

Selene had not come to the feast, but stayed at home looking at the things that were in her bundle. However, Joe had taken Marina, who no longer clung to him so closely, but went off to play with the other little girls.

After the feast he saw Thomas leaving with the woman and walking towards her house. He felt good about this development, although he was a little afraid on behalf of the woman. But he thought that since it was to her house that Thomas was going, if he beat her, he would at least not be able to drive her out, the way he had driven Selene out of his parents' house.

Father François died the following week. Selene was called up to the Mission to wash his body. She went, and Joe saw that she took the small bag of ochre out of her bundle. She was going to paint the old priest. It seemed somehow appropriate. It laid to rest many of Joe's mixed feelings about the old man. He was just a man, after all, and he had lived so long among them, he could be honoured in death like one of their own people.

There was a shortage of these French priests now and the mission house was closed after the funeral. A priest came on Sunday and one other day a week, travelling from a mission house on another reserve.

In the meantime, the Protestants sent a missionary to the Reserve. He and his blonde, pregnant wife and a flock of tow-headed children lived in a tent for a while, but were soon accommodated in a tiny house by their converts.

Joe talked to the missionary, who was a tall and handsome whiteman of about forty. On the surface he seemed flexible enough, but Joe thought that he was narrow and rigid in his ideas. There had been no Protestants on the Reserve during the war; this man had been an army chaplain, and had lived on a base in Alberta. They got along well enough, talking about the army.

The Catholic Church responded to this incursion by reopening the mission house and sending in a priest to live on the Reserve again. This priest, Father Lambert, a narrow, middle-aged man, who had not been with the army, attempted then to drive out the Protestants by direct denunciation. He told the people not to let the Protestants into their houses, not to talk to the minister or his wife and children, not to let them have the house they had been given.

Everything the priest said was such an affront to the people with their traditions of hospitality and sharing and tolerance that these orders from the pulpit were more or less openly ignored.

At the same time the warfare between the two churches made people cautious. No one knew whether the Protestants would stay for long, but they were glad in a way that there was a challenge to the iron grip of the Catholic Church. Joe was glad. And many people compromised by going to both churches, to the tent church of the Protestants in the late morning after mass. It was entertaining. Joe too went to both churches every Sunday and Marina was in the Protestant Sunday School.

In August, the Protestant minister paid a call upon Joe at home. He arrived so soon after Joe came in the house that Joe thought the man must have followed him home. No doubt it was hard to find out where the Chief stayed for he was never at home in his own house, which was now used only as the meeting place. Selene had already put away her bundle. She stood, smiling shyly, and looking to one side as Marina and Joe offered the man tea and made him a place to sit down.

"Is this your wife?" Reverend Mader asked.

Joe knew that if he said she was, other people could tell him she wasn't. Also, because of Thomas Mountain, he didn't know what to say. Instead he replied, "Her name is Selene."

Reverend Mader seemed to take it for granted that she was his wife now. He looked at her directly and said with a smile, "You should come to my church sometime. I won't bite you!"

Selene laughed. In fact, she went to no church, not to the Catholic mission either, as the missionary was supposing.

When she laughed, Joe noticed a flicker of admiration in the man's eyes. Then, as Joe was also looking at Selene, he suddenly saw how beautiful she had become. It had happened these last few months and he had become accustomed to it. Her face had ceased to be hollow-cheeked and sunken-eyed, but had filled out to a pure oval. Her eyes, which slanted slightly, delightfully, in towards her nose, were bright and curious. Her figure too had filled out and she was now slim rather than emaciated; her dress clung to the nice curves of her hips and her small bosom. Her hair had become glossy again and sprang up to cover the patches where it had been pulled out. She kept it in a bun at the back of her head and it fell down slowly during the day, in shining strands that hung around her face. To the missionary, Selene must look like a laughing young girl, for it was hard to believe now that she was even as old as Joe.

"I wanted to talk to you about the position of my church," the man said, turning back to Joe. He explained about the denunciations of the priest, although this was hardly necessary; Joe had been present to hear them himself. The minister perhaps assumed that people went to only one church at a time.

"What I am saying is, do I have your permission to stay here and preach? People have told me to ask you." This meant it all rested on him, but Joe was not unhappy about that. He had already noticed how much the presence of the strange religion undermined the authority of the priest.

Joe said that he had seen that the minister and his family had already been given a house, and that this was fine with him. "I come to your church myself," he said.

The minister nodded and again Joe thought that he was very naive to think that people would desert the priest completely, burning all bridges, before they saw that it was safe.

But Joe was curious about the new religion and he asked the question which now was in the forefront of his mind. "Is it possible in your religion for a man and a woman to become divorced?"

The minister was surprised to be asked this so directly, and he laughed. Then he looked thoughtful and replied, "No, it is not possible in any but the heathen religions for a man to divorce his wife. But why do you ask?" And again he cast his roving, admiring glance at Selene, sitting cross-legged on the floor in the lamp shadows.

"For no reason," said Joe. "I wanted to know whether you were truly different, that was all."

After the missionary had explained at some length about the Christian religion, he got up and left. Marina had already fallen asleep on the bed. Joe lay down with Selene on the pallet and they whispered together.

"I was afraid when you asked him that question," she said. "He might have guessed something."

"No whiteman knows about you and Thomas Mountain, not even the priest that is here now. And I think he is too busy to find out."

"Was it to keep the priest busy that you said this missionary could stay?"

"I couldn't stop him from staying," said Joe, smiling.

"You could have but you wouldn't." She was thinking of the power of the bear spirit, he knew.

"I didn't like the way he looked at you," he said.

"I think—" she laughed. "If I went to his church he would try to bite me!"

She was a playful woman, and Joe, who liked to tease, was

[361]

surprised and delighted to be teased in return. They would often lie in each other's arms, talking in this delightful way about things they both knew were serious and even frightening.

The pity he had felt for her had been totally supplanted; he loved her with his whole heart. And he knew that what she felt was not just gratitude; she loved him too.

He said now, "You have become very round and make a nice juicy mouthful. However, you are my mouthful, not his!" Then he began to demonstrate what he meant by this and they ceased talking.

Selene did not eat the next morning but sat down and opened her bundle first thing. Joe was a little worried by this. He still did not understand how the things in the bundle functioned, but he had to trust her, because she was intelligent. Perhaps she was even a seer. He was hoping that she was one.

The next morning he came back because he had forgotten his knife and he found Selene throwing up. She did not explain and he did not ask, but it was perfectly obvious to him what it was all about, and he waited for her to tell him, feeling very happy.

His career as a midwife had continued; it was his main source of income. Just at this time a woman came to term and gave birth to a healthy child and Joe came home rejoicing, to tell his family.

"I am pregnant," Selene told him when they lay down later. "It is your child, Joe."

"I know that! Of course it is mine. I am very glad."

"I was afraid that you might not believe me, because—"

"Do you think I am like Thomas Mountain?" But there was something he wanted to know, he realized. He said slowly, "Marina is not Thomas's child, is she? And is that why—?"

"She is Thomas's child," Selene replied. She spoke fiercely.

Joe was sorry to hear that Marina belonged to Thomas. He could be a little glad, though, because Thomas did not know it, and perhaps Marina would not believe it either when she got old enough to understand these things.

"Then why—?" he persisted.

"Because he was not the first man I had been with and he found out. I thought it would not be possible for him to tell, but he tormented me and finally I admitted it."

Joe was now thinking with jealousy himself about that other man, wondering who he was, although he must have lived on the reserve where she came from.

"He was killed in the war," she said. "When I knew he was dead, I married Thomas. I thought I would never love anyone again."

"So is he—the other father?" Joe asked. He was not sure that he should ask this. The other father had completely gone from what Selene said to Marina now, and even Marina mentioned him less frequently. He really belonged to the time when Selene was mad.

"The other father?" she said vaguely.

"Marina talks about him."

"Oh yes. It was something I made up to comfort her."

She had no idea, he thought, how powerful her vision was, and how strongly it had affected Marina.

"Marina is not like Thomas," said Joe thoughtfully.

"No, she is like my mother. It is too bad she will forget her."

"How do you know that?" Joe rose above her on one elbow, trying to see her face in the darkness. Did she know things about the future, then?

"She is so young," replied Selene, vague again.

Joe lay down and began joyfully to contemplate his own child. Boy or girl, it would grow up without the shadow that lay on Marina.

"What are you thinking, Joe?"

So she did not know everything.

"I am not sure that I was thinking. I was feeling happy."

She was bending over him this time. A warm drop of water fell on his cheek and rolled down past his ear, then another one.

"Perhaps it is already the time when I shouldn't touch you?"

"Not yet. The baby will come in March, I think. We can still touch one another now."

"Then let's do that!"

The Protestant minister continued to preach in the tent church to which Joe went every Sunday after mass. But he noticed that the constitution of the congregation subtly began to change and became more than half women. The real adherents, those who sang the hymns and contributed the food to the minister's family, were all women. Joe understood that no woman could like the priest, who was dark and narrow and rigid, with a long horrid face like a coffin—as unlike Father François as it was possible to be. But he also wondered how all those women could like the Protestant minister so much when there were so many of them. How would he choose among them and wouldn't it make all the others jealous when he did choose? Perhaps he would stay faithful to his wife and his power would come from that, but Joe doubted that he would be able to do so, some of the women were so young and beautiful.

It was the time of year that the pack trains formed to take the outfitters to the mountains. Thomas Mountain would be very busy from now until Christmas and Joe was glad, because it was good to have him gone where he would not even by chance be able to see Selene, now that she was pregnant.

The Indian agent sent for Joe. Joe considered and then decided to go. If he sent a message that the agent should come to his house instead, the man might not do it; and Joe needed to know what was on his mind.

It was almost the same set of men that he had met there the first time, but one of the ones from Edmonton was there as well: the one who had shown that he thought the agent was a bungler.

Joe had taken Antoine and Joseph Tall Grass along to be witnesses for he did not dare meet the agent alone any longer; there was too much bad feeling between them. Now he said to the agent,"Will you please tell me who these men are before we begin?"

The agent grudgingly began to say the names of the men. When he came to the one from Edmonton, he said that he was Theodore Morton, from the Ministry of Mines and Resources. Joe looked closely at this man, as he was almost certain that he was the one who had called for this meeting. He was wearing the uniform of a captain in the Northern Alberta Royal Regiment, and Joe was willing to give him some respect, for his medals and insignia said that he too had been in the war. Joe wondered whether he had worn his uniform for this reason, however.

The man spoke of the surveyors who had been killed by the bear. He referred to this as an 'unfortunate accident' and Joe nodded, not looking at the agent. Then he asked Joe whether he had ever met the men, and Joe wondered if this was a test, to see if he remembered what he had told the police.

Antoine broke in and said: "We only went to their camp to talk to them and to offer to help move their tents!"

Theodore Morton said that the government now realized that it had been a mistake to send such a small survey team into bear country, and they wished to organize a much bigger team, using a pack train and guides with guns from the Reserve, who would be paid the same rates the outfitters paid.

Although another pack train would be hard to muster at this time of year, Joe thought that there would be enough men and horses to handle the relatively easy work of a survey in the low foothills. He looked at Antoine and Joseph and he could see that they were in favour; it would bring more money into the Reserve.

It was, he knew, a trick, a bribe, to make them accept the survey. But nevertheless, he said, "Yes, we will find the men and horses to supply the team. It is a very good thing you came to ask us about this first—" He put emphasis on that word, "Because we are willing to help anyone who is honest and who treats us fairly."

"That is good then," said Theodore Morton. He looked at the agent triumphantly for a moment. Then he stood up to indicate he was a busy man. The meeting was over.

Joe had been standing all the while. He said, "I would like to ask you for something."

"What is that?"

"When the survey is complete, I would like you to give us the surveyor's report."

The man was surprised. Then he laughed. "A surveyor's report is not an easy thing to understand," he said.

"We would like to know the government's plans."

Theodore Morton shrugged. "Very well, of course you can have the surveyor's report," he said.

"The paper you gave me to sign in Edmonton said that the government would dam the River and use the water for irrigation," Joe said. "Is it for the dam that the survey is being done?"

Theodore nodded. He was looking closely at Joe now; and Joe was glad that he also had worn his uniform. They were the only two men in the room who had been in the war.

"Will the government move the people when there is nothing to drink?" asked Antoine.

Theodore Morton said to Joe, "I guess you know that the government of Alberta can't move you people. The River will still be there, only it will have a dam on it."

Joe said, "I think it is not that simple. Otherwise it would not have been necessary to try to trick me into signing the paper."

Theodore Morton again glanced at the agent.

"It wasn't I who attempted to trick you," he said. "I heard that you were willing to sign."

"I am only the Chief," said Joe. "I can't agree to something the people haven't even heard of. If you want our agreement in future, you need to tell us what we would be agreeing to. This is why I want to see the surveyor's report."

Theodore Morton bowed his head. He stood there for a moment like that, evidently thinking, and Joe wondered what would happen. For this kind of forthright speaking he would have been beaten at the mission school. And the man had been a captain; in the army he would not have spoken to a captain in this way. But he did not see why a whiteman would prefer trickery over plain speech.

"All right," said Theodore Morton, raising his head. "After the surveyor's report is finished I will come down here and help you understand what it means. Then you will at least know."

"Then we will at least know," agreed Joe, and for the first time their eyes met.

When he told Selene about this in a whisper that night, she was only interested in whether he would go with the pack train.

"But I wouldn't leave you when you are going to have a baby," he said in surprise.

"I did not know there could be a man like you on earth!" she cried.

After the pack trains left, there were so many men gone that there were only women in both congregations. In the tent church Joe watched the fervent young women when they sang the hymns. He was sure that the Protestant minister was taking someone out on the hills at night—and perhaps more than one. The weather was fine and dry and it wasn't cold yet. Selene was now visibly pregnant. She said to Marina, "We will be very happy when the baby is born in the spring."

"I would like to be the only girl. So it would be better if you made it a boy, Mama."

"I can't make it a boy!" said Selene, laughing. "But I think it is a boy," she went on.

"Will our father come and live with us then? Wouldn't he like to see the baby?"

"The baby does not come from your father."

"Who does it come from?"

"From Joe."

The little girl looked tranquilly at Joe. She said, "Joe is not my father, is he, Mama?"

"No, you have another one."

"I thought so. Sometimes I forget."

Joe felt that her confusion was still very great. However, it was only a matter of time and then she would understand. He was not looking forward to her knowing who her real father was, though, and what he had done. It was easier—perhaps it was better—to let the delusion persist a little longer.

They had a very good Christmas because so many families had a little money from the men going out with the pack trains. The money would help to get them through the months of snow, when people were sometimes desperate for meat.

At the feast Joe again saw Thomas Mountain standing with the broad-faced widow. They went out together again afterwards. This thing had almost settled itself, Joe thought. However it went with the widow, at least Thomas seemed to have turned his thoughts away from Selene. Feeling very happy, he took Marina home with him and they found Selene placidly sewing baby clothes by candlelight.

It turned out that she could sew very well in an ordinary way, now that she had his mother's sewing things. Also, she had put away her bundle and never looked in it any more. Whatever had driven her to take out and arrange and rearrange those things day after day had left her now. She was calm and happy and did nothing all day but normal household things, keeping the fire, cooking, dressing her little girl and plaiting her hair, as well as her own, and Joe's hair.

Their life together was delightful during these winter days. Joe himself stayed home; he no longer felt a need to hide the fact that he really lived with Selene and Marina. They never quarrelled despite the long days together. Sometimes they lay awake at night, talking playfully about the baby or merely looking into one another's eyes and thinking of him.

He had made a bed for Marina that fitted against the wall and served as an extra seat during the day. Selene now slept in her mother's bed and Joe slept there with her. It was understood by Marina that this was the way it should be, as he was the father of the baby.

It seemed that the arrangement of things in the cabin was helping her to understand. Joe wondered if this was really all that the bundle had done for Selene when she was emerging from her madness. It allowed her to think, and perhaps in rearranging the things in it, she could think differently.

One day he was out hunting for grouse when he met Thomas Mountain. They began walking together, as they were far from the village and the hunting was poor. Nothing was said about Selene or the widow, but Joe noticed that when they returned to the houses with the poor upshot of their hunting, Thomas went down the street past his parents' home, where he had lived with Selene. He was plainly hunting for the widow and her family now.

In March, the baby was born, after a short uncomplicated labour. He was a very wide-awake, alert baby from the start, and he had a shock of black hair standing straight up on his head that made him look like Joe in his army photograph. In other respects he resembled Joe too, and she named him Joe.

Everyone in the cabin was completely infatuated with the baby and there was hardly a moment when he was not being held by someone. Marina played with him and tried to teach him to hold things, and as a result, he was able to do this long before most babies. As for Joe, the hunting was very poor that spring and he was often out for hours to return empty-handed or with only a grouse or rabbit, and he would fall asleep on the bed, hugging the small boy child in his arms.

People were now quite desperate for food, as the money they had made in the fall had run out and there was no game. The agent had been away for the month of March, which was a desperate time, but people did not expect help to be forthcoming from him; the system of rationing they had depended upon before had stopped during the war, after this agent had come. Some men got work from the park service or doing odd jobs around Bitter Root for the farmers. It was a relief when April came and the flocks of ducks and geese began to travel through and land on the River—although the hunt was illegal.

Joe was busy, but he wondered what had become of the survey report, and whether he would ever see it. It was a great surprise when, early in May, he heard that a strange whiteman was in the village looking for him. He found Theodore Morton leaning against the fender of his automobile outside his parents' house, which was now the Band hall, looking rather helpless. He had come alone. But under his arm was a portfolio; Joe saw that he had kept his promise to bring the surveyor's report.

They went into the front room together and spread out the papers and drawings on the table.

"I should get the Band Council," said Joe, thinking that most of them would be duck hunting.

"No. You can show this to them later. I would like it to be just the two of us. You see, I came alone."

Theodore Morton was wearing a three-piece suit this time. His shoes were black and very shiny. Joe was in wool pants and suspenders, and a plaid shirt of his father's, his gun slung behind him, his hunting bag in his hand. He wondered why the man had not worn his uniform and if it meant he intended some trickery.

"You seem like a man I can talk to," said Theodore Morton.

Joe nodded, but still he was cautious.

"Then I will not pull any punches. This dam will not be built next year, or the year after, and perhaps not for many years, but it will be built. These plans only indicate some of the places where it might be built, but all of them affect the Reserve." He indicated on the drawings where the dam might be built and where the flooding would occur.

"What I want to know is, what is your bottom line?"

"My bottom line?" said Joe.

"I mean, there are many agreements that can be made."

"Money," said Joe.

"Yes, money."

It was the first time he had recognized that an agreement of substance might be made before the government took the River. Up until now it had seemed to be merely a matter of trickery. And it had been puzzling to him how Theodore Morton could appear to be an honest man, when the dealing so far had been transparently crooked.

For a short while, he wavered, considering. People had been desperate for meat all winter and this was because the Reserve alone was too small to support the game they needed for subsistence. The incursion of farmland was all around them. Joe was very well aware that the people had inhabited a range far larger than this little piece of land around the River in the past. If they could trade for another piece, perhaps further away from the developed areas … Or if they could make enough money so that they would no longer need to subsist on game …

But he quickly realized that it was useless to think of moving away from development, as it would simply follow them wherever they went. And no sum of money they were offered now would pay their children and their children's children. And finally, when he really thought about it, he realized that he hated farming, and the idea that the noble River could be used as a sort of irrigation ditch by farmers who were at the same time destroying all of nature was deeply repellent to him.

He attempted to say some of these things so that Theodore Morton would understand. "We don't want to see all of the land being farmed," he said.

"You can't turn back the clock," said the tall man.

"But people here will never become farmers."

"With enough money you could become whatever you wanted. You could send your kids to universities and they could become teachers and lawyers."

"But what if we simply want to live here doing what we have always done?"

"Then you will be poor. You are poor," said Theodore Morton, looking around the barren little room.

Joe thought of his cozy home, the woman he now thought of as his wife, his adopted daughter and his baby son. He thought he could not convey to this man how wonderful the life he was leading was to him, and how he had longed to have this all through the war.

"I get the impression that your reluctance has something to do with the water itself," said Theodore Morton. He was assuming that he had won the argument so far. "You said something like that when I first met you in Edmonton."

"I think it does," said Joe, remembering how Antoine had spoken for the River. The elders had their beliefs about the sacredness of water. But he was not an elder and it would be hard for him to articulate this; he had only inherited their reverence.

"But the River won't cease to exist," the man went on. "There is always more water."

Joe was wishing Antoine could be here to refute this.

"You should only take what you need of anything," he said. "You shouldn't take more."

"But that is exactly the point. It's a very dry land, but a superlative land for farming. The water is needed. We are only proposing to take what we need."

Joe was now stumped, for he could hardly say that the farming was abhorrent to him and that he disagreed utterly with all of those propositions that Theodore Morton had just stated as facts.

Finally he said, "We have only this small place that is ours. Can't you whitemen leave us be?"

After a short pause the whiteman said, "You know, I have never seen a place like this before, and I can't understand why you want it so much. But I guess the fact that you are so stubborn—" he laughed in a friendly way—"convinces me that you do want it."

This seemed like a fair thing to say and Joe smiled politely.

"So now I am going to give you two pieces of advice, because I like you and I want to see you people get a fair shake. One, play for time. Two, when the time finally comes, make them pay through the nose. Oh yes, and I have a third piece of advice. Get another agent. The federal government maybe doesn't see eye to eye with Alberta on all this and that could help you. But that man is not your friend."

He stuck out his hand for Joe to shake, and Joe was astounded. Apparently he was going to leave now with the report still spread out on the table and no real conclusion to their talk. He had not tried to make Joe sign something.

"Will I see you again?" Joe asked.

"No, because I have quit my job. I thought I would bring you the surveyor's report because I could see that you wondered whether I would keep my word."

"But where are you going?" said Joe, now feeling rather worried about the man.

"To the devil, probably," replied Theodore. "Things have not worked out very well since the war. My wife has left me and well—I will not bore you with all that."

"My wife died," said Joe, thinking of that stark day when he buried her. "But since then I have found another woman and we are very happy. We have a baby son." He wanted to comfort Theodore somehow, to give him hope.

"Thanks," said Theodore, laughing, although it was not a happy laugh. "Perhaps that will happen to me too then."

They shook hands and then Theodore walked to his automobile, got in, and drove away with a wave of his hand.

Joe remembered the advice to play for time because that was what he had to do all summer. It was a very hot dry summer, and the farmers were screaming even more loudly for water than they usually did. There were meetings upon meetings with agricultural representatives and the Alberta government, and the agent was as thick with these people as he could possibly be. Joe was asked to come to his house and he stood or sat, saying nothing, while they expressed over and over their greed and rapacity for the river water that flowed through the Reserve. They did not know he had the surveyor's report and often they told him lies.

When he saw how the agent stood with the farmers' organizations, Joe decided to follow Theodore Morton's third piece of advice, as he thought it was certainly the truest thing the man had said. In July the agent did not bother to send Joe the money and the shells and Joe remembered how he had been away during the worst part of the winter and had not helped them. So he sat down with his Band Council and wrote a letter to Ottawa complaining, and then mentioning the threat of the dam and saying that they would like to see the agent replaced by someone who could represent them better. Joe addressed this letter simply: Minister of Indian Affairs, Ottawa. He mailed it in Bitter Root at the end of the first week in August.

Then the thing he had been expecting to happen with the Protestant minister did happen. He was found with another woman and his wife ran screaming through the town with her apron flapping up in front of her face. Then she took her children and left in a taxi from Bitter Root, which came right out to the door of the house and collected the family and all their mattresses and other possessions.

The minister lived in the tent church for about a week, but then the woman went back to her husband because no more church services were being held and the ecstatic hymn-singing was over. The minister himself finally left on foot one morning, carrying a suitcase. The tent stood for a while, derelict, since nobody would touch it, then blew away in a high wind overnight.

Then there was a kind of Roman revival, in which many women went to the church and made their confessions to the priest. Joe wondered whether it could really be true that the man had had so many women, most of them married and religious people. The priest was very happy and gloated every Sunday in the pulpit.

The next thing that happened, however, was bad. The priest called for Joe to come to see him in the mission house and said that he must not live with Selene as it was immoral. Selene was the wife of Thomas Mountain and should return to her husband.

"But he beat her and drove her out of the house in winter," Joe told him.

"Nevertheless, she is his wife."

"But she will not go back to him. And now she has a child with me."

"Perhaps he will accept the child. Otherwise it should remain with you."

"But he does not even accept his own child."

The priest looked hard at Joe. He had been having such a good time lately after the rout of the Protestants that he did not expect resistance. He looked down at a list on his desk. "Marina is the daughter of Thomas Mountain? She should go to residential school."

Joe said, "I don't want to send her because she has been very unhappy and confused by the behaviour of Thomas Mountain to her mother. She should not go to school until she understands better what has happened to her."

The priest said, "It is the law that a child must go to school."

Joe replied, "I can teach her to read and write myself."

"I will talk to the father. You are not the father."

Joe went away from this interview very disquieted. The priest was powerful again and he knew it.

However, Marina would have to go to school eventually. He had gone to school, and so had Marie, and probably Selene had too, although she showed no signs of it. He would try to postpone it for a little longer and she would probably be all right.

In the meantime, no power on earth would make Selene go back to Thomas Mountain. And Joe did not believe that Thomas wanted her either.

But the priest evidently did go to Thomas and hector him about Marina. Joe was dismayed to see that Thomas had returned to living in his parents' house. The priest had learned of his liaison with the widow and put a stop to it.

Every week now they had sermons on hell and adultery. The priest continued to gloat, but now he was not just gloating over the defeat of the Protestants but at his power over all the people.

They were still very careful and Selene did not go out of the house. Really, she had gone nowhere all summer, and this was all right because of their happiness with the baby.

But next the priest brought Thomas to Joe's house. He was trying to get him to take Marina. "She is your child and she should be in school," he said.

Joe had not wanted to let them in the door, but he could not prevent it as they took him by surprise.

Thomas Mountain was not interested in Marina, whom he had long ago disowned. Instead he glowered at Selene, who stood pressed against the wall as far away from him as possible, with her arms around the baby.

No one said anything, although the priest went on hectoring them for some time.

After they left, Joe got out the knife and jammed it in the door. No one needed to say that it was very dangerous for Selene now.

Marina lay on the bed crying, and Selene held her in her arms, whispering to her. Joe thought that she was telling her that her father would protect her from Thomas and the priest and he did not feel happy about this. He sat feeding the baby soup and wondering what to do.

It seemed now as though he was living by his wits from day to day. Even though the Reserve was his place and he was the Chief, on every side the plans of the whiteman hemmed him in.

He could take Selene and Marina and the baby, Joe, and go live somewhere else, even in Calgary. But to live in peace in his own place was all that he had longed for through the years of the war; to try to do that was the only thing that made sense.

The pack trains left for the outfitters' camps but Thomas Mountain did not go with them. Joe was sure that this was because the priest was inflaming him, telling him that he should reclaim his wife and child.

Marina no longer went out to play with the other children and Selene had returned to looking at the contents of her bundle, sitting over it for long hours on the cabin floor.

Joe went to see Thomas Mountain in his parents' house. He said to Thomas, "Do you remember the day we spent hunting this spring? We saw only grouse that day and you were able to shoot two. You gave one of them to me."

Thomas nodded. He was sitting beside the stove whittling a stick and he looked at Joe; their eyes met.

"It was a good day in spite of the poor hunting," said Joe, remembering how hopeful he had felt.

Thomas nodded again.

They were both caught in the priest's trap, Joe felt.

"You are no longer hunting for that widow, is that right? But I am afraid she and her family will starve this winter without a hunter like you. There is so little game."

"Are you trying to trick me?" Thomas asked.

"No, it is just that I think we ought to talk this over ourselves. It is our business, not the business of the priest."

"He says I will go to hell if I sleep with that widow. And you will go to hell because you are sleeping with my wife!"

"But you did not want the woman." Joe was afraid to say Selene's name because it seemed that Thomas might fight him. He had put down the knife he was whittling with and stood up. "You remember she was mad."

"You told me you wouldn't touch her! I don't think she is mad now."

"She would go mad again if you took her," said Joe and they stared at one another.

The ancient mother of Thomas was nodding her head like the pendulum of a clock. Thomas's eyes rolled right back in his head as he tried to think about what Joe was saying.

"She has your child."

"But you don't want my child. And I think you don't want a

woman who has another man's child," said Joe. "Besides, if you took her, you would have to kill me."

Thomas sat down again slowly and looked at his hands. "It is just that when I see her I know I don't want any other woman," he said.

"Well, you don't have to see her," said Joe. "She has stayed away from you. You would not have seen her if the priest had not brought you."

"I'm unhappy and restless here and sometimes I think I'm going mad myself."

"Why didn't you go with the pack trains as you always do?"

"Because the priest said I could have my wife again."

"I think you should go to the mountains and hire on with an outfitter. When you come back at Christmas, hunt for the widow again. That family needs the meat."

"It seems as though you are tricking me."

"No. I don't want you to kill me," said Joe frankly.

"I will burn in hell no matter what I do."

"I would rather burn for sleeping with a woman than for killing a man," Joe remarked, and Thomas gave a bitter laugh.

It was the best he could do, and the following day Joe was glad to see that Thomas had brought in two of his horses from the hills. It looked as though he was going to take Joe's advice and go to the mountains.

That night the agent called for Joe to come to his house and Joe wondered whether he should go or not. By this time the letter he had sent should have arrived in Ottawa and the agent might have heard of its contents. He decided to go, since he needed to know what was on the agent's mind.

As he was taking the knife out of the door jamb, Selene got up from her bundle and came to stand behind him. He turned around and looked into her face, but she said nothing, only her eyes were full of tears and he knew that she wanted him to stay at home.

"It will be safe," he said. "Thomas has gone to the mountains."

"But it will not be safe for you," she said in a low voice.

"I am only going to see the agent. He won't kill me," Joe replied. "Although perhaps he would like to."

She shook her head, but he pressed the knife into her hand and said, "Stay inside, with this in the door, and everything will be all right."

The agent said nothing about the letter. He told Joe that unless Marina went to residential school after Christmas he would send the Mounties to get her. Joe was now sure that he knew about the letter.

He walked home very slowly, feeling sorry for Marina. There was no way out of this for her; and he knew it would be harmful, as it had been to him and to everyone else. He could not comfort himself with its inevitability. He decided to try to talk to the child about Thomas Mountain, to tell her the truth, once and for all. He wished he had done this earlier, even though it had seemed cruel.

When he got home he found that the door of the cabin had been broken down with an axe, and when he rushed in he found Selene dead upon the floor. Her battered body had been stabbed and then almost dismembered by many blows with an axe. The knife that had been in the door lay upon the floor, covered in blood. It looked as though it had been used to stab her; but there was no sign now of the axe.

Of Marina and the baby there was no sign either, but the cabin was awash with blood and Joe did not doubt that they were dead as well.

The fact that he did not go in search of his own child was held against him at the trial. In fact, Marina was lying behind the stove with the baby clutched in her arms. She had saved his life, although she had taken refuge in madness to escape the horror she had witnessed, and was waiting for her father to come and save her. When Joe came in she made no sign. This too, was used in evidence at the trial.

Joe ran out of the cabin and through the town to the agent's house to use the only phone to call the police.

When the Mounties came, they took Selene's body and the knife that had been jammed in the door to use as material evidence. The knife had only Selene and Joe's fingerprints upon the handle. Then one of them went with Joe to the agent's house to take a deposition.

"Where were you? Why were you not at home?"

"I was here," said Joe. "The agent called me to come meet with him."

"I called him, that is true. But he didn't come," said the agent. "I wondered why—till he came running in here covered in blood."

The other Mountie had found Marina in the corner behind the stove. He brought her into the agent's house. Joe had been trying to explain about Thomas Mountain. They stood Marina in front of him, still clutching the baby and Joe at first thought he was looking at a ghost or dreaming.

"This man says your father killed your mother," said the first Mountie. "Was it your father, little girl?"

A look of horror crossed Marina's face. "No, it was not my father," she said. "He could never do that."

"Did this man come into the cabin?"

Marina looked at Joe almost without recognition. She burst into tears.

As they were handcuffing him, he was still looking desperately at Marina. Her frail small arms were wrapped around his baby boy, and she looked, bewildered, from one whiteman to the other, weeping.

If he could have spoken for weeping just then himself, he should have asked her, "Marina, it was not I who killed your mother, was it?"

Because at that time she still knew it was not.

12

1994 · Harry and Rose

◖ "HELLO?"

"Hello. Is this Rose?"

"Yes."

"Oh! Well, this is Harry."

"Harry? Oh! Harry!"

"Gosh, it was hard to find your number. I didn't know how to look for it."

"Yeah. The Reserve. It isn't a town or anything. It's just—itself." She laughed.

He laughed too, it was such a relief to have got her. The operator only had one Cartwright: Cartwright, R, under Bitter Root. He had been afraid the telephone might be answered by someone else.

"I just called to—to ask you something."

"Harry, I got really good marks! There's only one I haven't got."

"Oh, wow! Law school marks?"

"Yes! They were all A's. So far. Except the one I don't know about yet."

"Well, that's great! I knew you'd do it Rose. You were working so hard. Remember our last walk? In November. That seems like a long time ago."

"Down by the river in Calgary," she said. "The Bow."

"Well, I mean, it just seems like quite a long time ago. Hey, Rose! I got really good marks too. I forgot to tell you."

"A's?"

"Yep."

"All of 'em?"

"Yep."

"Wow! But Harry, you know you're smart! I told you it would be fine."

"God. It feels like I'm recovering from a long illness though. First year law school. They say it goes on like this too."

"I'm coming! I'm coming! Three more years to my BA and then—"

"And now for something completely trivial. Do you want to see a stupid movie?"

"A movie?" She was cautious suddenly.

"Yeah. A movie. Some movie. In Abercrombie. I could pick you up. I've got a—a pickup," he said breathlessly. He was twenty-two, but he had never asked a girl for a date, audaciously like this, on the phone.

"You have a pickup?" she was repeating, bewildered.

"Well, it belongs to my dad really. It's the farm truck. You'll come, won't you?"

"Oh—!" She laughed. "Okay. But I'm on the Reserve."

"I'll find you," he said eagerly. "Goodbye." And then after he hung up he realized he would have to call her back to say that it was tonight he meant, and get some directions.

They had met on a law school tour during initiation that fall; he was already in Law, and she was planning on it, even though she was still just in first year university. She was very pretty; so he had gone over to talk to her afterwards. It turned out that she came from his part of Alberta; she even knew Vicky, his half-brother's sister.

They had not been dating, but they had been seeing one another. Walking from residence to the university library together to study. That walk down by the Bow River in the cold. Rose, thickly swaddled in her winter coat, hugging his arm under her breast and talking about anything that came into her head: social contract theory, the French revolution, quarks ... While anxiety about remembering a couple of dozen cases mixed freely in his blood with desire for this exultant girl.

"Rose?"

"Oh! Hello again."

"How am I going to find you?"

Harry was familiar with directions in the country. He was a
farm boy after all. Turn right. Third brown house on the left. Sure.
The only one without a sweat lodge.—No sweat lodge?

After the movie they had pop in a café; then he drove her home.

"Good night, Harry."

"Um. Is that all?"

"Okay!" She laughed, then leaned over and kissed his lips briefly.
A nice kiss. Not as nice as the one they had exchanged after their
walk by the Bow River.

"Don't I get to—" He gestured towards the house—"meet your
mother?"

"My mother?" She was taken aback. Did she have a mother,
he wondered again. "Oh, okay. You can come in. For a little while,"
she added dubiously.

They got out of the truck and ascended the steps of a rickety
porch. The house had antiquated metal siding and he thought
probably it was made of plywood. But it was not a shack; it was a
real house. She turned around suddenly, before opening the door.
"My mother is kind of weird," she said.

"Oh, so is mine. Absolutely."

"No. I mean—she's weird."

"Well, look. Maybe I can make up my own mind about that.
And besides—so what?"

"Okay, but—" She rested her forehead against his collarbone,
which was unfortunately padded with four layers—parka, sweater,
shirt, undershirt—so he couldn't feel a thing.

"Would you mind—?" He was already lifting up her chin, his
hand in some kind of Cary Grant formation against her cheek.

They kissed again and this time it was good, it was astounding.

In the living room were a crippled old man in a wheelchair and
an alarmed-looking older woman, Rose's mother.

"Ma, this is Harry."

"Did you have to bring him in like that?" she exclaimed irritably.

"He wanted to meet you."

The old man was gazing at Harry, a concentrated stare, porten-
tous, full of meaning, whether hostile or not he could not tell.

"This is William Hogan. Mom lives with him," said Rose.

"Hello, William. Yo," Harry said nervously. The man continued to stare like an owl.

"He can't speak," said Rose. "Where's Tim?" she asked.

Her mother shrugged.

"My little brother. He's ten."

It was so unlike his own family it took his breath away. The bare room, the speechless, staring old man, the little brother out somewhere—it was after 11:00—or in. She wasn't sure. How had exquisite Rose emerged from these awful surroundings?

"I'm going to make tea, Mom," announced Rose, leading the way to the kitchen, which was not a separate room, just an extension of the room they were in.

"Should I—get him?" asked Harry, gesturing at the wheelchair.

"Okay."

He went to push William Hogan into the dining room, a kind of no man's land with a chrome table and chairs. The mother came too, still looking frightened.

Harry drank two cups of tea. "I like tea," he remarked, speaking to William, who responded suddenly by smiling. His arms worked apparently, because he was drinking tea too.

"I—I met Rose," he went on to the mother, emboldened. "We met. In Calgary."

"Harry's really smart, Ma. He's at the university too."

The old man leaned over at these words and patted her arm. She responded by kissing his cheek.

"Vicky's his half-sister," she told her mother.

"Well, not really. She's my half-brother's sister," Harry said.

The mother was looking at him intently now. "Do you know Medicine Bear?" she asked.

"Medicine Bear?" Harry looked at Rose.

"My uncle. He's the Chief."

"Nope. Don't know him at all. Don't know any chiefs."

No one laughed. The mother got up and taking the handles of the wheelchair, pushed William Hogan away. They went out of the room altogether and down the hall—to a bedroom, he presumed.

"Sorry," said Harry.

Rose was looking at her slim brown fingers.

[384]

She got up suddenly and took a turn around the room while Harry helped himself to a third cup of tea. "It's all different here, Harry! I should never have let you come in."

"But I wanted to meet your mother. Did I offend her? I'm sorry, Rose."

"You didn't offend her."

"Are you sure? Please come and sit down."

She sat down across the corner of the table from him and their knees were touching. This would have been good, except that both of them were wearing denim jeans with long johns underneath.

He stared at Rose's face. She was unusually pretty, in his opinion. Girls tended to have very usual faces. But with Rose, when she thought, she thought hard, when she was fierce, she was very fierce, when she laughed, it was all over her face, on her mouth, in her eyes. And she knew all kinds of things; she could solve conundrums of law, even though she was barely out of high school. Besides that, she was a girl. With breasts. Small ones. Although he had never had the opportunity to see them.

"My mother—" she said now, visibly thinking—"is mentally ill."

"You mean she was in—?"

"Yeah," Rose replied fiercely. "She was. Harry, would you mind waiting here?" she went on.

He nodded. He would wait here, he was thinking, till he died, if it would help at all. As it was, she just went down the hall and came back.

"He's in bed asleep," she said.

"Your brother?"

They sat in silence for a moment or two. Then she said, "This isn't going to work. You can't stay. And there's nowhere we can go."

Amazed by the implication in her words, Harry replied. "I'll go home. I just wanted to see you."

He put on his parka. She put hers on too, and accompanied him outside to his truck. Which had four flat tires. Harry got down to look. They were not just flat. They were slashed. Someone had taken a heavy knife to them. Maybe a switchblade.

Rose was appalled. He was glad to see that. Apparently things like this did not happen all the time.

There was a spare. Unslashed. Only one, though.

"I'll have to call my father," said Harry, his lips numb. Robbie was going to say a few things, he knew.

"Oh, God." She was crying, to his surprise.

"Well, it's okay. Don't get scared or anything." Although he was somewhat scared and it was by no means okay, especially what Robbie would have to say.

"Come in the house," she said, not letting him embrace her.

Inside she let him, and leaned against him while he kissed her hair, which was done up in a clip on the back of her head. He liked it when she let it hang down to her waist. It was lovely hair.

He called Robbie, who was asleep. "What the hell did you do?" he shouted down the phone.

Harry had not said that the tires were slashed. Flat was what he had said.

"Stay where you are. I'll come get you in the morning. Where are you anyway?"

"On the Reserve."

"Oh shit!" said Robbie. "Maybe I'd better get you tonight."

"No—It's okay. Tomorrow would be good enough." He was still holding Rose lightly by the arm.

"Well—Sleep tight!" shouted Robbie, and slammed down the receiver.

"That was your father?" said Rose. "Does he always yell at you like that?"

"He was just mad."

Harry was wondering what was down the hall. There must be at least two bedrooms, maybe three. One for the old man and Rose's mother. She had mentioned a sister. And there was her ten-year-old brother. Did Rose have a bedroom?

"May I sleep on the sofa?"

"Okay. I'll get you some blankets and stuff."

"I'm sorry, Rose."

She gave him an astounded look, wiping her nose on her palm, then went out of the room. She returned with some blankets.

"I'll make it up."

"No, I will." Harry spread out the blankets, then climbed under. "Sit here. Talk to me," he said, patting the spot beside his knee.

"No." She went away and began turning off the lights, to his disappointment. He was still wearing his parka. He struggled out of it. If only she would sit down.

"Good night, Harry," she said, from across the room.

Someone had punctured—no, slashed, and with a knife—his tires. On account of Rose? But it might have been a motiveless crime. There were a lot of young punks who lived on the Reserve, who went to the bar in Steamboat. After a long while he went to sleep.

He woke up suddenly. It was still quite dark. He felt stiff as a board. Because of his height he had had to sleep on the tiny sofa in a kind of fetal crouch. Also, on waking, he had instantly remembered Robbie, shouting at him over the phone. This was not the way he had intended to get his father introduced to the idea of Rose.

Something had woken him up. Stretching cautiously, he realized someone was sitting beside his knee. He reached out and grasped a handful of soft hair. It was Rose. She said, "Harry, come in my room."

"Oh. Okay," he replied, feeling feeble.

"I made Jasmine go in with Timmy," Rose whispered, leading the way. "We just have to be careful not to wake them up," she continued, gesturing at the wall. She shut the door very softly, then turned around with her back to it.

"But—!" Harry was suddenly desperate. She was putting him on the spot now. "I haven't got—! Rose! I mean—I don't have—!"

"Oh, that's okay," she whispered. She was removing his clothes and her own—she was still dressed, he noticed—unbuttoning his shirt, then her shirt. "We won't, then. We'll just—!" She exhibited what she meant and he felt that he was going to faint, although it was only her body, pressed full length against his.

"I've got to make it up to you somehow," she whispered, against his lips. "I shouldn't have let you come here in the first place."

He was about six inches taller, which didn't impress him, but which, he knew, gave some girls pleasure. Besides that, he was white, and freckled, inclined to go scarlet when embarrassed or under pressure, which hardly even described the present situation.

She was brown, fierce, determined. He had no idea what this was really all about.

"Please! Stop!"

"Really?" She was staring up at him, puzzled.

"Look, for one thing—Oh God! I didn't mean to tell you this! Not this way!—I'm a virgin. And for another, you've got to explain, Rose. Why are you coming onto me like this?"

She sat down on the bed. It was a well-furnished bedroom, he had time to see now. A double bed—for both girls probably. Bureau. Posters on the walls. Corkboard. The works. Not like the rest of the house.

He sat down beside her. Neither of them was naked. She was wearing her underwear—long johns and a little bra. He was wearing a T-shirt and long johns. Mating in cold weather. A difficult business. Especially when the people were thin and prone to getting cold, as they both were.

"Listen," she said. "I have a boyfriend. Oh God!—he isn't my boyfriend! I just said that so you'd see—"

"He slashed my tires."

"His name is Black Snake. That's what he calls himself now. We always knew each other."

"Did you—?"

"Oh yes!" She nodded her head. "But that was a long time ago. And I can't explain anything. I don't understand it myself. He's gone! The person he was is gone! He's become—"

"Rose," he said softly. He put his arm around her.

She was crying. But it wasn't because of the stupid things girls usually cried about. "There's a warrior society. They call themselves the Dog Soldiers. But that's Cheyenne! It isn't our people! And he's taken that horrible name, Black Snake!"

"I love you," he said, not meaning to say it yet.

"Harry!" she cried. And instantly returned, still weeping, to doing the kind of thing she had been doing before. Rather timidly, he now noticed. Their underclothes were very much in the way.

He lay down on her bed and managed to get her to lie down too. She stopped crying at last. He said, "I want you, Rose. But not just because some guy you know slashed my tires."

"I'm sorry, Harry." She yawned suddenly. He had slept, even Robbie was probably asleep, but he guessed that she had not slept at all.

"No, no—don't be. I'm not. And we'd have done that, except that I don't have any—. And besides, I'm a—"

"Well, when you get some—? Then will it matter that you're a—?" she demanded mischievously, leaning over him. Her hair fell in a beautiful way across his arm. Her brown eyes were intelligent and lively.

"You can bet it won't!" agreed Harry. "Is it okay if I stay here? I don't want to leave." I love you, he added, under his breath this time.

She was going to sleep with her head on his shoulder. He snuggled her a bit closer, and then, to his vast surprise, found that he was going to sleep too.

When he woke up Rose was gone. He could hear voices, among them, hers. She sounded cross. He crept out of her room and went to the bathroom, then into the main room. Rose was there, her mother, the old man, a kid who must be her brother. He was sitting on the sofa, still made up as a bed.

It occurred to Harry, looking at the turned-back blankets that he could have been a non-virgin this morning if he just didn't have such a big mouth. He had actually talked her out of it. Why had he done that?

Rose came towards him silently with a mug of tea, her eyes cast down. No one was saying anything now so he guessed that he himself had been what they were talking about.

The sound of his mother's car could be heard drawing up outside, and Harry, his heart sinking, returned the half-full mug to Rose. He put on his parka and went outside.

"Jesus," said Robbie. "What is this. Gang warfare?"

Harry said, "I just brought Rose home. She invited me in to meet her mother, but then—"

"Well—!" Robbie was still walking disgustedly around the

[389]

truck, kicking each tire in turn. Harry walked behind him feeling humiliated, scolded. They came back to the beginning again and there was Rose in her parka between the two vehicles.

"I feel kind of responsible for this, Mister," she said.

"This is Rose."

"Yeah, okay. Hello, Rose," said Robbie irritably.

"I mean, in a way it was my fault it happened. I should have warned Harry."

"Harry should be able to use his own damn head," Robbie said, speaking to Harry, not Rose.

"Well, anyway, I've got two hundred dollars in my bank account. Maybe that would help pay for the tires."

"You know who did this?" Robbie was now actually looking at her.

"Maybe."

"Well, he should go to jail. And I won't take your two hundred dollars. I'm going to make him pay for it." He jerked his thumb at Harry. "First he's going to put on the spares I brought."

Harry was already getting a couple of old tires out of the trunk of the car. Then he got out the jack. He was in a haze of embarrassment. But Rose was still with him, he noticed. She came around the corner, rolling a tire. They worked their way around the truck. She was very handy with tools. Robbie leaned, frowning and blowing out his nostrils like a horse, against the fender of the car.

Rose put the jack in the trunk. She stood up straight, facing Harry. Her hair was falling down over the front of her parka in a messy way and she had a streak of dirt on her cheek. She looked utterly beautiful. Harry took her hands.

"Okay. Ready? Or were you intending to bring her home to meet your mother?" said Robbie.

"Look, Dad. That wasn't very polite. This is Rose!"

"Okay. I'm sorry," said Robbie. "Maybe I got the wrong idea. Nice to meet you Rose. I guess Harry would like to introduce you to his mother."

Rose was looking at Robbie in alarm. She began to shake her head.

"Please," said Harry.

"How will I get back?"

"Harry can bring you back," said Robbie. He looked at his watch. "You'd better stay for lunch."

"I'll have to tell them." She went inside.

"Nice girl," said Robbie, surprisingly mild all of a sudden.

"I'm sorry about the tires, Dad."

Robbie sighed and folded his arms.

"I'll pay for them."

"Forget it. I guess you know what can happen when you leave a truck here now."

Rose came out again. The dirty streak was gone. She was twisting her hair up under the clip as she walked towards them. Harry opened the door of the truck for her.

"I'm only coming so your parents won't think—" she said, as he got in on the other side and started up.

"He already doesn't think that."

"Is he always so mean to you?"

"No," said Harry in surprise.

"It wasn't your fault. And he said he was going to make you pay."

"Well, he's not."

"Oh." She gazed out the windshield. "It won't happen again," she said, after a moment. "I'm going to talk to Black Snake."

"Are you sure it's even safe to see a guy like that? And besides, what will you tell him?" Harry felt he was getting some direct personal insight into the words "insanely jealous," for the first time. The mere idea of her talking to Black Snake was making him drive all over the road.

"I'll tell him to leave you alone."

"Or else you won't see him or speak to him or something? A guy who slashes tires is going to go for a deal like that?"

"Well, that's what I'm going to say."

"Rose, don't you think—? I mean, if you're going to make some kind of deal, you have to ask yourself—what are you offering in exchange?"

She was silent, wearing her fierce look and Harry continued to drive, having to concentrate on it. She had not just talked to Black Snake in the past, she had actually gone to bed with him. It was an appalling thought. Even if they had been, as she had intimated, more or less just kids at the time. Harry didn't want her even to think about Black Snake, much less try to drive some kind of Faustian bargain.

They drew into the farmyard and Harry felt a modest pride, hoping she noticed how nice the place was. There was snow all over everything, but even so, she could see the neat lawn, the shrubs and trees, the house, the tidy barns, the fields stretching out smoothly to the windbreaks.

His mother was great too, as he had been expecting. She was rushing around making lunch for twelve people, since his older sisters were home for Christmas, but she stopped in the middle of everything, saying, "This is Rose?! Harry, how wonderful! I'm so glad to meet her, finally!"

"Finally?" said Rose in bewilderment, looking at Harry.

"Well, he did mention you a few times," Sonya went on, laughing. "A few hundred times."

Harry was bright red with embarrassment, but he felt, all the same, that it was kind of a nice way of letting Rose know that he hadn't been keeping her a secret from his parents; or at least, not from his mother, anyway.

The house was overflowing with people and he took Rose around introducing her—to his oldest sister Marian and her fiancé, to Laura, to Lizzie, who had a boyfriend too … Finally he managed to get her across the kitchen, through the living room, down the hall and up the stairs to his room.

"What are they going to think?" she asked. He had just got the door shut and was wondering whether she would let him kiss her.

"About what?"

She was standing in front of his bureau looking down at all the 4-H trophies. She turned around restlessly. "About me being up here with you."

"They'll think you're up here with me," said Harry.

"Won't they think we're screwing?" she demanded. "That's what my mother thought. She was pretty upset."

"Oh—was she? But you told her we weren't—?"

"I told her I was old enough and it wasn't any of her business."

"Oh yeah," said Harry, remembering that they would have been if it hadn't been for him.

It wouldn't have crossed the minds of the people down below that he might have taken Rose to his room to have sex with her before lunch, and he wondered why. Was something wrong with him?—or was it something to do with them, that they wouldn't think of that?

"The problem is—that I still don't have—"

"I know. I've been with you the whole time, Harry." A mischievous smile crossed her face. "Let's just kiss some more, if you don't mind."

"If I don't mind?"

After lunch he took her outside to see the farm. They went down the line of granaries to look out over the fields.

"I hate farming," she remarked.

"What?"

"Well, it's why you whitemen took the land away from us, isn't it?"

Harry was silent. It was hardly surprising she would take this viewpoint. But he had not expected her to apply it so directly, so personally, to him, to this ranch.

"It pollutes the rivers. All the topsoil flies away. The natural grasses and vegetation are all gone, the animals murdered. Do you think it's nice?" she went on in disgust.

Harry was trying to think of what he could show her next.

"Let's go see the horses." He led the way to the barn.

"This is my father's horse. They're all called Thunder. This is Thunder the Third. Ping Pong belongs to my mother."

"Can you ride?"

"Of course. Can you?"

"No."

"Look, I could take you out. Want to?"

"I think I'd be afraid."

"I could take you double on Thunder."

"Your father won't get mad?"

"Nope. Horses need exercise."

He helped her to mount by the fence. They went around the corral a few times.

"Want to go out? We could go cross-country."

"Okay. You're sure—?"

Harry was very sure. He was thinking about the ugly little house she lived in, the one without the sweat lodge. The best thing he could do would be to show her the country—which she seemed to think about only in the abstract. It would not be so obvious that it was a farm since it was under the snow.

It was the first time he had ridden pillion on a horse with a girl who was not one of his sisters. He found the close, tight way they were sitting, knee behind knee, her arms wrapped around his waist, incredibly pleasant. It constricted his throat; but there was no need to talk anyway, in the wind and cold air.

They went all the way around the ranch, using the farm roads, the section road at the back, and tracks and short cuts made long ago by him and Lizzie, playing. He felt he was conveying to her something about himself, about his happy childhood, just sitting in front of her on the horse.

By the time they got back and got the horse cooled off and groomed it was after 4:00.

"Stay for supper?" Robbie said to Rose, meeting her in the corridor by the stall.

"I should go home. They'll be worried."

"You could call."

"That would make them worry even more."

Robbie laughed.

"Well then, Harry can take you home. He'll just have to drive with that collection of odd tires you put on this morning."

Rose said: "Did you tell the police?" She spoke directly.

"No. What makes you think I'd do that?"

"You said the guy who did it should go to jail."

Robbie shrugged. "Maybe he should. But I guess the police couldn't catch him now. You and Harry got your own fingerprints smeared all over the truck this morning, didn't you?"

Rose gave him a sunny smile.

[394]

Robbie laughed again. "You're going to go to law school like Harry, I hear."

"You hear?"

"Well, his mother said he had a friend named Rose who wanted to go to law school."

Harry stopped on a highway layover outside the Reserve.

"Why are we stopping?"

"So we can kiss." Without your mother thinking we're about to screw, or Black Snake lurking behind the house with his switchblade, Harry thought—but did not say.

"When can I see you again?"

"You mean—here?" she said dubiously.

"Tomorrow?" he pleaded. "I could pick you up."

❡ "HARRY?"

"Oh!—Rose?"

"Who was that? Who answered the phone?"

"My sister Laura."

"I thought for a moment you had another girlfriend."

"Another girlfriend?" *Another* girlfriend, sang his heart. "No, I don't have another—"

"This is tomorrow, Harry."

"I know."

"Can you come over here? I mean, come here. To—to go to the school Christmas concert."

"Oh. Okay. I'll have to get someone to pick me up later though. Dad still—"

"I thought of that. You can spend the night."

"I can? What about your mother?"

"It's okay about her. I'll tell you later. You don't mind?"

"Mind?"

"About the Christmas concert? I have to go. My brother's in it."

"But I want to go to that. And then afterwards you're saying—?"

"Yes. There's something you need to bring too, Harry. Don't forget."

"God! No. I won't forget!"

[395]

Laura took him in the car. He went to the drugstore in Steamboat on the way.

"Why are you going out to the Reserve?" said Laura, raising her eyebrows. "Are you sowing some wild oats or something? Finally?"

"No. I introduced you to her yesterday, remember?"

"She lives on the Reserve?"

"What's wrong with it? I'll call you tomorrow," he said, getting out of the car.

Rose came out of the house in a hurry, her parka still undone. She took his hand. Laura waved briefly, then drove off.

It was a school Christmas concert. Rose kept apologizing about it, but it looked like a school concert to Harry. Maybe a little bit wilder than the usual kind because two thousand people were present. Also the Chief got up and delivered an address which was fairly far off Christmas, in Harry's view.

"My uncle," said Rose, nudging him.

"Looks like quite a good one. A good uncle."

She frowned at him and he remembered guiltily how he had joked about this guy being the Chief.

The thing went on to its tedious conclusion. Afterwards he and Rose were out in the cold clear night air, walking hand in hand in the wrong direction.

"Not going home, I take it."

"We're going to my uncle's place. I asked him if I could borrow it. He's going somewhere to do the same thing we're going to do. He's got girlfriends all over."

"This is a very good uncle you've got," said Harry, enthusiastic this time.

A moment later they went through a back door into a filthy kitchen.

"What a mess!" she remarked. "I should come over and clean this up for him. Do you want some—tea, or something, Harry?"

She had turned right around into his arms, and what they were doing now brought kissing to a new level, in his opinion.

"The bedrooms are downstairs," she whispered, once again leading the way.

She paused, pointing out the painting of Vicky. But Harry didn't really recognize her in it. He had seen Vicky a few times and she didn't interest him greatly. It occurred to him that Rose would probably like Dominique, however.

Downstairs, things were a bit cleaner. They went into an almost empty bedroom. Mattress on the floor, that was all. "This was my room," said Rose.

"You lived here?"

"When we first came. I'll tell you about that later." She was standing in front of him and he perceived that this time she expected him to make the moves. Which he began making. At his own speed. He had not approved of her hurry-up methods very much before. Removing their parkas. Removing both their flannel shirts. Removing her jeans and his jeans. Taking off his undershirt, then her bra. Which was when a lot of things suddenly started to happen. Then, finally, eliminating the long johns.

A long while later, Harry emerged from some kind of a trance that he was in, slightly melancholy, but by no means unpleasant, and found, strictly by feel, because someone had turned off the lights, that Rose was lying beside him. "Was that okay?" he whispered.

"It was nice."

"Really? Nicer than Black Snake?" Perhaps one was not supposed to ask, but he wanted to know. He rose on one elbow, but couldn't see her face. It was pitch dark.

"Oh—that was a long time ago. I told you. It was kid stuff. Later on—I didn't want to get pregnant."

Harry was thinking. He remembered how his sisters had become tremendous prudes after a certain age. It was a long time ago. But not long ago at all, from another point of view.

"Besides," she went on, "he wouldn't have cared about—Not like you, Harry."

He was suddenly feeling much happier. He still had the image of himself stammering out that he was a virgin first off, then putting up so much resistance when she was coming onto him. It made him feel like an idiot. But apparently she appreciated it, after all.

Harry lay down flat again and her head came to rest on his shoulder. He felt the soft brushing of her long hair all down his side. It occurred to him that he should feel triumph because he was no longer a virgin. But actually, he didn't care much about that aspect any more.

"You're very white, Harry," she whispered. "I can see you in the dark. You kind of glimmer."

"It's not really white," he said. "It's sort of mottled. With freckles."

She laughed.

"I think you're beautiful, Rose. Your face, your figure, your hair—I couldn't tell you before, but I always thought so."

"I wasn't sure you liked me that way. Till our walk down by the River. But then, after that, we were busy studying."

"It's why I had to call you. It took me a couple of days to think what to say."

"Why?" she demanded. She rose on her elbow now, steadying herself with a hand on his chest. "I just can't figure out why you didn't have girls and girls before this, Harry. You're so tall—and good-looking—and nice!"

"I was hanging around with my cousin Tony for a long while," he explained. "He found out about a year ago that he was gay. I mean, he didn't find that out with my help," he went on hastily. "But in the meantime, he needed me for—protective colouration or something."

"But you must have known you liked girls."

He felt that he couldn't explain how difficult a period the last two or three years had been for him. Trying to help Tony through the crisis of identity he was in. Trying to figure out where he stood on the family quarrel that Tony was becoming. And at the same time, trying to find out who he was himself.

"Well, I was looking longingly at girls all the time," he said. "But Tony—See, I felt kind of responsible for Tony. He's a lot younger than I am. His mother took off when he was a baby and I always— Well, anyway, maybe he's got it straight now, who he is," said Harry. "His dad doesn't like it much."

He couldn't really explain how this was going either. Dominique, so quiet, so private, so—Harry felt—fundamentally good, had not been able to understand or accept what was happening with Tony at all. Harry had had to turn himself into a mediator like his mother. In a way it had been a good experience. But only in a way.

"Who's his dad?"

"My half-brother Dominique. You know—Vicky Boucher's brother?"

"He can't be your cousin then, this Tony," she pointed out. "He's your nephew."

"Oh yeah, but he's a cousin too. It's pretty complicated. My family," he said.

"On the subject, your mother isn't weird. She's nice."

"She is nice," he agreed.

"You just said she was weird to make me feel better about my—"

"No. Absolutely not. Not at all. Completely possible to be nice and weird at the same time."

She laughed. "Well, it is possible." Then she said, "I think you spend a lot of time helping people, Harry."

This was true. But he wasn't quite sure it was a compliment. "Helping people?" he said cautiously. "You mean, like a Boy Scout?"

"No, I mean, seeing what people need and trying to get it for them. Like saying things they want to hear."

He still didn't think this was going in a good direction.

"I just want to point out one thing to you, Harry." She gave his chest a slight thump. "I'm not in need!"

Harry was bewildered now. Things had just been going as well as he could possibly wish and then suddenly, after canvassing Tony—and his mother—they had taken this sudden turn for the worse. "Not in need?" he repeated.

"No! I'm doing this—because I want you! Not because I need you!"

"Oh God, yes. I understand that. Absolutely.—Rose? Did you say you want me?" He rolled over, trying to see her face. The moon had come up and there was a little more light in the room.

"Yes." She also rolled over and embraced him fully.

Harry felt momentarily as though he might explode.

"Well, I want you too!"

❧ A LONG WHILE LATER THEY WERE IN THE DIRTY KITCHEN upstairs, having a cup of tea. Rose had made some changes while the kettle was boiling, so that it no longer fell under the description 'filthy' in Harry's mind. She had dumped out the horrible coffee in the filter pot, put all the mugs in the sink and filled it with soapy water, wiped off the table and kicked a pair of muddy rubber boots out into the porch.

She gave him a mug of tea and then sat down on his lap. She was clad only in her flannel shirt. Harry was wearing his long johns.

"This is the house Mom brought us to when we were kids," she said. "I'll never forget that day."

"Where did you live before?"

"Calgary. She had an abusive boyfriend. A stalker. She ran for it. With us. And Tim took us in."

She was so pretty, perched upon his lap, her hair falling down all over them both, down his chest, over her breasts, that he could hardly take in the horror of what she was saying. He was feeling as though he wanted to eat her or something. Or to merge like protozoa.

"Then they found out they were brother and sister. They didn't know. Something awful happened to their parents and they were taken away from each other and put in white foster homes. That was what you whitemen did to Native children!"

"Hey, wait!" he said. "I absolutely didn't do that! I wouldn't have done that. Really, Rose. I wouldn't have."

"Well, okay," she said, looking at him over the rim of her cup. "Maybe you wouldn't have, Harry. But it happened."

"So how does William fit into the picture?" Harry was thinking of the old man with his sweet smile, the way Rose had kissed his cheek. William Hogan was one of the only points of hope he had seen in that little brown house.

"Well, she got together with him later. After he got hurt. I can't tell you this all at once!" she complained. "I was telling you about Tim. His father was a great Chief. Back in the forties. He was the first one to oppose the dam. His name was Medicine Bear too."

"Medicine Bear? I don't think I've heard of him," said Harry thoughtfully.

"I don't know whether Tim will go down as a great Chief too," she said. "But he is a great Chief anyway."

"He made an interesting speech," said Harry, trying to sound sincere. He had actually been listening, unlike most of the others in the hall: babies, toddlers, old people, schoolchildren and their anxious parents. The speech had been about the relationship of the Reserve system to the concept of aboriginal rights. It was kind of a strange speech to deliver at a Christmas concert.

She made a giving-that-point-away gesture, smiling. "Well, that's who he is—Tim," she said.

He was beginning to get an angle on how Rose saw things. He wasn't going to say that was wrong till he had given it a try.

Her uncle, her grandfather were great Chiefs.

Child welfare was some sort of plot to force assimilation. Well, he had heard that before; and maybe they really had done that back then.

But then farming was wrong. On environmental grounds. He had to give her something there. But it was also wrong on moral grounds. Even on aesthetic grounds.

As for the dam: they hadn't got that far yet, but he had already grasped where she stood.

Maybe Rose herself was intending to be a great Chief some day. He wondered how he felt about that.

"I talked to Black Snake," she said suddenly.

"What did you say to him?"

"I made him admit he cut your tires. Then I told him I was going to sleep with you because he did that."

"Rose!" Harry got to his feet suddenly, nearly capsizing her onto the floor. He caught her by the elbow and then they were standing, face to face, staring at one another.

"Is it true? Is that why—?"

"No. But I want him to think so."

"But is that really going to turn him into a citizen? Telling him you're going to sleep with other guys? Maybe he'll want to break something else."

She looked surprised.

It was not the way he had thought it might be. There was no

bargain. But Harry was feeling even more worried about her now. Telling a guy like that that she was going to sleep around: it was a declaration of independence. What would Black Snake do when he woke up to that idea?

It was a tough environment she had grown up in. Having to deal with guys like Black Snake. He couldn't just take Rose's perspective for a trial run. He was going to have to get into this a lot more deeply than that.

He sat down. "Look," he said. "I just don't like the way you're trying to make this thing work. I want you to tell *me* that."

"What?"

"That if I'm bad you'll go off and sleep with Black Snake."

She looked puzzled.

"What would happen then? You want to know what would happen then?"

She nodded.

"I'd be very, very good."

She laughed. Harry took her wrist and pulled her down onto his lap again.

"It works. But only as long as I'm the boyfriend," he murmured into her little ear, which had ended up beside his lips. "If Black Snake is the boyfriend, I'm not sure what develops."

"You think I made a mistake?"

He shrugged. "What I want to know is, am I the boyfriend?"

She turned around and looked at him. There were tears standing in her eyes.

"Do you really want to be, Harry? When you know all this stuff about me?"

"Oh yes. God, yes. I want to be!"

He was happy about it, very happy, although bewildered, because it was making her cry.

HE WOKE UP AND FOUND IT WAS BROAD DAYLIGHT. THERE were some noises upstairs. Someone had come into the house. Rose sat up with a yawn and a stretch.

"It's my uncle."

"This is going to be okay, is it?"

"I told him and he said it was cool.—Well, that's the way he talks," she said, responding to Harry's look of astonishment. She was rapidly getting dressed, and he watched as the long johns were drawn up over her long slim legs, as her little bosom, which he had dreamed of seeing, disappeared into the white bra.

She went out of the room and he began to get dressed, wishing the night wasn't over.

He heard their cheerful voices up above. It sounded good. He went to the bathroom, then began to ascend the carpeted stairs. The Medicine Bear character was saying, "Oh yeah. It's Harry, is it? That's cool. Let's see—which Harry is that? Do I know any Harrys?"

He entered the kitchen, which seemed to have taken another quantum leap towards cleanliness. Coffee was filtering, creating an appetising brown scent in the air. Rose had just placed the last clean mug to drain. Bright sunlight came in through the windows rendering the spots and smears on them invisible.

"Harry Hallouran," said Rose.

"Hallouran!" The man had swung around with a friendly smile, which faded rapidly from his face, out of his eyes. "This is a whiteman, Rose. You didn't mention that."

"Tim! What are you saying!" She stopped wiping the counter and looked at him in reproach.

"Are you one of Robbie Hallouran's ...?" he was asking coolly. Harry nodded.

"Robbie Hallouran wrecked Eliza Boucher's life," he said to Rose.

"Tim! Even if that's true—what has it got to do with Harry?"

"I don't want him ruining your life, Rose. He's a whiteman."

"Now just hold on a second, Uncle Tim!" She put her hands on her hips. "For one thing, I'm part white myself. That seems to have slipped your mind. And for another thing, you sent me to university. Which is full of whitemen. What do you want me to do there? Act like a nun?"

"Couldn't you find any Native guys? There must be one or two of those?"

"I don't pick my friends on the basis of race!"

"Oh shit," he said. He sat down. "All right. Let's start again. How old is he?"

"He's in law school," said Rose, standing beside him. "He's very smart. I just really liked him—up until lately."

"Does he use a condom, Rose?"

Harry and Rose looked at one another and laughed.

"Well? Do you?"

"Oh yes. Absolutely. God, yes. Of course."

The man sighed. "I hate this," he said flatly.

"Well, it doesn't have anything to do with you!"

"No," he agreed sarcastically, looking into the cup she handed him. "Absolutely nothing to do with me."

Harry had a chance to look this guy over now. Everything about him seemed to say 1970s Indian radical. His braids, the western shirt, flashy rings on both hands. He also had that middle-aged look—Harry's father had it too—which said: "I've already made up my mind about everything, so don't bother arguing."

He began thinking again about the speech in the school auditorium. Maybe the guy actually meant everything he said. He was willing to carry a certain point of view to its extreme logical consequences.

Harry could appreciate the level of abstraction this guy operated on. He was some kind of original thinker, this was clear. He was probably Rose's inspiration. Her background didn't seem to contain anything else that could have produced a mind like hers.

It had got his back up, that thing Medicine Bear had said about his father and Eliza. And then, of course, he was a racist.

Medicine Bear spoke quietly. "You're going to like it, Rose."

"What?" She had subsided into a chair between them. The kitchen floor was still pretty horrible, Harry thought, looking down at their woollen socks—that was the only thing wrong with the place now.

"The acreage. You know—you'll have the family car? But he's a Hallouran. I bet he rides a horse. He won't be happy unless you get an acreage. He'll commute. In his Jeep Cherokee. To the office."

Harry was insulted. The ranch was his heritage—unless one of his sisters wanted it. He hated acreages. And he had been thinking about starting up a storefront.

"Tim—?" Rose paused. "Do you ever sleep with—you know—white women?"

It seemed like kind of an extreme question to Harry. Rose was this guy's niece, after all.

"Sure. Put on an old bearskin and go into the city. You can find yourself just about any kind of woman."

He was laughing. Rose began to laugh too.

Harry was getting the picture now, although it still shocked him slightly to hear her talking to her uncle like this.

"Okay, okay!" Tim wiped his eyes. "Sleep with him. Go ahead."

"Well, I will. I wasn't waiting for your permission or anything."

There was racism on the other side too, of course. Harry remembered being relieved when his mother was so direct and warm right away, when his father changed his mind. Somehow the thing that disturbed him most about the conversation between Rose and her uncle—aside from the fact that he wasn't used to having his colour and cultural background count against him— and aside from the fact that they were so completely open with one another—was the assumption they were both making now, that there was not, there could not be, a future in it.

A real future. With the storefront. Maybe a partnership between him and Rose. Marriage. Kids. Horses too. They were also part of her heritage, after all.

Or else she would marry Black Snake. And how would Uncle Tim like that, Harry wondered.

13

1994 · The Boyfriend Test

"ROSE?"

"Harry!"

"I'm sorry it took so long. My dad had a whole lot of things lined up for me to do. Getting ready for seeding, you know." They had barely seen each other during exams.

"Oh, that's all right. I was busy too. Can you pick me up? In your pickup?"

"For lunch here. Would that be okay?—Hey, Rose! I've got a summer job. With Steen and Barret! Just file clerk, but—"

"Oh, that's wonderful, Harry. I'm working for them too."

"You are?" He was surprised, stopped in his tracks, really. It was a good firm. And he was at the end of first year Law, while she had barely started university.

All the things he had been intending to say—he had been wondering whether they could get some kind of place together in Calgary, or whether he could and she could come and stay there sometimes—were dammed up inside him for a few seconds.

"I always work for them. I've been doing it, well—for years. Tim Steen is my grandpa."

"Tim Steen is your grandfather?" Harry was bewildered. He had been hoping to meet the grandfather, if she still had one of those, on the Reserve, this summer.

"I told you, my uncle Tim was fostered. He was adopted actually—by Tim Steen."

"God. Well, that's—" It was great, it was even better than that. Suddenly an apartment in Calgary was looking like a real possibility, not just a daydream.

"Harry? I can't stop thinking about that bed in your bedroom."

"My bed?" He glanced at it. He had just gotten out of it.

"Remember you said—at Christmas—no one in your house would think—?"

It was not true now that nobody would think of it. But nobody would care. His sister Marian had broken all the taboos at Christmas, when she brought home her fiancé.

"Could I come over and get you right away?"

◖ IT WAS AFTER LUNCH AND THEY WERE DRIVING INTO STEAM-boat. Looking at Rose beside him on the front seat of the truck, Harry realized that it was the first time in months that he had not been desperately wanting to have sex with her. At Christmas they had met a couple more times in Uncle Tim's house, despite Harry's scruples about that.

"I'll never live on an acreage, Rose."

"Tim was teasing me."

"Yeah, but that guy really hates me. He must, if he thinks I'd have an acreage."

After that, there had been no place to go. He saw himself studying beside Rose in the library, her shoulder only a foot away from his shoulder, as he tried to concentrate on a case he was memorizing—while another part of his mind was dwelling upon her breasts, the exquisite shape they were, the way they pushed out her shirt slightly, the way they looked in a bra, the way they looked out of a bra.

This morning had gone astoundingly well. He had finished getting dressed, thrown all his 4-H trophies in a box and carried them to the basement, notified his mother, who was going to church with his father, that Rose was coming to lunch, and then gone to get Rose.

A whole lifetime had then passed, after which they went downstairs for lunch. Everyone remarked upon how thin and pale they both were from studying; there was no other comment. And now he was feeling optimistic; he was feeling positively stupendous.

"Just think," she was saying. "We'll see each other all summer."

"I was thinking maybe we could get an apartment together."
Easy. Everything was easy today.

"Oh! But Harry, I'll be on the Reserve."

"How can you be working for—?"

"I always do. They keep a little office out there in the summer."

"Oh, I see. You run the office?"

"It's a whole side of the business. The advocacy work on the dam and so on. But then they handle most of the criminal cases too."

"A good firm," said Harry, feeling terribly disappointed.

"But it's all right. Don't you see? My grandpa comes out nearly every day. He lives in Calgary. In Mount Royal. We'll see each other all the time!"

"All the time," agreed Harry with a certain irony. He glanced at her. Their eyes met and they both smiled.

It was certainly better to have this job than any other, he realized with relief. Obviously they would hardly have been able to see each other at all if he had not got it; and she might not have approved of any other firm either.

"Vicky's coming back in July. They're going to do a movie premiere in the Band hall."

"Really?"

"She and that guy she brought down with her last year. They're doing a movie about Medicine Bear."

"A movie?"

Rose nodded "It's the real history of Alberta," she said. "Not the stuff you whitemen put in textbooks."

It was not necessary to protest any longer.

"I don't mean you, Harry. You know what I mean." She always got back to him sooner or later.

He put his hand out and touched her knee, which although clad in denim jeans, was delightfully near the surface. No long johns in May.

Harry pulled into the curb in front of Poppalushka's. Rose got out on her side, looking at the tree-lined street in curiosity. The other houses, most of them smaller than Poppa's, demonstrated a somewhat less generous imagination. This was Steamboat, unfamiliar territory for her. She had gone to the big high school in Abercrombie for grade twelve, and it would have been the town—almost a city—she had seen the most of.

Small towns—another part of the real history of Alberta, Harry thought.

"This is my brother Dominique's house."

They went around the side and up the steps of the back porch.

"Yo, Tony," said Harry, going inside, then stopping short and looking at his cousin in dismay. Tony had shaved his head.

Harry was familiar with the weird things kids did to their hair in high school. This hairdo made Tony look like a concentration camp victim, however.

"AIDS protest. Next Sunday. You'll take me, right? It's in Calgary," said Tony breathlessly.

"This is Rose," said Harry firmly. He had been anticipating jealousy. Competition for time and attention too. It was one reason why he had decided to bring her right over here first thing. To let Tony know how important she was. To let Dominique know.

Dominique now came into the kitchen. "You're Rose?" he said.

"Dominique Boucher?"

They stood smiling at one another and Harry felt that for once he had been able to show Rose someone he loved who would truly interest her.

Dominique was in his early forties, still good-looking, supple and slim. He had always been a quiet man. Something Harry had always loved about Dominique ever since he was a little boy was the way he could get right up close to him and just be there. Dominique didn't need to say anything; he hated arguments. He just went for the best way of doing things without having to talk about it.

He was completely reliable, or he had been, until Tony had started acting the way he was acting.

"I met Vicky last summer. I spent a lot of time with her. Tim's my uncle, you know," Rose was saying.

Dominique nodded. He was not a jealous person. Vicky had sidelined him last summer, coping with what had looked to Harry from a distance like a very complicated love life. But Dominique would be the last person to complain.

"Pop?" said Tony, suddenly producing a pop can, pulling the tab, and giving it to Rose. "Pop?" he said to Harry.

Harry perceived that Tony was nervous. He probably wanted to make a good impression. But he wouldn't know that to Rose pop was a poisonous drink, representing every evil thing that white society had to offer: an addictive non-food, forced upon third world peoples by a ruthless worldwide capitalist conspiracy. Harry thought this too, of course, but he often wondered how people could live in the modern world. It seemed impossible.

Dominique was making tea. Harry drank Rose's pop.

"I just found out, Rose and I are working for the same law firm this summer," he remarked.

"Well, that's good," said Dominique.

This would have been a wonderful place for them to meet, with her on the Reserve, if he had been working on the farm all summer. Dominique worked all the time, so he was never home during the day, even on Sunday. This Sunday visit was by pre-arrangement: he and Harry had been fixing a seeder in the machine barn all the previous afternoon.

However, Tony was always home, Harry reminded himself.

A vision of Rose brushing her hair came into Harry's mind suddenly. She had been sitting on his bed brushing her hair just before they went downstairs for lunch. Her arms went up above her head in a lovely arc, like the arms of a dancer. Then the hand that held the brush descended, with the other hand following, smoothing and straightening. Then both arms went up again, lifting her diaphragm, her breasts, while her face remained grave, absorbed. It seemed hard to believe that someone would be doing something so graceful, so serious, almost like a religious rite, just in his bedroom like that, for his eyes only.

They were back in the truck again, taking Rose home for supper. He had finally managed to show Rose the two people who meant most to him on earth, aside from his mother and father. It had been a good visit.

"Tim thinks Dominique is a real hero," she remarked.

[411]

"He does?" Harry knew what she must be alluding to, but he was somewhat surprised. He never thought of Dominique in any context outside his own affections, he was such a private person. However, when Rose used the word "real" in that way, like "the real history of Alberta," Harry knew what she was talking about.

"He could have been the Chief," said Rose. "That's what Tim says. He says he backed away from it."

"He had problems with alcohol, Rose." Harry could remember the long blank year when Dominique had been absent, the joy he had felt when he came back.

"Well, he became a farmer, in the end." A traitor; that was what she meant, actually.

"He saved himself. He had to save himself, Rose."

She smiled at him. "Don't worry, Harry. I like him," she said. "Besides, you're a farmer too."

"Well—not really," said Harry doubtfully. "It was just that yesterday I had to help Dominique fix the seeder. And then— we'll be seeding soon," he added.

All around them were the verdant signs of spring. The sky arched high and blue overhead, the warm and hazy blue of spring. There was a skim of green across the hills, and the windbreaks were leafing out. And on either side of the road stretched the black dirt fields, the richest land in the world, in the driest corner of Alberta.

Harry said, "You know, I bet my mother is going to put supper on the table the moment we get home."

"Yes, let's just stop here for a little while, Harry. This is going to be such a wonderful summer!"

◖ ROSE HAD TOLD HIM ON THE PHONE THAT SHE WAS COMING over to pick him up on Wednesday after supper. She honked the horn out in the yard.

Lizzie, who was drying dishes, remarked: "It's your friend, Harry. She's driving a Cadillac."

"Well, I guess I'll be—"

"Back tomorrow," said Lizzie satirically.

"I'm so glad you have friend like Rose, Harry," said his mother.

"Yeah. But the thing I'm really glad about," his father growled, "is that Rose turned out to be a girl!"

"Wow. What a car!" said Harry, stretching out his long legs, patting the leather upholstery appreciatively. "Did you steal it or something?"

"It belongs to Grandpa."

"Where are we going actually?" They seemed to be heading for Calgary.

"Do you have to work on the farm tomorrow?"

"Yeah. But I guess no one would care if I got back after breakfast."

"We'll just have to get up early."

"Sounds good," said Harry enthusiastically.

She drove him slowly down Memorial Drive beside the Bow River. "This is where I had an epiphany about you, Harry Hallouran."

"Isn't that some kind of religious thing?"

"Well, it was like that."

He remembered very well too. The cold clear night, silent and holy, the way they had got off the bus downtown, and then begun to walk down through the sleazy neighbourhoods, across the bridge. He had taken her arm when they were passing a rowdy bar. She had been telling him things that night—nothing about herself—nothing really personal—but things about her mind, about how, like his, it was overflowing with thoughts, with logical sequences, with facts and ideas. Finally they had been standing together on the dark hillside above the River. Then she had turned into his arms and kissed him on the lips, her closed lips on his closed lips.

After that, they had just walked back to the bus stop, his arm in hers, clasped against her side, under her breast. With any other girl, he felt, it might have been nothing. With her, it had turned the whole world upside down. Apparently she felt the same way.

Now she was taking him to Mount Royal, across another bridge.

"Are we going to see the grandfather?" he asked.

"I was here in the afternoon. He said I should get you."

"Is he going to give me some kind of a test?"

"Yes," she said. "But you'll pass."

By now they had left the car in the driveway. It was one of those horrible landscaped homes, with a lawn so bright green that under the spotlights that lit the facade it looked artificial. Surely Rose disapproved of this?

A mammoth—she was nearly as tall as he was—whitewoman swept down upon them. "Rose!" she cried. "Oh God! I love him already! So tall! So perfect! Where did you find him?"

"Well—he's in law school—"

"In law school? Darling! Rose's friend is in law school! Did she tell you that?"

Another enormous white person rose from a reclining chair by the gas fire. He resolved, after a moment, into Tim Steen, almost a legend, whom Harry had seen briefly after his interview for the file clerk job.

What had been said then:

"This is Harry."

"Oh yes. How do you do, Harry?"

What was being said now:

"My God, darling! Look at them together! Aren't they gorgeous? And Harry is in law school!"

"Did you say you were in law school?" asked the huge elderly person.

"This is Rose's *boyfriend*, darling! Now, which bedroom are they going to sleep in?—Are you hungry?" she went on.

"Starving," said Harry.

"Oh—!" She disappeared suddenly.

The big whiteman sat down. Rose also took a seat in the leather recliner opposite, tucking her feet under her. This left Harry standing in front of both of them.

Harry was now wondering whether it would be a boyfriend test or a law school test. He thought he might pass the latter.

"Grandpa," said Rose. "This is Harry Hallouran. Steen and Barret hired him last week. For the summer."

"Oh yes," said the old man, looking Harry over with a smile. "Now I remember."

He must be well into his seventies, Harry was thinking. Looking

[414]

at Tim Steen was like looking at two generations' worth of legal advocacy for Native people, plus the whole history of the Ochre River dam. His was, in Harry's view, the only rational voice that had ever been heard in that dispute. It had been an incredible honour to be introduced to him last week, passing by in the hall. Now he was actually talking to this mythic being.

"I'm—I just finished first year," said Harry. "I got a job as a file clerk."

"Well, Rose acts pretty well as one of the partners over on the Reserve. She's been doing it since she was ten years old," he went on, winking at Rose.

"I just answer the phone, Harry." Rose looked a little put out. She didn't like to be patronized, Harry thought.

"If Native people in this generation will start to do their own advocacy—"

Rose was nodding . "Their own criminal cases too—"

"Lawyers have a way of becoming judges. And judges write a lot of law."

Harry was beginning to get the picture. There was a mission being dealt out here, but it was being dealt to Rose, not him.

"I guess maybe you know. She's a pretty ambitious young lady."

Harry nodded. He was already aware that Rose intended to change the world. He just had no idea that she had this type of encouragement; that she had, in effect, already started.

At this point Valerie returned with a tray of food, including many things that Harry hated, like caviar, or had a hard time identifying as food items at all. Were they fungi, those things on the skewers, or some form of seafood? He also was offered a glass of whiskey, which he declined.

But Valerie's return made the situation instantly more human, from Harry's point of view, in spite of the wildness and constancy of her interjections. Rose had given her the reclining chair and knelt beside him on the hearth rug.

And there was a plan afoot, which Harry found absolutely delightful, for him and Rose to spend the night—in the blue room, apparently—and then for the old man and Rose to go out to the

Reserve together in the morning, dropping him off on the way at the farm in time to start driving a tractor.

Rose disappeared briefly with Valerie to scout out the blue room.

"Farm boy, eh?" said the old man, cocking an eye at Harry.

"My father and mother own a couple of sections in Steamboat," said Harry. "But there's no irrigation. Times have changed in dryland farming, you know. There's a lot more consciousness out there."

The old man nodded thoughtfully.

"Rose would kill me for saying it. But they're trying. They've even got half a section in organic stuff."

"I was born out that way myself," said Tim Steen. "My dad had a ranch. North of Abercrombie. Roseland, they call the place now."

Harry appreciated hearing it. At least he wasn't the only white-man Rose liked who had been born on a ranch.

"You don't know how we all love that girl," went on the old man. "When I first saw her she was eight and bright as a button. As far as I'm concerned, she's just perfect."

"Pretty perfect from my point of view too," agreed Harry.

"Using a condom, Harry?" he asked, his voice apparently casual.

"Oh yes. Absolutely. Of course," said Harry, startled, but by now no longer surprised by the question. The uncle, the old man. Tony, too, had wanted to know. Even his father had got around to asking.

◖ "THIS PLACE—IT'S ALL VALERIE," SAID ROSE, RAISING HER arms to take the clip out of her hair. "She's kind of over the top. You don't mind?"

They were in a palace-like room with blue draperies and mirrors. It had a beautiful girl in it, her hair tumbling down over her naked shoulders to her waist. "This place is like something out of the Arabian Nights."

She laughed. "Do you like my grandpa?"

"Like him? Well, God, Rose. Do you think I'm going to get to know him well enough to say I like him?"

"Yes," she said. "I don't know whether anyone could get to like

[416]

this bedroom, though. Even if he slept in it a couple of nights
a week all summer."

"Oh, I think I could get to like that—pretty quickly," said Harry.

❡ THE FOLLOWING WEEK, HARRY FOUND HIMSELF A ROOM IN
Calgary and started working for Steen and Barrett. The old man
was more or less a sleeping partner; he only came in when he felt
like it. But he could do whatever he wanted; he was God in the
office.

Harry had been at work for only ten days or so, and had just
started to demonstrate that he was too smart to be a file clerk.
But then suddenly he was plucked out of the grips of a junior
associate who had been starting to really use him to research a
case, and removed—physically—to the Reserve, by Tim Steen.

"I'd like to see you two youngsters get together on something
for me," said old Tim as they sat in Rose's office, which was in a
derelict house—a version of the storefront of Harry's imagination,
only in a very different locale.

"This is the year the government is threatening to operate
the dam. Even though there isn't the same type of demand for
it that there was ten years ago. The politicians want a show of
justification for the hundreds of millions they wasted on this."

"So they'll go up there with an RCMP escort in their official cars,
play 'O Canada' on the loudspeakers, have a speech or two, and
then go away and leave us with this environmental mess on our
hands," said Rose bitterly.

"I've been invited to Ottawa in September to make my final
contribution to the federal inquiry on this. I'm going to write
a summary document; and maybe publish it as a book. We must
have just about the best library on this issue—and on dams in
general, and on the worldwide infringement of aboriginal rights
by dams—right here in this room," he added reflectively, looking
around at the walls, lined with reports.

Harry had been wondering whether there was any work here
for a file clerk. The filing was already excellent—Rose's work,
he supposed.

"Do you think you can do the research for my report and carry on with the usual work?" he asked Rose.

"Oh yes," she said eagerly.

"Harry, you're going to help with this?"

"Yes, sir." Harry was astounded. 'Yes, sir:' it didn't say what he meant. It was the kind of assignment a person could dream of all his life.

"Well, can you live at home? You'll have to get over here yourself. I won't be here most days," the old man continued.

Harry was thinking rapidly. He could stay at home; he and Dominique could soup up some kind of old rattletrap for him to drive over in. But there was an alternative. "I think I could stay with Eliza," he said to Rose. "Dominique would fix it for me. And—I know her. I've known her all my life."

He hadn't had a chance to really tell Rose about that. And it was still a sore spot. What her uncle had said about his father ruining Eliza's life.

"Well, just remember, this is going to be a lot of work. I'm trusting you two to buckle down and get it done for me."

Walking over to Eliza's—they had the rest of the day off after the old man left—Harry was reflecting upon how such things happened. When he had got the job with Steen and Barrett, it had been strictly on his merit, he was sure of that: his grades, the impression he made on the junior partners. And he had thought that was a big break—because it was exactly the kind of firm he wanted to work for later when he became a criminal lawyer.

But now he had been taken out of the file room and given the Nobel Peace prize and he was aware that it was not because of his own merit. It was because of Rose; although it did not seem as though she had intervened directly. The old guy wanted Rose to have a hand in his presentation. Normally he would have employed a real lawyer to do the groundwork. But Rose just happened to have a boyfriend who was an employee. And he must have made some kind of minimally good impression. And then there was the boyfriend exam; he supposed that was in here somewhere.

Now they were standing outside Eliza's house. It looked as if Dominique was already there; his truck was parked outside.

"She just lives alone, doesn't she?" remarked Rose.

"Well, since Vicky—and Dominique—"

"Old people don't usually have to live alone here, Harry."

Their eyes met. They were both thinking about what Medicine Bear had said.

"You've got to realize, Rose—my dad was young. He was still in his teens," said Harry. "And I guess he's been sorry about it all his life." That was what his mother thought, at least.

"Your parents took Dominique." The way she said "took," it meant "took."

"I don't know. Maybe you have to see what this is like from the inside or something," said Harry helplessly. He was thinking that knowing Dominique a little bit better would help her to see that it wasn't all bad; it wasn't quite the way she imagined.

They were still at a little distance from the house, where they had stopped. Rose was now eyeing the pickup. "It's Dominique," Harry told her.

"Your dad," said Rose. "He makes me nervous."

"His bark is worse than his bite."

"No. It's because of Eliza. Some whitemen are—you know, they like Native girls. They think of them as prey."

"Dad?" said Harry, horrified. The whole subject was indecent to him. And she was classifying his father as a sexual predator.

"It's something in the way he looks at me sometimes."

Harry remembered the assumption his father had been making when he first saw Rose. And she would know—Harry believed Rose would know—how he had looked at her.

"But now he knows that you and I—And Rose?" It was an excruciating thought. "You don't think that I—?"

"I never thought that about you, Harry." She took his hand and they walked forward and went into the house.

A small sore spot had become a larger, unhealed wound in Harry's mind.

Seeing Dominique made him feel better. He was sitting in the small kitchen at the table in his green work shirt, the sleeves rolled up. Eliza had given him tea. Harry had been coming over here with Dominique since he was a little boy, and he remembered how they could sit by the table sometimes for an hour, not speaking, Eliza smoking one cigarette after another. But Harry was sure they liked one another's company; just as he liked being in the machine barn all morning with Dominique, neither of them having to say a word.

Eliza got up and began opening a can of stew when she saw Harry and Rose. They were going to have supper. Silently Rose went to help her, just as Harry would have if she hadn't started to do it first. She found a pot for Eliza and put the kettle on.

Harry had blurted out the whole story to Dominique when he was talking to him on the phone, so he didn't have to tell him anything now. He sat down. They smiled at one another.

"Will she put me up?"

"She won't take your money."

"Come on, Eliza. Maybe you could use the money for something."

"She says it would be like making one of her own kids pay her," said Dominique.

"Wow. Thanks, Eliza." Harry began to feel a lot happier now. Maybe it was true that his father had made a certain assumption. But Rose made assumptions too. At least some of which were wrong.

Canned stew. It was going to be a strange diet all summer, going between Valerie's lemon grass, edible flowers, hot peppers and raw fish, and Eliza's cuisine. Harry decided that he really couldn't starve to death on canned stew and beans, the way he probably could on the other stuff.

"Seeding's just about done," Harry remarked.

They needed all hands during seeding and for the past three weekends Harry had been driving one machine or another. It had been very hard to get hold of Dominique. Harry had left messages all over—at home, at Mollie's, with Tony.

"You're getting Vicky's room," said Eliza. "It has the bed."

"Vicky's coming in July, isn't she?" said Rose. Eliza made a noise of assent. They all knew Vicky would not be staying with her mother.

Silently, Eliza placed a small pile of blankets in Rose's

outstretched arms. Then Rose went down the hall, Harry following. They were going to be in a room alone together for a short while. Harry wasn't going to waste the time making a bed.

"This is going to be okay," she whispered eventually, enfolded in Harry's hot embrace, holding back his head to prevent him crazily kissing her. "I was afraid—"

Harry knew what she had been afraid of. It was one thing to drive him around in a Cadillac. She had been afraid that he couldn't take the Reserve, though. As usual, just the fact that Dominique existed made everything better, Harry thought happily. He was also looking forward to getting back to that brown house she lived in at the other end of the village, the one without a sweat lodge. He was pretty sure he wouldn't make her feel ashamed of him there either.

They met the following morning at Rose's office and worked all day. The old guy was a slave driver. He wasn't actually there, but he had already telephoned in some demands, leaving them on the answering machine. Harry had climbed a mountain of material before lunch, just to construct a footnote. Rose was reading something else and got up to answer the phone when it rang again: more instructions. Peanut butter sandwiches. Then another long call—a conference call this time—with the old man.

Rose had gone home by herself the night before; she wouldn't let Harry come, so he had spent the evening watching Eliza's tv. He had been hoping she would stay and sleep at Eliza's, but obviously she felt the need to be home in the evening. They needed to sort this out somehow. He decided to take the bull by the horns.

When it came time to quit, Harry followed Rose out the door of the office, waited while she locked up, and then began to walk home with her. "What's your sister's name again?"

"Jasmine." She wasn't letting him hold her hand. "She's seventeen."

"The Tim situation in your family is out of control," he remarked.

"Uncle Tim has really gone back to Medicine Bear," she replied. "A lot of people call him Joe, too. It was his father's name."

It was very complex, but he would find out. Eventually he would know everything.

Her mother greeted him with the same frightened look as before. Rose went straight for the tea kettle and the pot of stew, so Harry sat down beside William, who seemed to recognize him. They grinned at one another.

Jasmine came out of her bedroom and trailed down the hall. She was an even more beautiful girl than Rose, although Harry found it hard to admit that this was possible. Perhaps it was the kind of thought a sexual predator might have, he thought to himself wryly.

Jasmine had widely-set dark eyes, black rather than brown like Rose's, and they slanted in a bit towards her nose, which gave her a kind of dewy, amazed expression. Her face was oval, like Rose's, her hair long and thick, like Rose's, and she wore the same kind of clothes: jeans, T-shirt, canvas sneakers. However, he perceived immediately that she lacked Rose's force of character. She made no attempt to cope with his presence, nor did she help Rose and her mother, who were setting out bowls and forks on the table now. She stood still, gazing wistfully out the kitchen window.

"Where's Timmy?" asked Rose.

Jasmine shrugged.

"This is Harry," Rose went on. "You didn't meet him yet."

Jasmine smiled shyly, vaguely, in Harry's direction. Her smile made her look radiant, but Harry could tell that she hadn't really noticed him. He was probably just a kind of white blob, something strange that belonged to Rose.

They sat down at the table and began to eat supper. The little boy wasn't home yet. William couldn't handle a fork too well. He drank his stew out of a bowl. Rose wiped his face for him tenderly afterwards with a dish towel.

Harry said: "Should I get the tea?"

The mother looked up in horror. Rose nodded. "Thank you, Harry."

While he found some cups, Rose was asking Jasmine something about homework. School was nearly over. Jasmine didn't have homework, it appeared. She put on a jacket and went out. Rose looked after her with a worried expression.

"Want to go back to work now?" she asked Harry.

"No," said Harry firmly.

She sat down again restlessly with her tea.

"Harry's staying with Eliza Boucher. He's working for Grandpa too." Apparently she hadn't told her mother anything. "Harry's going to be a lawyer, Ma."

She might have said, 'Harry's going to be a poisonous snake, Ma.' The mother looked at him with dilated eyes, then turned her head away slowly, afraid he might strike.

"She's had some bad experiences," said Rose.

"I shot my brother. I didn't mean to. Lionel nearly killed William." The mother spoke tonelessly, her head still averted.

"Well—" Rose made a helpless gesture. "Now you know about that, Harry."

"Is that how William got—? And Lionel was—?" Harry could put it together pretty fast from some things Rose had already said. "She didn't go to jail for that, I hope?"

Marina had started to look at him again almost as though he was human.

"My uncle didn't get permanently hurt. But William did. Ma felt so bad about it that she moved in to take care of him."

William was grinning away, nodding his head. He followed along somehow.

The little boy dashed into the house now. His mother got up immediately and began reheating the stew. Rose gave him a hug.

"Hi, Harry," he said to Harry. The males in this household liked him, at least.

"Come on," said Rose. "We have to go."

It was beginning to get dark and he managed to take her hand this time.

He said, "Rose, do you think we're ever going to make love again? It wasn't last week—actually, it was the week before that. And now I've been here for more than twenty-four hours. It seems as though this is getting harder rather than easier."

"That's what I was—We don't really have to work all night, Harry."

"Then—where are we going?"

"To Tim's?"

"Oh no! Please! Not there. What about Eliza's? She gave me the room with the bed, remember?"

Dominique wouldn't actually have told Eliza anything. But he would have conveyed, just by sitting there the way he usually did, that whatever Harry was doing was all right.

They then started what was, from Harry's point of view, an excellent routine. After work every night they went to Rose's house for supper. Then they usually ended up doing a little more work, just because neither of them, by temperament, was able to stop. Then they went to Eliza's and slept together till early morning. Then Harry would walk Rose home, go back and get a little more sleep himself, then get up and have breakfast with Eliza.

That was a good routine too. He did the cooking, while Eliza smoked her way through a couple of cups of coffee. Toast, fried eggs, bacon, waffles, porridge. His mother had brought out a whole box full of stuff. He should have known there was no way he was going to go hungry less than thirty kilometres from home. The only bad thing was that Rose had to be eating cornflakes on the other side of town.

They worked all day. Harry liked the way that was turning out too. Little kids came into the office and stared at them while they worked. And old people would drift in and sit down, sometimes for hours, saying nothing, just watching Harry and Rose work.

Harry heard from the kids that he was "helping Rose." It was a bit insulting since he was already so much further along in his education, but in a way it was true. Rose was a specialist in the area of the Ochre River dam. She had been on this beat since she was eight. And she was on a direct pipeline to the old man.

They were doing this work right out front. It was on display. The Reserve loved it. It was their show—the only response they had left to the mountain of concrete in the River valley.

At the same time, the criminal work of the firm continued in the other room of the little house. Break and enter, vandalism, theft, assault, assault with a weapon—one by one, sometimes in twos and threes, the young men were sent through to talk to one of the lawyers sent over by Steen and Barret. It was one meeting, as a rule; the next one would be in court.

"Lucky bastard," remarked a young guy Harry had met when he was still putting in time as a file clerk back at the Calgary office. He passed into the inner room carrying a thick briefcase full of files for the lawyer he was with. The guy was in third year Law, not first. It must have seemed unfair to him, the way Harry had got jumped ahead.

The young men came in all morning. Rose looked up, she looked down, checking off the names. Harry kept wondering if one of these guys was Black Snake, but her expression never varied: cheerful, warm, friendly.

And all the while their work went on. Harry knew now that he was taking both tests at once, the boyfriend test and the law school test. He felt he was passing. But it wasn't an easy exam. Even though the third year student thought it was all just gravy.

Valerie came and took Rose away one afternoon to go shopping in the city. Harry worked on, watched by a couple of old guys on chairs against the wall; snuff takers, who usually dropped out when they had filled their cans with spit. A younger fellow then dropped in: hair in a ponytail, western shirt, jeans, Nikes—kind of clean-cut, good-looking.

"Anything I can help you with?" Harry asked. He felt a bit stupid suddenly, in his crisp, pinstriped short-sleeved shirt; wearing his glasses to read with. He must look like an office drone to this guy.

"Nope. I just came by to see what you're doing."

"Oh. Well—you know it's about the dam."

He nodded. "Dam's built," he said.

"Yeah, but maybe this Reserve gets to have the last word on the subject."

"Last word? Who cares?" said the young guy.

Harry decided not to get into that. "I'm Harry Hallouran," he said, sticking out his hand. The old people did a lot of hand-shaking. This guy looked at his hand for a moment, then sat down.

"Do you want to read this thing I'm doing right now?" Harry printed out a sheet of bibliographical information and handed it over. Working with the PC was his innovation. The old man would have nothing to do with it. He wrote his stuff by hand, with a fountain pen, on foolscap.

"I don't get this," said the guy, putting down the paper immediately. "For one thing, what are you doing here? You're a whiteman."

"Yeah, but what if I agree with you? The dam shouldn't be there."

"What if you do?" The young man shrugged. "You get paid both ways, I guess. Get paid working for us and at the same time, you whites get our water!"

"What's your name?" asked Harry. The conversation was getting too hot, too political. Nothing like this happened when Rose was around.

"Judah Mountain," he said.

"Nice to meet you, Judah," said Harry. "Maybe you'd better talk to Rose when she gets back." Another part of his mind was saying that he didn't want this guy within a mile of Rose.

The guy continued to sit there, so Harry went back to what he was doing just the way he usually did, whether it was an eight-year-old or an old granny in the chair in front of his desk. This one was restive, though.

"So what do you do in your spare time, Harry?" he asked.

"Work," said Harry. It came out like that, kind of involuntarily, but it was true, he thought. Even sometimes when they were lying in bed together, he and Rose would talk about the old man's summary. It was like a gigantic game of Go Fish to them. So many cards lying face down to remember and match. Meanwhile the deck kept getting shuffled and reshuffled.

"Ever go out and—you know—have a beer with some friends?"

"I don't drink," said Harry, beginning to feel that he sounded like a Mormon missionary.

"Really? Like—never?"

"Well—" Of course, sometimes he had a beer. But they never kept the stuff around at home because of Dominique.

"How about tonight, man? With me and my friends. I've got a car. Coming?"

He had changed his tone and sounded friendly. Harry was tempted. He wasn't afraid of this guy; he knew he wouldn't get drunk. And he didn't know this group. Young men of his own age. A demographic he saw only on its way to jail. However, Rose wouldn't like it.

Again, he felt a slight contrary pull. Rose was always the boss. But she had to be, out here.

"Sorry," said Harry. "I've got too much to do. Some other time, maybe."

"Scared?" murmured Judah. "Think we'll spill beer on your shirt or something?" His tone had changed again.

"Sure," said Harry, getting up. He was a good deal taller than Judah. "Have it your way." Rose had made the right decision for him.

"You're scared shitless," said Judah, also getting up. But he didn't hang around. He went out the door.

Harry sat down again, feeling breathless. It wasn't because of personal threat. It was just the idea, which he had never got before in this place, that someone hated his guts.

Shortly after that Rose's brother Timmy came in with a couple of other kids and he began to feel better. Timmy often hung around the office. He liked to draw. Harry dealt them out fifty sheets of computer paper from the tracks of his printer and they began to draw with the crayons Rose kept in a big ice cream tub on the windowsill.

"A young guy dropped by the office this afternoon and asked me to go to the bar," Harry said to Rose that night.

She sat up in bed and looked down at him. There was a convenient patch of moonlight in that part of the room at this time of night and he admired the beautiful shadows on her body.

"Who was it?"

"Judah Mountain, he said his name was."

"Oh." She lay back down, but he sensed that she was agitated.

"I didn't go, you notice," Harry went on. "He said that was because I was scared shitless."

Rose said nothing. She was determined to run her own show. He had noticed this before.

"Look, don't go talk to him; don't do anything," he said. "There's no harm done. Just tell me something. Was it Black Snake?"

"Yes," said Rose.

He lay down and put his arms around her. "I think the guy wanted to see me up close. Well, that's okay. I kind of wanted to see him too."

"It was because I wasn't there," she said. She was very tense. Harry began getting her snuggled in, one arm behind her shoulders.

"Look, this wasn't assassination," he said. "It was let's-take-the-guy-out-and-see-if-he-makes-a-fool-of-himself. He even said that. He said I was scared they'd spill beer on my shirt. I was actually kind of tempted to go. But I thought you wouldn't like it."

She shook her head violently. No, she wouldn't have liked it.

Harry began to wish he hadn't told her at all. He had just wanted to check out his guess—which had become a conviction anyway over the course of the afternoon—that Black Snake had been looking him over.

❦ THE DAM WAS ABOUT TO OPEN. THERE WAS A LOT OF controversy on the Reserve about what to do, how to mark protest. A Band meeting had been scheduled and Harry was looking forward to going to that, to see what one of those was like.

Medicine Bear came to their office for the first time that morning. "I just dropped in to see the sideshow you and Rose have got going here," he said to the old man, who was sitting in the chair in front of Rose's desk.

Tim didn't look at Harry, clicking away on the keyboard, and Harry began feeling the same way in front of Rose's uncle as he had in front of her ex-boyfriend. He had on the pinstriped shirt; his mother had given it to him when she'd heard he was going to work in the city. Every night he washed it and hung it up in Eliza's bathroom on a hanger; then he ironed it the next morning using an ancient steam iron that Eliza provided.

"It's a big job the kids are doing," the old man was saying. "Getting it on paper."

"On paper! A mountain of paper. Built upon a landslide—of paper! Why? Tell me!" Tim made a sort of throwaway gesture with his hands. But Harry was surprised nevertheless. He seemed to want the old man to answer the question.

"So it'll be in the textbooks, Tim."

"Read by whitemen!"

"Read by everybody, I hope!"

"Yeah. What's that got to do with this thing over there in the River valley, though? That'll still be there, messing up the River when the textbooks are dust."

The old man said evenly: "All we have here is the power of the word."

"Tell me about it! I've got a pack of young braves in this place who are talking dynamite; they want the revolution to start right here. I know about the word, all right! When for two cents I'd pull down a silk stocking and go over there myself with a truckload of ammonium nitrate!"

"Yes, but that's going to be a pretty pathetic ceremony they put on over there, you know that. To justify the unjustifiable. That's what people will say in fifty years."

"Okay," said Tim. "There's something to that. But maybe there are two kinds of people. I'm one and you're the other. To you the world is made out of what people say. To me it's—" he went off into a trance, not finishing the sentence.

Rose was watching him, transfixed. Even the old man was looking at him, a curious expression on his face.

A few moments later, Tim emerged from his fugue. "Hey, thanks a lot!" he said. "I've got something now." He went out the door.

❧ THE OLD MAN STAYED ON FOR THE BAND MEETING. ROSE went with them to the hall, but then deposited them, kindly but firmly, together in the back and went to sit up front with her mother and Jasmine and the little boy. The whitemen got to sit at the back of the bus.

"It's a far cry from the old days," said Tim Steen. "They didn't even have a hall when I first started working here. Just that little house you and Rose are in. It belonged to Tim's dad."

It was like being in a slice of history, to sit in the back of this hall with Tim Steen, Harry realized.

They fooled around for a while with financial details: monthly statements, the bank account. But the meeting was about Medicine Bear's speech, which he shortly proceeded to make. He began with a highly political précis of the negotiations over the dam and the history of its building—a tale of chicanery, lying, deceptive tactics, bribery and coercion—he used all these words.

This was not at all like his performance at Christmas, Harry was thinking.

Then Medicine Bear went on to say that the Natives had met all of this with nothing but honest refusal right from the start. And now—he went on—there was a new spirit in the place that wanted to go beyond the old passive resistance and fight the whiteman on his own terms.

At this a bunch of wild men in war paint—some in ski masks, like Sub-Commandante Marcos—got up and cheered and ululated and danced on the metal chairs, and Harry wondered whether a great mistake was not about to be made. Medicine Bear seemed to be broaching the truckload of ammonium nitrate openly.

Medicine Bear stood there patiently, waiting for them to tone it down. When he could be heard again he said, "My mother spoke to me this morning."

Suddenly the hall fell completely silent and Harry wondered why. Who was his mother anyway? Wasn't she dead?

"She said this," Tim went on. "We live in a world of things. Native people, we know that. We're not trying to change the world. We just want to know what each thing is and how to use it without destroying it.

"She said that water is a living thing," he went on. "It moves. It breathes. We should respect its spirit. We have to follow it, wherever it flows, to protect it, in peace. At least we still know that, even if we're the last people on earth who do."

"That's what she said," said Tim, spreading out his hands, and the hush in the hall was even deeper than before. "Take it. Use it if you can. I hope it helps you. It helps me." He sat down.

Harry had got it by now. The mother was dead.

He himself had been sitting there that morning, both hands poised over the keyboard, while this electrifying message was being delivered. Or composed.

The meeting was over. Slowly, people began to get up and shuffle out, murmuring, shaking hands. Almost everyone in the place shook hands with the old man on the way out. Harry got quite a few hands himself. He felt fine now about being in the back seat.

"What was all that about his mother?" Harry whispered to Rose that night in Vicky's bedroom.

She lay there, silent, for a moment. Harry realized that although there was a lot he wanted to know about that, he wasn't going to be able to ask. Rose wouldn't like skepticism.

"She was my grandmother," said Rose. "I sometimes—sometimes wish—" She didn't finish the sentence. Harry wondered whether she wished she had the visionary connection too. She obviously believed in it.

There was mental illness in the family. Marina had been in and out of mental hospitals. The last time she had been in was after she shot Tim. Rose had told him, by now, a good deal about that. Tim had barely woken up in the hospital before he was on the phone, badgering bureaucrats and arguing with doctors and psychiatrists to let his sister out of the ward for the criminally insane where she had ended up.

Rose thought her mother's problems stemmed from the violence in her life: she had witnessed a murder as a young child, she had had abusive foster parents, then there was the stalker, Lionel, who had shot himself after he nearly killed William. But looking at Jasmine, whom Harry thought was about as spaced out as possible, it occurred to him that there might be some hereditary element. And then there was this, of course. For if it was not a kind of political flim-flam; if Medicine Bear really believed his mother spoke to him, then what was that but insanity?

The official opening of the dam passed without event. No one from the Reserve attended. As Rose had predicted, a cavalcade of official cars with an RCMP escort, four cars full of policemen with flashing lights and motorcycle outriders went through on the highway. It was a local joke that the cops had outnumbered the politicians.

That night people went out, silent, drifting in small groups across the hills, and stood on the banks of the River, looking into the empty riverbed. Harry and Rose went to look too. Then they walked home with Rose's mother and put William to bed. Harry got along very well now with Marina who ordered him around in the same way she did the others. He came in handy doing things for William; it had taken two women to lift William before Harry came along.

Jasmine was still out when they went over to Eliza's. Rose was upset.

They got up at 3:00, somewhat earlier than usual, and Harry walked her home. Rose looked in the bedroom. Jasmine wasn't there yet. They sat together on the sofa; Rose sat bolt upright, as usual when she was worried, barely allowing him to hold her hand.

"I just want her to come home," said Rose. "Tonight—I think something is going to happen tonight."

"Why? What do you think might happen?"

"Oh, I don't know! But Jasmine—if she went off the Reserve—if the boys took her to the bar—some whiteman might murder her!"

"Or some whiteman might fall in love with her, Rose."

"I'm just scared, Harry."

Finally he managed to get her to go to bed. He lay down on top of the blanket so he could hold her while she went to sleep. It occurred to him to wonder, as he had wondered before, how Rose got information. She seemed to have a sense of what was going on here that he lacked, even though they were always together, and the people she saw and talked to were the same ones he saw.

When he woke up again it was 5:00. Jasmine was on the sofa, sleeping, and there was a fire somewhere. Sirens on the highway.

It was not fire, but police.

Rose came out of the bedroom, pulling on a sweater over the clothes she had gone to sleep in. She barely glanced at Jasmine, childlike and naive in sleep.

"We have to go to the office, Harry!"

She had no idea yet what had happened, but she was already on the phone with a lawyer who worked for Steen and Barrett, getting him out of bed.

"I don't know what's happened yet! Does it matter? It's something. Someone is going to be arrested. By the time you get here, I'll know."

So something had happened after all. The tension of the night had not been an imaginary terror. Jasmine did not seem to have been involved. She had probably just been out like many other people, watching the River drain away. But something had brought the RCMP back to the Reserve.

By noon they knew. The lawyer had not bothered to come to the Reserve. He had met the cops in Abercrombie, bringing in a carload of suspects for questioning. Since then he had been in on the police interrogation. Finally he called Rose on his cellphone.

"He says he thinks he'll spring them," she reported to Tim, who had come stalking in, late in the morning, and sat down without a word in the chair in front of her desk. The whole house was full of people, elders, parents of the four young men involved, their younger siblings, who went dodging around the older people's legs and in and out the door. Harry wasn't working; it was too confusing and noisy a scene, and there was too much tension.

"He'd better spring them," said Medicine Bear.

"But they'll still be up on charges," Rose told him.

"What charges?"

"Break and enter? Theft? Vandalism? He doesn't know yet."

The lawyer was probably trying to broker vandalism as the charge, Harry guessed. They had broken into the main operating room of the dam and spray-painted the walls with swastikas. It would surely count in their favour that the damage had been so trivial; it was more like a prank than anything else. And there was machinery in there that they could have broken. The theft had been liquor, apparently—from someone on the Reserve.

How had Rose known? Harry had been with her almost all day yesterday at the office and in the evening. Yet somehow she knew and he didn't, that something was going to happen.

"All right. He's bringing them back now," reported Rose. "There'll be a trial date."

"So what are the charges?"

"Break and enter. Theft. Vandalism."

He hadn't managed to broker anything but their release pending trial. Medicine Bear got up without comment and strode out the door.

Harry spotted a ponytail getting out of the lawyer's Lexus. He had been expecting to see it.

"Will they be—going to jail?" Rose asked the lawyer, who came in briefly.

"Oh yeah. Jail's in it. Most of 'em are troublemakers. Criminal records. No way to keep 'em out."

"But—but—it's a protest. They'll be political prisoners, won't they? Going to jail for something like this?"

"If so, most of the Natives in jail today are political prisoners. Stealing booze and breaking a window doesn't strike a judge as protest. Painting swastikas wasn't a good choice either."

Rose was silent.

The lawyer was looking for a bathroom. They didn't have one of those, just a falling-down outhouse behind the building. Harry took him out there and he looked at it, then raised his eyebrows and asked if there was a gas station in Bitter Root.

For the rest of the afternoon, Rose said hardly anything. They worked, and Harry hoped that the slight boredom of the job she was doing—editing a bibliography—was helping her somehow.

That night she wanted to sleep at home, and Harry guessed that she really needed to be alone, although the way she was acting worried him. He knew that she was thinking about the boys who were in trouble; she was thinking about Black Snake. And while she was thinking about it she didn't want him around; she didn't want him to touch her. He had to rely on her to think it through for herself; to get it straight.

He slept very poorly. He missed her in the bed beside him, rolled up the way she usually slept, but lightly touching, with her back, her knees. He missed that even while he was asleep.

As a consequence, when he woke up slightly before dawn, and heard something, just a little noise—a crackle—outside, he jumped straight out of bed and went to investigate. By the time he was halfway across the room the flames were leaping in through the wall. Harry picked up his bedding and hurled it, blanket by blanket, onto the conflagration by the windowsill.

Then he ran out of the room, slamming the door behind him and shouting to Eliza. The phone still worked. Half a minute later he was outside the house with the bucket of water they used to flush the toilet and the sofa throw. There was fire over the whole wall, however, by now. The fire siren started up behind him and a moment later he had some help. There were men running from all angles, with buckets, with fire extinguishers.

It was just a matter of minutes or they wouldn't have saved the house. The plywood building was like kindling, standing on cement piers, with a good strong updraft underneath through the broken skirting. The fire truck arrived in time to squirt water over the charred and smouldering side of the house; the fire was already out.

The Reserve police were there. So was Medicine Bear. Eliza sat in the front of his truck with a dazed expression on her face.

"Oh, there you are," said Tim, coming around the side. He actually looked at Harry. He usually just looked through him.

"Is Eliza all right?"

"She's okay. She took in a bit of smoke. Where's Rose?" he demanded.

"At home." The implication of the question struck Harry. Tim knew—probably everyone knew—that he and Rose spent nights at Eliza's. "It was arson, wasn't it? Someone who knew she wasn't here?"

Tim nodded. "Tell it to the cops, okay, Harry?" Tim turned to the Native policeman beside him. "This is Harry. He boards with Eliza, like I told you."

Harry went to the office and called Dominique. He came over and took Eliza to Poppalushka's. She went without protest and it occurred to Harry that she would have been there a long time ago—or else, as Rose had suggested, Dominique would have been here with her—if it hadn't been for his own family, for Tony and Mollie, Robbie, even himself, dividing up Dominique among them.

He had not had time to think yet about the meaning of what

had happened. He realized how closely he—they—must have been watched. Was it attempted murder? Or was it someone trying to spill beer on his shirt? He walked slowly back to the office, wondering.

Probably nothing would have happened at all, except for the opening of the dam yesterday and the arrests. If Black Snake was going to jail anyway, he had nothing to lose—trying to get Harry off the Reserve, getting rid of the house he was staying in.

When he got to the office he found that Rose had a Native cop in front of her and she wasn't fooling around at all. She named names, she gave a motive, she detailed occasions when Judah had talked to her; he had threatened to kill Harry. But as far as she was concerned, the real victim was Eliza. She didn't intend to let him get away with it.

Another cop brought in Black Snake for a moment. They were calling the RCMP. Rose said, "You nearly killed a helpless old woman, Judah."

She was standing right in front of him. He looked at her expressionlessly. "What the heck is this all about?"

He was a good-looking guy. Harry couldn't help noticing this again. And he looked right for Rose. He was taller, but not much taller, the way Harry was. He looked smart too—although Harry couldn't believe that he was smart.

"I'll never forgive you, Judah," she said. "Because of Eliza."

The cops took him away in their truck, going to Abercrombie. Rose turned to the phone and began arranging for a lawyer to come out from Steen and Barrett.

The police held Judah, briefly. There was evidence of arson, there was motive, but there wasn't anything that put him right there on the scene. Eventually they let him go. Harry heard about these developments all day as Rose reported them to Tim, who was hanging around.

At 5:00 the office was finally empty. Harry felt that he had shaken hands with everyone on the Reserve that afternoon. They went out the door and Rose locked up. Harry was standing beside her as she turned around. She looked up at him. "Where am I going?" he asked.

She laughed. "You're coming home with me, Harry." She took his hand.

¶ THE FOLLOWING WEEK, VICKY CAME BACK. FROM HARRY'S perspective this was about as irrelevant as a visit from the Queen.

He was living with Rose's family now. Eliza's house was being cleaned, the charred window replaced, and another family was poised to move in right away. This arrangement meant that rather than working for ten hours and thinking about work or talking it over with Rose for another four, then using the remaining ten to make love, sleep and eat, he was now working fourteen hours, talking it over for another four or so, then sleeping on the sofa, not making love and not getting enough to eat in the remaining six. However, he was not complaining. It was nearly the end of July and they weren't anywhere near the end of what they had to do. Harry was determined to finish it with Rose, and not let some whiz kid from the office in to help them—some guy like the one who had called him a lucky bastard.

Vicky went everywhere with Medicine Bear. She stayed in his house. She was on the passenger side of his truck all the time. From a distance she looked like an older version of Jasmine: hair loose or in a long braid, T-shirt, sneakers, jeans, dazzling beauty. Meanwhile, the dark Irishman who had produced and directed the movie they were going to premiere skulked around in the background. Harry wondered how he was feeling. He thought he could imagine.

The night before the premiere Valerie threw a huge party at her house to which she invited everybody who was anybody in Alberta. Harry drove the old man and Rose down in the Cadillac after a long day's work. The blue room began coming over the horizon towards him, shimmering like a mirage.

Valerie gave him an old tuxedo of Tim Steen's. Harry was surprised to find out that he was the same size as the old man. Or as the old man had been before he got into his seventies and became a bit looser around the middle.

Rose was wearing a blue calico dress like a Mother Hubbard, which tied with a sash. With it she wore a petticoat and black boots.

It was the first time he had ever seen her wear a dress and it wasn't what he had been expecting for this affair.

"Valerie showed me all kinds of stuff that day we went shopping," she explained. "But I just got somebody on the Reserve to make this for me. Tim has a photo," she added.

She looked like a girl in an old photograph. A Native girl wearing the quaint clothes of another era. It was only after he had seen the movie that he understood.

They went out of the blue room—which had not finished revealing all its mysteries and possibilities by any means, Harry thought—and swept into the party, arm in arm, a couple. Valerie descended upon them, shrieking. In the background, Medicine Bear, wearing a bearskin and a loincloth. Vicky, dressed in something sophisticated for a change, something that made her look like the woman in the magazines. The Irishman, scowling off in a corner. The old man in his current tuxedo. A thousand flashbulbs going off.

Rose turned out to be shy at parties, so she stuck close to Harry; this was okay with him. The old man introduced Harry to every one of his partners. It seemed as though he was already a lawyer; and in addition to that, he had the smartest girl in Alberta on his arm. There was no sign at all of the guy who had called him a lucky bastard.

They rose late the next morning, and after a fabulous buffet breakfast composed largely of lemon grass and seaweed, swept off to the Reserve—by Cadillac—to watch Vicky's movie. The blue room was disappearing behind him, but Harry felt that no moment he had spent there had gone to waste.

The movie was attended by everyone who had been at the party in addition to everyone on the Reserve. This time Harry was not at the back of the bus, but right up front in the celebrity seats, Rose on one side, Jasmine on the other, and a Native boy he didn't know on the far side.

They walked home afterwards. No one said anything. There was a huge feast and celebration going on in the Band hall, but Rose's family went home. For some reason Harry thought at first that this was because of William. Whom he quickly set up in bed, got washed and made comfortable. When he went out to get the tea, he saw that Marina was seated on the sofa stiffly, one daughter on either side of her, holding her hands.

Medicine Bear came in suddenly. He wasn't wearing the bearskin and loincloth any longer, to Harry's relief. He went straight over to Marina and knelt down in front of her. She began to cry, covering her face.

Tim said: "You saved my life, Marina!"

She gave a great sob and Rose and Jasmine made way for him on the sofa.

"I just had to tell the story, Marina. She made me!" He had his arm around her and there were tears on Medicine Bear's face too. Which suddenly made Harry like him a whole lot better.

They began to do some ordinary things. Harry ate a peanut butter sandwich Rose gave him. Rose and Jasmine put the little boy to bed. Meanwhile, Medicine Bear sat on the sofa holding Marina. Rose and Jasmine went to bed. Harry went outside, rather miserably, and down the road towards the office. Medicine Bear was going to stay on the sofa with Marina for as long as it took, apparently.

Outside the house a boy fell into step with him. "Are they okay in there?"

"They're as okay as they can be—I guess." Harry looked at the young guy. "What's your name?"

"I'm called Tall Grass."

Another Dog Soldier? Harry glanced at him again and noticed that he really was young. He was only about nineteen or twenty, like Rose.

"It's my last name actually."

Harry realized suddenly that Tall Grass was probably hanging around because of Jasmine. It was not the first time he'd seen this guy outside the house.

"She's okay," he said. In fact, he thought she was the most completely okay person in the house, after that movie. Besides William.

The guy didn't say anything. But he looked a lot happier. They parted in front of the office and Tall Grass started back in the direction of the house. Harry went inside and made himself some sort of a bed on the floor with a dictionary and a couple of law texts as pillows.

The next morning Harry got up early and took advantage of already being at the office to do a few hours work. Then he went to Rose's house, thinking there would probably be something he could eat: cornflakes, or maybe there was peanut butter left. He met Tall Grass, who finally went inside with him, out of desperation.

Harry was still thinking it was astounding how successfully Vicky had played the mad Selene. She had actually looked a lot like Jasmine. Of course she had had plenty of time to study this family and decide upon whom she was going to model herself.

Medicine Bear was still there with Marina. Harry got William up. Someone—Rose again, probably—made everybody a peanut butter sandwich. The house had now begun to fill up with old people. It reminded Harry of the office, but even more so. They sat all around, on chairs, on the floor, lined up with their backs against the wall. It was a kind of collective outpouring of grief—and sympathy and love—all offered in silence.

Jasmine had disappeared—with Tall Grass, probably.

Harry said to Rose, "Come on, let's go to work. It will do you good."

She was looking really dragged down. The situation at home was more than depressing.

But working didn't do her good, Harry noticed. She could hardly concentrate on anything. She walked around the office, making convulsive little gestures. Then she would sit down and jump up again.

"Rose. Talk to me. What is it?"

She shook her head. She looked as though she had not slept at all. She wouldn't let him kiss her. She would hardly let him touch her.

In the afternoon, the old man came. He saw at once that there was something the matter with Rose. "What is it, Rose? What's on your mind, sweetheart?"

She wouldn't tell him either.

Harry was getting desperate. It was impossible to work, but he no longer wanted to work. He wanted to have somewhere to go with her where he could hold her, the way Tim had been holding Marina. There had been something in the movie that had deeply upset and disturbed her.

"Get Tim," said the old man briefly.

Harry went to Rose's house. Marina was asleep. Medicine Bear had finally gone home. The place was still full of old people. William was fine.

He went to Tim's house. Vicky was in the kitchen, eating a piece of buttered toast. It was 3:00 in the afternoon.

"I'm Harry," said Harry. "Remember me?"

"Of course I do."

He remembered what she was like now. She wasn't like the Queen. She was Dominique's sister.

"Rose needs Tim," he said.

"Oh. Okay. It's urgent, is it?" She was already going to get him.

"Rose?" Tim was talking to Vicky. "Oh no. Why did I do this?"

"Because you had to, Tim. And by the way, I was the one who did it," she replied. "Harry, stay here. Have some toast."

"No, no!—Thanks!" He went out the door in time to get in Tim's truck. They drove down the street and around the corner to the office. Tim was looking haggard.

Rose and the old man were standing there in tableau. He was holding both her hands. She was merely looking at the floor.

"Come on, Rose," said Tim. "I'm checking you out of this paper factory. We'll go for a drive out by the River."

Harry looked desperately after them, but the old man restrained him. "He'll take care of her," he said. "Just let him handle it, Harry. Ready to do something?"

Feeling like a tool, Harry spent the rest of the afternoon taking dictated notes and looking things up. It was the sort of thing he did most afternoons, but with Rose only a few feet away, looking over at him with a smile. Neither he nor the old man smiled once all afternoon.

Tim and Rose did not return. The old man departed around suppertime and Harry started for Marina's house. They had already eaten there, but Harry was able to put together a few slices of bread and jam. Marina seemed to be okay again. William and the boy were fine. The boy was drawing. Jasmine's boyfriend removed her shortly after Harry came in. The old people had disappeared. He thought he might get the sofa again.

But more than anything, he wanted Medicine Bear to come back with Rose. He was jealous. His closeness with her all summer, close and getting closer, he didn't want her to have that or anything like it with another man, even if he was her uncle, and old enough to be her father.

He was lying down on the sofa when Rose finally came in. She looked better. Harry sat up right away and she came over and sat down beside him. He put his arm around her. She was fine. The shivering tension she had been under in the morning seemed to be all gone.

"Where's Jasmine?" she asked.

"Out with her boyfriend. Rose—?"

"Her boyfriend?" Rose turned around and looked at him in dismay.

"Guy by the name of Tall Grass. He's been hanging around here—well, for a week or so. He seems like a citizen."

"Jonas?" She was thinking fiercely. "The one I was in grade twelve with?"

Harry shrugged. "Rose—?" he said.

"Well, that's all right," Rose leaned against his shoulder, yawning.

"Let me in," said Harry. "Something was wrong. Maybe I couldn't help. But I just want to know—what was it?"

"Oh," she said. She started thinking again. He could feel her, thinking.

"You were gone a long time. Where did you go?"

"Up in the River valley. They're letting some water down now. Tim wanted to see what it was like there. We drove way up and then we walked for a while. No one here knows how the River is going to change."

"But what was it, Rose?"

"It seems kind of—I don't know—selfish. And I should have realized anyway."

"Realized what?"

"That I don't come from Medicine Bear," she said. "I don't have those genes. I've got—I've got the other ones."

Harry tightened his grip on her shoulder. But she still seemed fine. The tension had gone out of her.

"Tim is like her. He's even in touch with her somehow. Well, you saw it," she said. "The speech he made the night before they opened the dam. But I don't have her either. I can't even draw." She laughed.

He could see now why she had been so upset.

Proud Rose. On her mission, which she had felt came to her from destiny. But what was really in the background? A grandmother whose inspired, artistic side had not descended to her. Her grandfather a murderer. A mentally disturbed mother. Her whiteman father a drug addict.

"What did he say to you?" Harry asked in amazement. Somehow, Tim had fixed it. But how had he done that?

"He just talked to me about the River. It's still there. Water is eternal, however the whitemen screw it up."

"But, I mean, what did he say about that other thing?"

"I didn't tell him," said Rose. "I would have been ashamed to tell him. He spent his life wondering if his mother was murdered by his father. I guess I can face this myself."

Proud Rose.

Harry was feeling very happy all of a sudden. She hadn't told Tim. But she had told him. Not to get help; she wouldn't ask for help. She had let him in, though.

The old man was there next morning first thing. Rose gave him a sunny smile and a hug. A huge happy grin spread over his face. He seemed reluctant to let go of her. All morning he kept glancing at her, just to make sure. Harry was checking on her himself. But she was fine.

"Did she tell you anything?" the old man asked in an undertone later on. Rose was on the phone with the office in Calgary.

"Genes," said Harry briefly.

"Ah so! Well, if that was it—! I knew someone else you couldn't talk to about that," he said.

◀ A SURPRISING, AND FROM HARRY'S POINT OF VIEW, VERY GOOD thing happened then. Eliza came back to the Reserve. The family that had been poised to take her house retreated rather angrily to their old cramped quarters. Harry didn't understand how housing worked at all. Eliza could have her old three-bedroom house because she had always had it.

He made breakfast for Eliza the next morning. Dominique had delivered another couple of boxes of food when he brought her home. Harry started with porridge. Bacon and eggs. Toast and jam. He fried himself another egg when he was frying one for Eliza.

Eliza was conveying what she had disliked about Steamboat. "Dominique never home."

"That's true."

"That boy of his always home."

"Yeah." Tony would be way too talkative for Eliza. She liked to sit with people.

"You don't have no neighbours."

"No neighbours?" said Harry, amazed. There were houses all down the street on either side of Poppalushka's.

He put another piece of toast in the broiler. Recent events had deprived him of his naive faith in the availability of food.

"Whitemen," she said.

"Oh yeah." His own whiteness had become invisible to her.

He and Rose and Jasmine and Tall Grass went out together that evening for pizza in a café in Abercrombie. They took Tall Grass's car, a large North American model from the late seventies. Harry had always felt these cars expressed the style of the Reserve. He had often seen the old rust buckets conveying large parties, sometimes as many as eight young Native men, to the bar and the cafés in the big town. Now he found himself sliding out of the back seat after Rose.

His whiteness was not invisible here. He was stared at in the pizza parlour. The other whites were wondering what he was doing with the Natives.

Tall Grass turned out to be quite all right, just as Rose had said. He was a thoughtful boy, inclined to pauses and silences, which Harry could see fitted in well with Jasmine's feyness. Obviously they had been hanging out together for some time without quite knowing what to say to each other. Rose was by now completely matter-of-fact about their being a couple, which was probably— in Harry's view—helping them to understand that they were one.

◀ THEY HAD CLIMBED THEIR MOUNTAIN OF PAPERWORK AND were beginning to slide down the other side. It was the second week in August. They were going to make it, Harry was sure of that now.

Over at the farm they would be starting their pre-harvest repair of all the machines. But Harry had no time even to think about what they were doing there. He had not been home all summer.

His life was bliss. It was bliss to be with Rose all day. The old man knew he was smart and said he was doing good work. He had got to know Rose's family and they all liked him; even her mother liked him.

Then one day, his father had a heart attack.

Dominique came and got him. His mother, the girls, were all at the hospital. It had happened the previous night. Just a small heart attack, according to his mother on the phone. A warning.

"Do you want me to come?" asked Rose.

Harry shook his head.

"He won't want to see me anyway," she said. She was looking at him anxiously, however.

"Stay here, Rose." The old man was present most days now. He did the writing; they had done the research. Now they were fine-tuning the blend. "If Harry needs you, he'll say so, right, Harry?"

Harry was looking down at Robbie. His father looked different in a hospital bed, smaller, pale, not so sure of himself.

The girls had made him go in by himself. Laura had already taken Sonya home to sleep. The emergency was over.

"So—been working hard?"

Harry nodded. He had been working harder than he had ever worked before in his life. But still, he felt guilty, as though he hadn't been doing a thing all summer. They needed all hands for harvest—and where had he been? Maybe his father wouldn't have had a heart attack if—

"Sorry, Dad. Maybe I should have been home."

Robbie made an irritable, don't-mention-it gesture. Harry wondered if they were going to talk about the heart attack at all. Probably not, if he didn't bring it up.

"Somebody told me you're making a name for yourself already."

"What? Who was that?"

"Oh, Rich Marten. He says you're right in like this with old man Steen." Rich Marten was their MLA. It was not necessarily a compliment, coming from him.

"So this law school thing is what you really want to do, is it?"

"Yes. But Dad—?"

"Sure about that? You'd make a pretty good farmer if you put your mind to it." This was a compliment, coming from Robbie.

"I think—I have to be a lawyer, Dad." Especially after what he had learned, what he had seen, this summer.

"Well, Marian is teaching at the university, Laura's nearly a doctor. You're doing law. Whatever the heck Lizzie decides, it won't be to stay home, that's for sure. Where's the farmer?" his father complained.

"Dominique," said Harry.

"Yeah. Okay. That's what I wanted to talk to you about," said his father. "If I die—"

"You're not going to die, Dad. The doctor says—"

"Oh yeah. The doctor says. Are you paying attention, Harry?"

"Yes." Harry was paying very close attention.

"There's your mother, obviously. I talk this over with her all the time. She says, if you're going to farm it, you'd better own it. You've got to have a stake to want to do something stupid like that. So what if we leave it to Dominique, Harry? Got any objection?"

Harry shook his head. It was exactly what he wanted. Dominique would run the place as a farm until he died—no matter what happened to the freight rates. And after that—? If there was no one in the next generation who wanted it—and Dominique could be trusted to find the one who did and give it to him—then it would slowly go back to being prairie, with the natural grasses, the wild birds and small animals. None of them would ever see it turned into acreages.

"So. Okay. But as it happens I intend to stay alive for a while. Even if I have to have this thing where they rip your chest open and replace your heart with polyethylene tubing. I just thought I'd get that one little thing settled. So your mother doesn't have to worry."

Harry went home for supper, which was a fairly constrained meal. Marian had arrived from the airport in the meantime. She intended to go to the hospital in the evening with their mother.

Lizzie went out for a long ride on Ping Pong after supper. Laura and Harry did the dishes; then she disappeared too. Harry mooched around for a few minutes, picking things up and putting them down.

The fact was, he wanted Rose. He didn't just want her; he needed her. Somehow, being at home was not enough to make him feel better. He called her up. She was still at the office.

"I'm coming over right away," she said. She could hear his desolation; he didn't even need to tell her.

"How will you do that?" Harry had already been mentally reviewing the various farm vehicles he could use to get her.

"I can borrow Jonas's car."

"Oh. Okay."

Harry thought of the pair of giant fluffy dice that hung from the rear-view mirror of Jonas's car. If one of his sisters made a comment about that he thought he might get mad. This thought in itself was so uncharacteristic of Harry that it surprised and alarmed him to be having it.

Rose arrived about half an hour later; it was almost dark. Harry had put on some barn clothes to feed and water the horses.

"Is he all right, Harry?" Rose was embracing him, dirty clothes and all.

"I guess so. No one really knows yet."

"With these bypass operations nowadays you can live to be a hundred," she said.

One of the things that had been on his mind was his own genes. If his father could have a heart attack when he was still only in his sixties ... He didn't want to let go of her. She felt good. She smelled good. She was exactly right. He began feeling a lot better.

Marian and his mother drove into the yard. Harry put away the horse buckets. Everyone was in the living room watching TV when he came in. He sat down on the sofa beside Rose. She was right there.

He looked at the faces of his sisters, so woebegone at supper. Rose was making everything better. They were curious about her. Marian had only seen her once, at Christmas. But the other two didn't know her any better. His mother was quite animated, almost her usual cheerful self. She would have been prepared to love Rose no matter what she was like, of course.

"I read about that movie of Vicky's, in Toronto," Marian was saying. "Is it really about your family?"

Rose nodded, her face tranquil.

"Vicky plays Rose's grandmother," said Harry, thinking of the half-mad Selene-Vicky-Jasmine. It was the most amazing thing in the film, in his opinion.

"You've seen it?" said Marian in surprise.

"We went to the premiere," he replied. "The week after they opened the dam."

"You did?"

"I was invited. With Rose."

"Well, I'm going to see it as soon as it opens in Calgary," said Laura.

"Where is Vicky now?" asked their mother. "Did she come to the premiere?"

"Oh yes," said Rose. "She's on the Reserve now. She and my uncle—"

"Rose's uncle is Medicine Bear. The Chief," said Harry. They were all listening to this as though it were extremely exotic stuff. Whatever concerned Vicky had always fascinated them, of course.

"Vicky and my uncle—. Well, she's staying with him now. But they can't be together, even though—"

"But she has a huge career," protested Marian. "I mean, especially after this movie—"

"She couldn't just go and live on the Reserve," said Laura.

"No, she can't," said Rose. "But she'll be back. That's what I like about her. "

There was a chorus of romantic sighs. Vicky would be back even though she had been on the cover of *Vogue* magazine. Even though she was poised to become a film star. Harry was thinking about Vicky standing in Tim's kitchen in jeans and her bare feet, a piece of toast in her hand.

"So they opened the dam?" asked Marian. "Everyone is saying it's an environmental disaster."

"Tim Steen is going to have the last word on that in Ottawa this fall," Harry told her.

"Tim Steen? Oh yeah. The lawyer?"

"Harry's been working for him all summer," said their mother.

"With Rose. Rose and I have been working for him."

"You have?"

"He's Rose's—. You see—"

"He's my grandpa."

"He *is*?"

"You know, we like to think we're related to Vicky because of Dominique," interposed their mother.

"Where is he, anyway?" asked Harry. Dominique would normally have been around all evening this close to harvest.

"He stayed on with Dad. They were talking about the harvest."

Harry nodded, thinking of that conversation this afternoon. He didn't think it was just harvest they were talking about now.

◖ THEY HAD A WEEK TO GO. THE PRESSURE WAS ON TO FINISH the old man's presentation before school started. Before Harry had to go to work on the harvest in every spare moment he had. Before their long summer together was over.

Harry felt a great deal of optimism over what was going to happen in the fall. He and Rose had been talking about trying to rent a house together with Tall Grass, who was going to take a film and TV technician's course. If that happened, Jasmine might come to stay with them too and do grade twelve at a city school. Rose thought this would be a great improvement over either the Reserve or Abercrombie.

Vicky had left. The Irishman had disappeared right after the premiere, but Harry, thinking about it, decided that he was probably still somewhere in the picture. No one who had an artistic connection to Vicky would ever want to let go of her. And he thought the connection might be more than just artistic, even though Vicky had been staying in Medicine Bear's house for weeks and went everywhere with him, in jeans and a T-shirt on the Reserve, in a cocktail gown to parties and receptions in Calgary.

Medicine Bear disappeared for a few days. Rose said that he had gone camping up the River.

Rose seemed rather preoccupied. It was Thursday afternoon and she suddenly announced that she intended to go into the city the next morning. Harry supposed she had some arrangement with the old man, who was nearly always with them these days. They had supper at her house as usual, then after William was put to bed, she came to Eliza's. Harry walked her home, the way he usually did, at about 5:00.

At 7:00 he got up, made himself an excellent breakfast while Eliza had her usual quantum of coffee, and then went to the office. No one was there yet and he got a lot done before the old man turned up at around ten o'clock.

"Where's Rose?"

"She went to Calgary," said Harry. He was puzzled, however. Didn't Tim Steen know she was going? How was she getting there? Rose always went to Calgary in the Cadillac.

They worked until noon. Harry was becoming slightly concerned. He went to Marina's house to get a peanut butter sandwich. He made William and little Tim peanut butter sandwiches as well. William was not terribly good with peanut butter, but he liked it.

"Did Rose say when she was coming back?" he asked Marina, who shrugged.

The old man was talking to Valerie on the phone when he got back to work.

"She's not there," he remarked, hanging up. "She didn't say when she was coming back?"

"No," said Harry. "She just kind of—told me. That she was going. I assumed it had something to do with you or Valerie."

"How did she go?"

"I can't understand that either. Maybe she took Jonas's car."

He went out to look for Tall Grass, who hadn't heard anything. His car was still parked beside his mother's house, out of gas.

"This isn't like Rose," said the old man.

Harry had begun to think about Black Snake again. He couldn't help it. Even though he had heard Rose say that she would never forgive Judah, Harry's mind tended to take him off into the old path of jealousy whenever there was even the slightest excuse for it. Could Black Snake have kidnapped her? But she wouldn't have told him she was going if she had been kidnapped.

Medicine Bear dropped in suddenly—unexpectedly. He was looking very brown from the sun and much more relaxed, not as strung out and unhappy as he had seemed after Vicky left.

"Where's Rose?" he asked immediately.

"We don't know," said the old man. "She said she was going to the city. But she isn't with Valerie."

"What? Rose is gone?"

"Well, maybe we're panicking over—"

"You're panicking? All right. What did you say to her? Did you have a fight?" He was looking oppressively at Harry.

"No! I mean, no. We didn't have a fight. She just said she was going to the city." Harry's lips were numb. He and Rose never fought about anything.

In fact, it had been an especially tender night. He was realizing that now. As though she were trying to make up for something. Something like having a crazy boyfriend who slashed tires and stole booze and defaced buildings. And who would set fire to the house of a helpless old woman. This was the way Rose had come to him in the beginning. He could never forget that.

"Oh shit!" said Tim, sitting down abruptly. "If anything happens to Rose—! Look, I don't even want to live here any longer, do you understand that? I hate this place! The only thing I really care about here is Rose. And that's all you'd care about too," he went on, speaking to Harry, "if you had any sense. But fuck you! I don't care about you!"

"What are we going to do?" asked the old man. He asked Harry.

"I think—I think we shouldn't do anything. Till tonight, at least. She's pretty independent." If there was something Rose felt she had to do, she would just go ahead and do it. Harry knew that.

"Is it that thing about—the Mountain connection again?" asked the old man. He and Tim were both treating Harry as though he were an oracle. Or to blame, alternatively.

"The Mountain connection?" said Tim. "Were you talking to her about that? What did you say to her?"

"I don't—I don't think—" stammered Harry. It had come to him that they were thinking about Rose's reaction to being Thomas Mountain's granddaughter. To him, the Mountain connection was a different matter. Black Snake was Judah Mountain.

"Stop giving Harry the third degree!" snapped the old man. "He doesn't know any more than we do. Maybe she just took the afternoon off and went shopping."

Tim lit a cigarette. He drew on it twice, then put it out in a piece of silver paper which he threw in the wastebasket. Then he threw the whole package of cigarettes in the wastebasket, and stalked out.

They all knew that Rose would not have taken the afternoon off to go shopping. They did some more work.

"Know what? This thing is done," said the old man. He let a thick slatch of reports drop out of his hands onto the desk.

"We're just giving them more and more of the same stuff now."

"It ought to be readable. That's the main thing, really."

"Well, it's readable, all right," said Harry. "I'd compare it to the Bible. Horrible, but enlightening."

"Am I to take that as a compliment?"

"Oh yes! Absolutely! The Bible was written by God, wasn't it?"

The old man laughed. "You're a first class man, Harry," he said.

"Really? I mean—thanks."

"When Rose showed you to me, I thought, well, what the hell, the office is full of know-it-alls. Why not see whether this young fellow can do it instead? The worst that could happen is that he can't. But it didn't really occur to me, Harry—" He gestured with his old freckled hand at the open door of the office.

Harry nodded, thinking of all that had happened on the Reserve that summer.

"That movie—" the old man said. "It was almost too much for me."

"It was pretty powerful," agreed Harry.

"It made me relive that time. Medicine Bear was my first big case, you know. He was innocent. I thought I was pretty smart. But he lost. He was the one who lost everything. Have you ever seen a hotshot young lawyer sitting in his car in the driveway, crying? Well—maybe you will someday, Harry. Maybe you'll be there too."

Harry looked at him in silence. The old man was giving him another slice of history.

"The prosecution had all their ducks in a row. The real murderer had disappeared off into the mountains for the winter. By the time we caught up with him it was spring, the trial had been over by three months and he was dead, drowned in the River. The axe was gone, Joe's fingerprints all over the knife. No alibi—it was made out at trial that he lied about that. And then there was the child, Marina. Back in those days, when they got to work on a child witness—She didn't even remember who Joe was by the time they were through. There was nothing I could do about that."

He took off his glasses and passed his hand over his eyes. The lump was in Harry's throat as well.

"The fact of the matter is, the powers that be wanted to kill any opposition to the dam, and all of it was coming from Joe— at that time. So—they killed it. And, you know what, Harry?"

"What?"

"When you see something like that happen—When you look into the man's eyes—You simply can't imagine! Well, it changed my life, at least. I never forgot the lesson I learned there. It made me a lifelong opponent of injustice. I think I put my money where my mouth was—at least as far as this Reserve goes. I did my damnedest anyway."

"Well, you absolutely did," agreed Harry.

"But it didn't change the outcome, did it?"

"Oh, I think it did." History was suddenly appealing to him.

"People will be reading your book next year and the year after. They didn't just do it and get away with it."

The old man smiled. "Well, at least we did our damnedest," he said. "I'm glad you were on board, Harry."

"Well, God, sir, I mean—I was glad to be on board."

The old man was still smiling at him. "After I pass on, this place is going to need a first class man. You've got the stuff for it, Harry. You know that yourself. Rose'll probably end up being the Chief," he went on. Harry nodded. The scenario was surprising, but still, it didn't surprise him. According to the Department of Indian Affairs, chiefs were elected; the position wasn't hereditary. But if something happened to Medicine Bear, Rose could get elected tomorrow. No one would even stand, if they knew she was running. He had seen how people here loved her, the way they trusted her.

The old man was looking troubled suddenly. They had both begun to worry about Rose again.

Medicine Bear came stalking back into the office. "Wherever she went, it was probably with Judah Mountain," he announced. "His car is gone."

The old man wrinkled his forehead and looked out from under his bushy eyebrows at Tim. "Friend of hers?" he asked.

"Are you kidding?" said Tim. "That young brave is more trouble than you can imagine. Just keeping him in his chair took up all my time this summer."

Harry said: "Doesn't Judah have a trial date coming up?"

The old man lifted the phone. "Who's the lawyer, Harry? It's our brief, I guess."

Harry remembered the name of the man who had refused to use their outhouse. It was a lucky thing. Rose usually handled all the criminal stuff and since he was not in the Calgary office he didn't know anyone—except the senior partners.

"Well, this Judah and a couple of others were up this afternoon. Man's not back from court—probably just went straight home." He looked at his watch. It was 5:00.

Harry was pondering. Judah was going to jail. If Rose had gone with him—Why had she gone? She wasn't a witness—not in the case he was being tried for.

Maybe he hadn't gone to court at all. Maybe he and she had gone over the border. There were some reserves in the U.S. where he wouldn't be found. He remembered what Rose had said about those graffiti charges. Judah would be a political prisoner.

And then there was something else too. He knew she already felt responsible for Judah; but he also remembered how she had finally understood her connection to Thomas Mountain, how bitter that had been for her. She might be trying to save Judah from the cycle of violence and degradation that had resulted in the crime and then the suicide of her grandfather.

"Harry—?" said the old man.

He and Medicine Bear were both staring at him as he thought.

"I don't know!" said Harry. He felt like bursting into tears. What if she was gone? With her strong sense of justice. But she had good sense, too, he reminded himself. She expected him to trust her.

"All right, let's find that lawyer," said the old man.

He tried, but it was still too early. The lawyer was nowhere, not in the office, not at home. Friday night—he had turned off his cellphone. Lucky bastard, thought Harry. He was taking his girlfriend out for dinner, probably.

Medicine Bear took the old man out to eat in a café in Abercrombie. Harry went to Marina's.

Jasmine was always out these days. Harry put together a meal for all of them and helped William to eat it. Marina didn't know where Rose was and she was worried too, by this time. She didn't eat anything.

Tim and the old man came in. For a short while they all sat bolt upright on the straight chairs by the table, drinking tea. They were still not able to get hold of the lawyer.

"I'm too old for this. I'm just going home," said the old man. Tim was obviously staying. He and Marina had given up talking. It was another night when the sofa was taken.

Thank God for Eliza, thought Harry morosely, going over to her house. It occurred to him to worry about his father, but his mind didn't have room for that right now. If Rose had just gone along to Black Snake's trial—with him—she should be back by now. It was not the type of trial that would take very long.

It was dawn and he must have slept, although he could not be sure of that. It seemed as though some sort of noise had awakened him, however. The back door, which Eliza never locked—had he heard that being opened? He was sitting bolt upright to listen as Rose came in.

Harry jumped out of bed and grabbed her. "Rose—!"

"Harry," she replied, kissing him. Her lips were soft and fresh, her breath smelled faintly of toothpaste. She was acting as though she had just gone out of the room for a moment and then come in again.

"Rose! We all—! Your uncle—! The old man—! Your mother—!"

"I went with Judah. You guessed, didn't you?" He let go of her reluctantly, but only because she was rapidly skimming out of her clothes.

"Did he go over the border or something?"

"No," she replied, astonished. "He went to jail, Harry."

"Then why—? Why did it take you so long to get back?"

"I needed to be by myself for a while," she replied, getting into bed. She yawned. "I needed to think, Harry."

Thinking was the last thing he wanted her to do. Or was it? Harry stared at her, bare-breasted, totally desirable, her long hair spilling all over the pillows. Obviously, if she had needed to think, whatever it was about, she had arrived at a favourable conclusion.

"Please," he said. "Just tell me about it." He sat down on the edge of the bed. "You drove him down to his trial. Was that because—?"

"I wanted him to get there," she said. "I knew you would guess. And I didn't want to make us both unhappy arguing about whether I should."

"Did you go in?"

She shook her head. "I just gave him a hug and told him I'd see him when he came home again. Then I waited outside. It didn't take very long."

"God! Well, and then?"

"And then I couldn't just—go to a restaurant and drive home.

I had to think about it. Really think about Judah going to jail. About what it's like for him, what he's going through now. So I went down by the River," she said. "Where we went that night—remember? It made me feel better. It isn't our river now but once upon a time maybe it was. A cop came along in the middle of the night and asked me what I was doing. Judah's car probably attracted him. I said I'd been having a nap, but I was just going. On the way home I stopped in Abercrombie to get some gas and go to the bathroom."

Harry was nearly wild with irritation and jealousy and love. He was naked and the air was cool. It was the end of August and beginning to be cold at night

"Harry—you're shivering!" She lifted up the blanket and he slid in beside her.

"You weren't really worried, were you?" she said.

No, no. He hadn't been really worried. Was he going to tell her that he had been frantic? That he had been mad with jealousy? That he still was jealous? That he wanted to order her to leave Judah Mountain strictly alone in future—to receive his own richly deserved punishment by himself? He wasn't going to say any of those things.

"We have to get some sleep," she whispered after a while. "We have to go to work in a few hours, Harry."

"No, we don't. The old man said it was finished. He said that yesterday afternoon."

"But I wasn't here," she said.

"Well, you can't be everywhere at the same time, Rose."

"No." She spoke sleepily. She was rolling herself up as usual, curved in against his side. "It was just that I had to do that."

Obviously, wherever Rose was going she was determined not to leave anyone behind. Black Snake was coming. Jasmine was coming and Tall Grass. Everyone on the Reserve was coming. Harry was coming too.

———————

Dante was designed by Giovanni
Mandersteig (1892–1977) and cut by
Charles Malin (1883–1955), a talented
Parisian punchcutter, in 1954. Originally
a private foundry type for the Officina
Bodoni at Verona, Dante was later
released by the Monotype Corporation,
for machine composition in 1957, and
in digital form in the early 1990s.
The letterforms of Mandersteig's
Dante were greatly influenced by his
study of types by the fifteenth-century
Italian punchcutter Francesco Griffo.
The version of Dante used here has
been slightly modified to better reflect
Mandersteig's letterforms.   A.S.

The lyrics of "The Rose of Tralee" are attributed to William
Pembroke Mulchinock (d. 1864). The lyrics of "'Tis the Last Rose of
Summer" are attributed to the Irish poet Thomas Moore (1779–1852).

Typeset in Dante by Andrew Steeves and printed offset by
Gary Dunfield and Marilyn MacIntyre at Gaspereau Press.

Gaspereau Press acknowledges the support of the Canada Council
for the Arts and the Nova Scotia Department of Tourism & Culture.

6   5   4   3   2   1

NATIONAL LIBRARY OF CANADA CATALOGUING IN PUBLICATION

Haley, Susan Charlotte, 1949–
    The murder of Medicine Bear : a novel / by Susan Haley.

    ISBN 1-894031-77-6 (BOUND).
    ISBN 1-894031-76-8 (PBK.)

    I. Title.

PS8565.A4334M87 2003   C813'.54   C2003-903938-2

GASPEREAU PRESS
PRINTERS & PUBLISHERS
ONE CHURCH AVENUE
KENTVILLE, NOVA SCOTIA
CANADA B4N 2M7